ABOUT THE AUTHOR

Xiao Bai was born in 1968 in Shanghai and began writing in 2009. He quickly made a name for himself as a writer of fiction and essays. His first book, a collection of essays entitled *Horny Hamlet* (2009), was a prize winner in China. His debut novel, *Game Point*, followed in 2010, and *French Concession*, his second novel, appeared in 2011 in China. It is being widely translated and is his first book to appear in English. In 2013, his novella *Xu Xiangbi the Spy* won the Tenth Annual Shanghai Literary Prize. Xiao Bai lives in Shanghai.

ABOUT THE TRANSLATOR

Chenxin Jiang was born in Singapore and grew up in Hong Kong. She lives in Shanghai.

FRENCH CONCESSION

Xiao Bai

**Waterford City and County
Libraries**

Translated from the Chinese by Chenxin Jiang

A Point Blank Book

First published in Great Britain & Australia by
Point Blank, an imprint of Oneworld Publications, 2016

This paperback edition published 2017

Published by arrangement with HarperCollins Publishers, New York, U.S.A.

Originally published in China in 2011 by Shanghai 99 Readers Culture Co Ltd.
under the title *Concessions*.

ISBN 978-1-78607-000-5
ISBN 978-1-78074-903-7 (eBook)

Printed and bound in Great Britain by Clays Ltd, St Ives plc

And walked like an assassin through the town,
And looked at men and did not like them,
But trembled if one passed him with a frown.

—W. H. AUDEN, *In Time of War:*
A Sonnet Sequence with a Verse Commentary

In fact, when the moment came, power had not so
much to be seized as to be picked up. It has been
said that more people were injured in the making of
Eisenstein's great film *October* (1927) than had been
hurt during the actual taking of the Winter Palace on
7th November 1917.

—ERIC HOBSBAWM, *The Age of Extremes:*
The Short Twentieth Century, 1914–1991

TRANSLATOR'S NOTE

This story is set in 1931, or Year 20 of the Republic, the twentieth year after the revolution that overthrew the Ch'ing Dynasty and created the Republic of China. It takes place in the foreign concessions established by Britain, France, and the United States in the mid-nineteenth century, extraterritorial jurisdictions in the heart of Shanghai. The British and American settlements were soon combined to form what was known as the International Settlement, whereas the French Concession remained independent. Both concessions were returned to the Chinese government during or shortly after the Second World War.

Spelling of Chinese names throughout mostly accords with the Wade-Giles system in use at the time, except where certain conventional names or spellings (such as the Whampoa) are more widely used.

LIST OF CHARACTERS

Weiss Hsueh/Hsueh Wei-shih, a French-Chinese photojournalist who becomes an unofficial detective for the Political Section of the French Concession Police

Therese Irxmayer/Lady Holly, a White Russian firearms dealer and Hsueh's lover

Leng Hsiao-man, a member of a revolutionary cell and Hsueh's lover

Ts'ao Chen-wu, Leng's second husband

Wang Yang, Leng's first husband

Ko Ya-min, a member of the cell

Lieutenant Sarly, head of the Political Section of the French Concession Police

Inspector Maron, head of a detective squad under the Political Section of the French Concession Police

Ku Fu-kuang, leader of the revolutionary cell

Park Kye-seong, a Korean member of the cell and Ku's right-hand man

Lin P'ei-wen, head of one of the cell's units

Ch'i, an ex-prostitute and Ku's lover

Zung Ts-Mih, Therese's business partner from Hong Kong

Yindee Zung/Ch'en Ying-ti, Zung Ts-Mih's sister

Ah Kwai, Therese's maidservant from Hong Kong

Tseng Nan-p'u, a functionary in Nanking's Central Bureau

Cheng Yün-tuan, a secretary at Nanking's Investigative Unit for Party Affairs

Secretary Ch'en, a senior member in the Communist Party and former leader in the student movement

The poet from Marseille, a member of Inspector Maron's detective squad

Commissioner Martin, an English commander at the International Settlement's Municipal Police

Baron Franz Pidol, Luxembourg United Steel Company's chief representative in Shanghai

Margot Pidol, Baron Pidol's wife and Therese's close friend

Brenen Blair, Margot's lover

Consul Baudez, the French consul in Shanghai

Colonel Bichat, head of the Shanghai Volunteer Corps

Sergeant Ch'eng Yu-t'ao/Pock-faced Ch'eng, head of North Gate Police Station

M. Mallet, Chief of the French Concession Police

Sawada-san, First Secretary at the Japanese consulate

Li Pao-i, a newspaper reporter at the *Arsène Lupin*

Tao Lili/Peach Girl, a prostitute at Moon Palace Dancing Hall

Barker, an American

The Boss, head of the Green Gang

Morris Jr., prominent member of the Green Gang

Ch'in Ch'i-ch'üan, a member of Lin's unit

Fu, a member of the cell

Li, a member of the cell

Chou Li-min, a member of the cell

Pearl Yeh, a famous actress

Yan Feng, a cameraman at the Hua Sisters Motion Picture Studio

Pierre Weiss, Hsueh's father

Mr. and Mrs. Romantz, proprietors of the restaurant Bendigo

Hugo Irxmayer, Therese's deceased husband

The walls of the cabin were trembling. A steam whistle piped two short blasts. Hsueh opened his eyes. He still had the covers pulled over his head, and the ebb and flow of waves sounded like thunder in a distant world. The world beneath the covers was warm and rocked gently. Therese's naked back shivered in the darkness. The ship's engine must be restarting.

A thick fog had blotted out the stars. Going out onto the deck right now would be like stepping into a freezing dark dream. The deck would be treacherously slippery, and he would have no sense of direction—he would barely even know where his own hands and feet were. He would hear the waves but be unable to see them in the endless darkness. He might see a buoy flickering dimly several hundred yards away, as if through uncountable layers of black gauze.

The *Paul Lecat* set off at full steam. In only a few hours, it would be high tide on the Yangtze, the only time when a large ship could sail safely through the Astraea Channel. There was a sandbank on the northern side of the channel, and the whole channel was sand-logged. When the tide was at its lowest, the shallowest stretches of river would be less than twenty meters deep. The *Paul Lecat* weighed 7,050 tons, and displaced about twenty-eight meters of water. It thus had two hours to reach the next anchorage site at Wu-sung-k'ou, the mouth of the Wu-sung River.

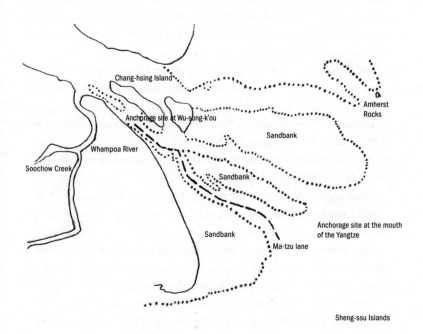

Chang-hsing Island

Amherst Rocks

Anchorage site at Wu-sung-k'ou

Sandbank

Whampoa River

Soochow Creek

Sandbank

Sandbank

Anchorage site at the mouth of the Yangtze

Sandbank

Ma-tzu lane

Sheng-ssu Islands

Sea lanes at the mouth of the Yangtze River

Halfway through the journey up the river, it had a close brush with disaster. A German cargo ship sailing out to sea passed it very narrowly—"pass port to port" was the entry the pilot would make in his logbook that day. The river was foggy. The pilot did not hear the other ship sound the horn at its bridge, and by the time he saw the red light on its port side, they were on course to collide. The *Paul Lecat* hastily turned fifteen degrees starboard to let the other ship pass. In so doing, it was nearly forced out of the channel and onto the muddy sandbanks.

With the door just a crack open, a sliver of red light filtered in. Hsueh opened the cabin door and was immediately terrified by the sight of the other ship advancing toward him like a huge building.

He crept back under the sheets. Therese was sleeping like a mother hog, her snores long and gentle.

His fingernails brushed across the cloud-shaped purple birthmark between her shoulder blades.

Although they were traveling together, he knew little about her apart from her name. After all, she had engaged his services as a lover, not as a spy.

She likes to chain-smoke, especially in bed. She knows a lot about antique jewelry. Her ink green garnet stone has a pattern like a horse's mane. She knows some mysterious people in Hong Kong and Saigon. Granted, some of these were his own inventions—strangers always stimulated Hsueh's imagination. He was a photographer, and he made his living peddling photographs to all the newspapers and magazines in Shanghai. If he was lucky, a single photograph of a burglary-murder scene might fetch fifty yuan.

The first time they had met was at the scene of a shooting, standing over the corpse. The second time was at Lily Bar in Hongkew, next to a massage place with lanterns outside that read *PARIS GIRLS*. She wasn't all that different from the Paris girls inside, he thought.

In fact, only recently had he learned her name, in the Hotel Continental in Hanoi, when he heard that man call her Therese. Before then, all he knew was that people called her Lady Holly. He gradually worked out that she was White Russian and not German, as she was said to be. She fascinated him. They spent their nights in places like the Astor House Hotel in Shanghai or the Hotel Continental in Hanoi. Spacious balconies, wide corridors, electric ceiling fans whirring discreetly. The air would be thick with the lascivious smell of overripe tropical fruit. The wind would blow open the pale green curtains and dry their glistening backs. He was almost in love with her.

It was now low tide, and the *Paul Lecat* would have to be moored in a temporary anchorage for twelve hours, until another pilot boarded the ship at the next high tide and navigated it into the Whampoa.

He yanked off the sheets, leaped out of bed, and got dressed. Only when he stepped outside did he realize that they were nowhere near their destination. The horizon grew bright, and the wind pierced his shirt. He decided to go to the restaurant for a cup of hot tea.

The railing, starboard side. Another first-class cabin. Leng Hsiaoman was about to steal out of bed. She could not risk disturbing Ts'ao Chen-wu, sound asleep beside her. According to the plan, she had to go to the telegraph room and send a telegram.

Ts'ao, her husband, had been sent to Hong Kong on a secret mission to arrange the visit of an influential man in the ruling Kuomintang party. He was now returning to Shanghai to meet that man in the French Concession, and accompany him back to Canton via Hong Kong and Shen-chen.

Ts'ao's snores rose and fell, like his temper. He was brusque and yet gentle, hard to pin down. She was in a pensive mood, though not because of him. She had scoured her memory of their life together, struggling to find things she loathed about him, good reasons for hating him, yet nothing she could think of justified what she was about to do. But surely she had to have a higher cause to live for.

Anchored Wu-sung-k'ou await high tide STOP onshore before ten STOP pier as agreed Ts'ao

The telegraph operator sent these words to a Shanghai wireless shore station with the call letters XSH, to a Mr. Lin P'ei-wen, who identified himself as the man responsible for welcoming the delegation. Half an hour later, at the Telegraph Office on 21B Szechuen Road, the night shift operator opened the glass door and went up to the counter. He handed the telegram to Mr. Lin, who had been waiting there for more than two hours.

The door to the main dining room was shut. Hsueh returned to the room, where Therese was still sleeping. In Hanoi, he had rushed out of the hotel toward the pier in a rage. He had made up his mind to ignore her, to stop sleeping in her room or her bed. But even when he booked himself a berth in third class, all she did was mock him. At the pier, he realized he had stepped on a piece of chewed-up betel nut. Standing beneath a palm tree, he looked at the Vietnamese hawkers dressed in black on the pier, and the stench of sweat made him feel queasy. He found himself wandering back to the hotel.

She hadn't bothered to pursue him at all—she had known he would come back of his own accord. He was young, and she was seven or eight years older. She had the upper hand. Who is that man? Who is he? he had asked. Mr. Zung, she said. In Hong Kong, she had gone out alone and left him at the hotel all day. At first he assumed she had gone to meet more of those White Russians forced to sell their last few pieces of jewelry. Then on the journey from Hong Kong to Haiphong, he'd seen this Mr. Zung on the boat. Therese pretended she didn't know him, but he had traveled with them all the way to Hanoi. In the hotel lobby, as he was coming downstairs to buy a packet of cigarettes, Hsueh overheard that man call her by her name—Therese—and saw her slip into his room. She had not come back to the room until midnight. He had questioned her angrily, pushed her against the wall, torn her skirt and silk drawers off, and reached his hand in to touch her. She had not even bathed. She kept smiling at him until he asked, Who is he? Why has he been following us since Hong Kong?

She brushed him off, laughing at him. Who do you think you are? she asked. He thought he was in love with her. He loved the way she smoked. Instead of using one of those agate or jade cigarette holders, she would let the tobacco stain the bright curve of her lips, while her short black tousled hair cast flickering shadows on her pale face.

Now he was sitting on the side of the bed while she slept. Her handbag lay on the bedside table, and he opened it. He had never looked through her things before. A ray of early morning light sliced through the cabin window, illuminating a dark metallic outline. He put his hand inside the bag. It was a pistol—

The bag was snatched from his hands, and someone kicked him so hard he thudded to the floor. It was Therese, sitting on the pillow. The gray sky outside had turned a shade of vermillion, and she sat looking at him, backlit by the morning sun, her bare shoulders almost transparent. His eyes watered. He got up, snatched up his camera, and went outside.

The fog had lifted, and the river was sparkling. The white deck was stained bloodred with the dawn. He went down to the lower deck and toward the front of the ship. Coils of rope, sheets of canvas, and all the odd-numbered lifeboats were lined up toward the front of the boat by number, with the odd numbers on the starboard side while the even numbers were on the port side. A crowd had gathered by the railing to watch the sunrise.

There were a handful of tables and chairs, but the canvas seats were wet, and no one was sitting down. The bow of the ship was even windier, and it was empty. He leaned against the railing. Eight ships were anchored here in a fan-shaped formation, each with her bow pointing southwest toward Wu-sung-k'ou. An American passenger liner, the *President Jefferson*, was moored nearby. Waves beat on the ship, water droplets spattering its orange body just above the waterline. They looked like beads of sweat on a massive, hairless beast. Floating garbage collected near the surface of the water, while the gulls circled, looking for rotten food. He cursed aimlessly at the sky, and his self-pity turned into anger.

A shadow floated by. It was a silk handkerchief, dancing just beyond the railing like a white jellyfish swelling in the wind. He turned and saw a woman leaning against the railing. She wore a black wool coat, beneath which her dress, a green-and-white-checkered cheongsam, peeped out. The sun shone onto the port side of the ship from beyond the Yangtze, glinting off her hair. Her face was wet with what looked like tears. He had seen her somewhere before. She was pale, and the light shone into her eyes so that her tears glowed. He must have seen her in a movie, but which one? He couldn't stop himself from staring at her.

The bell rang for breakfast. Leng Hsiao-man wiped her cheek with the back of her hand. She glanced at the irate stranger, and as she was about to leave, she noticed a camera hanging from his long shoulder strap. The lens cover sprang open, and a finger pressed down on the shutter button. She hurried away.

The pilot boarded at 8:30 A.M. from a ladder mounted on the port side of the ship. He was responsible for navigating the ship into the narrow mouth of the Whampoa through Ch'iang-k'ou Channel. The ship would sail a little farther along the Whampoa to its destination, Kung-ho-hsiang Pier, just east of Lokatse on the northern shore of the Whampoa. He was not the only man getting ready to board the ship. At the floating pier just outside the port commissioner's office, four men in short sleeves were boarding a speedboat bound for the *Paul Lecat*—most likely gangsters, as they were carrying guns.

When the men sent by the Green Gang arrived at his cabin, Ts'ao had breakfasted and was fully dressed. Two of the bodyguards lugged his trunks out onto the deck. He reclined on the sofa in the cabin while Leng stood by the railing outside. He had no idea why Leng didn't just stay home. She insisted on traveling with him, but when she came she always had that mournful look. She shivered, went up to the trunk, opened it, and retrieved a red scarf, which she tied around her head.

The *garde municipale*, the police force of the French Concession, had been notified of Ts'ao's secret mission, but he would also need the Green Gang's protection. So instead of disembarking at Kung-ho-hsiang Pier in the International Settlement, he took a speedboat to Kin Lee Yuen Wharf, south of Lokatse. That was in the French Concession, within Green Gang territory.

Two boats were let down from the ship at the same time. One carried a Frenchman, a messenger who regularly traveled from Hanoi by train and sea via Haiphong to Shanghai, with documents that had to be personally signed for by the head of the Political Section of the French Concession Police. The other boat carried an important member of the Nanking government, his wife, his own bodyguards, and four bodyguards sent by the Green Gang. Before long, his wife started complaining of seasickness and insisted on sitting at the cabin window to get some air.

The sky was bright. Lin P'ei-wen was sitting on a rusty ladder that dipped below the waterline. The waves foamed around the pier, while bits of wood and leaves floated downstream. From where he was on Fishermen's Pier, he could see the porters on Kin Lee Yuen Wharf wearing their copper badges—only registered workers were allowed onto piers permitting overside delivery. He looked out to Lokatse, a bit of land on the eastern shore of the river that jutted out where the river took a sharp turn south. Someone said that it was called Lokatse because there used to be six families living there—*lok* meant six. But there were far more than six families there now. All the foreign trading houses were claiming land along the waterfront and building warehouses there. The few remaining rapeseed fields between dirty black walls looked like gaps in a mouth full of rotten teeth. There's no way I can keep track of all the boats rounding the corner past Lokatse, Lin thought. The papers said that the authorities were planning large-scale works to fill in deep fissures in the riverbed there.

Lin had collected a telegram in the early hours of the morning using forged identity papers. He had reported the contents of the telegram to Ku: their target, the hero of the day, would be arriving as planned. In a sense, Lin and his associates were merely the supporting cast.

In the early morning, Ku Fu-kuang had been at Mud Crossing in Pu-tung, waiting to cross the river with two other men. The Concession authorities prohibited boats other than the licensed Chinese- and Western-run ferries from taking passengers across the river, but there were always boatmen willing to risk the passage across the narrow, winding river for a fee.

Now they were sitting in a chestnut-colored Peugeot sedan parked at the entrance to Kin Lee Yuen Wharf.

Lin saw two boats round the corner, one after another. A woman stood at the entrance to the cabin of the speedboat, the chrome-plated railing glinting in the sunlight, her red head scarf flapping in the wind. Slipping out of Fishermen's Pier from a hole in the wire-mesh fence, he went up to the Peugeot and waved.

Ko Ya-min jumped out of the car and melted into the crowd. The entrance of the wharf led out onto the crowded Quai de France. Lin immediately picked out the reporter Li Pao-i, whose shifty air gave him away.

The *Arsène Lupin* had never employed more than three people at a time. It was printed once every three days, and each paper consisted of a single broadsheet folded up into a tabloid paper, so calling Li Pao-i a newspaper reporter was a stretch. But he had somehow gotten a tip and arrived early to get a piece of the action. This was a big scoop, and he didn't have the nerve to hog it, so he had also sold the tip to a handful of more reputable newspapers whose reporters he saw regularly at the teahouse. Now they were standing next to him, while men with cameras waited about ten meters away.

Sergeant Ch'eng Yu-t'ao strode through the entrance to the wharf with several of his men from North Gate Police Station. Someone important was disembarking today. The Green Gang had under-taken to protect him, and the sergeant's job was to shoo busybodies away and seal off the floating dock connected to the jetty, so that the motorcade could drive directly up the jetty onto the dock. When the cops arrived, the Peugeot drove slowly away from the entrance to the wharf.

Ku was now standing on the southern end of Rue Takoo with a Browning No. 2 pistol tucked under his shirt, in the left pocket of his gray serge trousers. The pocket had been specially sewn on, and it was extra deep so his gun would fit snugly inside. The strange windowless building behind him was a cold storage warehouse belonging to Shun-ch'ang Fish Traders. Ku was frantic. He realized the flaw in his plan. The jetty had been sealed off and no one was allowed to enter the floating dock. If the party had a motorcade, or if the blinds on the cars were drawn, then all was lost.

Lin P'ei-wen was standing at the opposite corner and looking toward him. Behind Ku, a narrow street called Rue de la Porte de l'Est ran south along the Quai de France, two blocks from Rue Takoo and parallel to it. On the side that intersected with the Quai de France, there was an iron gate with a police guard post. Farther south, where the French Concession ended and Chinese territory began, the road was called Waima Road, and the building on the intersection where the Quai de France became Waima Road was the headquarters of the Shanghai Special Marine Police Branch. Lin's job was to watch those two buildings closely. Ku himself was standing at the spot with the best view, and he had a clear view of the entrance to Kin Lee Yuen Wharf. The Peugeot was parked on the other end of Rue Takoo, near Rue du Whampoo.

Leng had already disembarked. She too realized that things had not gone according to plan. There were three eight-cylinder Ford sedans waiting for them, and they got into the middle one, with Ts'ao sitting next to her. She did not know whether anyone could tell which car they were in, and the blinds were drawn.

She made a decision without thinking twice.

Sergeant Ch'eng Yu-t'ao was standing on the floating dock to welcome his guests. He had Ts'ao's personal bodyguards hand over their Mauser rifles. Civilians were not allowed to carry unregistered firearms in the Concession, and what mattered was that they had the Green Gang's protection.

The car drove slowly up the jetty, turning past a building toward the entrance to the wharf.

It was just past ten. Li Pao-i would claim that he had heard the clock at the Customs House chime, or at least that was what he later told Hsueh at the teahouse.

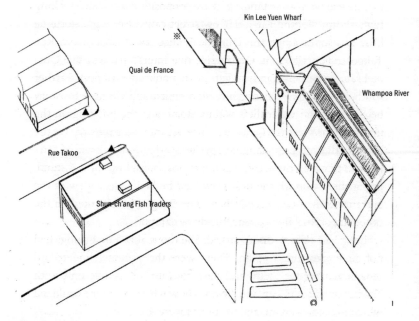

Kin Lee Yuen Wharf

Quai de France

Whampoa River

Rue Takoo

Shun-ch'ang Fish Traders

※ : Ts'ao is assassinated here

▲ : Lin and Ku watch from here

◎ : Shanghai Special Marine Police Branch

The assassination at Kin Lee Yuen Wharf

Just then, a string of firecrackers exploded with a deafening boom behind the rickshaws lined up on the northern side of the entrance. Later, the police confirmed that a string of firecrackers had indeed been hanging on the iron fences surrounding the wharf. The ground along the wall was strewn with tiny bits of paper, and the place stank of nitrates and sulfates. The Concession Police had developed a conditioned response to firecrackers—although harmless, they had often been used in recent protests and riots to sow chaos at the scene.

A rickshaw broke out of the lineup, cutting off Leng's sedan. Its window was open. Leng rolled her window down and stuck her head out. She poked her finger down her throat, and began to throw up the milk she had had for breakfast on the ship. The car stopped abruptly, her head jerked, and vomit spattered onto the body of the car. She did not see Ko Ya-min waiting behind the rickshaw. The door to the car was yanked open, and she fell out onto the ground. The gunfire pierced her eardrums like a screwdriver.

Firecrackers were echoing all along the tall buildings on either side of the wharf. But Ku had no time to enjoy the spectacle—he was focused only on witnessing its effect. As he watched Leng fall out of the car, he thought he could imagine how she must feel.

When it was eventually decided that Ko Ya-min would be the assassin instead of Leng, no one breathed a sigh of relief for her. Leng had argued that she was every bit as brave as Ko Ya-min, and the cell believed this man, Ts'ao Chen-wu, had in all likelihood ordered the murder of her ex-husband in prison. Ts'ao had been an officer in the Kwangsi Army, and he was now head of the Military Justice Unit for the forces occupying Shanghai. But Ku chose Ko as the assassin. His priority was to make sure that Ts'ao's execution took place in public, in a highly visible location. Luckily he had not planned to have Ts'ao shot on the floating dock itself, or the police blockade of the jetty would have thwarted his plan. Ku knew why Ko Ya-min had fought so hard for this task. Wang Yang, the man who had been shot in prison on Ts'ao's orders, was not only his half-brother and mentor, but also the person who had definitively conquered Leng's heart, especially now that he was dead.

Ko reached his hand into the backseat of the car to fire. All three bullets hit Ts'ao, and the last one penetrated his temple.

For Ts'ao, that bullet was the final blow. But for Ku, it was only the first blow, the first of a series of powerful signals he planned to send to the Concession and to Shanghai.

The Concession Police stood by. Later, at a meeting to discuss the incident, they would say that everything happened too quickly for them to react.

The eight bodyguards sent by the Green Gang were also caught by surprise. They had just gotten into the other two cars in the motorcade. Just as an audience relaxes for a moment when the curtain falls and before the applause begins, they let their guard down as they settled into the car, and the assassin had seized his chance.

An investigative commission representing the Nanking government in Shanghai also began to look into the incident. In one of their internal meetings, someone suggested that there was something fishy about the fact that the police had demanded Ts'ao's bodyguards hand over their rifles. Others suggested an investigation into the Green Gang bodyguards—who else could have known when Ts'ao was due to disembark, and how was this information leaked to the assassin? But all these speculations petered out when they discovered that Ts'ao's wife had sent a telegram from Wu-sung-k'ou when the liner was anchored there. Investigations into her quickly revealed one startling piece of evidence after another: her unusual background, the telegrams she had sent to Shanghai from Hong Kong, her red head scarf, and the vomiting. The woman herself had disappeared. Her photograph appeared in all the newspapers, and the Concession tabloids made a big show of using many question marks to suggest something scurrilous had happened.

Someone brought in the form that the man who collected Leng's telegram had filled out at the Telegraph Office, but they could not identify him, and the trail went cold. The tabloid reporter called Li Pao-i was a more promising lead, but there was little Nanking could do about that. As a resident of the French Concession, the man lay within the jurisdiction of the Concession Police, and the interrogation reports they sent to Nanking had clearly been doctored. One Sergeant Ch'eng from North Gate Police Station had written a report stating that Li had nothing to do with the assassins, and that Li had simply received an anonymous phone call at the newspaper's editorial offices, as well as a brown paper envelope that afternoon after the incident took place. But Li had connections to the Green Gang and was known for his cunning. He had tipped off several other newspapers, and sold his story and the contents of the envelope to several of the most reputable newspapers in the Concession instead of printing them in his own small paper, so he wasn't technically in breach of press regulations. No one in Nanking gave much thought to this setback, as they were already in the process of making plans to cooperate with the Concession Police.

And neither Nanking, nor the Concession Police, nor even the Green Gang could get anything out of the assassin, because after firing three shots at Ts'ao, he aimed the gun at his own temple and fired. The police coroner later found that the man had also bitten through a wax cyanide pill under his tongue. The bullet was just a safety measure.

CHAPTER 1

The Morris Teahouse was decorated like the interior of a ship's cabin. This was not unusual in the foreign concessions, where middle-aged European businessmen liked to install portholes and ship wheels in their houses, and style themselves captains. To be more precise, the teahouse looked like a floating hexagonal pagoda with its narrow stairs and copper-plated railings. The third floor had large windows on three of its walls, through which the Race Course could be seen, northeast of the teahouse.

The teahouse was as raucous as a stable. In fact, the building had housed a stable before being converted to a teahouse. Two large pieces of iron shaped like horses' hooves hung on the door, and Li Pao-i touched them every time he went inside.

The Morris Teahouse was where all the smalltime journalists in the concessions met to trade tips because it was so near the Race Course. On a clear day, if you stood at one of the windows facing north, you could see all the way to the ticket booth and even make out the colorful numbers announcing a raffle or listing betting odds. The crowds waited by the entrance, milling about in threes or fives. Li looked out onto the racecourse. On the inner dirt track where the horses warmed up in the morning, a stable hand was taking a small black mare for a lazy walk. When nuggets of horse shit dropped from her round ass, the stable hand would snatch them up as though they were worth something and put them in his bamboo basket.

Pppft! Li spat tea leaves out of the corner of his mouth. Even the tea here tasted like horse piss. The previous Saturday, the North Gate police had barged into his room early in the morning. Li lived in a tiny room above the shared kitchen, which meant his room always stank of fried salted fish. He was still half asleep when they dragged him outside and shoved him into the dingy backseat of a car. And then they dragged him out of the car and threw him into a room with white walls. It was true he could lock the door at night. But why should he? It wasn't as though he owned anything valuable. And how had they burst into the courtyard and marched straight through the kitchen and up the squeaky wooden stairs, all without waking meddlesome Mrs. Yang downstairs? Granted, they were cops, unstoppable in their uniforms, with whistles and batons, and police badges on their lapels.

That was why he had slept soundly right up until the moment when his visitors pulled the covers off and asked him politely to get dressed. The car made several sharp turns and pulled up in front of a red brick building. Only when he was pushed roughly out of the car did he think to ask: who are you anyway?

And then they stopped being polite. One man punched him on the back of the head. He recognized the man waiting inside as Sergeant Ch'eng of the North Gate police. He knew old Pock-faced Ch'eng. Like Li, Ch'eng was a Green Gang man from a wealthy Shanghai family. Unlike Li, the sergeant was a big shot. Li tried playing the gang card, mentioning his capo, but they kept kicking and punching him. He was forced to tell Ch'eng everything he knew. Except that he didn't know anything. He certainly did not know ahead of time that a man would be killed or he would have told the police—he was a good citizen. Ow! All right, he wasn't a good citizen, but he still wouldn't have had the nerve to keep that secret. He'd gone to the Kin Lee Yuen Wharf because an anonymous caller had told him at seven in the morning that something big was going to happen there. But what was he doing in the newsroom so early? Li said he hadn't gone home in the first place—he had spent the night playing mahjong. And why would he believe a single anonymous caller? What made the other reporters believe him? Here Li hesitated, and his interrogators pinned him down by the shoulders. Maybe it was the other man's tone of voice, which had sounded deadly serious, like cold air emanating from the phone receiver. But then how had he convinced the others? Oh, that was a piece of cake—he got another punch in the head, apparently Sergeant Ch'eng's men didn't like it if you sounded too casual—aren't reporters ready to believe anything in case there's a scoop in it for them?

Sergeant Ch'eng let him go. He did warn Li that if it weren't for his capo, and if it weren't for the fact that Li had been clever enough to sell the manifesto to other newspapers instead of printing it in the *Arsène Lupin*, he would be spending the next couple of years in jail at Lunghwa Garrison Command. The media had had a field day covering the Kin Lee Yuen shooting, and many newspapers had printed a manifesto addressed to Shanghai residents by the assassins, without the slightest regard for the authority of the Shanghai Party-Government-Army Press Censorship Bureau, which was housed in the East Asia Hotel.

The teahouse began to fill with people, and he sat at a window facing north. Hsueh sat opposite him, while his camera lay on the small table.

"Where were you that day? I spent all night looking for you. I even came here to catch you in the morning, but you weren't anywhere to be found!"

Li Pao-i was telling the truth now. He had not told the truth to Sergeant Ch'eng.

Hsueh seemed to regret missing out on the scoop. Of course, Li then had simply sold the tip to someone else. Hsueh flipped through the photos again. Several of them had already appeared in the newspaper, but there were a few others that Hsueh hadn't seen. These were the ones by the *China Times*, and the photographer had developed a set for Li to keep.

Hsueh's favorite subject of photography was the crime scene. Here, the gunman's corpse took up the right-hand diagonal half of one photo, lying beneath the spare tire that hung at the back of the car. There were black pools of liquid and a gun on the ground. *Shun Pao* identified it as the semiautomatic Mauser C96 rifle, while other papers used its nickname, the box cannon gun, to make it sound scarier. Another photo was a close-up of a cop's face. Beyond the rim of his cap and his raised tin whistle, which was so near the lens it looked like a wilted black flower, you could see the door swung open and the body on the backseat. The corner of a black coat peeked out beneath the door. It belonged to the woman, the victim's wife. One photo captured her vacant expression as she lay there, propping herself up with her hand and struggling to lift her head, with vomit on the corner of her mouth. Li had seen another photo in *Millard's Review*, an old photo from the newspaper announcements of Mr. Ts'ao's wedding. Word was that Ts'ao's death had had something to do with his wife, who was now wanted by the police department.

"I saw this woman on the ship. I've got a photo of her that's much better than this one. That guy did a shoddy job. His camera won't do, and his technique is terrible," Hsueh said critically. In the chaos, the *China Times*'s photographer had clearly been unable to keep his subject in focus.

"Show it to me."

"No, I don't think I will." Hsueh sounded a little distracted. "You'd have to pay me. Fifty yuan."

Li promptly lost interest. The assassination was old news. A whole week had passed, the Concession newspapers had devoted pages and pages to the story, and now everyone was getting tired of it. Only Hsueh was still enthusiastic about it.

"So, this woman. Was she really a Communist?" Hsueh said. "How did they find you anyway?"

"They stopped me on the road and asked me to get into a car with them." Li was lying again. He had been walking down the street when a woman had slapped him in the face and started hurling abuse at him. Then someone had stopped to break up the fight and shoved him into a car. He had been kidnapped. But he didn't want to admit that—it was a little embarrassing.

"What did they look like?"

"What do you think, they all had red hair and green eyes? Haven't you seen a Communist before? Only a few years ago they were on every street corner."

Just thinking about that man made his skin creep. The man had been forty or so. He always had his top hat on, even indoors. His eyes pierced through you from beneath the rim of his hat, and he smoked one cigarette after another. Li wouldn't dare mess with him—he could see that this man was much more dangerous than the police. He didn't have to ask what you were thinking because he knew. And the more polite he was, the more terrified Li became, as if he could be shot for one wrong word. The man put the gun on the table.

He warned Li not to go getting any ideas, not to even think about tipping the police off quietly. Li was to comply fully with his demands. At nine in the morning he was to show up at the Kin Lee Yuen Wharf, watch carefully, and write a good story. The next time we visit, we'll bring you something, he said. But instead of visiting, they merely sent him a brown paper envelope containing a manifesto announcing the execution of the counterrevolutionary element Ts'ao Chen-wu, signed by the Special Operations Unit of the Chinese Communist Party in Shanghai and Their Comrades of People's Strength. A bullet lay in the envelope, proof that his correspondent meant business. He could have sent two bullets, but would two bullets say anything that one didn't?

He dared not simply print the manifesto in the brown paper envelope, so he pulled an old trick and sold it to several of the more reputable newspapers, reasoning that he had more than complied with his visitor's request. Of course he made a tidy profit—that was his job. He even managed to sell the tip to a foreign newspaper. The Communists couldn't object to getting some international attention. The wealthy Chinese in the Concession only read foreign newspapers, paid for monthly by check. They all had servants who would retrieve the paper from the letterbox and bring it to the living room in the morning. If they came after him, he could reasonably claim that having the Concession's foreign newspapers print their manifesto was the equivalent of loosening a screw on the

Press Censorship Bureau's gates. The next day, it would be in all the Chinese papers. Wasn't that exactly what these men wanted?

He didn't tell Hsueh all this. It was time they forgot about this story. It was stale news by now, and he was quite sure his visitors would leave him alone. Apart from Hsueh, no one else had come over to ask him about it all morning—and Hsueh was clearly more interested in the woman than the story. When he left, he asked Li Pao-i to give him the photos of this woman, even though he thought little of the *China Times*'s cameraman. Sure you can have them, it's old news. Have them all if you want. I've already made more than eighty yuan off this story. Care to know the woman's name?

"I know, she's called Leng Hsiao-man."

Hsueh turned and walked quickly down the stairs.

CHAPTER 2

As Hsueh walked along, he could not stop thinking about that woman. She looked like someone he knew, but he still didn't know who she was. All the movies he had seen starred Western actresses. Maybe it was a certain expression, a scene, a line of dialogue she reminded him of. He hadn't even spoken to her. Now that her photo had been in all the papers, he could barely tell whether the face he imagined was the one he had seen by the railing.

On Mohawk Road, someone thumped him on the shoulder. His shoulder strap slipped, and he quickly hooked his arm to catch his camera. It was Barker.

Barker was American. He had fat fingers covered with layers of skin that made them look like Cantonese sausages, and his fingernails were dull.

"Acetic acid," Barker had told him one day in the bar.

He had spread his hands, palms facing downward, on the little round table in the bar. The tablecloth was stained with tea, as if he had just rubbed his hands on it. You could invent an alias or grow a beard, but you could not swap out your fingertips. The police had a new way of dipping your fingers in ink and pressing them on a piece of paper, which would go in a big book in a filing cabinet. Then you would never be able to get in trouble again—the cops would find you wherever you went. It's not as though you could cut off your fingers. Soaking them in vinegar worked and didn't hurt, but it took a couple of weeks. When Barker was telling him all this in the bar, they had known each other for only about a month.

Hsueh had met him at the roulette table in the saloon. When gambling was outlawed in the International Settlement, all the dice joints and gambling dens had migrated to the narrow alleyways of the French Concession, but foreigners hardly ever came to this kind of place. Barker hovered by the tables, tall and lanky with long arms like a mantis. He stuck out. Hsueh made a point of being inquisitive in the Concession, which he considered his territory. He kept tabs on anyone who stuck out.

A wanted man in America who had fled across the Pacific, Barker now stood in the saloon with the air of a diplomat fresh off the ships. His right elbow was cupped in his left hand, and he was ostentatiously tapping his forehead with his right index finger, like a British public school boy.

Barker pulled Hsueh into the Race Course. Word was that the final steeplechase had been fixed, said Barker, and the horse owner himself was said to be betting against the Cossack jockeys. The jockeys had decided to trap Chinese Warrior between two other horses to prevent it from reaching full speed, and Black Cacique, a literal dark horse, would win. The crowds crammed between the iron gates and the viewing deck were hysterical, as if the Lord himself had decided not to wait for Judgment Day and was judging the saved from the damned on the basis of their betting slips.

A whistle blasted, and the loudspeakers on either side of the viewing deck began to crackle. Someone was making an announcement in English followed by Shanghainese dialect: "The Race Club Committee hereby announces the hosting of an additional steeplechase race this afternoon."

Cheering, the crowd rushed toward the viewing deck. In the frenzy, a single cry could create a maelstrom that would suck the whole crowd in.

Hsueh changed his mind abruptly. He did not want to join them after all. He bid farewell to Barker, and walked toward Avenue

Édouard VII. He would lunch at the Manor Inn, and later that afternoon, Therese would be waiting for him at the Astor Hotel, in a
fourth-floor luxury suite that cost twelve yuan a day.

Hsueh was the illegitimate son of a Frenchman who had boarded
a boat in Marseille with a suitcase full of tattered clothes. The
Frenchman had loitered in bars in Saigon and Canton, bragging
about his exploits, until he found a job in Shanghai. It was the best
time of his life. Hsueh's Cantonese mother had a dull complexion.
She wore a traditional jacket with dull patterns, her curls jabbing
into its stiff collar. She had never worn clothes like that before meeting Hsueh's father, and she then refused to wear anything else. She
rattled constantly around Hsueh's pale collarbone, in an egg-shaped
cloisonné box that he wore on a heavy silver chain around his neck.
The chain had long been stained black with his sweat. Even when he
was at his least self-conscious, whispering dirty phrases in Therese's
ear in Chinese she didn't understand, his mother was still rattling
between their bodies.

Moved by a passion he had never experienced until then, Hsueh's
father rushed to the trenches at Verdun during the Great War, leaving behind in Shanghai all his possessions, his Chinese lover, and
Hsueh. He never returned. Hsueh was only twelve years old. But it
could not be said of Hsueh's father that he did not love his family. He
wrote to them from the battlefield, and the letters that reached them
from across the oceans often contained a small package of photographs. In one of them, a Zulu regiment was performing a religious
ceremony. Hsueh's father had never seen that many black men in his
life. Wearing nothing but a piece of cloth around their waists, they
waved their sticks, dancing with rapt expressions. Hsueh's favorite
one was of his father smoking a pipe in the trenches in summertime,
his chin covered with stubble, shirtsleeves torn short at the shoulders. In another photo, a man posed stark naked at the entrance to
the shower cubicles while his uniform hung on the wall. It was his
father, grinning at the camera with one hand covering his pubic hair.
His mother had stashed this photo away, so he did not see it until
after her death. There was a line in French on the back: *Poux—Je n'ai*

pas de poux! Lice—I have no lice! He suspected this photo was partly responsible for the fact that his mother never remarried.

That winter, his father posed for a photo next to a row of corpses. He wore his jacket and a water canteen slung over his shoulder. There were so many corpses that it looked like a slaughterhouse. Some were laid out side by side, while others were piled on trucks like garbage. In fact, the injured looked even more horrific than the dead. One man was wrapped from head to toe in bandages, excepting three holes for his eyes and nose.

Not only had his father's amateur photography influenced Hsueh's choice of career, but the very photos that he sent them from the trenches were also an artistic inheritance that had shaped Hsueh's tastes. Hsueh's penchant for snapping photos of dead men, crime scenes, maimed, stabbed, and bullet-ridden bodies, frenzied gamblers, drunkards, and all forms of human perversity could likely be traced to the photos his father sent home.

When she died, Hsueh's mother had left him a small sum of money, most of which he spent within a month. He had an American firm on the Bund order a camera from New York for him, a 4x5 Speed Graphic with a 1/1000s Compur shutter, the best press camera to be had. It could capture the instant before a bullet pierced a human skull.

Before he met Therese, photography had been his greatest love, with gambling only a distant second. Then Therese had nearly replaced photography in his affections until he tried combining his two loves and found that they were both the better for it.

He had fallen for her right away, that night in Lily Bar.

"Half a glass of kvass topped off with vodka. Hey you, Duke! You know what I want." She had been a little tipsy. Duke, the waiter she was shouting for, was the White Russian owner of the bar.

Her voice was husky and tender, a voice made for old songs. While the Victrola turned slowly on the bar table, she sat at a table by the window. The black of the wrought iron grilles stood out against the blue diamond-shaped glass, and a naked woman was engraved in yellow on the glass. It was raining, and the pavement had an oily red sheen. When the song ended, she would clap hysterically.

He had thought he was seducing her, so he was startled to find that she had turned their relationship on its head, conquering both him and his camera in the space of a week. His own passive tendency to go along with what other people wanted was to blame.

This afternoon, Therese would be waiting for him in her suite on the fourth floor of the Astor. She might even be in bed, if she had already spent enough time soaking in the bath, warm like a mug of cream swirled with pink fruit juice. Like a filly clambering out of a pond, she would climb out of the bath and skip right into bed. She had an aristocratic air that the White Russian men who claimed to have been dukes or navy admirals rarely possessed. Their huge bodies cowered in the dark corners of the Concession's bars, members of a defeated northern tribe. Therese, on the other hand, pushed Hsueh onto the bed, had him lie straight, and sat astride him, swaying and waving one arm, as though she were waving a Cossack dagger.

If he didn't love her, he wouldn't be losing his temper or interrogating her. He imagined the sultry Southeast Asian breeze whetting her appetite. One day she would decide he couldn't satisfy her. She would slip out of the hotel room and into someone else's room. He pictured the man in the other room as an old friend, whereas he himself was only a fling. He imagined her lifting her legs under someone else's body. The very idea tormented him.

He began to think he didn't love her after all. He preferred thinking of himself as a dandy taking advantage of the fact that Therese was both wealthy and generous. That made him feel better.

But he still wanted to know whom she had met in the hotel. She would not tell him. If he began to ask, she would get mad, or pounce on him, or even pretend not to hear him and ignore him altogether. He began to daydream about investigating her, but he wouldn't know how to start. He had no wiles. Li Pao-i might, but Hsueh did not.

It was the White Russian woman who first attracted Lieutenant Sarly's attention. The French Concession Police had a file on every foreigner in Shanghai, and it recorded that she was known as Lady Holly, but the name had nothing to do with her real name or provenance. Only the Chinese used that name, and she had often dealt with Chinese.

She had come to Talien by boat, and before then she had probably lived in Vladivostok. As a southerner, Lieutenant Sarly had never been that far north. He was Corsican; Corsicans controlled all the important posts in the police force.

There were a few documents in her police file, among them a report signed by Foreign Agent 119, which gave her real name as *Irxmayer, Therese* and noted that Irxmayer was her late husband's name. The German name concealed the fact that she was a Russian Jew. There were some faded notes, the earliest records of this woman. Most of them dated from the two months after she first arrived in Shanghai. After that, she seemed to have slipped out of sight. No one in the police's network of agents and investigators mentioned her.

A month ago, on the lawn adjacent to the police headquarters on Route Stanislas Chevalier, thirty meters or so from the women's rattan tea tables, Commissioner Martin had told him something interesting. Martin was his English counterpart at the International Settlement's Municipal Police. The other officers had been playing a game of *pétanque à la lyonnaise* on the lawn. The lower ranked officers never tired of playing this game. That day, the prize was a trophy and a three-star bottle of brandy. Gripping the iron boule with his palm facing down, Inspector Maron threw the final boule. A man ran into the playing area and traced out a circle with a piece of string to count out the number of points scored by the winner, and all the families got up from their bamboo chairs. When they counted to the fifth boule, the onlookers cheered.

The colonial police and administrators formed their own social circle that congregated at tea parties and various joint conferences. At these events, Sarly often received veiled hints of local vested interests, and it was as important to satisfy them as it was to placate London or Paris, thousands of miles away. Business in the colonies was conducted informally, as it had always been. So you couldn't always take what Hong Kong's British colonial police force said on paper seriously— even they might not be taking themselves seriously. And what was anyone to make of their ambiguous choice of words? *You may have noticed*, or, *It would appear from subsequent investigations. . . .*

Martin was dressed in full hunting gear that day, but the paper he drew from his pocket was not a map of some unknown country. It was the last page of a long letter about the suspicious activities of one Zung, a businessman from Hong Kong who had been spotted at deserted villages around the bay. Since no opium, alcohol, or the usual smuggled goods appeared to be involved, the case was passed on to the Special Branch of the Hong Kong Police. The letter closed by making casual reference to a German woman and the firm she ran, Irxmayer & Co. She lived in the French Concession, the Hong Kong police learned. Not long thereafter, one of the letters that the colonial police force in Hanoi sent each week by sea was found to contain a detailed description of a botched police sweep. Careless Indo-Chinese terrorists (all the plotting could wear these people out) had left a note under a pillow in their hotel room. Solid information, the Hanoi police concluded—*assez généreux, nous voudrions dire*. They sent the original note to their English colleagues in Hong Kong without opaque formalities or polite equivocations. It simply contained a post office box number: P.O. Box No. 639.

From there it was a short step to discovering that the post office box belonged to a businessman in his early thirties, one Zung Ts-Mih. The Hong Kong police realized immediately that this man had long been a subject of interest. Further investigations revealed that the respectable-looking Mr. Zung had a complicated background and obscure ancestry. In the sailors' taverns it was rumored that despite his Chinese name, Zung was at most half Chinese. Even his father was said to have been a British subject "of mixed blood." These words had been circled in red in the report, and a big bent arrow, like a circus clown's tilted hat, pointed to a rectangle containing the word *Siamese*.

At least three of Mr. Zung's close contacts were under surveillance by the Hanoi Police. And yet the British insisted that their policy permitted them to investigate the suspects and photograph them but not arrest them. Lieutenant Sarly considered this so-called policy an instance of British arrogance, appeasement, and sheer neglect. The real subject of their investigation was one Alimin, a roaming wolf whose travels had taken him all over East Asia, to Bangkok, Johore, Amoy, and Hankow, and reportedly even to Vladivostok and Chita, where he was said to have received some form of technical training. The photograph was indistinct, but in it he was wearing a shirt with a jacket and black bow tie, together with a pair of those baggy knee-length shorts worn over a *sarong* of the kind the natives wore. He had a thick brow and huge nose.

Someone had written across the top of the first page of the document:

—*selon la décision de la IIIème Internationale, le quartier général du mouvement communiste vietnamien déménagera dans le sud de la Chine. Ses dirigeants arriveront bientôt dans notre ville (Shanghai), leurs noms sont Moesso et Alimin.*

It turned out that Mr. Zung was the Chinese agent for a foreign trading company registered in Hong Kong and run by a German woman whom the police later determined to be White Russian. She lived in an apartment in the French Concession, on the third floor of the Beam Apartments on the corner of Avenue Joffre and Avenue Dubail. A detective from Marseille, who fancied himself a poet, had described the building as an "ornate box with the scent of cape jasmine and osmanthus." Lieutenant Sarly ordered an investigation into the occupants of the Beam Apartments, which turned up a report entitled "Personnalités de Shanghai," a sixteen-page document that the secretariat nicknamed the VIP file. So it turned out the police did have information on this woman after all, buried in a list of Concession dignitaries. No one had taken the time to link her to the inconspicuous woman noted in the port customs files. The VIP file did not contain much information beyond an address, occupation, and phone number. But the detectives in the Political Section immediately began a preliminary investigation, and started writing their reports, a stack of which now lay at Sarly's fingertips. On his table, rather, in his sunlit document tray.

The red brick building at 22 Route Stanislas Chevalier was the police headquarters. Sarly's Political Section was on the northern side of the second and third floors. The building reeked of rosin and paraffin wax. Lieutenant Sarly dealt with the unbearable smell by endlessly smoking pipes. On humid spring days, this made the air in his office even more rancid. But in the afternoon, sunlight streamed into the room. The shade of the mulberry trees inside the walls extended onto the street, and two children in tatters stood on Route Albert Jupin, staring up at the tree. Afternoons in the South Concession were usually quiet apart from a couple of dogs barking from inside the jails on Rue Massenet.

The woman who lived in the Beam Apartments was a thirty-eight-year-old White Russian woman whom the Chinese referred to respectfully as Lady Holly. She apparently ran a jewelry store opposite the apartments on the corner of Avenue Dubail, under the sign ECLAT. The door faced Avenue Dubail, whereas the side facing Avenue Joffre was a storefront window shaded by curtains. The store occupied the ground floor of a two-story building, and when the family living upstairs hung their gray Chinese gowns out to dry without wringing them out, water would drip onto the *ECLAT* sign, said the report. Sarly recognized the hand of the poet from Marseille in this writing. Sarly himself was always encouraging his subordinates to write official reports with more flair. Details, he always said, stick closely to the details.

The jewelry store did mediocre business. Ever since the Russians flocked to Shanghai, the market had been flooded with large quantities of precious stones all said to be from the mines of the Urals, and it was hard to tell which ones were genuine. The Russian jewelry stores had Jewish storekeepers who all sported a scraggly beard full of crumbs and spit, like large furry animals with an air of Central Asia about them. The locals were skeptical of claims that distant off-shoots of the tsar's family had come to Shanghai with their wedding jewels tucked carefully away in trunks. Sergeant Maron, a man who sank his free time in Sherlock Holmes novels, pointed out that the jewelry shop could not possibly be making enough money to cover rent, much less subsidize Lady Holly's lavish lifestyle.

Someone later put a list of names on his desk, with a note identifying it as a list of passengers on that French ship involved in the Kin Lee Yuen incident. He tossed the list onto the sofa, and did not look at it until the poet started screaming at the top of his lungs. Yes, that's her, the White Russian princess of the Beam Apartments—that's her beautiful ass! Only a poet could look at a name list and think of ass.

Of course, it could be a simple coincidence. But Sarly's Corsican imagination told him that if one woman kept turning up everywhere you looked, and you persisted in thinking there was nothing to it, you must have some nerve to be denying the existence of God, of the great hands that arrange all earthly affairs.

Sarly knew that nearly everyone in the building called him "bow legs" behind his back. Like a retired jockey who had stopped caring about his weight, he pounded the black floorboards of the police station and made them creak. Not long after Sarly was posted to the Political Section, the atmosphere there changed. His predecessor had been on good terms with the local gangs and secret societies until someone had circumvented the colonial authorities and ratted him out to the Paris newspapers, after which the man had to be posted to Hanoi.

Sarly had two habits that distinguished him from his predecessor. To begin with, he liked tobacco pipes. From the document tray on his desk to the two telephones, a row of briar, agate, coral, and jade pipes adorned the room. This was a private hobby and had no impact on the rest of the Political Section. Rather, it was his predilection for paperwork that drove his subordinates crazy. Sarly liked to circulate documents in the office, as though he could only comprehend something when it had been written down with a name and rank attached to it.

Sarly sat placidly in his office, smoking and reading documents. The new leadership of the Political Section had ramifications beyond its walls. In the summer, the mulberry trees that shaded Route Albert Jupin attracted a crowd of urchins who often scaled the walls surrounding the police headquarters to reach the mulberries. The junior officers on duty had gotten in the habit of slipping out of the back door and catching a few boys, boxing their ears, and putting them to work polishing shoes, washing cars, sweeping floors, and scrubbing windows. That afternoon, they were hiding in the alleyway and ready to pounce when Sarly poked his head out of a third-floor window and stopped them.

The various subdivisions of the Political Section were further divided into smaller units. The Chinese men all worked for the Chinese police inspector, who also had two Chinese detective sergeants under his command. Foreigners were foreigners, whether Vietnamese or French, and Chinese were Chinese. So if a Frenchman wanted something from a Chinese detective, he would first have to speak to the Chinese inspector, who would then give the appropriate orders. Sarly cut through all the bureaucracy. His powerful bow legs kicked open the doors to every office in the building. He would assign work to anyone he saw fit, and he selected detectives from every division for a newly created detective squad that met every

morning in a room on the end of the third-floor corridor. Everyone
else called this meeting "morning prayers for the lieutenant's bastards." The French were infuriated by the fact that half the bastards
were Chinese. Sarly's theory was that the Political Section could not
only be an elite force. To protect French colonial interests, it must be
in touch with the local community.

Something occurred to Sarly, and he looked more closely at the
list. He noticed that the White Russian woman had not been traveling alone. She had a companion, Hsueh Wei-shih, Weiss Hsueh. The
discovery irritated him. At morning prayers the next day, he would
chew his detectives out for not having done a thorough job.

The evidence suggested that Irxmayer and Co. were doing some
alarming deals. Official documents listed the company as trading
"household metal tools" and "commercial machine equipment,"
which sounded less like a pretext than a rueful excuse: times are
hard, so we had to specialize to stay afloat.

In fact, Irxmayer and Co. traded across Asia in ammunition and
firearms. Beneath the hay and durable oilcloth in its wooden crates
lay deadly weapons that could be used to assassinate a man, intimi-
date him, play Russian roulette, or even to start a war.

Margot ran toward Therese's Ford car as soon as it had driven past the fence.

They were at the home base of the Shanghai Paper Hunt Club, north of a stream called Rubicon Creek on maps. The rules of the hunt were as follows: the club nominated a master who laid a paper trail by scattering scraps of colored paper from a large bag he carried across country, and the riders would have to follow the route he laid out to the finishing point. For thirty years now, the master had been Ah Pau, who had an endlessly inventive Chinese sense of humor. He scattered scraps of paper in the crannies between rocks, under tufts of grass, hid them in ditches and under bridges. Once he strung them across the river on a piece of fishing line, causing several contestants to fall in. No one could guess what Ah Pau had up his sleeve, which was why Brenen had Margot study the map closely.

The map had been drawn by early pathfinders in the club, who invented names such as Three Virgins' Jump and Sparkes Water Wade. Margot once asked Brenen out of curiosity: "But what do the Chinese call these places? They must have Chinese names—they aren't even inside the concessions."

Brenen had given her an answer in the true colonial spirit: "Who cares what they call it? Once we give it a name, it's ours."

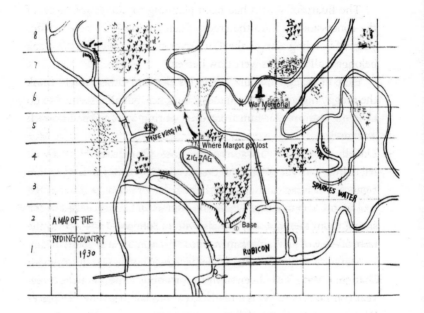

The Shanghai Paper Hunt Club's race at Rubicon Creek

Her husband, Baron Franz Pidol, would have approved of that answer. The Luxembourg United Steel Company's chief representative in Shanghai, he spent most of his energies speculating on land, and he currently had his sights on a field near Rubicon Creek. "Even that old cripple, Sir Victor Sassoon, has his eyes on the creek," said Franz.

The Board of Works had been planning to build roads west of the concessions toward the creek. Their timing was perfect. After years of flooding along Lake T'ai's river system, to which the creek belonged, all the fields were now barren.

Here in Shanghai, Franz was in his element. Others might think the muggy nights and mosquitoes a nuisance, but all it seemed to do to Franz was prevent him from ever visiting Margot's bedroom. It was unlikely that he never slept with anyone else. The talkative Mrs. Liddell told Margot that all the men took Chinese lovers. They all fell in love with the place, with the social scene, with smoking Luzon cigars and playing cards, and with the superior goods on offer at the brothel on Avenue Haig, where the women did not sit naked in the sitting room the way they did elsewhere. Subtlety was more to the taste of the worldly businessmen whose circle Franz was about to join.

Margot was lonely. Until Franz declared that he was in love with Shanghai, Margot had been counting on going home when his three-year contract ended. Was it really so easy to fall in love with a place? Wasn't it much easier to fall in love with a person, like Brenen?

Brenen Blair had fallen in love with Margot the moment he saw her. Margot only had two friends in Shanghai, and apart from Therese, Brenen was the only person in whom she could confide. In the tearoom at Arnhold & Co., Brenen had suggested she buy parchment lamp shades bordered with dark gold, as she was looking to change the lamp shades in her bedroom. It was the first time they had met. Only much later would he have a chance to admire the lit lamp shades, when Franz had begun to travel inland frequently by train.

Mrs. Liddell said that although Mr. Blair was young, he was a veteran diplomat, who had proved himself capable of handling tricky

situations during postings to Australia and India. He was currently
a political adviser to the Nanking government. As the go-between
for the colonial British government and the Nanking government,
he had the right to convey his views directly to the Foreign Office in
London without going through the British consul in Shanghai, Mr.
Ingram, or through the British temporary representative office in
Beijing.

Brenen suggested that Margot join the Shanghai Women's
Equestrian Club, and Franz supported the idea. The two of them
accompanied her to the stables of the riding school on Mohawk
Road, and picked out a gray mare flecked with white. Franz could
not understand why Margot wanted to name the horse Dusty
Answer. The odd name was actually Brenen's idea. Franz had been
cordial to Brenen until they had summered together in Mo-kan-
shan, the mountains near Shanghai, where Franz had just bought
a plot of land and built a summer resort. When they got back, he
began assiduously to avoid all social occasions at which Mr. Blair
might appear.

Margot showed Therese into the club grounds. The grass had
been freshly mowed. The Chinese servant at the club had been busy
since dawn, carrying bamboo chairs out of storage and wiping them
down, filling silver buckets with a cocktail made from rock sugar
and gin. The grass was dotted with wildflowers that attracted bees
and butterflies to buzz about your ankles. A water buffalo burned
black by the sun lazed on the southern shore of Rubicon Creek. The
club used to wait until the end of November to put on its official
competition. By then, the beans and cotton would have been har-
vested, the winter crop of wheat planted, and the weather would be
at its mildest. But since the arable land had all turned to wasteland
after the flooding, the committee had been happy to arrange a few
more contests. After all, the Depression meant the men had more
free time, and they needed the exercise.

They found a bamboo table beneath the oleander tree. The
men were arguing by the stables. Mario, the man with the loudest
voice, was an Italian illustrator who drew cartoons for the foreign

newspapers in the Concession. They said he had been beaten up in a bar in Hongkew by a band of Japanese *rōnin*. The illustrator was arguing with people, among them the British businessman whom Margot knew to be in Franz's set. "It's time we taught Nanking a lesson," the British man cried. "We should have the Japs do it. They could even start a little war. We'd get new treaties and new boundaries for the concessions, maybe even fifty kilometers on either side of the Yangtze!"

"Wouldn't that be a windfall for you," Mario replied frostily. "With all that land you've bought, a war would keep you out of bankruptcy court!" His voice grew louder. "You idiots, wake up. There's no more striking it rich out here. The Great War was the end of that. If the Japanese get here, they'll ruin us all."

Compared to the rest of the crowd, Brenen was tall and thin. He came over to keep them company while they examined the horse.

The crown of the chinquapin tree hung over the fence. The gray mare stood beneath it while the stable hand in his blue jacket stroked her neck, tightened the girth, and lifted the saddle to reveal her mane, which had been neatly braided. The scent of bay leaves wafted toward them, and the mare grew fidgety, snorting and pawing vigorously at the ground. To join the club, Margot had had to buy a horse, because competing horses had to be the bona fide property of club members. They had to be Chinese horses, though strictly speaking, that meant they were small Mongolian horses, crossbred from English purebreds and Mongolian horses, as Brenen had once explained to her. Her mare was a crossbreed too. Look at her hips, he explained, smacking the horse's ass in front of the Cossack horse dealer on Mohawk Road. Purebred Mongolian horses have sloping hips, while English horses have arched hips. This horse is descended from the herd of English stallions that the tsar bought, because he was convinced that his Cossack cavalrymen would defeat Napoleon as long as they were mounted on horses with the wide hips of English purebreds.

"In fact, Dame Juliana Berners of Sopwell Nunnery said as long ago as the fifteenth century that a good horse possesses the back of a donkey, the tail of a fox, the eyes of a rabbit, the bones of a man, and the chest and hair of a woman. A good racing horse is proud and holds its head high, like a beautiful woman."

Brenen repeated this speech, looking at Therese.

A bay horse came galloping in from the north side of the field.

"Ah Pau! Ah Pau!" the onlookers cried.

Ah Pau was indeed galloping down the hillside on the bay horse. The Chinese servant was the central figure of the Paper Hunt Club. Several of the club officers had retired and returned home, while others had lost their lives in the Great War, making Ah Pau the only constant: now in his fifties, he had served the club faithfully for thirty years.

The jittery racehorses crowded along the fences on the northern edge of the field, and the gates were finally opened. Margot climbed into the saddle and waved at Therese, who was standing in the field. A gust of wind lifted her hat, and as she dropped the reins to catch her hat, the gray mare suddenly started forward.

Margot lurched in the saddle, but Brenen steadied it for her, picked the reins up nimbly from the ground and placed them in her hands.

"Ladies and gentlemen, on your mark, get set, go!"

The horses rushed out the gate. One of them crashed into the fence and knocked the post askew so that it ripped out of the ground, tearing up clods of mud. Hundreds of hooves thundered down the hill. The grass glinted in the breeze, and someone called out: "Tally-ho!"

Previously, when he was explaining the rules of the game, Brenen had told her that the expression was borrowed from the cry the Indians used for their hunting hounds. In the paper hunt, riders who found the strips of paper hidden in the hedges or under pebbles cried tally-ho to alert the official observers.

They raced down the hill into a cabbage patch. Margot tugged at the reins, steering her horse into the cabbages. Suddenly, a Chinese man appeared from the bushes, stamping his feet and shouting at her. Startled, her horse took a step back and began pawing at the ground, flinging up mud. Brenen caught up with her and flung a silver coin on the ground. The shouting stopped.

They had lost the group, and there were no scraps of paper in sight. They were standing on a small plateau hemmed in by a stream. Margot got the map out, and Brenen pointed to a Z-shaped stream called Zigzag Jump.

They steered their horses east along the stream, past a wooden bridge, and stopped in front of a mound of yellow earth next to a copse. On top of the mound lay an obelisk built of rubble, the club's war memorial plaque.

It was almost noon, the sun was shining on the bottle green stream, and insects darted among the poisonous leaves of the oleander. Margot felt that she could not allow Brenen to touch her. She melted a little whenever he came close. It was she who had fallen in love with him. She felt like a bee with its wings caught in nectar.

Hsueh thought of Therese. He pictured her hair, which was curly like a shock of cornflower petals. Curiously, the darker the room was and the more pain he was in, the more clearly he could picture Therese. But that was only to be expected, since he had taken dozens of photographs of her.

He did not know what they wanted with him or why they had brought him here. From where he lived on Route J. Frelupt, the car had only made two turns, which meant they must be at the police headquarters on Route Stanislas Chevalier. They drove through the iron gates and into a passageway on the north side of the building, between the red brick wall and a high fence lined with glass shards, where they dragged him out of the car. It was cold and there was no sunlight.

They pushed him into the building. The walls of the corridor were dark green with black paneling, and the floors were painted black. He was brought into what looked like an interrogation room and forced onto a chair fitted with high boards. As soon as he sat down, the boards were rotated so that they were positioned right under his arms.

The Chinese sergeant sat behind the desk, asking questions and filling out the printed form he had in front of him. When he had finished with each page, he handed it to the secretary who sat beside him, a Chinese man who knew French and who was busy translating and typing up the document.

The questions slowly began to focus on his trip with Therese. The sergeant stopped filling out forms and began to write down Hsueh's answers on a piece of grid paper.

Where did you go in Hong Kong? What about Hanoi? Haiphong? Can you only remember the hotels? Did you go to the pier? To bars? Restaurants? Did you meet anyone?

But he had little to say. No, he was not lying. I'll give you ten minutes to think about it, said the sergeant, and walked off, probably because he needed to piss. He came back, his clothes smelling of Lysol. Hsueh still had nothing to say.

"Ah yes, she did go to see a man in another room in Hanoi," Hsueh said. Of course the thought had been in the back of his mind all this time. A Chinese man. I don't know him, I know nothing about him, but he looked a little shady, said Hsueh, glad of the chance to disparage his rival.

"Well, then let us help jog your memory," the sergeant cried.

They dragged him into an empty room. Pushing him onto the ground, they tied him up and held his head down. Huddling on the cold cement floor, he watched apprehensively as the men brought a tin bucket. Then they jerked his head upward and pushed it into the bucket. It felt as if there was something clenching his heart. He heard loud voices, footsteps, and before he had time to process all this, his head was smashed first one way and then the other. He could feel the force of the blows through the bucket.

The pain was concentrated at one point to begin with—his nose, which happened to have been bashed into a ridge on the inside of the bucket. That was just a dull pain, like walking into a pole in winter. But then his entire face started burning, and someone was clubbing the back of his skull, making it swell up. His shoulders ached. His head was being kicked this way and that, he was nauseated, and all his joints hurt. His throat felt as though it had a dried pepper stuck down it.

Eventually his joints were pushed to their extremes and began to give out. A pleasant numbness replaced his exhaustion, and there was a roaring in his ears, as if a crowd of people were shouting and talking into the bucket.

After what felt like ages, the bucket was shaken hard, and his nose hurt sharply. He could taste and smell the rust. The bucket clanged to the ground behind him, and sunlight glinted on the windows, blinding Hsueh momentarily. Then the stench of rust went away. The setting sun played on the edges of clouds and reflected on the glass. Hsueh thought he could almost smell the sunshine.

He was taken to another room, where his linen jacket, tailored at Wei Lee, had been hung carefully on the coatrack. He had quite forgotten when he had been stripped down to his shorts, and as he was putting on his pants, he examined the bruises on his bony knees with self-pity. He couldn't tell whether he had gotten them from being kicked around or from kneeling on the ground.

Someone lifted him up and put him on a chair, as if he were a photograph being fished out of developer and hung up to dry. Things became unblurred, took on straight lines, and came right side up. The man smiling at him was not the Chinese sergeant who had been grinning and screaming at him before his head was stuffed into the tin bucket, but a Frenchman.

The burly Frenchman introduced himself as Sergeant Maron. Maron's love of Indian food was evident from the scent of curry about him and the yellow-black stain on his lapel. His laughter echoed in the little third-floor room facing north on Route Stanislas Chevalier. Hsueh was brought a stack of documents to sign, and asked to sit on the chair.

No one asked if he wanted a cigarette, but they forced one between his teeth. His ears were still ringing.

Let's start over again, said Sergeant Maron. Let's say we're just chatting like old friends, and it turns out I have a few questions that you might be able to help answer. Remember to give me as much detail as possible.

He started with the journey. When Hsueh admitted that Therese had paid for the whole trip from Shanghai to Hong Kong, Haiphong, and Hanoi, that she had booked their passage and paid for hotels as well as restaurants, Sergeant Maron clapped him on the shoulder. Good for you! he said.

But why did she pay your way? Surely not just because she's rich—why wouldn't she pay me, Sergeant Maron, to accompany her instead? Are you saying you're a better man than I am?

Or did she pay for you because you are her lover? What did you do when you weren't in bed? Did you take her for walks, or go to the beach in bathing suits? If you spent all day indoors, does that mean you were in bed all day? Let's talk about something more interesting. What is she like in bed? Tell me—you'd like to help me, wouldn't you?

Hsueh remembered the warm subtropical wind, the humid bed-sheets, and the way the overhead fan turned slowly. You bastard, you know I have to keep you happy because of that tin bucket of yours. He called his photographs to mind.

"Sometimes we'd smoke in bed and have the servants bring us meals. She could never have enough sex. If I got tired, she would get on top of me. She loved to lie on the edge of the bed and stretch her feet upward."

Like official newsreels of soldiers in the trenches, putting up their arms to surrender. His gaze would travel upward from her red knees and painted toenails toward her face, on which shadows of the ceiling fan flickered.

"Go on," said Sergeant Maron. He lit a match and began tapping lightly on the surface of the table. He seemed to believe Hsueh. He looked as if he were trying to picture the scene.

"As soon as we stopped, we would light a cigarette. Just one, and we'd take turns taking puffs. She likes Garricks, and you can get a whole tin of them for one yuan. They have no filters and are thicker and shorter than 555s. She would take the cigarettes out of the tin and keep them in a silver cigarette case. I always lit the cigarettes because she said she had better things to do with her hands. If the case wasn't right there, she'd have me hunt everywhere for it. Some days I could turn the room upside down and not find the cigarette case. She probably hid it on purpose because she liked watching me walk about the room naked. My 'Chinese ribs' turned her on, she said. That was her private nickname for me. Later I would discover the cigarette case bundled up in the bedsheets with her sitting on it. She'd laugh and say, it was wrapped in black sheepskin and I was numb all over, that must be why I didn't notice it was there."

Hsueh kept inventing things he thought Sergeant Maron wanted to hear. Desperation can be the mother of invention, he thought. He and the sergeant were beginning to share the conspiratorial pleasure of the interrogator and the interrogated. Words came flooding to him as if he were an author whose writer's block had evaporated at the end of a sleepless night.

"So you'd been through her bedroom and never came across anything suspicious?"

"You mean a gun?" Hsueh didn't mean to say that, but the words slipped out.

"Does she own a gun?"

Sergeant Maron looked at him with a curious expression. He seemed to be momentarily fascinated by the buttonhole of Hsueh's thin linen jacket, from which a withered cape jasmine sprouted. Then, as though awakening from a daydream, he began to ask Hsueh more questions.

"How much do you know about her? They say she's German."

"No, she's Russian."

Sergeant Maron waved his hand dismissively. He disliked being interrupted. "Have you seen her documents? Does she have a Nansen passport or travel papers signed by the tsar? How dare you call yourself her lover when you know nothing about her?"

He paused, as if he were about to announce something important, to rebuke Hsueh for his ignorance.

"The woman the Chinese call Lady Holly, your Therese, is Therese Irxmayer, an extremely capable woman who owns a company based in Hong Kong. She is far more dangerous than you think, and the Concession Police is presently investigating her undesirable activities. We believe she has crooked friends running a shady business. We would like you to help us by getting involved, and give us news of her friends. It would be in your interest to cooperate—the police department will not forget your assistance, and I will personally be grateful."

Two policemen took him to the hotel. The Frenchman drove, and Hsueh sat in the back with the Chinese man. The car stopped outside the Astor in the rain. When the engine started up again, the Frenchman saluted him playfully with two fingers of his left hand held crooked. He was wearing a raincoat with a matching hat at an angle.

"*Mes couilles*," Hsueh muttered under his breath, tossing his cigarette end into a puddle.

The gate was closed, and the elevator shaft rumbled. He walked across the lobby to the stairs, to stretch his legs. He was tired and hungry. At nine o'clock they had gone to the Cantonese eatery on Pa-hsien-ch'iao. Eat, Maron had said, but Hsueh had barely eaten. It was the break between shifts, and the place was full of cops.

The men had stared at him while he was making a phone call to Therese. One was standing inside the phone booth, about three feet behind him. The other stood outside the phone booth, facing him from behind the glass. Then they dropped him off and politely said good-bye.

Hsueh's muddy shoes made squelching sounds on the patterned wood floor.

All day long, those voices had mocked him, menaced him, and tempted him. He almost thought he could hear them coming from the paneled walls in the hotel. It was those voices that convinced him he would do it, not the terror he had felt that morning when he was tied up in an empty room, lying on the floor with his head in a tin bucket.

CHAPTER 6

Therese did not mind being called Lady Holly by the Chinese. At least Holly was shorter than Irxmayer. Besides, even Irxmayer wasn't really her name. A blond Austrian man had given it to her in Talien. She preferred this name because she preferred to forget the past. She often said to her assistant, Yindee Zung: if you can't forget the past, how can you keep going? Yindee Zung was Zung Ts-mih's sister, and he once wrote his Yindee's name in Chinese and showed it to Therese—Ch'en Ying-ti. He told her *Yindee* was Siamese for *happiness.* Zung himself was Yindee's "fifth brother" in a large clan that seemed to span Hong Kong, Hanoi, and Saigon. Yindee had tried time and again to explain the complex web of family relationships to her, but Therese never seemed to get it.

In Hong Kong, Zung could find a buyer for just about anything, and he could source anything you wanted. Immaculately dressed, he would go into any dark walk-up, push the door open, climb the narrow wooden stairs, and extend his soft, delicate hand. He could cut deals with smugglers, the gangs, or even with Communists.

As soon as she had left the Viennese sausage shop on Route Dollfus, Therese could sense that something was not quite right. She kept glancing at the opposite sidewalk, or looking surreptitiously over her shoulder by pretending to rearrange her hair, but she could not see anything. She did feel a pair of eyes on her.

She had spent the morning at a tailor's on Yates Road. Gold Tooth

P'an was an old friend of hers, and Therese had recommended him to Margot. The man can make a perfect copy of any dress from a faded movie poster, she had said. Margot had brought a light blue piece of taffeta that reminded Therese of her childhood—her tenth birthday, in fact, when she had worn a dress with a thick hemline and silver bells under the hem. Or was that a scene in a movie? She had told so many stories about her past that she could no longer remember which ones were true.

The dress was not ready yet, but they would try out the fit.

"Look-See, Missie?"

P'an spat pidgin English in a hoarse voice that sounded like fingernails scraping across taffeta. He stitched a dress together loosely and handed it to Margot, who came out of the dressing room looking like a blue daisy. Brenen would love this open-back dress. It would allow his hand to slide down the small of her back all the way to its natural resting place. Margot always reported exactly what went on between herself and Mr. Blair, so Therese had heard all about that afternoon when they had gotten lost by Rubicon Creek, under the Great War memorial. She could picture them there, Margot in her English equestrian outfit, leaning against the wobbly branch of a tree, Brenen's hand, and Margot flushing the whole time as if the branch were still brushing against her cheek.

This made her think of Hsueh, whom she had not seen in a week. That young half-Chinese man. She figured she could be ten years older than he, probably more like five or six. But he was a Chinese man with smooth skin, and she had to admit she liked him—she even liked that clean baking-soda smell he had.

Therese had slept with singers, illustrators, tipsy men from Lily Bar. She was used to intimacy with strangers. One of them was a Czech Jew who did cartoons of naked men and women on the Astor's notepads, in which the men's dicks stuck out as sharply as the black chimneys on English battleships on the Whampoa. But as far as Therese was concerned, not even the artist's pencil was a match for Hsueh's camera.

Hsueh, the amateur photographer, the sham dilettante. He loved fumbling around in the dark in her room at the Astor—the Chinese half of him refused to switch the light on, open the windows, or draw the curtains. He did not like the breeze off the Whampoa at night. Like all Chinese people, he was wary of catching cold. Even in the dark, Hsueh's fingers were perfectly accurate, as if he were measuring out chemicals in the darkroom. When he photographed her in the darkness, Therese would glimpse his pale face for a split second when the magnesium powder flared.

Route Dollfus was short and curved slightly. A network of narrow alleyways, the *longtangs*, crisscrossed the French Concession, real estate developers claimed tracts of land at will, and even the Municipal Office's urban planning was in disarray. The Concession was perfect if you had something to hide.

At the fork in the road, Therese changed her mind and turned onto Route Vallon. She stubbed her cigarette out on the iron grille outside a Russian bookstore, and threw the cigarette end into the semibasement window just below the display. Without turning around, she walked up to the adjacent Russian-owned art studio and stopped in front of its display window.

A sign in the window said ART DECORATION STUDIO, ORDERS TAKEN in ugly cursive print. It contained shelves full of multicolored boxes, and framed oil paintings hung above them. One of them was of a large black bird staring obliquely out the window from its only eye. The bird's beak looked like a sickle. It was pointing at a sculpture of a naked woman, who was entirely white except for a helmetlike shock of black hair.

Between the beak and the naked woman's breast hung a mirror with a gaudy frame. Just what she wanted. She studied the mirror carefully. Sunlight streamed onto the wall. The rickshaw man had left his rickshaw on the curb while he squatted in the corner, smoking a cigarette. There was no one else under the parasol tree.

Back at her apartment, Therese turned the key in the copper Eveready lock. Yindee stood in the middle of her living room while Zung was sprawled on the sofa. Ah Kwai put a cape jasmine on the round side table by the window, filling the room with its dank scent.

Zung had just arrived from Hong Kong. He was examining a book of movie posters with his chin pressed to it, peering at the photographs from different angles. He had a sharp chin that reminded Therese of pictures of Chinese concubines.

Running in to serve them tea, Ah Kwai laughed and dashed out again. She had come to Shanghai with Therese from Hong Kong, and Zung sometimes brought her Cantonese sweets. The room was heavy with the scent of Chinese jasmine tea, which Therese loved. Zung was always teasing her, claiming that Russian tea stank of camel piss. Apparently the Russians had complained that tea tasted different when it was shipped in by train, having gotten used to tea saturated with the sweat of camels carrying merchants across the Gobi Desert from Shan-hsi. Wily Chinese merchants consequently began soaking their sacks of tea leaves in camel urine for a few days before delivering it.

Zung typed out invoices on a stack of light-blue paper with his Underwood typewriter. Each month he brought large sums of cash from Hong Kong and deposited it in her personal account. She never asked him how much he kept for himself. For the past hundred years, foreign businessmen who prospered in China had refrained from asking such questions of the *compradors*, their middlemen, and everyone had done well out of the bargain.

Therese herself sourced the goods. Recently a man called Heinz Markus had written to her on behalf of Carlowitz and Co. from Berlin. He reported that Carlowitz was prospering, especially now that it was officially sponsoring the National Socialist Party. As long as Therese's firm brought in the orders, Carlowitz could fill them. The Germans had lost a large share of the Asian market during the Great War, and they were anxious to make up lost ground. It was rumored that the National Socialists didn't much like Jewish people, but Therese ignored them. This was Asia. If you made money, no one could touch you.

At least she no longer had to sleep with the skippers in exchange for lower shipping rates. They all came ashore horny and exhausted from steering their run-down freighters all through the Indian

Ocean and South China Sea. Once her shipping lines had been set up, the money started flowing in, and she now had a steady stream of business. In Hong Kong, Shanghai, and even in Hanoi, Zung had friends he could count on. He and his family had collaborated with foreigners for a century. As long as the Europeans were willing to contribute their cash and connections, they could cut a deal with anyone: the government, warlords, the police, the gangs, and an assortment of big-time and small-time crooks.

In Hong Kong, Zung ran a wholesale hardware store on Chatham Road that also dabbled in retail. His light-blue records listed a curious transaction.

"Why did it have to be customized? And did it have to cost that much?" she asked.

"It was a birthday present for the mistress of an eccentric Indian businessman," he explained.

The pistol had been set with precious stones and covered with gold leaf. The businessman specially requested that a piece of ancient Chinese jade with an etching of a belly dancer be set in the stock of the gun. The man smelled of curry. He wanted a thin line etched into the jade inside the folds of her dress—he apparently believed that his mistress had been a virgin until they met, which was what her mother had told him.

Zung told Therese that he had to arrange a delivery to a Korean client in Shanghai. He drew another invoice from his pocket, a white piece of paper with three lines typed on it:

Mauser 7.63 Auto Pistol
Spanish type .32 Auto pistol
Chinese (Browning) .32 Auto pistol

"Five thousand seven hundred and thirty-two yuan altogether," Zung said. "And of course, there's Sir Morholt."

Sir Morholt was Therese's private nickname for the Prussian businessman, because he had a scar on his right wrist, a memento of fencing in his youth, which he liked showing to people. It reminded

Therese of a certain picture book for children to read on sunny afternoons, which contained an illustration of Tristan cutting off Sir Morholt's right hand. She had once mentioned this picture to Zung.

Carlowitz and Co. had put Therese in touch with Sir Morholt, and they arranged to meet in a bar on Chatham Road. He told her he worked for a German metals firm. As he spoke, he sketched out a diagram of a weapon she had never heard of, noting its name in German in a corner of the notepad. Before getting up to leave, she slipped the piece of paper into her handbag. He had talked incessantly about the gray mist on the Rhine.

Now Zung was handing her a real blueprint that was not a hasty sketch on a bar-table notepad. It had been cut carefully from a larger roll of drafting paper, like a child's geometry homework or a sample diagram in a furniture catalog. There were three parts to the diagram.

"Looks dangerous all right. Who would buy it?"

"Yeah it's dangerous." Zung wasn't really paying attention. He drew out his silver cigarette case.

"Everyone knows everyone in this business, and this will make us too conspicuous. It will get us in trouble."

Since she got back from Hong Kong, Therese had been unable to shake the feeling that someone was following her.

Therese had a green eight-cylinder Ford Model B.

The car was usually parked in the backyard of the jewelry shop. A spare tire hung on the rear of the car, draped in white canvas. Dusk was settling on the longtang, someone had put a vinyl record on, and the sound wafted down the street from a second-floor window. It was a girl singing in a southern Chinese accent. Her shrill voice sounded syrupy—someone might have put too much wax on the Victrola needle.

Therese herself was driving, and she had not brought her bodyguards with her. She was going to the Astor House Hotel. It was a Friday, and she would be spending the weekend there. If she and Hsueh got hungry, they could simply take the car and drive along North Szechuen Road to find a restaurant near Lily Bar.

She drove north along Rue Paul Beau. The rusty gates to the longtangs along the road had been left ajar, and the scent of canola oil wafted out. Therese rolled up the windows. She soon turned onto a wider road. The light reflected illusory movie posters onto the windows of the car: the RKO Pictures musical *Tanned Legs* and *His Glorious Night* with John Gilbert in a mustache. In a lit shop window, a polar bear held a sign in his mouth that said SIBERIAN FUR.

Then the road grew narrower and the dark shadows of buildings loomed ahead. At night, the walls of flint and marble looked as though they had been hewn directly from the hillside. She drove across

Garden Bridge, passing the Soviet consulate to her right, its tall tower resembling a gigantic helmet with the Soviet flag for a crest.

A few years before, the Cossacks who arrived in Shanghai with Captain Stark's navy troops had attacked the consulate. Their wild revelry had ended feebly with a few old drunkards gathered outside the Astor, singing Orthodox hymns, and throwing rocks at the windows to revenge themselves against their class enemies. They had been reduced to drinking vodka that was crummier than the stuff workers swigged from their enamel mugs. The women crowded round to watch, but Therese could not be bothered to join them. She watched from her window in the Astor, sipping on half a glass of vodka with kvass while the Czech painter lay naked on the bed.

The consul himself had led the charge to protect Soviet sovereign territory. He shot and killed the Cossack captain who was trying to tear down the hammer and sickle flag at the gate. Therese would have loved to fit out and arm the Cossacks, but they were penniless. That was the day she first saw Hsueh, who was still taking photos when the Concession Police burst through to the consulate gates and the crowds had scattered. As soon as she saw him, she got dressed and rushed downstairs to ask for a copy of the prints.

Two days later, Hsueh gave her the photos in Lily Bar. She didn't look closely at them until they were in bed at the Astor. Just leafing through them made her horny.

From then on she saw Hsueh occasionally and made love to him. Their trysts grew more frequent. She loved looking at the photos he took. She had never seen herself that way, watched her body dissolve into countless shifting parts, as though she were suddenly not one woman but many, all strangers to her. Some of the pictures made her look uglier, and some more beautiful than she really was. She was not even embarrassed by photographs of her ass sticking up in the darkness, like the ass of a spirited white mare.

She often asked Hsueh to meet her at the Astor, which resembled a ship with its maroon-paneled maze of corridors leading to hundreds of rooms, and delicate wrought iron flowers inlaid with frosted glass set in the doors. Her usual rooms were in what the steward called the forehold, which faced the waves and humid breeze of the Whampoa. When mist rose from the river at night, you could feel as if you were floating. A curved beam arched across the living room, which was furnished with solid teak furniture. There were rattan armchairs, a coffee table, and a mahogany floor lamp. Behind these living room furnishings, a set of double doors led to the bedroom.

The bedroom had an Oriental smell of fog on the Whampoa, moldy mosquito nets, and camphor wood, sandalwood, or cinnamon wood. The bottoms of the heavy teak drawers were made of scented wood, and whenever she opened one to retrieve a bathrobe and towel, its scent would fill the room. She opened the windows to let in the cry of gulls and whistle of ships.

The bathtub stood in the middle of the bathroom, surrounded by soft chairs, a ceramic basin, and a toilet bowl in the corner. The bars of the radiator had been polished by the hotel's servants until they gleamed. A retractable chandelier hung so low that its arms almost touched her head. She dozed off.

Then the phone rang, waking her abruptly. Dripping wet, she stepped into the bedroom to answer it. It was Hsueh, calling to say he would be late. He sounded nervous and his voice was hoarse. But before she could ask why, he had hung up.

She didn't hear from him again until after ten at night when he knocked at the door.

Therese looked at him in astonishment. She was sitting crosslegged on the bed while Hsueh lay fast asleep with his back to her. Bruises covered his face, legs, and waist, and there was a cut on his lip. It was not the bruises that surprised her. The type of man she could have for the price of a couple of drinks in a bar often appeared in her room battered and bruised.

No, she was surprised by how aggressive he was. He seemed to be angry about something.

He pushed her to the edge of the bed, lifted her legs roughly, and squashed her, ramming her face into the pillow. He wanted to turn her over, to expose her crotch to the light of the hanging chandeliers, as if she were a dancing insect that would freeze when in the light. She lifted her taut legs high in the air, and the light played on the sleep marks on her knees. Pleasure swept across her abdomen like a wave as she grasped at his arms and ass.

When he turned, his dick flopped over like a worm. She reached out to touch it, and it became hard before he even awoke.

His voice came from near her feet, sputtering as though it was bubbling up from somewhere near the muddy bottom of the Whampoa.

"Tell me, tell me, do those wicked friends of yours do this to you?" She caught his head between her knees, as if she could capture that brain of his that constantly distracted her. She wanted to rub the wet sponge of her body against the bridge of his nose. She refused to stop and listen to him. If he was jealous—well, let him be.

Half an hour later, she thought about the "wicked friends" he had mentioned. Did he think she was having sex with Zung? Then he was mistaken. All this time she had resisted Hsueh. He wanted to unsettle her, and the more she resisted, the more deeply he seemed to penetrate her. She could not force herself to like him any less, but she was afraid of leading him on. She did not want to disappoint him. Recently she had found herself mellowing with age, becoming reluctant to let go of things that made her happy. She was afraid of loss, and happiness no longer seemed to lie within easy reach. She had come to see that happiness for her consisted of a certain inward thrill.

"He's not a wicked man. He's just my business partner," she explained.

"What kind of business?" As he leaped off the bed, his spinal dimple was visible and bruised all over.

"It's not important," she said angrily. "It's none of your business. It wouldn't do you any good."

"I want to know all about you! I have drinks with you, sleep with you, and travel with you. But you make me feel like a gigolo—I don't know what you're doing or where you're going, and you always slip out of the room when I'm asleep."

He had started shouting. "I don't even know where you live or the line of business you're in. What's the gun for, buying emeralds?"

"I told you, that isn't an emerald, it's a garnet stone from the Urals."

He reached into her handbag for her cigarette case and tipped out its contents. The cigarette case, a pistol, and a pale blue sheet of paper fell onto the wet sheets—a blueprint for a machine gun that looked not unlike an elaborate clotheshorse. A present from Sir Morholt, who had cut it out carefully and entrusted it to her in a bar in Hong Kong.

She snatched it up along with her gun and stuffed it back in her handbag. Glaring at him, she thought of the kick she had given him on the ship. She thought about how much she liked everything about him.

"Okay, a garnet stone. That doesn't call for a gun." Lighting a cigarette, he handed it to her.

"Maybe one day you can come with me to see him, but not now. I'll tell you more about my business some other time. But you'll have to behave. Don't ask questions. Don't talk too much."

She had reached her hand between her legs and was playing with his dick, kissing his nose and ears. Her mouth tasted of smoke. Now his body smelled of her body. Defeated, he collapsed onto the pillow, and the bruise on his shoulders made him gasp in pain. She stroked his bruises and the scars on his neck.

It was past midnight, which meant it was Saturday, and they were about to spend the whole day in that room.

"Now, tell me who did this to you?"

CHAPTER 8

The restaurant was called Bendigo. It lay on the corner between Route Cardinal Mercier and Rue Bourgeat, on the ground floor of the Cathay Mansions. The window seat in the northwest corner faced the French Club and Lyceum Theater across the road. It was the best Western restaurant in Shanghai, and it was owned by a Jewish couple.

The steps behind a set of glass doors led down to the restaurant. Its semibasement had not been constructed according to any particular architectural style, or to prevent lowland dampness, or to keep servants from being distracted by goings-on outside. Rather, the contractor in charge of building the foundations had chosen the cheapest steel bars he could find, causing the entire building to begin sinking into the ground not long after it had been built.

The owner of the restaurant was a German Jew whose portrait hung on the wall by the steps leading to the restaurant. He used to have a magnificent beard, which made him look like Karl Marx in one of the posters that used to hang on every street corner, but he had shaved it off when he opened a restaurant. He was a legendary figure, and there were many stories about him. For instance, it was said that he had made the first rent payments on the restaurant using money he made as a young man panning gold in Australia—didn't the name Bendigo suggest as much?

But longtime residents of the Concession could tell you a different story. More than twenty years ago, old Romantz had been a penniless Jewish tramp who did not have so much as a suitcase to call his own. It was said that every one of the wretched foreigners who arrived in Shanghai traveling below deck in great ships came ashore with a couple of tattered trunks, but that wasn't true. Romantz had been pacing along the Whampoa, close to despair, when Fate thought of him, and a large wallet fell from a rickshaw. A chance like that is what you make of it. If Romantz had kept the wallet, it might have paid for a couple weeks' worth of beer. Instead he snatched up the wallet and dashed after the rickshaw, and things turned out very differently.

The owner of the wallet was the old captain who managed Astor House Hotel. He was so impressed by Romantz's honesty that he offered him a job on the spot. Romantz spent twelve years at the hotel as a steward, in charge of the silver cutlery and French porcelain. After ten years, Fate thought of him again, and this time she sent him a wife. Mrs. Romantz was a Russian Jewish woman who kept rooms in the hotel to entertain single foreign men. Finding that Romantz could be as attentive to her as he was careful with the captain's French porcelain, she agreed to marry him. They decided to marry in secret, outside the synagogue, because as long as they did not declare their marriage before the Lord, Mrs. Romantz could continue pursuing her lucrative profession. They would tell Him when they had scrimped and saved enough money for the restaurant. Sure enough, on the very same day Bendigo opened, they had a proper Jewish wedding at the synagogue.

Romantz was a legend. Perhaps because the Concession was something of a floating city, rootless, without a past and with no guarantee of a future, it functioned like a huge vat of dye that tinted all its characters with the quality of timelessness, which turned them into legends.

But Zung had not come to Bendigo to listen to Concession stories. He was neither a journalist nor a tourist, and besides, he had heard them all before. He was meeting someone here. It was Sunday, and the restaurant was almost empty.

His rooms were in the Oriental Hotel, facing No. 5 Horse Road, opposite the bright lights of Ch'ün-yü Alley. The main door of the hotel opened northwest onto Yuyaching Road, as if its architect had hoped that the wealth of the Race Course would rub off on it. Zung had to sign himself into the hotel guest book using a Chinese name, so he called himself Ch'en Ku-yüeh. Of the fountain pen and calligraphy brush provided, he chose the brush and signed his name in excessively florid cursive, an honest form of dishonesty. He presented neither the proof of residence issued by the colonial Hong Kong government to Ch'en Chi-shih, nor the travel authorization granted by the Hanoi Police to Mr. Paul Ch'en. The Municipal Police required all hotels to record the names of guests, but few hotels did so.

That afternoon, Ch'ien, the steward from Hopeh, beckoned to him from the hotel counter and told him to leave by the back door instead of by Yuyaching Road, which was jam-packed because the famous storyteller Li Po-k'ang had jumped ship to Eastern Bookstore, and every rickshaw in town seemed to be coming here to hear him perform.

Zung put his skullcap on the counter. He was wearing a gray jacket that came down to his knees, cinched black trousers, and a length of silk for a belt, the ends of which hung over the back of the chair, as though he had draped a pouch over it. The police were here at noon, Ch'ien said. They inspected the sign-in books and asked questions about a certain Mr. Ch'en.

"You're kidding."

"I swear I've never told a lie in my life."

Therese was right, he thought. I should be careful. Maybe I should move to another hotel right now. At the YMCA swimming pool, Zung told Therese what he had heard at the hotel. But she did not seem concerned. She did seem tired. On the weekends she disappeared, and Yindee told him that Therese was spending her weekends with that half-breed photographer. To top it all off, it was Maslenitsa that weekend, and Therese always made a point of taking Maslenitsa off. But he had pressing news for her. He had just closed a deal, and that night they would have to agree on a time and place for delivery.

The young man sitting to the left of Zung was wearing a black leather jacket and round-rimmed spectacles. He had many names, and Park Kye-seong was only one of them. In Hong Kong he had been working for a trading company based in Busan, and he had placed an order with Zung for them. He could even speak the Cantonese dialect just as fluently as he spoke Mandarin Chinese.

The other man was even younger, and he sat up very straight opposite Zung, with both his hands placed flat on the table, as if he were a Boy Scout or a student awaiting a boarding school inspection of fingernails. Zung had deliberately chosen this expensive Western restaurant to make his guests feel slightly uncomfortable. He picked out a table in the center of the restaurant, the better to observe how his guests' wary glances darted across the room.

Park introduced the youngster as Mr. Lin P'ei-wen. Just call me Lin, the other said. They barely spoke, and the restaurant was quiet. It had no bar, no gramophone, not even a mirror on the wall, lest it dampen the guests' appetite. But there were flowers everywhere, and even the picture frames contained flowers and fresh fruit. Before the first course was served, Mr. Romantz himself came to the table, smiled, bowed, and laid the table.

Park was not shy when it came to food. He plucked out the spine of an entire smoked trout with his fingers, and his knife and fork sparkled like weapons.

There were five small tables, and a foot-high platform on the far end of the room held a larger table surrounded by an iron railing, beneath which potted roses had been arranged. A curved corridor to the left of the platform seemed to lead into another room.

The sweetness of Alhambra cigars filled the room, and between the warm and cold desserts, Zung cut Luzon cigars. "La Flor de la Isabela," he murmured, offering them to his guests politely, as if they were flowers from the Spanish royal gardens. But Park's mouth was full of pudding, and he did not want a cigar. Nor did the over-powering cigar smoke agree with Lin, who leaned back on the soft leather cushions of the chair.

None of them was in a hurry to talk business. This was a small restaurant, and you could smell the tang of a new bottle of pepper when it was opened at the next table. They said a bottle of pepper here cost more than a whole meal would elsewhere. Who would talk about a deal here, right in the middle of the room? Everyone would think you were a bunch of imposters—unless they took you seriously and started paying attention, which was worse.

The coffee cup was the size of half an eggshell. It was hexagonal, like everything else in the room: the saltshaker, the small table, even the room itself. Mrs. Romantz appeared next, bearing a flat rattan fruit basket containing two mangoes and two American oranges. She bowed and smiled as she presented it to them, and then bowed and smiled again, as if congratulating herself on a successful performance.

It was already nine o'clock at night, and the sound of a band playing on the rooftop of the French Club wafted toward them. Zung was waiting. He couldn't tell whether his guests had the authority to make decisions about their deal. He had been expecting Mr. Ku, but Mr. Ku had not appeared, even though Zung had chosen the restaurant in part because it was near his quarters. The smoke played mysteriously in the electric light, and the air quivered with the rhythm of the Charleston. Zung asked his guests whether they wanted to go to a dance hall, but no one responded to his ill-timed joke.

Park left the restaurant first, alone. Ten minutes later, Zung and Lin left together.

When they came out onto the street, the Lyceum Theater was still playing. The Ford cars in the garage belonging to the cab service next door, Moody Inc., were arranged in two neat lines, like two rows of beetles staring with their large compound eyes, caught in the bright white light and unable to move. Zung and Lin stood on either side of the cavelike entrance to the garage. On the opposite side of the street, only one window was lit on the third floor of the Cathay Mansions, and its white window frames glowed pale blue in the night. Under the windows hung a large pair of glasses with arms that could be extended outward onto the street. Just then the arms were completely extended and suspended over the sidewalk, as though someone had smashed them. The left lens read LEUNG MAN-TAO; the right lens read MEDICAL DOCTOR.

Zung did not know where Lin wanted to take him. Maybe his good faith had finally earned him the right to meet Mr. Ku. Maybe they were only going to keep him waiting elsewhere. He was on the verge of losing his temper, but he kept his cool. The car drove south along Route Cardinal Mercier and past Route Vallon. Then Lin motioned for the driver to stop.

Park hid in the driveway of a luxury bespoke tailor on Route Cardinal Mercier. The lowered shop awnings kept out the glare of streetlights. He saw a car drive past with Mr. Zung and Lin in the backseat, and waited until it was a couple of hundred meters away before hurrying in its direction. During the half hour between nine and nine-thirty, the streets were empty, like a stage at intermission. Nothing moved among the shadows of the parasol trees except the wind. It was warm and dank, and there was a putrid smell, as if a hidden monster had belched. Their car was the only one to drive along Route Cardinal Mercier for a whole two minutes. A cat meowed in the copse behind the walls of the French Club.

Park saw the car gradually come to a halt at the side of the road. Then he waited a few more minutes to make sure they weren't being tailed before walking up and getting in next to the driver. The car started up again. Park unbuttoned his top button and lit a cigarette. Before long he had smoked a third of the cigarette, as if he had been sitting there with them the whole time.

Park was Korean. He had been a young actor playing bit parts in Shanghai when he joined a group of Korean Communists, among whom he soon came to play a leading role. He traveled to all the coastal cities of southeastern China: Chou-shan, Hong Kong, and sometimes even Haiphong and Penang. Moscow funded the group's activities and gave him three months of training in Khabarovsk. But before long, other Korean cells active in Irkutsk and Vladivostok began to ostracize Park's cell. In Moscow, they were debating whether it was more important to protect the Soviet Union or to continue the task of world revolution. In the resulting bureaucratic reorganization, Park's cell lost its financial support and ceased to receive orders from Moscow. They decided to send a delegation on the dangerous journey through Manchuria to Moscow, to defend themselves at the debates taking place there. The discussions grew so heated that someone started a fight, and word was that it was Park's older brother.

One night, the Municipal Police sent a large police squad to storm a meeting of Korean revolutionaries on Avenue Dubail. Park's brother pulled out his gun, attempting to resist arrest, and was killed on the spot. It was rumored that the police had been tipped off, and some suspected the Korean Communists in Vladivostok, but Ku warned Park against believing the hearsay. The British police in the International Settlement were known to be crafty, and the rumors might be a smoke screen. In any case, Park's cell suffered great losses, and if Ku had not accepted him into his own cell, he would have had nowhere to go.

The car made a U-turn and headed east, toward the brick villas and the wooden-gated longtangs of the French Concession. As Park gave the driver directions, he kept glancing in the rearview mirror. At the restaurant, he thought he had seen a dark shadow flit past outside. He was suspicious. At any rate, he did not want to be careless. His training had taught him how to follow someone.

The car turned onto Rue Amiral Bayle, and stopped at the entrance to the longtang. The corner store opposite it was still open, and two men stood inside: the shopkeeper, busy with sums on an abacus, and his errand boy, who stood shirtless by the counter, wearing a piece of black cloth tied around his waist, even though it was only June. Bundles of wooden clips, a row of metal spoons, assorted metal frames, and bits of wire hung above them.

As soon as the car stopped, Park got out and melted into the shadows of the alley. Lin took his guest into the unlit longtang, turning

left into the horizontal alley, and going into a house. Hiding behind
the house across the alley, Park heard two sets of footsteps on the
stairs. He knew those stairs were narrow, steep, and pitch-black.
Then he heard rapping at a door, more footsteps, and the sound of
furniture being dragged across the floor.

He emerged ten minutes later and slipped into the house. The
apartment was directly above the street. He pushed open the double
doors at the entrance to the stairs. Leng sat on a stool, keeping
watch, and staring at a kettle about to boil on a little gas stove. She
looked up at him, and down into her own thoughts.

He went into the room. Their guest was sitting at the table near
the window. Ku sat across from him in long gray traditional dress,
an oak hat on the desk. Lin stood behind their guest. Lifting a corner
of the curtain to look down onto the street, Park took a seat at the
table, facing the window directly.

The cell was getting bigger, and Park noticed that Ku's recruit-
ment methods were not always upfront, but that did not trouble
him. He trusted Ku. Like Park, Ku had been trained in Khabarovsk,
but he was far more experienced than Park himself.

Ku was a natural leader and careful planner. His cell was divided
into several smaller units that operated in isolation and only collaborated occasionally. The master plan was written nowhere but
in Ku's brain.

Firearms would be crucial. In Ku's plan for revolution, firepower
was everything. Money bought guns, and they had money. After the
Kin Lee Yuen operation, they had done a few more assassinations to
put the group's finances on firmer ground.

At a camp on the outskirts of Khabarovsk, Park had learned the
techniques of persuasion, how to give your counterpart the illusion
that he was winning you over rather than vice versa, how to frighten
a man, how to tempt him, how to make him follow you, help you,
put his life in your hands—with words alone.

Their guest passed a piece of paper to Ku and looked at him as if
he expected Ku to leap up and seize it. Instead, Ku took it from him
calmly.

"Our inventory is all in Hong Kong. We can have the goods shipped to Shanghai by a Blue Chimney Co. passenger liner. As usual, the delivery of goods will have to take place at the pier."

"Sure," Ku said.

"Payment on delivery. That's what we agreed on in Hong Kong."

"Sure."

"Five thousand seven hundred and eighty yuan, in silver."

"No problem."

The tea had now been served. The room grew quiet. Tea leaves swirled in their cups. Their guest knew what he was doing, he knew the rules, and would say no more than was necessary. Park was reassured to see that Mr. Zung did not stand on ceremony and had not brought a bodyguard. He would not need one. The most dangerous moment was the delivery of goods, but that could be arranged without their even having to meet. Of course, payment would have to take place in person, but the very fact that they were meeting here signified that many important people in the complicated black market in firearms had vouched for both parties.

Park's own favorite rifle was the "box cannon" rifle, the Mauser C96 with 7.63 mm chambering, of which Ku was ordering a new high-velocity model from their guest. In a shootout, firing off all twenty rounds at once always had a powerful effect. The gangs also liked the Mauser. It was said that a defeated northern warlord who was lying low in Shanghai once engaged high-ranking members of the Green Gang for protection, and that his personal bodyguards were tricked out of their Mauser rifles as a result. The gangsters had demanded that they turn over their guns, claiming that unlicensed firearms were prohibited in the Concession, and when the men eventually got their guns back, the rifles had been swapped for rusty old pistols.

Lin drew the curtains, closed the door, and left the room. He stood in the hallway and chatted with Leng. But the voices within fell silent before long, so Lin opened the door and went down the stairs.

Their guest was about to leave. He reminded Ku that once they had received and paid for the goods, the two parties would be strang-

ers to each other. Irxmayer & Co.'s policy was to ask no questions
about how customers used their goods. Hunt wild ducks, murder
unfaithful spouses, or hang your guns on the wall—just forget you
got them from Irxmayer & Co., especially if things go wrong.

"Mr. Zung, please rest assured, we'll do more business in the
future. Your company is selling us a bunch of goods, and we now
represent a significant chunk of your business. You might as well
have our entire ledger. We know you have to cut off a finger with
gangrene right away—you can't afford to do this deal if there is any
chance it could go sour."

Honesty can be the best policy. Their guest looked pleased. Lin
had already ordered a car for him from the hardware store opposite them, and this time it was Lin who took him back to their
meeting point.

Park waited until long after the car had taken off before he turned
and left. Instead of going upstairs, he patrolled the dark streets for a
while. When they were first escorting their guest into the car, he
had noticed a shadow in a longtang about fifty meters away. It was
the second time he had seen that checkered shirt today, and this
time he clearly saw it flapping in the wind beneath a dim streetlamp
suspended from the arched beam of the longtang. By the time he
hurried over, the long alleyway was empty. He knew it led out to
another road. It was possible that he had imagined the shadow, but
he doubted it. Rue Amiral Bayle was the safe house for Lin's unit and
an important meeting point for the cell. In a little while, he would go
back and report this to Ku, but not yet. Waiting on the street corner,
he figured that Ku would soon notice that Leng was distracted, and
her mind was wandering. Ku would speak to her the next time he
had a chance. The leader of a secret organization must pay close
attention to the mental focus of its members; the greatest threat to
the cell's security was distraction. He grew slightly worried for Ku.
Leng herself seemed unaware that something was troubling her.

The dog howled. Leng looked at the clock on the dresser—it was only 3:30 A.M. Again she began to ask herself the questions that had tormented her for days.

Ts'ao Chen-wu, the man who had been killed at the wharf, was indeed her husband, but he was also her enemy. Her first husband had died at his hands. She didn't know which fact trumped which.

A few months ago, she had come to Shanghai from Kweilin. At the time, Ts'ao was privately representing a senior figure in the Nanking government, a man active in the Kweilin army who was building a secret political coalition. If she had not run into Ko Ya-min that day, she might be in Paris by now. She had not seen him, but he had seen her. She was walking down Route Joffre to Route Ferguson, and he had followed her there. She was living in the Shanghai quarters of the Kweilin army, which had an armed police guard post outside. Military guards stood inside the gate, though they were unarmed because the Concession authorities did not permit firearms to be carried openly. He did not dare follow her inside.

The next time she ventured out, it was to a small bookstore on Route Gustave de Boissezon. He came up to her and stood behind her. They used to study Russian with the same tutor, the old Bolshevik. Even before turning around she knew that someone behind her was looking at her with hostility.

The Bolshevik was not old, but everyone called him that because of all the stories he told about his days in Moscow, St. Petersburg, Paris, about how he used to run circles around the policemen and spies. None of them had taken more than half a year of Russian classes, so he always spoke the simplest Russian in class. But every anecdote came to life as he recalled the expressions on people's faces, the rustle of leaves falling to the ground, the color of a medicine bottle. He could turn the most ordinary things into the stuff of legends.

Wang Yang, her ex-husband, was a young tutor at the Russian school, just a few years older than she was. He had spent time in the Soviet Union, and he was lucky not to have been caught in the Peking University dormitories when the military police had burst in. He fled to the Soviet Union, and upon returning to Shanghai, he gave her and Ko tutorials. He was a gifted speaker, and a phrase in Russian or German would occasionally slip into his lectures. He used mimeographed copies of a textbook called *Introduction to Marxism*, which she later recognized as a translation from the Russian, of Bukharin's *The ABC of Communism*.

Ko had always idolized Wang. That happened a lot—she had idolized Wang too, at least until they got married. Ko would do anything Wang asked him to do. In fact, he too had fallen in love with Leng, and he only kept his distance because he realized that Wang was already pursuing her.

Now Ko was gone too. He had chosen suicide, the highest form of sacrifice, the only one worthy of the word—choosing death rather than being killed.

The mission to assassinate Ts'ao should have been hers. She fought for it, but they had questioned her courage. It's not that we don't believe you're capable of putting the revolution ahead of family ties, Ku had said. *Family* wasn't the right word. But what would she have him say? After all, it was true that Ts'ao was her husband.

What she really wanted to say was, let me die with him. Sitting at the window of the apartment and looking out onto Rue Amiral Bayle, gazing at the dark outline of the city, she could hardly believe she was alive.

6. Be cruel to others and to yourself. All emotions, affections, friendship, romance, gratitude, even the love of honor, must be suppressed as forms of weakness, and replaced by the single-minded cruelty of revolutionary zeal.

She found this line in Ku's manifesto for People's Strength incomplete. It wasn't friendship or love she had to suppress—it was self-loathing. If single-minded tyranny had the cleansing power Ku said it had, it should free her from self-hatred and despair.

"But when did he ask you to marry him?" Ko asked again.

I don't know. I really don't know. I was being held in a cell at Lunghwa Garrison Command. No watch, no woman in a green cheongsam to smile at me from a calendar, no sunlight. Sometimes a gust of wind would carry the smell of sun, grass, and fried stinky tofu into the corridor.

None of them responded. They were all quiet, even the boy in the white linen suit, who kept curling his bangs around his finger. Only later did she find out that his name was Lin. Ku too was silent. He became unusually hospitable, and kept offering her cups of water and tea. I've got Tiger Balm in case you have a headache, he said.

I just don't know. Every morning, the wooden doors would open, and a slight breeze through the corridor would dispel the stench of an entire night's sweaty bodies—who knew women could stink like that. Then an iron gate would open with a clink, and even though this sound promised the smell of sun and grass, it was terrifying. If you were to be interrogated, then you would still be alive; if not, you would be taken out to the prison yard and shot. They executed prisoners nearly every day. I had no news of Wang. The guards were gentle with us. "You aren't bad people, you were just doing what you thought best for our country," they said. But they were far from gentle with the other women, and if any of them were insubordinate they would be taken outside and savagely beaten up. I'd never have thought that women could be so cruel to other women. But they never told you anything, and the men were in a completely different wing of the prison. How could I possibly have had any news of Wang?

When she said this, Ko suddenly grew angry. She could tell that rage was welling up inside him. He stood before her, biting his fist, almost as if this were his way of declaring his love. If he wasn't able to love her, he would have to hurt himself, and if he could not harm himself, he would hurt her—

His fist shot out and sprang back, testing, before he punched her hard on the forehead and cheekbone. Lin rushed up and held him back, but Ko's eyes bulged as he struggled to free himself and pounce at her, like a sculpture of a man throwing himself at a pyre.

She felt humiliated. Not because Ko had hit her, but because Ku had said nothing. Actually, at that point she did not even know Ku's name. All Ku had said was that he was gathering intelligence about her on behalf of the Party. He represented the Party. And the Party had stood by and said nothing while someone was punching her, or when she was arrested. That was humiliating. It showed that she was not important enough for the Party to bother rescuing her. She would have to rescue herself. The law student from the Communist Relief Society had said ambiguously: No, I do not represent the Party, but I am here on behalf of a Society, and I can offer you legal advice. You are free to take my advice as being from the Party, from your own cell. If Ts'ao asks something of you, you may acquiesce, he said, you may play along.

So she had played along, even though she felt despicable. Ts'ao arranged for the guards to give her exercise. He brought her food. He acted like a gentleman, and he didn't ask her right away. They knew each other from growing up in the same small provincial capital, where they had been classmates at the teacher training college. Then they had left that suffocating inland city at the same time, both young people who craved revolution, except that one of them had gone to the south, and one had gone to Shanghai. The one in the south had joined the National Revolutionary Army, and now headed the Military Justice Unit belonging to the occupying troops. And she was his prisoner.

But slowly, he began to hint at it. This place is part of the Garrison Command's Military Justice Unit, and it's not within my purview, he said. It's no secret that the Committee to Purify the Party is headed by madmen. Of course I know them well, and I did talk to them, arguing that the government should give a chance to a woman who made an honest mistake. But they asked me—is she family?

Do you understand? Is she family?

The coffee he had brewed for her was steaming. He had thoughtfully put one lump of sugar in the coffee and two more on her saucer. Somehow he had managed to get his hands on real china in the prison. This was the superintendent's office, the best room in the building. It was sunny outside, and the room was cool even at the height of summer. He was a few years older than her—I only turned thirty last year, she thought. He told her he would pay for her to spend two years studying in Paris, as a birthday present.

Of course I knew what he was suggesting. I didn't respond. Until the Communist Relief Society came again, and I asked for their opinion. I thought—they must be acting on behalf of the Party.

Ku had been deep in thought. He looked up and said to her: no, the Society does not represent the Party. They are only a charitable organization that offers necessary help to friends of the Party in prison. They are an organization affiliated with the Party.

I see that now. But then I said yes. I agreed. This was when he asked me again, directly. He told me Nanking's new policy was to be tougher on revolutionaries, and another round of political prisoners would be killed. Don't wait any longer, say yes, marry me, he said. If I can tell them you are my family—surely we wouldn't destroy families in the name of revolution?

I only made one request: release Wang Yang at the same time that you release me. I can't do that, he said—if you're my wife, then what does that make him? That I cannot do. Then he hesitated for what seemed like ages, and told me that Wang Yang had been executed a month ago, in the prison yard. I cried for a long, long time.

Had she cried? she wondered. She seemed to remember that she had cried. But maybe she only cried because she was weak and despised her own weakness. She didn't remember ever having loved Wang Yang, and if she had ever loved him, it was only because she had been young then.

Wang Yang once told her that a professional revolutionary didn't need love, and could not permit it. If intercourse was a physical necessity, a revolutionary who felt that need should address it in the most straightforward way possible. No, a revolutionary couldn't afford to waste his time flirting like a bourgeois.

Did she have doubts? If Ko had not asked her this question, would she have thought about the timing of Wang's death? Had Wang Yang already been executed when Ts'ao proposed to her, or was he only executed afterward? That doesn't matter, Ku said. Either way, Ts'ao is a counterrevolutionary army officer who slaughtered revolutionaries. But the question was of utmost importance to her, and to Ko as well.

Ko seemed to believe that this was a test not only of Ts'ao's character, but also of Leng's loyalties.

Ku spoke next. "Think carefully. The first time he asked you this question, did you give him a clear answer? This morning you said you didn't give him an answer. Does that mean you didn't say anything? We're running out of time, and we'll have to escort you back to Route Ferguson soon. All right, you didn't say anything. Wasn't that a clear signal that you wouldn't agree to his request?" His tone of voice signaled that this was a mere formality, and all he needed was an answer to complete his interrogation notes.

Outside the window, boards clattered and the lonely sound of hooves echoed down Rue Amiral Bayle.

CHAPTER 11

JUNE 8, YEAR 20 OF THE REPUBLIC.

5:18 A.M.

She heard someone sigh outside the window. Peering out through the gap between the curtains, she saw that the sky was much darker than the streets beneath it. The streets were wet with dew, like wet blotting paper on which cartwheels clattered. A donkey was harnessed to a cart full of night soil, and the driver had been yawning, not sighing.

The morning of the next day, the interrogation went on in the back room, right next to the room she was living in now. The back room had a sound-absorbing partition, and its window faced the courtyard. Her room, on the other hand, overlooked the street. One window opened out onto the longtang and the other onto Rue Amiral Bayle.

Ko had brought her here. Telling the officer assigned to her that she was going shopping alone, she had gotten into the first of two rickshaws, while Ko got into the one behind her. If someone comes in, I am Chang Tung-sheng, and I used to manage your father's silk store, Ku said as they were going into the room. We met each other by chance on the street, and I brought you here so that we could have a quiet chat about old times. That may seem strange, but it isn't really. After all, I did watch you grow up. When you were little, and I was working in the store, I used to hoist you onto my shoulders to buy peanuts. You don't know where I live, but I don't live here. These are my friend's rooms, and he isn't home. A young man—

here he pointed to Ko—opened the door, and you heard us say that he is my friend's new apprentice.

During their last month of Russian tutorials, Leng had audited the Polish man's classes. He was an old Bolshevik who said he had been to Bombay, and gave classes on "the techniques of undercover work." The class was mesmerizing, because all the stories drew on his own experience. She had paid attention in class, and she could tell Ku was fabricating a story they could use if they got into trouble. Ku must be an experienced revolutionary, she thought. He must have a senior position within the Party.

She was still unable to answer the questions they had asked her the previous day. She didn't know whether silence constituted denial. She could not guess what they would think. Did you ever say, let me go away and think about this?

And what if I had said that? Did Ts'ao have Wang killed because he wanted to marry me? He didn't have authority over the Garrison Command. *But you couldn't have known whether he had the authority. So you are all questioning my loyalty to the Party, and to Wang. But were you loyal to him? After accepting this marriage proposal, or even before you accepted it, did you ever once think of Wang? Remember how frightened you were, how the fear of death tormented you. You were too distraught to think of Wang. It was sweltering, the food was terrible, you washed once a day, and they only gave you enough water to wipe yourself down, so you didn't even have a clean pair of underwear. Without sunlight, you would rinse your underwear with your last drops of water before hanging it on the iron fence to dry. You longed to get out of there, to escape the huge gates and enjoy the sunlight you craved.*

Even after marrying Ts'ao, you never thought back to this time. Maybe you didn't dare, or you didn't want to. By the time you left prison, you had become a new person. If no one had asked you what happened, would you remember? Did you hesitate? Did you ever turn him down? Didn't things just happen of their own accord? Ts'ao wanted to rescue you, and he needed a reason, so wasn't making you his wife the best reason there was? When did you even ask him about Wang? Did that cup of coffee even exist? The cup of steaming coffee in your memory?

The Party finally, abruptly, made its decision: We trust you, said Ku, breaking the silence. The cell believes you. *You were immensely relieved. Actually, you were overcome with gratitude. Your loyalty had been confirmed.*

But from then onward, the comfortable life you had led since leaving prison vanished. The house with a garden in suburban Kweilin, the ormosia tree, the servant Hwang and his family, failed attempts at getting pregnant, and Paris . . .

Without warning, Leng was plunged back into her old lifestyle, which was so frenetic she was almost happy. She had not rediscovered revolution—it had rediscovered her.

No. 13: He who has any sympathy for the world cannot be a revolutionary. The revolutionary cannot hesitate to destroy the world and everything in it. He must hate all things equally.

In accordance with Ku's directions, she and the other members of People's Strength memorized the manifesto, recited it aloud, and debated it. When they first started, she found the exercise ludicrous, but slowly she came to see that it was actually strangely effective. Words can purify you, uplift you, make you strong. But she was weak, and when she went back to living with Ts'ao in Nanking and Kweilin, she began to have second thoughts. Whenever she wavered, she would argue with herself. At the pier in Hong Kong, she even thought about trying to stop Ts'ao from getting on the ship, though she would not know what to say or how to explain what was going on. Even when the passenger liner stopped at Wu-sung-k'ou, and they were waiting for the boats to pick them up, she was still wondering whether it was the right thing to do, whether she had imagined it all. She found herself weeping by the ship railing because she despised her own indecision, and as the sun shone on her, she kept whispering the words of the manifesto to herself. A wealthy young man had stared at her inquisitively.

Daylight.

She hardly ever ventured out. She felt abandoned. They had

asked her to stay in this room on Rue Amiral Bayle and not to leave, especially during the day. She yearned to be given a mission, but she didn't get one, and no one came to see her. The neighbors proba- bly thought she was an abandoned wife or a single woman. There's nothing wrong with spending all day at home, but if you never leave the house at night, or ever, people start asking questions.

They told her that since she had disappeared exactly when Ts'ao was assassinated, the newspapers were full of reports of her, and her photograph would be everywhere. She was a top-priority suspect on the police's wanted list, and they could be pinning her photograph up on notice boards in police stations this very moment. Anyone who bothered to look up her name would know everything about her—Lunghwa Garrison Command had a complete file on her.

The apartment on Rue Amiral Bayle had been rented in Lin's name. When Leng first moved in, they had told her that this was one of their safe houses. Ku appeared frequently, and whenever he did he would set up a table by the window and tip mahjong tiles onto it. If they heard the clatter of mahjong tiles, the neighbors would ask fewer questions about the unfamiliar faces upstairs.

Lin looked like a wealthy young dandy. For one thing, he walked around with a couple of books under his arm, like a university stu- dent. For a man like him to rent a room and keep a pretty woman in it was not unheard of, even if she did happen to be a few years older than he. At most, the neighbors might smile knowingly at him. Be careful of this kind of woman, young man, their looks said.

But then her comrades stopped visiting. Her days were strangely quiet, and at night she had trouble falling asleep. She woke late, and even after waking up, she couldn't go out, so she usually sat by the window daydreaming, whiling the day away. Finally, last night, they had come back. No, the cell had not forgotten about her. They knew she was here, and Ku said they had only temporarily stopped using the apartment as a safety precaution for her own good.

This morning, she felt alive again. She felt that she could not go on like this. She had to be part of their work. She would speak to Ku. She decided she would go out for a walk, because if she kept hiding in fear of being recognized, she would really turn into a coward. She would forget what it was like to walk fearlessly on the outside. She would be terrified of strangers and panic whenever someone so much as glanced at her. Then she would really be unfit for urban undercover work.

She got dressed, put on makeup, and decided to buy some vegetables at Pa-hsian-ch'iao Market. When she stepped out of the longtang at nine, Rue Amiral Bayle was its usual sleepy self. The corner store had just opened, and the hardware store was still shuttered. The storekeeper's assistant was squatting on the sidewalk washing his face. She stood at the gate, waiting to flag down the first rickshaw that passed.

It was eerily quiet. The sunlight fell cold at her feet. The water in the man's basin splashed onto the asphalt and was absorbed immediately. All eyes were on her. She felt intensely uncomfortable, but she knew it was because so many days had passed since she last ventured out. Even so, shivers ran all the way up her back, from her knees upward, giving her goose bumps beneath her cheongsam.

The men standing on the street corner must be enemies of the cell too. They certainly were not ordinary passersby. They lounged about, one pretending to study the physicians' ads on the wall, while another was smoking with his arms crossed and looking toward her side of the road.

She turned around and decided to hail a rickshaw on the other end of the street.

But then she saw a man she knew. On the opposite sidewalk, turning east. He glanced over his shoulder, and she saw that he had a camera. She recognized him, but she could not tell if he had seen her. She quickly turned and left.

CHAPTER 12

JUNE 8, YEAR 20 OF THE REPUBLIC.

9:30 A.M.

Don't look right at her, Hsueh reminded himself. He had become a
self-taught private detective. His target kept shifting, and it was currently the woman he had seen standing by the ship's railing. He still
could not remember which movie he had seen her in.

Don't stay on the same side of the street as your target or follow
them from behind. You're more likely to lose them that way. Walk
on the opposite sidewalk, parallel to your target, even though that
doesn't guarantee you won't be caught. You'll find yourself sneaking
around as if everyone on the street despises you, as if casually lighting a cigarette might attract your target's attention.

He could always just leave on the next train to Nanking, or the
little steamboat to Soochow. Nanking might be better. He could
get a job there. But he quickly dismissed the idea. Where could he
go? He was half French, half Cantonese, and a bastard. The half-
breed cities of Asia were the real homes of bastards: Hong Kong,
Saigon, Shanghai. And even in Hong Kong or Saigon, he would be
well within their reach. Maybe he was staying put simply because he
didn't want to move. He was used to this city. He was the parasite,
and it was the host.

Sergeant Maron, who smelled of curry, said he liked him.
Inspector Maron, rather. He told Hsueh he had been appointed
the head of a newly established detective squad within the Political
Section of the Concession Police. He confided that he had worked

at the Concession Police for seven years without ever winning the
esteem of his superiors and peers. As a result, he became the least
corrupt foreign detective in the entire police force. He looked down
on the policemen who were buddies with all the gangsters and spent
their days in gambling dens and brothels, and they had looked down
on him—until Lieutenant Sarly became head of the Political Section.
Lieutenant Sarly is a good man, he told Hsueh. If you do a good job
for him, he will look after you.

But Hsueh was petrified. His targets sold guns for a living—
that was what Inspector Maron had said. In fact, Hsueh wished he
could bring himself to run away. He quickly turned the corner into
another longtang, and as he was hurrying into the alley at the end
of the longtang, he realized why he was still here: he belonged here.
Born a Concession man, he would die a Concession ghost. That was
a good line. He could have it engraved on his tombstone. Actually,
he should write it on a piece of paper and keep it in his wallet, so that
if he were ever found dead on the streets, they would bury those
words with him.

When they left the Astor the previous afternoon, Therese had
driven to the door of the YMCA. They parted there, and she went
inside while he crossed the road.

Thirty seconds later, he remembered what he had to do. He
turned and followed her surreptitiously into the YMCA building.
Luckily for him, it had been open to Chinese since the previous year.

She went into the changing room, while he went through a different corridor to the side door of the swimming pool. It was the
beginning of June, a little too cold for swimming, so the pool was
almost empty. He saw Therese's body shimmer in the water like a
white-green fish, the hem of her swim skirt floating just beneath the
surface like an aquatic plant. Her legs thrashed about in the water as
though they were in bed in the Astor. At this moment, he could not
imagine how she could possibly be a dangerous woman. She was
happily swimming around and getting drunk.

But then that man appeared. Just seeing him made Hsueh's
blood boil.

He was definitely one of Therese's wicked friends. The whole thing must have been his idea. Hsueh knew these characters when he saw them. If the man hadn't tricked Therese into getting involved, she would still be running her jewelry business. First he had tempted her into a dangerous business, and then he had seduced her. He must have slept with her. Therese climbed out of the pool, dripping wet, and the man began to towel her off. She put her feet up on a chair, nonchalantly, and the man actually dried her thighs with his towel, like a lover making a point of being attentive.

Now he stood at the side of the pool, chatting with Therese as if they were old friends. For the first time, he began to think that Inspector Maron's orders might not be such a bad idea—this man was a shady character. Forget Therese, he would follow this man instead.

The man came out of Peter Poon Tailors and went into De Luxe Shoes, and then into a White Russian tobacco and alcohol store that sold Luzon cigars. Hsueh could deduce this man's tastes, and it infuriated him that they were nearly identical to his own.

Finally, the man went into a restaurant. Hsueh had to roll a newspaper up, stuff it in his pocket, and duck into a shop selling magical props on Rue Bourgeat, feigning a sudden interest in its stacks of empty boxes. Apparently, you could make all kinds of things appear from the boxes: a bunch of fake flowers, a toy car, a porcelain bird, anything at all.

He should have folded earlier when he'd been playing poker that night. He should have known that the Japanese guy—Barker had said he was a Hawaiian—was up to something funny. That odd Japanese name came to mind, Zenko. Zenko should have folded, and so should the Portuguese player, in which case Barker would not have gotten the ace. Barker was definitely a cheat. Maybe all three of them had been playing him. He sometimes thought of that card game as the root of all his troubles. If they had not won hundreds of yuan off him in that one card game, he would not have vowed not to touch a playing card for three months. Had he not vowed not to touch cards for three months, he would not have agreed to go with Therese to Hanoi—except that the logic did not work, because he immediately had to admit that he would have gone anyway.

These were dangerous men, Maron had warned him. Gun dealers. Hsueh had watched many people die from gunshot wounds. He could picture their legs twitching like the legs of dying insects. He didn't understand himself. He was terrified of death, but that didn't stop him from being quite reckless. Yet come to think of it, the world was full of people like him—the Concession was full of people like him. He once read in a magazine that some people had a tendency to self-destruct. These people couldn't seem to just settle down and live perfectly good lives. They were earnest young students who had to go and become revolutionaries, diligent shopkeepers who couldn't stay away from a roulette wheel, prim society wives who spent their days reading women's magazines full of quack articles about painless delivery, who had to go and have affairs.

A bespectacled Frenchman from Marseille who worked for Maron had told Hsueh: don't worry, we've got your back. You matter to us more than the other hired snoops—you have French blood in your veins.

At the door to Bendigo Restaurant, he was almost discovered. In retrospect he realized that the man in a black leather coat must have seen him. Although the man's mouth was obscured by a huge beard, you could tell he was quite young.

They were having dinner at an expensive restaurant while he shivered in the night breeze. That irritated him, and he stood at the vestibule of the theater staring at them, almost daring them to spot him. He wanted to know whom his man was meeting for dinner. He guessed they would be keeping an eye out for him. The man in a black leather coat stood in the shadows with his back to the wall for a long time, scanning the street corners.

Yes, they must have seen him. Now they would be careful. He dared not follow their car, and he could not keep up with a cab on foot. As for hiring another car to follow them, that was for the movies. No, Hsueh had another plan.

He ran up the steps of the Lyceum Theater, and watched the road from its vestibule. He waited for their cab to drive by and memorized its license plate. When it returned to the garage, he ran up to the counter to hire the same cab. He sat in the passenger seat next to the driver, and by paying only double the standard price, two yuan, he got the driver to take him to Rue Amiral Bayle, where his previous passengers had alighted. The driver even remembered which longtang the men had gone into.

The previous night, Hsueh had hidden at the end of the longtang until they all left. He went back the following morning.

At just past nine, he was standing outside the hardware store on Rue Amiral Bayle opposite the entrance to the longtang, pretending to make a phone call, when he looked up and something unbelievable happened.

Unbelievable! Much later, when Hsueh thought back to it, it still seemed incredible. Above the curved beam that stretched across the alleyway and the peeling red paint of the walls, a second-floor apartment had been built directly across the alleyway, bridging the two buildings on either side. The flowery curtains at its window opened, and a face appeared in the darkness. It was a woman, poking her head out of the window. She withdrew hastily, slammed the wooden shutters, and drew the curtains. Hsueh recognized her!

She was the woman who had been standing by the railing. He had developed that photograph of her, but even staring at it he still could not remember where he had seen her. It dawned on him that this was the place he had been looking for: this second-floor window. Despite being an amateur, he could tell it was no coincidence that a firearms dealer and the chief suspect in an unsolved murder could be found haunting the same longtang.

That was when he decided to follow this woman instead. She came out of the longtang, and he followed her along Rue Amiral Bayle, walking nearly parallel to her. Then he watched her walk west along Rue Conty and stop at the street corner, forcing him to turn east instead.

Therese's wicked friend was interfering with everything good in his life, and yet he did not even know where and when the man would turn up next.

Many years later, Sarly would come back to visit Shanghai. He had
since become like a father to Hsueh. The Concession had been
devastated by war, and because Hsueh was in contact with an assortment of people, as usual, the Nanking authorities began to investigate him. At one point, they even had him secretly imprisoned.
Hsueh's many friends stood up for him, producing evidence that
Hsueh was innocent of their charges. Lieutenant Sarly even drew on
old files from the French Ministry of Foreign Affairs to advocate for
Mr. Weiss Hsueh's acquittal.

When Hsueh was released from prison, Sarly organized an elaborate celebratory dinner. He pressed Hsueh to visit him in France;
indeed, the French government would welcome Hsueh to relocate
to Paris if he wished, in recognition of his long years of service
to French colonial affairs. Hsueh could also come to the south of
France, where Sarly had bought a plot of land with the money he
had saved from working in Shanghai. He had been paid well for his
colonial postings.

As the night wore on and the wine began to have its effect, they
started reminiscing about the past. Sarly said that he wouldn't have
noticed Hsueh if it weren't for the White Russian woman who had
caught his eye. By chance, or perhaps because she was beautiful, he
said self-mockingly, he had ordered an investigation into her. And
then, in an intriguing turn of events—as though some higher power

had planned it—the investigation had led directly to the assassination at Kin Lee Yuen Wharf.

One morning after Hsueh's trip to Rue Amiral Bayle, Inspector Maron found Lieutenant Sarly clutching a half-eaten croissant in his left hand and a cup of coffee in his right, while attempting to open the door to the meeting room with his knee. He leaned over and pushed the door open for Sarly. Our man has found a lead! Maron said.

The detectives were waiting for them. Inspector Maron did not announce the breakthrough at morning prayers. Instead, he passed a note to Lieutenant Sarly, who glanced at it and tucked it into his file. When he left the meeting room, he asked Inspector Maron to collate all the files that had anything to do with this Hsueh character—interrogation records, the reports he had been filing, and the police department's files on Hsueh himself—and bring them to his office.

The note Inspector Maron gave him was a tip written in nearly flawless French by this amateur photographer, and containing startling news. The man had followed a friend of the White Russian firearms dealer to a house on Rue Amiral Bayle. (Maron had penciled a note in the margins explaining that this was Zung, the middleman.) The following day, when he returned to the house, he had discovered its unlikely occupant, whom he recognized from her photograph in the papers. She was the wife of Ts'ao Chen-wu, that man who had been killed on Kin Lee Yuen Wharf, and she had disappeared right after the assassination.

When investigating that assassination, Lieutenant Sarly had been intrigued by the killers' interest in media coverage. Police information suggested they were dealing with a rigorously organized assassination squad, which had leaked the news to reporters ahead of time, and given them a manifesto calculated to cause panic as well as an outline of events, to make sure the story remained in line with their message. Sarly was impressed that they had not only planned the assassination but also intended to shape its media coverage.

He found the killers' approach thought provoking. At a morning prayer meeting several days after, he admitted to a few of his subordinates that there might not be a truth to be discovered about these events. Maybe the truth was a heap of documents, newspaper cuttings, and interrogation notes. Maybe it was what people whispered to each other in the alleyways, what the plainclothes investigators wrote in their daily reports. Maybe the truth existed only in their files.

Years later, Lieutenant Sarly would remember the storm clouds hanging over Shanghai that year. He didn't just mean that metaphorically. The heavy rains had flooded neighboring provinces, and only in early April did the skies clear. Then the Political Section of the Concession Police unexpectedly became the center of attention. As Sarly remembered it, he had never been quite so popular in his life. Even the British confided in him. His counterpart, Commander Martin from the International Settlement, invited him to his country club for lunch. They ate medium-rare steak and lamb kidneys heaped on a plate. The young British diplomat who dined with them was very quiet. Whenever Commander Martin brought up something important, such as the suggestion that they should set up a system for exchanging intelligence, he grew even shyer, staring down at his wineglass and cigar. Sarly had been the best-informed man in Shanghai in his time. Years later, he still remembered that this man was eventually embroiled in a sex scandal, and forced by public opinion to slink off and leave Shanghai quietly.

Martin said he hoped they could "reach a private agreement" to cooperate since, as Sarly knew, London was being run by a bunch of thugs led by Ramsay MacDonald. The prime minister had previously been a Foreign Office man, and here Martin glanced apologetically at the young man—there were rumors from London that Soviet spies had infiltrated the Labor Party cabinet, which was simply outrageous. In any case, the British government had resumed foreign relations with the Soviet Union and was withdrawing troops from the colonies. This was evident even in Shanghai, where the British seemed to be passing the buck to the Japanese Army. So Molotov had been right, said Martin: France was the great enemy of socialism and the Soviet Union.

The steak was two inches thick, grilled over a gas stove and garnished with a cream sauce and Lea & Perrins Worcestershire sauce. Sarly had had a formidable appetite back then, but strangely, his appetite had shrunk as soon as he left Shanghai. Back then, everyone in Shanghai seemed to have a huge appetite.

"And that, Lieutenant, is why some of the more sophisticated set in London would like us to work more closely with the French Concession Police."

Which was how it all started. Of course, Hsueh knew nothing of this. How would he? He was an idle young man who had gotten himself caught up in a firearms investigation, like an insect struggling in a spiderweb.

Earlier that year, the Ministry of Foreign Affairs had sent Sarly a message via private channels, advising him to run a couple of high-profile operations targeting Communists, to dovetail with their trade embargo policies against the Soviet Union. Unlike Martin's lot, the Political Section of the Concession Police had previously taken the view that doing less was more. The police's job was to protect commercial interests, collect their share of the profits, and keep everyone happy. Lieutenant Sarly was sometimes tempted to think that they should all learn to get along with the Communists. These radical groups kept the French colonies from getting too dull. Whereas the International Settlement wanted to curb the power of the gangs, and stamp out the brothels and gambling dens, the French embraced them, scoffing at the Brits. And while the International Settlement cooperated with the Nanking government in arresting Communists, the French Concession deliberately turned a blind eye. The French were slow to act, and word of their police raids always leaked ahead of time, giving the Communists time to retreat and transfer their bank accounts. As long as they did not cause too much trouble, the Concession Police would tolerate them. Crafting a colonial policy that distinguished them from the British would serve to demonstrate how liberal the French were. This had always been the French way of doing things.

But then everything changed. Officially this was because the

French intelligence agency had received reliable information that Comintern and Moscow were sponsoring subversive radical groups in Indo-China, via Shanghai-based organizations that offered financial and practical assistance. The mail from Haiphong brought all kinds of news in documents from heavy bound reports to scattered notes discovered in raids. Lieutenant Sarly decided he would have to do something about it, if only to placate Paris. Perhaps he wanted to beef up the line on his résumé about supervising a colonial police force. In any case, he began to read the files. The biggest problems will resolve themselves if you look away, Lieutenant Sarly liked telling his men. But even a trace of something fishy can turn into a case if you look hard enough. All it takes is imagination.

Sarly himself had an active imagination, and he prided himself on knowing the city well. How many of the goings-on in the Concession's maze of longtangs really escaped his gaze? People thought of the French as being idle and free-spirited, but there was more to them than that, he thought. They could govern just as competently as the English could, or better, and their colonies would be more interesting places for it.

All the detectives in the Political Section had their own team of informers, and every informer had his eyes and ears on the ground. They penetrated every tissue of the city like a network of veins. They each had to file a report every day, even if it was scribbled on the foil from a cigarette packet. If they were illiterate, they could also give an oral report to be recorded by their superiors. All those bits of paper in dubious handwriting would end up on the secretarial division's desk, to be sorted through and translated, and the juiciest stories found their way to Lieutenant Sarly's desk.

That was how the assortment of handwritten notes that Hsueh wrote on scraps of paper—several, in fact, on Astor letterhead printed for the hotel's guests—wound up on Lieutenant Sarly's desk an hour later, in a fat file delivered by Inspector Maron. Not only did Lieutenant Sarly notice that this amateur photographer could write entire reports in French, he also found a familiar name in the records of Avenue Joffre Police Station: Weiss, Pierre Weiss.

Weiss had been a Frenchman doing business in the Concession when war broke out. He had returned to France to enlist and had never come back to Shanghai. He and his Chinese mistress had had a son, one Weiss "Wei-shih" Hsueh, who was now an informant for the detectives of the Political Section, taking part in an important investigation.

Inspector Maron told Lieutenant Sarly that he had ordered a search of Hsueh's rooms on Route J. Frelupt. Lieutenant Sarly looked up from his papers. Cancel it, he said. But Maron replied that Ta-p'u-chiao's Chinese policemen were already on their way.

CHAPTER 14

Hsueh was outraged. He wanted to get even with Maron. He was glad he hadn't told him everything he knew that morning at the police station. When he got home, he was startled by the sight of his wardrobes flung open and drawers tipped onto the floor. His clothes lay scattered everywhere, but bundles of newspapers and letters, and—yes, photographs, were all stacked on his bed. A picture of the French executing a spy at the corner of a trench was propped up on the toaster rack, the rifle pointing toward a pot of jam. His father had leaped out of the trench to take this photograph, standing on the edge of the trench just above the head of the man who was about to be executed.

Upon inspecting his possessions, he found that all of his important letters and photographs had disappeared, including his father's photographs, and pictures of his mother and Therese. He was mortified. Those were his most private possessions. He was enraged by the thought of how Maron would sneer when he saw those photos.

An observer might be forgiven for thinking that Therese didn't look all that sexy in his pictures. In some, she was leering so widely that her nostrils flared. In others, the perspective made her thighs look fat, and her ass looked flabby. But he thought they were beautiful shots and true to reality. He remembered one overexposed photograph in which Therese's legs were curled up, and she looked like a white sapote fruit cut open to reveal its pulp. She was aroused, and her pubic hair was visibly wet, though Hsueh would have to admit that the wetness was partly his saliva.

He could not imagine what someone who saw those photographs would think of him. They recorded moments of pure abandon. He had given Therese the photographs that portrayed her accurately and not as a strange creature. The rest, the ones he'd kept, were the ones the police had taken. It had to have been the police. Maron was behind this.

All afternoon he seethed with rage and humiliation. He had spent days making up stories to satisfy Maron's appetite. That man slurped Hsueh's stories down like spaghetti, and kept shoveling more in. Strung together like cheese, Hsueh's stories all ended up in Maron's insatiable stomach. He wrote about what Therese liked in bed. He invented an entire daily schedule for her: where she ate, where she had her dresses tailored, whom she met and where. To please Maron, he was forced to lie about some things. He said he was Therese's closest business associate, that there was no one she trusted more. He accompanied her everywhere, and when she was not able to attend a meeting in person, he would attend it on her behalf. He even wrote his reports in French, afraid that a careless translator might leave something out. He scoured the Concession's bookstores for detective novels that would contain the firearms terminology he needed.

Of course he was selective in what he told Maron. He heaped most of the blame on Therese's wicked friends. She herself might not be aware of what was happening, he wrote. Her real expertise was in jewelry, and she allowed Zung to take care of other business. (Inspector Maron had told him that the man's name was Zung.) But sometimes he told the truth, like that morning. Inspector Maron had been grumbling that Hsueh was all talk and no action, so Hsueh told him about following Zung and the other two men to Rue Amiral Bayle. He even mentioned the woman who had disappeared in the Kin Lee Yuen assassination case. But although he could easily have said more, he did not. He did not mention that the woman lived in the apartment overlooking the longtang. He even concealed the location of the apartment—it was late, he claimed, he could not remember which longtang it was in, and she had only appeared briefly at the entrance to the longtang. But he had seen her picture in the newspaper, and he had a photographer's memory for faces.

When he left the police building, he had still been feeling indecisive. He had been afraid. He hadn't had the nerve to do what he had to do. By the time he turned the corner of Route Stanislas Chevalier, he had begun to regret the whole thing. He knew his reports could hurt Therese. He considered telling her everything, but he was afraid of Inspector Maron, afraid of the darkness and smell inside that bucket.

Now he was no longer afraid. He walked downstairs to his landlady's rooms to borrow a phone. She looked concerned. What were those policemen after when they barged in this afternoon? she asked. He was unafraid.

But when the call went through, he suddenly found himself tongue-tied. All he could think to say to Therese was that he missed her. His landlady was listening through the living room door. Therese laughed. He heard something clatter onto the floor on the other end of the line, and guessed that she must be pulling on the long telephone cord.

The Vietnamese traffic cop wearing a red-tasseled hat looked like a puppet. Hsueh stood at the crossroad, waiting for the man to pull his card and turn the wooden sign mounted on a revolving pole. When the side painted red faced a particular street, the people and cars on that street would have to stop and give other traffic the right of way. But before the sign turned, a car pulled up, the window was rolled down, and Therese waved at him from the passenger seat.

"So, you're alive then?" she asked huskily once they were alone in the Astor. The mahogany four-poster bed was hung with a gray mosquito net that smelled moldy in the breeze. The sun had set, but the floor next to the bed was still warm with the sunlight.

Therese was lying on her side on the edge of the bed near the window, with two pillows tucked under her arm. She curled up comfortably, stuck her ass in the air, and began to stroke his groin.

A British warship sailed past, its steam whistle sounding a long blast. Therese cocked her head as the dying rays of the sun played on the edges of the cloud and shone into the room so that the tiny hairs on the skin of her hips grew bright.

He wanted to tell her right away, but he didn't get a chance. She tore his clothes off and started playing with his dick until it sprang up like a punching bag assailed by blows.

His ribs were still sore, and he was so tightly wedged between Therese's legs that he could barely breathe. Her knees were hooked around his waist like clamshells. Her muscles became visible when her legs stiffened. Hsueh had just watched them tighten around his cheekbone. He thought he was screaming, but he only produced a moan.

She took his fingers and brushed them along her crotch. He had to make up another story. He had to come up with something he could get away with. Nothing convincing came to mind. Instead, he found himself chasing her to a climax. . . . Afterward he stayed hunched over, to avoid looking directly at her.

As he fell onto his back, a bold idea occurred to him.

"Zung has to leave Shanghai immediately."

The panting stopped. He had to go on.

"He's in danger, and you'll be implicated. He thinks he's doing business with the gangs, dealing in firearms," he said, staring bravely at her shoulders. "But his customer is actually an ambitious assassination squad active in the Concession."

"How do you know all this?"

"I'm one of them," he said, figuring that she would fall for that— after all, wasn't everyone in Shanghai connected to the gangs in some way? He was proud of his invention. "I happen to know the head of this gang, and—well, actually, we're old friends."

This was absurd, he thought, no way would she believe him. He felt discouraged, but he went on: "You know I'm a photographer. They sometimes engage photographers, and that's how we met—he used to hire me to do investigations. That's why I investigated Mr. Zung. I followed him."

She reached toward the bedside table, rummaging about in her handbag, as if she wanted the lighter, and produced an exquisite pistol. It happened so quickly he had no time to be frightened. The next thing he knew, the barrel was digging into the soft space between his chinbone and Adam's apple. He was about to vomit.

Petrified, he opened his eyes wide and raised his arms in a gesture of surrender. His fingers were shaking.

"Tell me the truth."

There was a long silence. The clock ticked, and seagulls could be heard foraging for rotten food along the river. Time passed so slowly he could barely stand it, as it does when you've got to piss. He was so terrified that he was about to piss right then. He had seen what a bullet could do when it pierced a man's chin and tore off his lower chinbone, as if it was simply opening a box. He dared not answer, afraid that if his chin moved, it would trigger the gun. Strangely, his brain began to go through the terms he had been learning. Trigger? Or was it hammer? He wanted to remove himself from the situation by recalling those terms, as if remembering them would make what was happening to him seem far away, like a scene in a novel.

Therese began to laugh again. She looked at his face, and plucked a crooked piece of hair from his nose. It was her pubic hair, and he could still smell its scent, like cheese with a little apple vinegar. Sometimes a gun can get you out of a tight spot, but sometimes all it takes is a single damp pubic hair.

"Why did you follow him, and where to? I want the time and place. Why is he in danger?"

"It was Sunday evening. I followed him from the YMCA to a restaurant, and then to an apartment on Rue Amiral Bayle. It was a safe house for the assassination squad. The gang leader already knows something's up. This lot is disgruntled. They've turned to contract killing, and they've been pocketing the bounty. He's decided to have the police deal with it—you know the gangs always work with the police. So the police have been watching this apartment, and since Mr. Zung went there, they'll be watching him too.

They'll start making arrests any day now. I was going to tell you right when I got here."

This is ridiculous, he thought. This story is full of holes. Boy, am I an idiot. He watched Therese lift the mosquito net and open the cigarette case lying on the bedside table. He was in deep trouble. A single phone call would reveal his lies.

"Was it the gang leader who wanted you to spy on me and follow Zung?"

"Yes."

"Tell me his name."

Hsueh's mind raced. He tried to remember the names he had seen in the newspapers. After the Kin Lee Yuen assassination, a small paper with links to the gangs had suggested that the leader might be named—Ku. Yes, that was it.

"Ku. We all call him Mr. Ku."

"And was it Mr. Ku who had you follow Zung?" Therese's voice had grown cold. It was the first time Hsueh had mentally connected this name to the people he had seen the other night. He pictured their faces. It had been dark, but the middle-aged man could have been Mr. Ku. He realized he had made an irretrievable mistake—if Ku was doing business with Therese, why would he have Hsueh follow Zung? Then he thought, if you believe me, it follows that Zung must be deceiving you.

"How dare you spy on me for someone else! How dare you follow Zung!"

The barrel jabbed upward again. He thought about the ridiculous mess he was in. His eyes watered with self-pity. The barrel jabbing into his skin sharpened all his senses. His tear glands began to itch, and his vision blurred. His voice came out as a whimper and he found himself speaking French, as though a softer, less forceful language would help him avoid triggering the hammer on the other end of the barrel. Even he himself could not hear what he was saying, but Therese seemed to understand him anyway:

"I followed him because he is a wicked influence on you, because I like you. I . . . I love you."

CHAPTER 15

All that time, Lieutenant Sarly was homesick for France. He did not really belong in Shanghai. There were Europeans in the city who had long since forgotten where they were from. Not long ago, they had gotten on ships somewhere else and acquired new identities upon landing in Shanghai. These men had come to Shanghai with nothing, made their fortunes here, bought houses, married their wives, and started families in Shanghai—people called them Shanghailanders, and it was no wonder they considered Shanghai their home.

Lieutenant Sarly wanted to bring his family to Shanghai, but his Corsican wife could not stand the humid Asian weather, so she took their children back to Marseille on a ship via Saigon. He did not keep a Chinese mistress, preferring to travel home once a year on vacation. By contrast, M. Baudez, the French consul, had brought his entire family to Shanghai, even though diplomats were posted to new locations more frequently than were the police.

That evening, Lieutenant Sarly was sitting in the study in the consul's villa. Huge balconies lay outside the French windows, and behind the railings you could see the great lawns. A sharp cry came from the direction of the parasol trees. Consul Baudez stood up and looked outside. A boy was lying on the path between the lawn and the trees planted along the wall, entangled in his bike. But it was the girl standing on one of the lawn chairs who had been screaming. She was rocking the chair back and forth, her leg straddling the back of the chair, with its peeling black paint. Meanwhile, the boy on the ground struggled to free himself from the rubber tires and bike frame.

"They gave us all the testimony they collected," Lieutenant Sarly continued. He was giving the consul his customary briefing on intelligence received by the Political Section.

A Nanking intellectual who claimed to be a professor had come to him with the report, which consisted of testimony followed by an analysis of intelligence collated from various sources. Sarly flipped to the signatures on the last page, which appeared to indicate a sort of investigative research group, probably staffed by a handful of young intellectuals culled from the thousands who were fleeing inland towns for the large coastal cities, ambitious types willing to submit to the direction of a middle-aged professor. Nanking attracted scores of young people like that with its proliferation of study groups, associations, and societies of learning. The card they had given him carried one of those curious names. What was it again? A research society, or was it an investigative institute? Lieutenant Sarly glanced at the report on the table.

"We were eventually able to persuade that man to talk," the man had said. He had been wearing a Chinese suit, his eyes gleaming behind his spectacles. He did resemble a diffident university professor. "It's better for Chinese matters to be taken into Chinese hands. You are guests here, and guests will always be too courteous. Besides, according to the terms of the lease, one day you will leave." The shy professor began to laugh, as though the laughter would prove he believed in Sun Yat-sen's nationalist principles.

The Nanking investigators concluded that Mr. Petroff Alexis Alexeievitch, who was registered in the Political Section's fingerprint records as Mr. Brandt, File No. 2578, was not, as he had claimed, a thirty-nine-year-old German businessman. He refused to answer any questions when he was being interrogated at police headquarters. Nanking insisted on having him transferred first to Lunghwa Garrison Command, and then to the Nanking military prison. Sarly decided that the consul probably did not want to know what had happened to Mr. Brandt in prison. He himself did not want to know. He had heard that a prisoner there would be made to kneel in front of a large iron clamp and have his head placed inside it. For every three notches the screw was turned, the clamp would grow one centimeter tighter.

Mr. Brandt's testimony was recorded four times. He handled the situation admirably. Each testimony was flawless and internally consistent, and each time it completely contradicted the testimony he had previously given. The interrogators had easily been fooled into thinking that each of those testimonies was a real breakthrough. Sarly doubted that even the last of them exhausted what Mr. Brandt knew. He could not even be sure that Alexis Alexeievitch was his real name. Not that that mattered, since Mr. Brandt probably did not know his real name either.

In any case, this was valuable intelligence. It demonstrated conclusively that Shanghai was becoming a center for the firearms trade. Large numbers of bank documents and deposit slips had been found in Mr. Brandt's apartment, totaling some 738,200 yuan.

Documents showed that the bank account was extraordinarily active, yet Mr. Brandt could not produce any invoices or receipts. This did not work in his favor. He had enough money to buy a whole house, and he could not explain where the funds came from, or to whom he had paid them. He insisted that he was representing a German trading company based in Hamburg, which planned to buy property in Hong Kong or Shanghai as the first step toward establishing an Asian presence.

In Nanking, Mr. Brandt kept changing his story. First he said he was trading opium, and then it was firearms. In his third testimony—Sarly figured this must be the tenth turn of the screw— Brandt said that the German company was a shell belonging to a shadowy Moscow firm, one of the firms that had sprung up when Comrade Lenin discovered that his newly established Communist country would have to use the exploitative imperialist methods of international trade if it was to feed itself.

But the Nanking investigators did not believe this story. The Concession Police never arrested foreign businessmen without incriminatory evidence—not that Brandt would know this—and two sources had fingered him separately. Brandt later admitted that while his mother was a born and bred Berliner, his father had been born in Moscow. Then, in a raid on revolutionary cells in Hanoi, the French police there had found Brandt's correspondence address in Shanghai. The Political Section of the Concession Police initially thought he might be the leader of the Pan-Pacific Association of Unions. But not long thereafter, in a botched military operation in a small city in Kiangsi province, the Kuomintang discovered documents that the newly established Soviet government had forgotten to destroy in its hurry to retreat. Clues in the documents had led to a series of arrests made by the Kuomintang military in Kiangsi. One of them had caved when threatened with torture and divulged the numbers of a few bank accounts in Shanghai.

According to the interrogation notes from Nanking, in his fourth testimony Brandt had admitted to leading a new Communist organization with a mandate to support the socialist movement across Asia from Shanghai. The organization would provide expertise, strategy, and, crucially, funding to other radical groups. Lieutenant Sarly had his doubts about that confession too. The manuscript was too logical, too well written. It read like a carefully crafted masterpiece pretending to be a draft. The writer hesitated, contradicted himself, crossed out large sections, and yet when he got to the point it was unambiguous and succinct.

But although the Brandt case raised many questions, all parties involved agreed on one fact: they had a common enemy, one that was disciplined, well organized, and well funded. After setbacks in Europe, particularly in Germany, their enemy had refocused its strategy on the Far East, which the Comintern considered the weakest link in the capitalist chain. The best place for them to detonate their bomb would be Shanghai, Asia's most heterogeneous and ungovernable city.

In their private conversations, Consul Baudez and Lieutenant Sarly agreed that the French Concession was the most vulnerable part of Shanghai. A few Shanghailanders, mostly real estate developers, had strong opinions about the Communists. Although the consul had thus far remained neutral, he would seize this opportunity to take action. Baudez too had received a private letter from the Ministry of Foreign Affairs in Paris via diplomatic mail, hinting that the Concession authorities should make a few high-profile arrests in line with France's shifting policy toward the Soviet Union. The animosity between the two countries was no longer a mere trade dispute.

The narrative taking shape in Lieutenant Sarly's mind linked the recent assassinations to a firearms company that operated across Asia and an amateur photographer in the Concession. Further intelligence suggested that the head of the assassination squad in question had a Soviet background. He thought he could see Fate winking at him.

Best of all, it turned out that the photographer, Hsueh, was the son of an old friend. Hsueh's father and Lieutenant Sarly had served in the same company of a colonial regiment during the Great War. They had spent all summer smoking Lieutenant Sarly's beloved pipes in the wet mud of the trenches. Hsueh's father loved to take photographs, and Lieutenant Sarly still had a few of them. That winter, Pierre Weiss's trench had been bombed. Sarly had forgotten all about him until the police station sent him a stack of photographs culled by Inspector Maron from Hsueh's collection. Maron said this Hsueh character had other, more vulgar tastes.

There was no way Inspector Maron would have recognized the much younger Sarly in the photographs. In them he was shabbily dressed, having torn off his uniform sleeves at the shoulders, as men often did in the trenches. Left to steep in sweat, the flesh of their underarms could develop sores and rot.

He did not mention any of this to the consul, partly because it involved a personal matter, but mostly because his opinions were as yet unformed.

CHAPTER 16

Leng was lonely. No one had given her anything to do, and she also hadn't had a visitor in days. She felt abandoned. The night before, she had called Ku from the telephone in the hardware store across the street. This was a clear violation of the rules, but she could not help herself. She sounded like she was about to cry. Just stay put and Lin will be along tomorrow, Ku said. Leng felt a rush of hope.

She slept better than she had in days. Anyone would be miserable, left alone like that. The next morning, she put on makeup, and picked out a checkered cheongsam and a pair of white leather shoes. She would go to the market and buy fish. Lin liked fish. She considered him a real friend, the only person in the cell in whom she could confide.

As she drew the curtains, sunlight streamed across the table. She pushed the window open to let in the crisp morning breeze. Then she poked her head out and got a shock. That man was standing on Rue Amiral Bayle, at the end of the longtang next to the hardware store, looking up at her window. It was the man she had seen a few days ago—or rather, the man who had been standing at the railing of the *Paul Lecat*.

She calmly withdrew her head and put on her shoes. Don't close the windows or draw the curtains, she told herself. She reflected for a moment, and reached out to hang her thin blanket outside the window. Don't turn that way, don't look, she warned herself.

She hurried downstairs. There was only one way out of the longtang, which opened onto Rue Amiral Bayle. She had no way of knowing what this man wanted. They said her picture was in all the newspapers, and anyone could recognize her.

On the intersection of Rue Amiral Bayle and Rue Conty, she ran into trouble.

She picked Lin out right away. He was in a white canvas suit and clutching a magazine. Then she saw the two other men with him. She was dismayed to see a policeman standing in front of Lin, but immediately realized that this was a routine search. Lin's bourgeois appearance seemed to irritate the Vietnamese man in a bamboo hat, who searched him thoroughly. He grabbed Lin's magazine and gave it to the Frenchman with him, but the Frenchman only shook his head. At the end of the search, he paused before reaching his hand out to pat down the back of Lin's waist, as though he had saved the most important step for last, to catch Lin off guard.

On the other end of the roadblock, the Chinese detective opened up the seat of a rickshaw and rifled energetically through its contents. Passersby cursed and grumbled. The police soon lost interest in Lin, and waved him on.

To Leng's puzzlement, Lin did not leave right away. He hesitated, looking at the ground, and rolling up the magazine in his hand. He stared into space, as if he were wondering why the police were performing searches so early in the morning. Then he looked behind him and tapped his head with the rolled-up magazine, as though he had just thought of something and had to go back for it.

She had already raised her left arm to wave at him, but Lin was not looking toward her.

Just as he turned, a gunshot rang out, and everyone looked past Lin in the direction from which the shot had sounded.

Only she was looking at Lin. He turned around, the gun went off, and in the confusion he nearly tripped. For an instant Leng thought he had been shot.

Some people fled south along Rue Amiral Bayle, while others ducked into doorways and gaped at the runners. The police had recovered from their shock, and the sound of police whistles and warning shots rang out. Chinese plainclothes detectives raced after the shooter.

He was still firing off rounds and looking over his shoulders at them. Then he began to skip along sideways, taunting his pursuers like a mischievous urchin. He twisted around to fire into the air behind him, obviously to create confusion.

Leng saw Lin run toward Rue Conty, and she hurried after him, trying to catch up. The shooter, who was trying to escape, had to be one of her own comrades, someone who had been there with Lin. More people appeared, crowding at longtang gates to see what the fuss was about. People poked their heads out of second-floor windows, as if the street were a movie set and gunfire were nothing to be afraid of.

Then, suddenly, no one was running any longer, and Rue Conty reverted to its usual morning stillness.

Lin had melted into the crowd. Leng had to slow down. Her mind was racing. She didn't know whether she could or should go back to her room. Luckily she had seen the man and left immediately, or she wouldn't have witnessed this incident. Right now the apartment would be a dangerous place to be.

She was annoyed that Lin hadn't gone straight there to give her the news and tell her what to do.

She was still scanning the backs of people walking ahead of her. Perhaps she should find a telephone and call Ku. But she dared not just borrow a telephone from a corner shop. She mustn't let anyone overhear her. She thought about calling from a hostel on the street corner but decided the phone at the reception was not safe—a few extra cents would not keep these people from talking. The Concession was crawling with police informers.

She cut through a longtang toward Avenue Dubail, figuring that she would find a public telephone booth there. During the day, the iron doors leading into the longtangs were all open, but the sunlight never penetrated beneath the third floor windows. Despite the breeze, the air was moist with the smoke from yesterday's dinner and the smell of chamber pots left to dry in the sun. The narrow alleyways stank like the city's intestines.

She heard footsteps clicking on the glazed tiles behind her and echoing through the quiet longtang. When she turned the corner she stole a glance behind her and saw the man again, although this time he was not carrying his gigantic camera. She quickened her footsteps. Who was that man anyway? Why was he following her? She knew he had recognized her.

She suspected that the unusual search on the corner of Rue Conty had been no coincidence. It must have had something to do with the man. She was irritated at Lin for having made off so quickly. If only he were here, they could ambush that man, attack him with bricks or a stick, or somehow knock him unconscious.

He was clearly her enemy. He must have drawn the police there. Perhaps he was an informer. But she could not imagine how he could have found the meeting point on Rue Amiral Bayle unless he had seen her leave the safe house. They had been right, then, when they told her she was instantly recognizable. She had to get in touch with Ku. This was an emergency, and she must report it to the cell right away.

The next longtang led to Rue Lafayette. She stepped out of the longtang and waited impatiently for the Vietnamese policeman to turn the sign so she could cross the street. A fence painted black stood beneath the parasol tree, and behind it she could see the shrubbery inside the Koukaza Gardens, the sunlight glittering on grass behind the wooden lattice gates. The telephone booth lay to the west of the gates.

Two gangs of French urchins were fighting for control of the booth. When its hinged door swung into one tousled blond head, the boy collapsed next to the telephone booth, and the children scattered immediately. The old man who sold telephone tokens sat inside the booth, observing them impassively.

Only when Leng walked right up to the booth did the fallen warrior let out a loud cry, leap up, and scamper in the direction of the park gates.

The street was quiet, except for the breeze rustling the leaves of the parasol tree. Leng had no money. She had not brought her handbag, and she did not have a single cent on her.

Later, Hsueh would tell her that she had been standing in the telephone booth looking frantic, like a bird trapped in a cage.

And there he was, smiling through the windows of the telephone booth, just as he had smiled at her not too long ago at Wu-sung-k'ou, when the early morning sun was shining and there was a breeze on deck.

"I saw you on the ship."

He opened the spring-hinged door, poking his head in to speak to her.

Leng thought it best to deny this. "What ship? I don't know you."

"Sure you don't. But I can give you this."

He retracted his head and held a telephone token against the window with his finger, making it slide up and down the glass.

She swung the door open and walked out. Yesterday's dew hung on the thick beams of the fence. He cut her off at the gate.

"Who are you and why are you following me?" Leng said loudly while a couple two feet away walked into the park, one after another. The young man turned to look at her, unmoved. Clearly he had his own troubles and no time for anyone else's, or why would he be in the park so early in the morning? Leng caught a glimpse of a red tassel out of the corner of her eye. The Vietnamese policeman was standing at a pavilion by the gate and yawning. The sunlight glinted off the wet grass roof of the wood and brick Romanesque pavilion. The policeman took an interest in them and began to meander over.

She panicked. Should she scream? Her photograph was in all the newspapers. In fact, it was probably in the police files and pinned on the wall of the police station with photos of all the other suspects. She turned around and walked into the park. She was furious that they hadn't given her a pistol. If she had one, she would shoot him dead right now, she fumed.

It was a Sunday, and the park was bustling with visitors. She paid no attention to the people strolling about; it was the policemen she was worried about. The Vietnamese and Chinese policemen kept appearing from the wide path that ran north-south through the park, and a small policeman rode along on horseback, fully armed. His line of sight stretched from the south to the north gate of the park.

And the man was still walking two steps behind her.

CHAPTER 17

Hsueh did not lack the imagination that Sarly was always saying a good agent had to have. Not that Sarly gave him much advice about intelligence work when they met that afternoon. He was nostalgic for the war, for muddy trenches, for the smell of burned grass mingled with the deep earthy scent of the fields after rain. So he spent most of the afternoon reminiscing about the trenches and his friendship with Hsueh's father, whom he referred to as Pierre, and whose photographs lay on the table. Anything I do for you, I'm doing for Pierre (may he rest in peace), he said. The Concession Police always needs new blood, and of course—Lieutenant Sarly had always valued patrilineage—you are French.

"To be a good agent, you must use your imagination," said Lieutenant Sarly. "The facts won't just present themselves to you— all you've got are a couple of clues and your imagination. The sergeants each have dozens of agents working under them, and the inspectors have even bigger teams. But you will be different. You'll report directly to me."

He had been terrified when Therese pointed her pistol at him that day, and had consequently told her a boatload of lies. In retrospect, he realized that a woman who sold explosives to Communists and the Green Gang could not possibly have been fooled by his amateurish excuses. That night he began to suspect it was only a matter of time before someone blew his cover. Therese would question Mr.

Ku the way she had questioned him, and between them they would soon work out that Hsueh had been causing trouble for them. Then they would come for him. They could batter the door down while he was fast asleep, they could ambush him at the end of a dark alley, they could even surprise him in the steamy public baths, and hold his head under the hot murky water to drown him.

In the middle of the night, he suddenly broke out in a cold sweat. He began to figure how much time he had left to escape. Therese would tell Zung about her suspicions, and then, like a zigzagging billiard ball, this story about an inquisitive young good-for-nothing would reach the ears of the two young men he followed in the cab, and Mr. Ku himself.

On the other hand, things were also going well for him now that he had become a police investigator with secret privileges. He was anxious to prove himself. Lieutenant Sarly wanted him to locate the dark longtang to which he had followed a Hong Kong businessman and a couple of other men, who then suddenly disappeared.

He used to make up stories to satisfy Inspector Maron, tell him whatever he thought he could get away with. But Hsueh was moved by Lieutenant Sarly's determination to honor his friendship with Hsueh's father, and he agreed to take a police squad to the apartment on Rue Amiral Bayle. When Maron started mobilizing his men, however, Hsueh began to have second thoughts. He still held a grudge against Maron, and he didn't want him getting all the credit for this case. He was gratified to realize that he would not be able to pinpoint the exact location of the apartment anyway, since all the longtangs on that street looked more or less the same.

Early that morning, he paced back and forth from one end of Rue Amiral Bayle to the other. Even the ordinarily composed Inspector Maron grew impatient. He had a few of his men set up a roadblock and frisk pedestrians. This was an old police trick: turn up the heat and flush out anyone who looks nervous.

He saw the woman stop in her tracks. A young man in a white linen suit was waiting by the police roadblock. Hsueh recognized him immediately as his old friend from Bendigo.

When chaos broke out, the woman did not stop to find out what was happening like other people on the street. She turned and began to walk away quickly, slipping past the police blockade. She tried to follow the young man, and he watched her lose her mark.

Lieutenant Sarly's comment about using your imagination came to mind. Hsueh thought the woman in the second-floor window might have something to do with the firearms deals, in which case the meeting the other night could have taken place in her rooms. He was pleased with himself for coming up with that. He had originally been forced to spy on Therese, and all the other people he came across were only characters he resorted to when he needed to make something up. But when he saw this woman, all the other figures began to find their proper place in the story taking shape in his mind.

He imagined how she must feel right then—frightened and bewildered.

While the police were falling over themselves chasing the shooter, he began to follow her. She walked briskly through dark alleyways lined with red brick walls half coated with rust-stained, mossy cement. In the sunlight, he could see wisps of cotton drifting onto her short, permed hair. On the ship, she had pinned her hair up in a braided bun. Her light wool coat was just a little shorter than her checkered yellow-and-green cheongsam. When she turned the corner, she would tip her head forward and sway slightly, as if she had caught sight of someone she knew and wanted to surprise them. When her arm swung and disappeared around the corner, her beige coat rippled as if a carp were squirming under it.

When he returned to Rue Amiral Bayle that morning and saw her standing at the window, he could already guess most of the story. But for reasons even he himself did not fully grasp, he had not told Maron the truth.

Hsueh caught sight of the Vietnamese policeman who was always grumpy, but even he didn't scare Hsueh anymore thanks to Lieutenant Sarly. He stretched out his hand, grasped her wrist, and cheerily yelled something in French in the direction of the policeman, but no one understood him, or cared.

She glared at him but allowed him to lead her along a pebbly path lined with knee-high fences, which cut through the field toward the lotus pond.

He barely knew why he was doing this, perhaps because he had seen her weeping on the boat, or perhaps because he did not believe that a beautiful woman could also be dangerous, because he always observed danger through the lens of a camera. Even though Lieutenant Sarly had told him that a Communist cell was behind the Kin Lee Yuen assassination.

"Why didn't you bring your camera?" she turned and asked abruptly. She seemed not to have noticed that this was tantamount to admitting that she recognized him.

Then she stared down at a magpie, at the rushes growing by the pond.

"I see you've been thinking of me?" He himself had thought back to that moment on the ship, shoals of fish gleaming in the sunlight, lifeboats draped in gray-green canvas, the walnut tables on the deck. She had been unhappy, his camera had surprised her, and then she had left angrily.

She looked just as angry now. She said nothing, giving him an icy look, and walked away.

"That's my job, I'm a photographer, a photojournalist," Hsueh called behind her.

He was telling the truth, of course. He had always sold his photographs to newspapers and news agencies, and now he even had a newspaper job. You'll need another job, Lieutenant Sarly had said. I could give you a police badge, but then you'd have to work your way up from being a lowly junior detective, and earn your promotions based on years of service. Since this is the Political Section, I have discretion in hiring intelligence operatives. If I add a few words to your personnel file at the right time, the Concession Police could hire you directly as a sergeant, perhaps even as an inspector. So the best way to go about this would be for you to have an unrelated profession in public and work privately for me.

Lieutenant Sarly made a couple of phone calls and had drinks with his friends at the French Club. The next day, the editor of the French newspaper *Le Journal Shanghai* sent word inviting Hsueh to visit their offices. As soon as he arrived, he was handed a contract to sign and a box of gold-edged name cards, printed in French on one side and Chinese on the other.

She stopped in her tracks, hesitated, and spun around with a gleam in her eyes. Hsueh's flippant words had gotten him in a dangerous situation.

The Concession tabloids had spent a whole week rehashing the Kin Lee Yuen assassination for scandal-hungry Shanghai residents. This woman was said to be an accomplice to murder, or perhaps even its mastermind. The editors produced photographic evidence that she was both beautiful and wicked.

A few of the foreign papers and the more serious Chinese papers speculated that the killing might be connected to Communist assassination squads. They also printed a statement provided anonymously by one such group claiming responsibility for the assassination.

He knew they were Communists. Lieutenant Sarly had told him so.

At this point, they were both standing by the lake, or rather, the pond. He took a few steps toward the pavilion in the center of the pond, which was supported by wooden planks planted in the mud at the bottom. On summer nights, the pavilion often hosted concerts featuring Debussy, Rachmaninoff, and the debonair composer Satie. Butterflies and other insects darted about in the sunshine.

He was not very afraid of the Communists. They belonged to another world altogether. For all he knew, they were hiding in a remote province somewhere outside the Concession. They were reckless students who had caused a great stir and terrified all the foreigners in Shanghai a few years back. The commotion had been amusing to watch, but it had soon died down. Their schemes had nothing to do with his. If anything, the Concession was his territory, and he should receive them like guests.

"You must know that I sympathize with your cause." Hsueh regretted these generous words as soon as they left his mouth. The wind blew, and his shadow began to shudder on the face of the pond, as though it were an informant, listening.

"I can see where you're coming from." He tried a different way of putting it.

"I don't know what you mean." That's right, don't admit to anything. He looked at her mischievously. The longer they were silent, the more flirtatious the silence became.

He liked imagining he was an incorrigible Don Juan. It gave him more confidence.

She arranged her hair with a gesture like a Boy Scout salute, four fingers pressed together and the thumb bent.

"What do you want?" She looked dispirited, and her question sounded not threatening but resigned.

"I've been following you all this way."

"What do you want with following me?"

"I want to help," he said earnestly. "I don't know what you are doing, you obviously don't want me to know, and I guess I don't want to know. But I know a few things you don't, which I would like to tell you. In any case, you can't go back to the apartment now."

"Why should I trust you?"

"Well, why haven't I already turned you over to the police? Why do you think they were searching people on Rue Amiral Bayle? And why do you think they haven't found out where you live yet? How do I know you are a Communist? Why shouldn't you trust me?"

His series of rapid-fire questions sounded like part of a monologue, and he felt as though he had pulled off a successful performance and deserved a round of applause.

"What I know will be useful to you. You must let me talk to you. Wait for me here. Today is a Sunday, and you can pretend you came here to read. I'll go find out what's happening on Rue Amiral Bayle."

He turned to leave, but after a few steps he turned around, pointed at the pavilion, and cried, "Don't go anywhere. Wait for me here."

He felt like a protective lover telling her to be careful. But she still looked worried.

Ta-sheng-yu Candle Store was the second storefront on Rue Palikao, just after Rue de Weikwé. An-le Bathhouse took up the whole street corner and the first storefront. Between the bathhouse and the candle store there was a longtang called Yu-i Alley, and coal for the baths lay piled at the entrance to the longtang. Rainy days were the worst, but even on a sunny day like this, Lin had unwittingly tracked black footprints onto the candle store's green tile floors.

"Are you sure they don't know about this place?"

"I never told them about it."

Ku was silent for a while. The attic was filled with boxes that smelled of dry dust and gunpowder. An arrhythmic sound of hammering came from the direction of Yung-he-hsiang-pai, the blacksmith. Deep in the alleyway, a girl training to be a Chinese opera singer accompanied a *hu-ch'in* in a raspy voice.

"Why were you carrying guns? I know they don't have any brains, but don't you use yours?"

Ku spoke in a low voice. He had lost his temper, but in the dead of the afternoon, against the backdrop of the singer's shrill voice, his anger sounded unreal.

He was waiting for Park to call. He knew something like this was bound to happen with this lot. They were little more than children. Most of their peers were still in school, fetching water for their teachers, scampering through the streets, and getting into fights.

There was an upside and a downside to working with young people. The downside was unexpected misadventures like this one. The upside was that they were naïve, bold, energetic, and treated danger like a game. In some respects, they blew trained operatives out of the water.

He took the phone from the storeroom up to the attic, and told a young member of the cell named Ch'in to mind the store. The attic was stocked not only with candles and foil, but also with matches, firecrackers, and fireworks. Sitting among the boxes was like sitting on a heap of explosives. But Ku was perfectly at ease lighting his cigarette with a match. He knew all about explosives. He had learned to make them from scratch in Khabarovsk.

No. 10 Yu-i Alley was visible through the tall wooden windows, over the back wall of the candle shop. Scallions grew in a battered aluminum basin on the wall of the rooftop patio south of them.

Whenever he was in a new place, Ku would take note of all the doorways and passages, mentally working out escape routes. This was part instinct and part rigorous training. Instructor Berzin had said that a good undercover agent must be as wary as a victim of claustrophobia, but more assertive and aggressive.

Here, for instance, the south-facing window had been boarded up against thieves, but Ku took the boards down so that the window now opened directly onto Yu-i Alley. In a corner of the alley piled high with An-le Bathhouse's coal, there was a single brick in the wall which could be removed to reveal a loaded German-made Luger pistol wrapped in wax paper. The storeroom also had a back door leading into the courtyard of a *shih* house, one of the gray brick town houses with interior courtyards that lined all the alleyways. If you went through the courtyard you could come out of the entrance to No. 10 Yu-i Alley, take a left, go through the longtang leading to Rue de Weikwé, and turn onto Boulevard de Montigny. Once you were inside the Great World Arcade, you could melt safely into the crowds. In a pinch, you could always open the window facing west, climb onto the balcony and out onto the roof, and then look for your chance to escape.

Avenue Édouard VII

Rue des Pères

Rue de Saigon

Rue Palikao

Kuan-sheng Yüan

Rue du Consulat

Boulevard de Montigny

Boulevard des Deux Républiques

Chinese-administered territory

Whashing Road

French Concession

Rue Eugène Bard

①: Candle Store
②: Bathhouse
③: National Industrial Bank
④: Singapore Hotel
⑤: A French Concession Police Station
⑥: Police Station
⑦: Safe house for Lin's unit
⑧: Ch'i's rooms
⑨: North Gate Police Station

Boulevard des Deux Républiques and environs

There's always one threat or another, but you can cope. You are a trained marksman and were taught how to fight with your bare hands, to disguise yourself. You have been involved in dangerous business all your life. So you'll take a deep breath and suppress your anger. Even if that man does get caught by the police, he won't know where the Rue Palikao safe house is. And if he breaks under interrogation and gives them the address on Rue Amiral Bayle, the most they can do is arrest Leng, which would be a heavy but not a fatal blow. Leng only knows one phone number, which would take a full day to trace, and the Concession Police are slowpokes.

At almost two, the phone finally rang. It was Park, calling from a public phone. He spoke in a low voice and the line was crackly. His voice hissed into Ku's ear like an echo carried by the wind, or rather, an echo shattered by impurities in the copper telephone lines.

When he put the receiver down, Ku lit another cigarette.

Lin shifted uneasily, watching the match burn out into a crooked stick of white ash in his hand. As it melted in the wind, he finally asked:

"Well?"

"Park confirmed that Comrade Chou Li-min has given his life for the cause as a result of this morning's altercation." Ku screwed his eyes up, and the corner of his eye twitched, as though irritated by smoke. "He wasn't sure of the rumor, so he went to Chao-chia Creek, where he found the police dragging the creek for Chou's body. It looks like he was pursued there, leaped in, hoping to swim to the other side, and the police opened fire."

Silence.

Lin said nothing. Ku watched him carefully. Was he afraid? A lighthearted morning excursion had ended in death. Or was he angry? Anger could be useful if it was channeled into courage. They would need it—they were about to make another move.

"Comrade Chou had the courage to sacrifice his own life to protect his comrades. After mourning him, we must press on and avenge him." He suspected his words were not forceful enough. He swallowed the cigarette smoke into his throat, allowing it to seep out from the corners of his mouth. His hoarse voice became smokier.

"The problem now is that Leng has disappeared. She is not in the apartment on Rue Amiral Bayle. You agreed she would wait for you there, and I'm afraid she may have run away because the gunfire frightened her. It's too dangerous for her to be wandering around alone during the day."

Lin started, as though waking from a dream, and got up abruptly. "I'll go and find her." He bent over to pick up the rope ladder.

"Where do you think she might be?" Ku mused. Then he said out loud: "She will call. If she does not call by five o'clock, we should evacuate this place."

Lin couldn't just sit down. He wanted to do something to avoid being overcome by grief. He didn't stop to ask himself whether Chou's death had frightened him. He was young. As a student, he had been just in time for the tail end of the revolutionary times. Before he knew what he was doing, he had been swept up by an unthinking frenzy and gone along with it. Then the violence of the struggle had surprised him like a sudden rainstorm. One of his comrades was shot dead by the army in a demonstration—the man had been his point of contact with the Party, and just like that, he had lost touch with his cell. Sometimes he thought to himself that if he had managed to stay in touch, he would have been killed. The thousands of young people swept up by the revolution hadn't had time to organize themselves, and when the counterrevolutionaries retaliated, many of them simply lost touch with their cells and hence with the Party. Some of them resisted, and were killed. But he was not afraid. He was angry. He had actually been contemplating a suicide mission of some sort when he met Ku. Ku was a prudent, experienced revolutionary with meticulous offensive and defensive plans. He and his comrades were pinning their hopes on Ku because they thought he could win.

Now Lin was looking at Ku expectantly, trustfully. All his muscles were tense, as if he were a hunting hound awaiting a command, or a coil spring that would bounce back as soon as Ku loosened his grip.

Ku screwed up his eyes and took a draw of his cigarette. He was fascinated by the restless passion of the young man in front of him. Strangely, he was not even discouraged by the threat of death.

It was time to announce the next operation. If this energy wasn't channeled into an operation, it would explode. Allowing these young people to wait idly would be a recipe for disaster. They couldn't be suppressed—they must be allowed to take action.

He had already been plotting his next operation, which would be even more visible than the last. It would be a defining moment for the cell and earn them lasting recognition and respect. People would remember it not as a headline in a few two-cent tabloid newspapers, immediately overshadowed by the next day's news, but as a legend.

He began to spread the word via various channels. He allowed versions of the story to intersect, appear, and disappear. He did contact a few journalists, but his message was chiefly directed at the various powers operating in the Concession, and the armies of part-time informers who worked for them. He used the network to send a simple message: Ku is here.

Ku is here and to be reckoned with. Whatever your job is, even if it's starting revolutions, people have to know who you are. He did not think of himself as having tricked these young people into joining him. They had a goal, and he could achieve it.

He had long wanted to give the gangs a fright, if for no other reason than that they had helped to massacre the Communists. Now that he was back, they were ignoring him. He would have preferred not to communicate with them via a woman if he didn't have to, and at first he had thought Ch'i could not possibly know anyone in the gangs, but eventually he used her to send them a message: they were underestimating him and People's Strength.

He had not yet settled on his next target, but he was considering either 181 Avenue Foch or 65 Gordon Road. Both were Western-style mansions with a lawn, a fence, a garage, guards, a complicated network of corridors, and police stations not a hundred meters away. The only difference was that Avenue Foch was near a French Concession police station, whereas Gordon Road was near an International Settlement police station.

"Avenue Foch," Lin said.

Lin wanted revenge, Ku thought. He pictured vengefulness as a liquid that could be poured out into measuring cups. It would certainly be a justifiable target, as the owner of 181 Avenue Foch had been directly involved in the 1927 massacre of Communists. But he would have to consider it carefully, as the guards at Avenue Foch were far better armed.

That meant there would be a gunfight, a significant challenge for his squad. They could handle guns all right, and they would sometimes go to deserted beaches in Pu-tung to practice on scarecrows as they chewed and spat sorghum. Or they might rent a boat and take it out to sea, to use a few of the unlucky seagulls circling around Wu-sung-k'ou as target practice. But real fighting was about fear and conquering fear: could his people do that? By contrast, an assassination was a mere performance, like a mischievous practical joke. You strode up to the unlucky victim, took your gun out, pulled the trigger, and watched him collapse to the floor. Years ago, when he was involved in union activity, he had made his way through the outhouse to the factory yard, and dumped a sack of night soil on the foreman's head. The foreman had been standing complacently at the factory gates with the protesting workers shut outside, fiddling with walnuts in his hand until night soil suddenly rained down on him, and he was humiliated. No one was afraid of him from that day onward, and all the stories of his cruelty evaporated.

In principle, an assassination, or even the grander operation he was planning, worked the same way as that sack of night soil. They toppled an old authority or source of fear, establishing a new one in its place. In the labor camps in Azerbaijan, he had spent days going back to these memories. The more he thought about this moment, the more significant it became for him. It proved that fear can unseat existing powers and install new ones. And by the time he escaped and made his way back to China across the Dzungarian Gate, he knew exactly what he would do.

CHAPTER 19

JUNE 14, YEAR 20 OF THE REPUBLIC.

6:18 P.M.

Leng nearly ran headlong into a rickshaw, and stopped to catch her breath. She had altogether forgotten about calling Ku. If it weren't for that man, she would already have made the call. In fact, this morning she had already been standing inside the telephone booth when he—

She finally remembered about making the phone call when it was growing dark.

She got to the candle store on Rue Palikao based on the directions Ku had given her over the phone. She hurried up the stairs, and as soon as he saw her, Ku asked: "Why didn't you call?"

She had to admit she had panicked. It hadn't occurred to her that in a city of a million people she would run into this man, the photojournalist. There was no way to explain it. And she had to tell Ku what she had learned.

What could she say in her defense? She should have called Ku right away and told him about the incident on Rue Amiral Bayle. Instead she had waited for the man at a pavilion in the Koukaza Gardens for hours, like a nervous lover, and gone with him to the White Russian restaurant. He was the journalist who had tried to take a photograph of her on the ship. He was enormously curious and remembered every face he saw. He liked pretending to be nonchalant. She trusted him instinctively, but she couldn't explain why.

All those days alone in the apartment built across the alleyway had enervated her, as if she'd spent days lying in the afternoon sun. No one knew she existed, she thought, no one knew the part she had played in that assassination. Both her comrades and her enemies had abandoned her, almost as if they had plotted together to forget about her.

She told herself it was her duty to banter with him, to have dinner and flirt boldly with him. She had to find out who he was and what he wanted. For some reason, instead of telling Ku about their first encounter on the ship, she found herself telling him that Hsueh was an old acquaintance working as a photojournalist, a trustworthy and sympathetic man who only wanted to help.

But none of that mattered in comparison to what this Hsueh Wei-shih knew. He said he had close friends in the Concession Police, and he warned her not to return to the apartment on Rue Amiral Bayle. He had insider knowledge that the police suspected it of being a safe house for Communists, and once they knew the precise location, they would start making arrests there. His newspaper had been tipped off, and he had gone to Rue Amiral Bayle this morning together with the police, in pursuit of a scoop. He had recognized her right away, and wanted to warn her, but there was no time. The frisking on Rue Conty was an old police trick to draw out malefactors.

"And why would he share this intelligence with you?"

"He knew the police were looking for a woman. The minute he saw me, he put two and two together. He knew me, and he could guess from the newspapers that I had to have been involved in the Kin Lee Yuen operation."

"And you admitted to it?"

"He didn't believe that I could kill anyone—that I could really have been involved in the assassination of a counterrevolutionary army officer." Strangely, she almost believed her own words. She had prevaricated to make her story simpler, but it was only getting more complicated. And she was surprised at herself for hiding their meeting on the ship from Ku. Was it because it sounded too unlikely, like a chance encounter invented by a romance novelist?

"But he must have suspected you had something to do with it, or why would he have told you about the police?"

"Yes. He thought I had to be involved, but he couldn't accept it. I told him that things were not as simple as he thought they were, but that I didn't want to talk about it. He said that if talking about it stirred up painful memories, he would rather not ask."

"As an old friend, did he give you any advice?"

"He said I should leave Shanghai right away, as quickly as possible. But he did not know whether I was at liberty to just leave, so he did not want to impose his opinion. He said he would make further inquiries at the police station."

"At liberty?"

"If there was some reason why I could not leave, was what he meant."

"And you couldn't call because he was right there?"

"Yes."

"So you spent the whole afternoon with him."

"I did."

"Where?"

"In a Russian restaurant with a name I didn't recognize. On Rue Lafayette."

It had been on the intersection with Avenue du Roi Albert. The restaurant had a sign on the corner that said ODESSA, after the port city on the Black Sea. Steps led down to the door, which he opened for her. The Russian waiter seemed to know him well, and they discussed the menu brightly, as if it were an important ritual.

"Whom does he know at the police station? What are their titles?"

"He didn't say."

"You must find out. That could prove to be important to us."

Despite being exhausted, she was aware that Ku's words constituted a mission with which the cell was officially entrusting her.

"You did well to stay calm. Keep in touch with him. His contacts at the Concession Police could be useful to us."

"He isn't one of us."

He had been in high spirits, showing off his knowledge of cameras and Russian food. He had ordered *barjark*, fried beef, and *shashlyk*, lamb chop cut into round pieces and grilled. She had always been with ambitious, idealistic young men; even Ts'ao had fit that description. This man was good-looking—almost handsome—and impertinent, though he could also be gentle.

"What do you think he thinks of you?" Ku blew out the matchstick in his hand.

He had stared at her all that time. He ordered wine but did not drink it. She could tell he wanted to ask her questions but didn't dare to. He pretended to rummage in his pocket for something, but all he pulled out was an expired betting slip. You must give me a way of contacting you, like a phone number. That way if something happens I can let you know right away. Then he produced a pen, as if he had a bottomless pocket, but he was too clumsy to be a magician. The pen was out of ink and drew nothing but white lines on the old betting slip. When she refused, he argued with her.

"He thought the police must have evidence against me, or they wouldn't be coming after me. But to him I am only a frail woman, and he never did ask whether I had anything to do with the Kin Lee Yuen case." She tried to make her reply sound objective.

"So did you figure out how to stay in contact?"

"He gave me his phone number at the editorial offices, but he's hardly there. He's a photojournalist, so he's always out and about. He told me he would have some news for me tomorrow. We're meeting at noon at the gate of the Koukaza Gardens."

When they parted ways, she was careful to avoid being followed. Using the techniques she had learned, she would sometimes stop abruptly, or duck into a shoe shop and scan the passing crowd through the glass window. The trickiest thing was managing to shake off three operatives triangulating to pursue you. The man walking parallel to you across the road was the easiest to spot, and likely to be the most careless of the three. Because he had to keep his eyes fixed on you, even his stride would often fall into rhythm with yours.

Not until she was certain of not being followed did she make the phone call.

There were voices downstairs, but she could tell Lin's laughter from all the other voices. Rue Palikao was noisier at night than during the day. She heard the crackle of vegetables being fried, the whirr of the stovetop fan, and a curious sound of running water that came from somewhere else.

Ku smiled the artificial smile of a humorless man who finds himself having to force a smile: "He's in love with you, isn't he?"

"We've known each other for a long time."

"If he would risk giving you intelligence, he must have feelings for you."

Her reflexes were always slower in the evening. She stared blankly at Ku.

The photojournalist had been wearing two-tone shoes stitched together from white and brown leather, and she could tell that he took pride in dressing well. He bent over, lifted the hem of his trousers, and retied the elastic band on his socks in a single knot, folding the top of the sock over so it would cover the purple flannel band and leave only a single strand hanging down. He was really quite handsome, much more attractive than she had noticed on the ship, and he knew it. To him, she must seem gawky and subdued. He sprang down the steps, turned to hold the door open with his elbow, and backed into the restaurant while beckoning at her.

"If your comrades are all this beautiful, I'll have to join the revolution," he had said loudly, appearing to have forgotten that they were in a small restaurant. She instinctively reached out and caught hold of his gesticulating hands to stop him from going on.

"You must think about how he can be useful to us," Ku said soberly. "Of course, it all depends on whether he really does have connections inside the Concession Police. But if he does, they could be helpful to our cause."

Before they left the restaurant, the man had warned her again not to return to Rue Amiral Bayle. If you don't have anywhere to go, I'll come up with something, he had said. "But of course, your people will have somewhere safer in mind."

Just then there were noises downstairs, chairs being moved and boxes turned over. Lin's steps squeaked up the bamboo ladder and his face appeared.

"What is it?" Ku asked sternly.

"A rat." He grinned.

Leng felt numb to everything around her. She sat there, blankly, clutching a cup of tea that had gone cold, that feeling of bleakness spreading like a chill across her body.

As a matter of fact, Therese did not think Hsueh was lying. She believed him. After all these years living in Shanghai, she still hadn't got a handle on the gangs, who really were everywhere. But she could tell he had lied about being friends with the gangsters. She remembered the night when Hsueh had arrived at the Astor covered with bruises. Clearly, they'd had him beaten up and forced him to spy on her. She relented.

She had always liked Hsueh, that half-Chinese bastard who smelled of jasmine. She loved his photographs. They were pictures of blood-covered corpses, vomit reeking of alcohol, female bodies. They exhibited an obsessive love of cleanliness, a sort of harmless irreverence, a bizarre sense of invulnerability.

The relationship also felt more real to her since Hsueh had intruded on the other half of her life. The bastard now stood out from all the other men whose pale naked bodies she had seen in the darkness. He wasn't just a certain position, a scent that made her horny, a cock with a birthmark on it. She had handled many different cocks, some crooked like eagle beaks, some with foreskins that could be stretched endlessly like a nylon sock.

If you make this one exception, you'll never be ruthless again, she told herself. She could have simply killed him. She could have had him killed. She had loyal bodyguards and good friends in the White Russian gangs.

That day, as she threatened him with a gun and pushed the barrel into his chin, she had watched the tears well up in his eyes. She jabbed the barrel in farther behind his chinbone. He had to be punished. As she pushed harder, she could hear him moan and try to swallow, and she felt sorry for him. She knelt on the bed, naked, still sweating, but the torturer's cruel smile played across her face. As she stroked his dick with her other hand, she could tell how petrified he was, how frustrated and vulnerable. He wouldn't give in. But he couldn't help getting aroused, and for Therese, that signified a form of surrender.

She was overcome by affection for him, and later she thought that might have been when she had fallen in love with him, perhaps because she had never had to think about whether she loved Hsueh until she was forced to decide whether to kill him. For more than three years, they had met every weekend at the Astor, and if she hadn't had enough sex, all she had to do was give him a call. He was always there, and the thought of never being able to see him again had not crossed her mind. Never before had she thought of Hsueh as an actual human being, rather than a male body who gave her pleasure. He was jealous that she had other men, and had even stooped to spying on her. For the first time, she had learned of something that had happened to him outside their relationship: someone had beaten him up and forced him to report on her.

She started thinking of him as her lover, and the thought filled her with tenderness. When her gun was jabbing into his chin, hadn't he almost wet himself from fright? Didn't he tell her that later on, when she was fondling him? But he had said he loved her anyway.

She ruefully admitted that she was a woman just like the rest of them, like her friend Margot—love was the bane of their lives. She had survived war, famine, and revolution. She liked to think she wasn't easily duped, and she knew insincerity when she saw it. But she also knew that everything in the Concession had a price. So she was choosing to overlook Hsueh's lies because she could tell he was for sale, and she could afford to buy him. She thought her lover far superior to Margot's. Equality couldn't exist in any relationship that took place in this city full of adventure seekers, gold mines, and traps. One person was always in control of the relationship, and if it wasn't him, it was you.

She directed Zung to leave Shanghai immediately, telling him she had reliable information that the gangs and even the police were aware of his latest deal. But she did not tell him about Hsueh. Zung was her business partner and trusted employee, but even so, how could she broach the subject of her private life, never mind reveal that she had been sleeping with a man sent to spy on them?

Earlier that evening, nouveau-riche Shanghailanders had arrived at an Edwardian villa in the west of Shanghai for an elaborate party. They had all been nobodies when they first came to Shanghai, but they had at least been ambitious. And now that they had made their fortunes and become the masters of this place, they had all bought worthless titles of nobility from their home countries back in Europe. They ate three-course meals. With the money they had made speculating on land, they hired tutors and nannies for their children. They spent huge sums of money on Russian jewels for their wives, and smaller sums of money on Asian mistresses whose lips revived their dicks. They permitted their half-Chinese sons to work in their friends' companies, and abandoned them when their own speculating failed.

It was just past seven, and the dew on the grass had not yet softened the ground. The swimming pool was still sparkling in the dusk. Since it was a fancy dress ball, the villa and grounds were teeming with all kinds of odd characters. A group of Arab nobles leaned on the second-floor railing, the men wearing scimitars and the women wearing head scarves. The theme for the day was the sinking of the *Titanic*.

The captain—the founder of the American company the Raven Group, the evening's host—announced that the ball had begun. The Arabs howled as though they were standing at the edge of the desert. Margot was wearing an elaborate fin-de-siècle pleated dress that trailed on the floor. Even her drawers had been specially stitched by Chinese tailors according to the fashion of the period, she whispered to Therese. They were long silk drawers with the type of open seat pants that nowadays only toddlers wore.

"You'd better find somewhere quiet and let Mr. Blair get under that dress," Therese mocked gently. Margot's husband was dressed as a general. He had managed to procure a number of medals and a gold-embroidered red sash with a large stain that looked for all the world like an old borscht stain. Baron Pidol was clearly fitting right in. He was acquiring the Shanghailanders' leisure habits, and he already had a genuine antique sash.

An up-and-coming young poet from London tied a purple shawl around his head that covered his chin and was draped over his shoulders, in an impression of a Berber chieftain. Shanghai was his first stop on a journey through China, and he hadn't yet traveled farther inland. The men who were learning how to be rich—or their wives, rather—all ordered literary magazines from London and knew of him from there. They invited him to banquets, keen to see the young prodigy from Cambridge. His companion was even younger and skinnier than he was, and had smeared his face black with paste. To avoid having to paint his shoulders black, he had drawn his tartan wool shawl higher around his neck to hide his pale skin. A man called Madier commented in what he meant to be a worldly tone: "I suppose the Moroccan gigolo costume suits him. The poets, Gide, I mean, didn't they all use to go off to Morocco for this sort of thing?"

The poet and his companion couldn't hear the people gossiping about them. The former was too busy grumbling about the music. The band was playing last year's hottest jazz standard, "Body and Soul," a perfect song for a slow dance with an arm around your partner's waist. They always played new songs for this crowd, just to prove they were *au fait* with the latest musical trends. But would the poor dead musicians on the *Titanic* in 1913 have been playing jazz back then? The poet didn't stop to think that if this had been 1913, people wouldn't have been content to whisper about him and his companion—some busybody might have hauled them into court.

Shanghailanders were like that. While they might be fooling

around, they despised and gossiped about anyone else who did. If things ever got so far that they made the newspapers, the whole Concession would enjoy a few evenings of *Schadenfreude* at the dinner table. Shanghai prided itself on setting trends, but it was also a stickler for conventional values. Someone said out loud that the woman singing in the band should be expelled from the concessions for being a disgrace to the British Empire. Apparently she had jumped up on the table at a businessman's private bar and danced naked in the style of the Tiller Girls, kicking her feet up so high that they almost reached the chandeliers. The inebriated young men who were present all got an excellent view. They said even a prostitute wouldn't do what she did after getting drunk: lie on the table, kick her legs up in the air, and even piss into a wineglass. Her husband, a failed speculator, had jumped off a building. He hadn't been able to keep her under control, but couldn't the Concession Police do anything about her?

Someone said loudly that his second cousin had written to him saying London had no plans to withdraw its troops. Since 1927, every time the Nanking government had made anti-imperialist noises, London had sent a company or two to Shanghai from India. The Concession would flourish for the next hundred years! The land west of Shanghai would be worth a hundred times as much in five years, and everyone should snap it up. His listeners cheered.

Baron Pidol was drunk, while Margot occasionally swept into view among the dancers. She couldn't resist spiking the foxtrot with a few kick steps from the Charleston, the latest dance craze to hit Shanghai, even though her long dress was ill suited to dancing it.

"I don't like the Charleston," Baron Pidol told Therese. "A wellbred lady shouldn't be dancing the Charleston. Crossing her hands over her knees like a monkey from Szechuan."

His own dance steps were a little ragged, so Therese steered him off the dance floor. Chinese servants in lemon-colored silk shirts with short sleeves made their way through the crowd. The baron reached for another glass of gin and tonic.

"I could have another twenty glasses of this. In twenty glasses' time I'll be sober again, twenty times soberer than when I'm sober. Soberer than that Mr. Blair."

"You don't look soberer than Mr. Blair right now."

"Oh yes, Mr. Blair is sober. Sir Blair. He's sober. He could cross his hands over his knees and he'd still be a sober gentleman. She, on the other hand, is a whore."

"She's your wife."

"That's true. She is my wife. Margot, will you take Franz to be your lawful wedded husband? That's my wife all right, sleeping with another man."

"That's a lie."

"I'm not lying. She thought I didn't see what they were getting up to in Mo-kan-shan, but even if I hadn't, wouldn't it be written all over her face? She hadn't showered, and she still smelled of him. Did she think I couldn't tell? Did she think I couldn't smell the sperm on her? Women have all kinds of smells, but semen only has one smell, like almond milk tea left out overnight."

"You didn't see a thing. You're just guessing."

"I saw everything. They didn't even shut the door. They couldn't hear me race up the stairs. I had taken my gun but forgotten my hat, and what kind of gentleman forgets his hat when he goes hunting? Anyhow I tiptoed downstairs and gave them another five minutes. Then I shouted for my hat in the yard, as though I hadn't seen a thing, when of course I'd seen it all. She came rushing down the stairs, her face flushed, her eyes watery."

The party was in full swing. The drunken bachelors had formed a long line, each with their hands on the shoulders of the man in front of them, hopping through the hall with their knees bent like frogs. They skipped around the pool in the lawn, came back through the hall, and hopped up to the second floor and back. More and more people joined them. Therese took the crestfallen baron out to the lawn. It was windy, and moonlight played on the servants' silk sleeves. Baron Pidol was still pouring his heart out.

"I'm going to buy a ticket and go home. I hate this place," he whimpered.

"Surely a gentleman wouldn't just run away."

"Oh, I'll be back. I want to go home and tell the board that there's money to be made here. Then I'll come back with cash and buy and buy."

Someone rang an alarm bell they had borrowed from the Board of Works' fire department, and someone else was making an announcement in the hall. Therese could only just make out the words. "The ship has hit an iceberg and it's about to sink," he said. The crowd began to scream.

Inspector Maron must have complained to Sarly that Hsueh had disappeared at the most crucial moment. The scene of the shooting was
a mess, and the plan to search the apartment had to be abandoned.
But when Hsueh eventually turned up, he did lead the policemen
to the correct apartment. Unsurprisingly, they found no one there,
but they did find some valuable evidence. The Chinese detectives
discovered a forged Concession residency document under a pile of
drawers, and as soon as the poet from Marseille saw the photos, he
cried: "Isn't this the woman who disappeared from the *Paul Lecat*?"

They also found a Browning pistol and five rounds of ammunition. "If Hsueh had not run off on his own and we'd gone in right
away, we would have nabbed that woman," Maron told Lieutenant
Sarly in front of Hsueh.

When Sarly asked just what Hsueh had been doing, he said he had
been searching all the longtangs on Rue Amiral Bayle for the right
apartment. And when Sarly lost his temper, Hsueh only rubbed his
nose and said that he would find her again.

Sarly didn't ask how. Which was not to say that he had perfect
faith in Hsueh. But he did know that the concessions were governed
by a set of rules to which the police had no access. For instance,
both the French Concession and the International Settlement
contained a handful of places—an alleyway, a yard surrounded
by black picket fences, or a maze of old wooden huts—that were

miniature fiefdoms, concessions within concessions, controlled by the gangs or the Communists, and defended by their own armed guards. All the Chinese knew where these places were, and none of the French detectives did. Unless he absolutely had to, no Chinese detective would reveal this information to his superiors. There was a wealth of information to which only the Chinese had access, and even a Shanghailander who had spent thirty years here might never figure it out. That was why Sarly was willing to invest in Hsueh. He believed that Hsueh's Chinese face would give him access to what Sarly thought of as Shanghai street savvy, and that his French heart would prompt him to report it to Sarly.

When Hsueh later thought back to that day, he realized he had been feeling vaguely confident that he held a pretty good hand. Like any keen gambler, he prided himself on his intuition. He refused to admit that he was affected by anything like being attracted to a woman he felt as if he'd always known. He thought of the information he had as something like an inside tip that an unknown contender would be allowed to jump the gun. Now he was waiting for the odds to rise before placing a bet.

Despite knowing that Therese often lunched at that White Russian restaurant, and that the waiter knew her so well that it had almost become her second home, he took the woman there. It was either showing off or a gesture of protest—actually, he wasn't sure which. But running into Therese there would certainly have been something.

That night, he put half a tin of Garrick cigarettes in his cigarette case, and went out to look for Li Pao-i. He took him to Moon Palace, a cheap dancing hall where one yuan bought you five dances with a girl. He wanted to ask Li about the Kin Lee Yuen incident.

Li Pao-i's take on recent events shocked him. It wasn't an isolated incident, said Li. The whole underground intelligence network of the Concession was chattering about this new assassination squad. No one knew where it came from, but at least three assassinations had already been linked to it.

"Didn't your paper say they were Communists? There was that manifesto too."

"The Communists don't work that way," Li said. He had smoked half of Hsueh's cigarettes in no time at all.

Tao Lili came to their table. She loved journalists, and it was said that her stage name, Peach Girl, had been Li's suggestion. "Why a peach?" she was said to have asked him. He drew his hand back and sniffed at it. "What do you think?" he said. Upon which she was said to have pounced on him: "Eat me out, then!" Not all the dancing girls offered extra services on the side, but Tao was well known not just for her willingness, but also for her indiscretion. All of Shanghai knew which of her clients cut it, and which didn't. A tabloid journalist had apparently uncovered one young dandy's embarrassing secrets by hiding in an adjacent cubicle. She looked at Hsueh, and whispered something in Li's ear.

"You idiot!" Li muttered.

"The Communists don't do assassinations," he said to Hsueh. "They take care of their own traitors, sure. And they might kill someone who poses a serious threat. But they wouldn't have to hound a small-time journalist like me when they can use their own publications. They wouldn't shift gears like that overnight."

"What's your stake in this anyway?" Li asked, gesturing with his wineglass. The deep glasses were said to have been invented by the captain of a Scottish pirate ship, to make sure that the wine wouldn't spill even if the seas were rough. Nowadays, of course, the pirates had all become bigwigs in Asia.

Hsueh produced one of the official name cards he had gotten from the newspaper, and handed it to Li.

"The French are keen on it. They think there's a story here. They think it could be a big deal."

"It could be a pretty big deal, that's true . . ." Li stopped midsentence and looked at Hsueh, as though he had just realized something.

The table was low, and Hsueh could see Li stroking Tao's thigh from across the table. Tao glanced at Hsueh, adjusted her posture slightly, and smoothed out the slit in her cheongsam. The line of white flesh that had been visible just above her stockings vanished.

"What I'm about to tell you, now that's a big deal," Li said mysteriously.

"You cunning old fox. Stop pretending you know anything," Hsueh said, deliberately refusing to give Li any face in front of Tao.

Li was provoked. He got up, shrugged his shoulders, rubbed his nose, lit a cigarette, and let slip a piece of information that could have been worth a hundred-yuan check:

"You're not the only person who's been coming to me asking about this. And it's not just the police. You wouldn't believe it. At the teahouse by the Race Course, even Morris Jr. came to me. Not on his own steam—you guessed it, the Boss himself sent for me."

"Wait, the Green Gang cares about this?"

"Word is that someone paid the Green Gang a lot of money to find the killer, so yes, the Boss does care. Of the three killings so far, one isn't important. One has to do with the coup in Fukien. Three days after the assassination, the commander of the fort at Safuchou was arrested and sent to Nanking. The most important of the three is the assassination at Kin Lee Yuen Wharf. Ts'ao Chen-wu was in Shanghai making arrangements for the arrival of an important figure, and he was killed to stop that man from going to Canton. It had something to do with public debt, but even I don't know the whole story."

He said "even I" as though it should all have been reported to him as a matter of course. Then he put his hand complacently around Tao's waist, and pinched her.

It was Li's own fault he didn't know the whole story—he'd never done an honest day's work in his life. To find out whether public debt had played a role, all you'd have to do was read the papers for the week of the assassination. Once they were done talking, Hsueh resolved to go straight to the editorial office's reading room and read all the foreign newspapers from the past month.

The dance hall didn't seem to be doing well that night. Even Peach Girl, their most popular dancer, wasn't hauled off to join any other tables. A singer shrieked the song "Drizzling Rain" at the top of her voice, while a fire-eating acrobat performed in between songs, juggling three flaming beer bottles that rose and fell in the air. Li was groping Tao; Tao's deep eyes were fixed on Hsueh; Hsueh couldn't stop thinking about Leng.

"Leng is your real name, isn't it?" he had once asked her. She had ignored the question.

Hsueh didn't really trust Li. You had to take all the tips horse-traded in the Concession with a grain of salt. He could have sworn Leng belonged to a Communist cell because she was so focused, and he felt she must be ideologically motivated. Mere flirting seemed not to distract her at all.

But the next day, he felt less sure. He had stayed up all night reading old newspapers in the editorial offices until the early hours of the morning. Even the editor had praised his diligence:

"Whatever the big scoop is that you're looking for, after you go to the police, you're coming to me. Whatever you've got, you're publishing it with me."

He went to the Jih-hsin-ch'ih Bathhouse for a bath and a full-body massage, and took a nap. He also kept an ear out for the latest news of the Green Gang.

"There's that new assassination squad, of course. People something?" The bathhouse was the best place for gangland news—even the boys who gave foot massages were sworn gangsters. They knew exactly what tips to leak and what to bury. The Boss had it all under control.

So when he met Leng at noon, the first thing he did was to try and worm more information out of her.

"I didn't think financiers could be Communists."

"What do you mean?" Leng was puzzled.

"Nothing." Leng was getting used to Hsueh's random questions. If she ever thought back to these conversations days later, she would realize that things would have turned out quite differently, had she told Ku about every exchange between her and Hsueh.

Hsueh's chief talent was being creatively untruthful. Last night I went straight to Moon Palace Dancing Hall on North Szechuen Road, he said. I was looking for my police friend. *This barely counts as a lie.* I pretended I didn't really care, and I was only asking questions to make the dancing girl think I was in the know. *This isn't too far-fetched either.*

"Your friend, is he a Frenchman?" Leng asked.

"Yes, but he's lived here for years and he speaks Shanghainese." Hsueh blushed at having been caught out.

"It's funny you speak French and know so many French people."

"My father was French," he said without trying to boast, although being French had its advantages in the Concession.

"I see."

Hsueh was surprised that Leng was in such a lively mood. She had been silent and nervous the previous day, like a hedgehog curling up when prodded.

Yesterday afternoon the Concession Police ransacked the apartment. They found identity papers with your photo and a fake name, unless that's your real name and Leng isn't.

Leng grew irritated. Those sons of bitches, she muttered.

He had nothing left to say. That's all for today. Dismissed. Hsueh touched his brow in what he imagined to be the international Communist salute.

He was even more surprised when Leng suggested watching a movie. A movie? Sure, why not. Let me buy you a steak dinner too.

Before Ku could make his next move, they made a move on him. That was his own fault. Under the circumstances, he shouldn't have gone to Ch'i's place. If they hadn't yet decided to buy him off, there was a chance they might be sizing him up, and he should have guessed they would use Ch'i to get at him. When he first negotiated with them, Ch'i had been their go-between.

He got home in the early hours of the morning and rapped on the door. Still shaken, he told Ch'in to go to sleep. He wanted to think.

On the way to Ch'i's apartment the previous night, he had had a funny feeling. The apartment was on Rue Eugène Bard, and getting there from Rue Palikao usually took about fifteen minutes, but today it took more than half an hour. He could have taken Rue du Consulat toward Boulevard de Montigny, which would have allowed him to stay within the bounds of the French Concession and not go through the iron gates. But for some reason he ventured into Chinese territory via the gates on Rue Palikao. He was always telling the cell that they had to breathe deeply and stay calm, and maybe he had been jittery. But that meant he had to cross the northwest corner of Chinese-administered territory and enter the Concession at the gate between Ming Koo Road on the Chinese side and Rue Voisin on the French side, where two policemen stopped him and frisked him.

No big deal, he looked calm and hadn't been drinking. But he was uneasy, and the policemen gave him an unusually thorough search.

This wasn't the usual Chinese policeman with too much time on his hands deciding to give someone a hard time, a Frenchman taking it out on a Chinese man, or even a regular cop just going through the motions of a search.

Luckily he never carried anything important with him. But the search made him so tense that his back muscles ached. Maybe it was because it was windy and the moon was blotted out by clouds. He thought he saw a shadow behind the tree on the other side of the longtang. He stopped, lit a cigarette, cocked his head, and cupped his hands around the cigarette to keep the wind from putting it out. A silvery moonlight filtered through the knotted branches of the parasol tree and lit up the dark shape under the tree—it was only a pushcart. In the moonlight, even the words painted on the push-cart were legible: SOYBEAN MILK FORMULA, which the Kuomintang Municipal Government's Department of Health was promoting as being nutritious and cheap. As he slipped into the narrow longtang, he heard a rustle behind him and spun around. It was a wild cat, which stopped to stare at him for a moment, two beads of green gleaming in the dark, before it vanished.

Ch'i's expression when she opened the door surprised him. He couldn't tell whether she was startled or eager to see him. Were they both feeling nervous, or was it just him?

But as soon as he went inside, the scene that welcomed him made him relax. A large bowl of congee and two plates of pickled vegetables lay on the table, and Ch'i's floral curtains kept out the draught. She took off all her clothes, except a tiny bodice. Squatting behind the bed, she pissed and washed her behind.

He sat by the table, smoking, and when she was ready, she came over to undo his buttons. Her shoulders smelled of jasmine.

He decided he had gotten himself worked up over nothing.

He would smoke a cigarette before dinner. Taking the cushion from his own chair and putting it on the seat next to him, he patted it to signify that Ch'i should keep him company instead of getting into bed. Who knew that Ch'i of Fu-chih Alley had a meek side. "I always thought you sit like you're a tycoon," she had once told him.

When he was about to laugh out loud, she said: "Then I realized you weren't a tycoon—you were a hit man."

Local newspaper headlines always gave him a false sense of security. Police Raids Chingho Road Saloon after Bartender Seduces Owner's Wife. The subtitle was Boss Finds Lover under Bed, Adulterous Couple Arrested.

Brothel in Tung-sheng Hotel Fined.

Chief Culprit in Wang Yün-wu Kidnapping Executed Yesterday.

Rue Amiral Bayle Gunman Shot Dead by Police.

He occasionally glanced at the newspaper as he ate his congee, barely noticing Ch'i. She was just like a pet dog. She wouldn't mind. All women are obsessed with some man, and besides, Ku had saved her life. A gang of men had come after her for adding an extra zero on the end of a check. If they had asked nicely, she might just have given the money back. But they had bullied her, and in a rage, she threatened to expose that man in the tabloids and humiliate him. The next thing she knew, his men were storming into her apartment, and if Ku hadn't been there, they would have killed her on the spot. If he hadn't happened to be in Fu-chih Alley—and she had wondered for the past eight months why he happened to be there— they could have disfigured her with limewater, or stuffed her in a sack and thrown her into the Whampoa. But he had rapped his pistol on the table and forced the men to negotiate with him. As they talked, one of them had crept up behind him with a chef's knife, but he had gotten up suddenly, pushing his chair back and tripping the man over, and then felling him with a well-aimed punch to the chin. At that they had said: "Don't mess with us and we won't mess with you!" Then they had stormed out.

That was why she did everything he asked. She knew he liked watching her, so she would walk around naked and fix him tea as though the June night were not cold at all, as though she were a White Russian prostitute. She hid a gun under her mattress because he asked her to. If his life depended on it, then so did hers, and if it made him feel safer then she would feel safer too. She could give him a sense of familiarity, but she also knew how to make him feel special—when he was depressed, she would pant harder and shriek louder to boost his ego. She had taken the gangs a message because he wanted her to, although he knew Morris Jr.'s bloodshot eyes gave her the creeps.

Ku got under the blanket, and pressed his stomach up against Ch'i's cold bum through the thin cotton blanket and shirt. He waited for her to turn around and tug mischievously at his pants as though she couldn't wait, which was part of their usual routine. Her being naughty gave him an excuse to pretend he despised her, but the more he did that while pleasuring her, the more she enjoyed it.

His loosened trouser band lay twisted on his stomach like a caterpillar. She was stroking him, but her mind seemed to be elsewhere. She opened her mouth, as if to say something. She pinched him too hard by mistake, making him gasp in pain. He caught her by the hair and said: "What's the matter with you today?"

"They came here looking for you," she squealed.

"When? How many of them?"

"Just after dark. Three. They looked everywhere—in the closet and under the bed."

He sat up and reached under the mattress for the gun. There it was. He felt better.

"And what did they say?"

"A lanky man with a scar on his cheek slapped me in the face!" She told him the fact she considered most important first. Her hand brushed her cheek, as though to indicate the slap, or the scar.

"What did they say?"

"They said they would be back."

His back ached. He was nervous and angry. He turned over, gripped her wrist, and reached one hand under the mattress toward that cold piece of metal. He could feel his armpits sweating, and the sweat ran down his ribs to his belly, dripping onto Ch'i's bodice. He ripped it off as if he were ripping off the scales of a carp to reveal its white belly.

His fingers were stretched taut and pressed tightly together. Her strained vocal cords let out a long moan like the cry of a seagull on the river at night. That was how they missed the rapping at the door.

The strange noises outside had been going on for a while. Heavy, sloppy footsteps on the stairs, someone knocking and then battering at the door. By the time he finally turned to look, it was too late. There were two men in the room, and one standing at the doorway between the sitting room and the bedroom. Between them they had an axe and two guns, a Browning in the room, and a Mauser at the doorway.

The Mauser straddled the doorway, one foot inside the room and one out. He pursed his lips and brandished his gun. Ku could see that it was set to fire a single round.

He ignored the two men in the room, and focused on the Mauser. He wanted to get out of bed.

"Don't move," the Mauser said, pointing at him. Then he motioned to Ch'i: "You, get off the bed."

Ku steeled himself. He swallowed, and forced himself to smile. "Don't you want me alive?"

"For a couple days, maybe." The voice was calm, as though speaking to a dead man.

Ch'i stretched out her legs to get off the bed but hesitated, and tugged at the blanket to cover—

"Don't move the blanket. The two of you, tie him up inside the blanket."

So all she could do was reach for her bodice to cover her crotch, and stand by the side of the bed.

Behind her, Ku reached for the gun, careful not to let his shoulders move, and edged toward the side of the bed to get into a better position.

Now Ch'i was standing on the ground by the bed, and to the right of her pelvis he could see the Mauser. She edged toward the right, and her pale ass had never looked curvier or more beautiful. Her green birthmark shivered. Strangely, he was not afraid. He wanted to reach his hand out and plunge it between her legs again. He wanted to pull her back toward him and make her cry out like a lonely seagull on the Whampoa at midnight.

When the Browning appeared to her left in front of him, he fired. He didn't need to worry about the empty-handed man on the right, who had tossed his axe on the ground by the door, assuming that the Mauser had everything under control.

He fired straight at the Browning's chin, shooting his chinbone off. He pushed Ch'i aside to look for the Mauser. Ch'i stumbled, but she suddenly turned toward him, spreading her arms out, as though she wanted to make her body into a wall.

The Mauser fired a single round that pierced her from the tail-bone through to her belly. But her body changed the trajectory of the bullet as she turned, so that it penetrated the blanket and lodged in the wall.

Ku stretched out his right hand to break her fall, pulling the trigger with his left. One round, two, he aimed again, a third round. His targets slowly collapsed onto the ground, and for a moment there was complete silence. You could hear the wild cats in heat, and blood bubbling from wounds. Only now did he notice that his hand was pressed against Ch'i's pubic hair. Her pubic bone, which usually felt soft, now felt sharp like a rock, making his wrists hurt. He withdrew his hand. He could feel the warmth in her body as it grew cold.

Ku was now sitting in the attic of the candle shop, smoking endlessly and plotting his revenge.

CHAPTER 23

From the roof of Te-hsing Hotel, Ku scanned the mansion opposite him on Route Ratard with a pair of racecourse binoculars. He had booked the entire third floor of the hotel. Half an hour earlier, he had been busy working on the third-floor balcony disguised as a technician installing electric lights. But the roof was a better vantage point. From it he could see not just the mansion, but also its extensive grounds farther north, along Avenue Foch.

At 181 Avenue Foch was Fu-sheng Casino. It was one of the Boss's top sources of income, and also where he made all his friends. Everyone had heard of it, but not everyone was allowed in. There was no shortage of gambling dens in the Concession. When the British banned gambling in the International Settlement, they had all picked up and moved south. But Fu-sheng was reserved for high rollers, and new gamblers had to be vouched for by existing members. Anyone who qualified was handed a thousand yuan worth of chips at the door and wouldn't have to settle the bill until he left.

It was a three-story villa with red tiles and wide eaves, high walls and low walls. A squadron of fully armed guards posted at windows and balconies controlled every inch of the nine-acre grounds from their positions. The walls were decorated with intricate wall carvings, the perfect firing position for a shootout. Ku saw Morris Jr. standing behind a second-floor window on the corridor. He knew that that was the guardroom. The night before, he and Park had wormed their way into the building dressed as two high-rolling gamblers. Park, the former actor, was much better at coming up with disguises. The entire grounds could be seen from the guardroom. The casino guards could defend the main gate and walls from the three vertical windows facing north toward Avenue Foch, and use automatic rifles to secure the yard and back gate from the windows facing south.

Morris Jr. was about to leave the grounds. There were more than thirty bodyguards at Fu-sheng, huge sums of cash, and scores of important guests who couldn't be touched. It was three in the afternoon, and he could afford to take off for a few hours, until the Boss himself got there in the evening. He always arrived punctually at eight and played the domino game Pai Gow for four or five hours, humming to himself as he played. Then Morris Jr. would not be able to step away even for a moment. Lin had found all this out by talking to the gardeners.

Morris Jr. was not tall, but he was as sturdy as a turret on an armored police vehicle. His nervous tic was squinting, but he wasn't squinting right now. Although Ku had killed all three of the hit men sent to dispatch him the previous Sunday evening, that did not seem to worry the thug at all.

Morris Jr. had disappeared from view. He must be inspecting the rooms. The smaller rooms would be empty, with only a handful of guests milling about the roulette and dice tables. But Ku's binoculars picked him out again inside the bar where guests came for a breather or a bite to eat. He was stuffing cigars into a leather pouch, bantering with the waitresses, and looking out the window. The back gate on the far side of the lawn was shut, and guards sat outside the greenhouse, dozing in the sun.

He went over to the iron gate, and disappeared behind a wall. That did not trouble Ku at all. Lin would be watching him from there. They had already spent a few days staking out this place, and they knew Morris Jr.'s routine by heart. He always cut diagonally across Avenue Foch, ignoring the cars that sped past as though he were the only man on the road. Then he would walk straight up to the counters at the Continental Car Service and hire a cab. Once he had paid, and the attendants said his cab was ready, he would saunter out, maybe light a cigarette at the door. He would turn the corner into the longtang next door, and walk toward the garage at the end of the alley.

The whole process from hiring a cab at the counter to walking into the garage would take him about three minutes. That gave Lin's unit plenty of time to get ready. In those three minutes, they would board a car, having already hired one and claimed that they were waiting for a friend in the garage. Then they would direct the driver to make a turn at the gate, the only blind spot that could not be seen from the drivers' waiting room. There they could hustle him off the cab with a gun to his temple, shoving him into the storage room just to the left of the exit, where they would truss him up and stuff his mouth with absorbent cotton balls.

No one in Lin's unit knew how to drive a car, so Ku directed Park to join them for this operation. At this moment, Park was sitting in the driver's seat, wearing his absurd knitted cap, its edge folded all the way back to the bobble, making it look like a dumpling with too much skin.

Ku ordered all his operatives to wear ordinary clothes with one really outrageous accessory. Lin, for instance, had wrapped his amber-colored glasses, nose bridge included, in white medical gauze. If there is one thing about you that stands out, people tend to focus on it and forget what your face looks like. A small trick, but it always works.

Killing Morris Jr. would rid Shanghai of a gangster known for his cruelty, but Ku also had other motives for targeting him.

As soon as Morris Jr. appeared, squinting at the car and making his way toward it, Park was to push the door open and shout over the black Czech-made car:

"Your usual opium den, sir? Hop on board, please." Ku had wondered whether Park's northern accent would give him away, but he decided it would have to do. Luckily Continental employed plenty of drivers from Shan-tung.

Morris had an opium habit. Although the casino provided it to guests as a courtesy, he kept his little vice a secret, especially from the Boss. He always directed the cabdrivers to take him to North Szechuen Road.

Later, when they debriefed, Park mentioned that he had backed the car along the wall several times, so that the passenger door would be right next to the wooden door to the storage room: "We didn't want to give him another second to squint." Lin jumped in from the right passenger door, and Park opened the window between the front and back of the cab, telling his passenger to stay calm and not get jumpy. Not that he could move with a Mauser pointed at his brain—or rather, jabbing into his eyelid. Having your eyeball burn while your eyelashes itched must be uncomfortable, Ku snickered.

At night, 181 Avenue Foch lit up from all its windows like a huge lantern or a gold furnace. Cash flowed like molten gold at the tables.

But Ku wasn't after the money at Fu-sheng—he was smarter than that. Besides, if they could pull this off, wouldn't every other casino in the Concession be showering People's Strength with protection money? He might not be working toward a Communist revolution, but he did think of himself as revolutionizing the power dynamics of the Concession.

Right now, he wanted revenge. Not only had the Concession powers underestimated him, but they had also killed his woman, and if she hadn't taken a bullet for him, he might be dead too. He did not tell the rest of the cell about his grudge against Morris Jr. and goal of revenge. But whenever he thought about it, his whole body longed for Ch'i.

While the others were preoccupied, he kneed the captive in the groin, slamming his balls from beneath, so that the man fell over and rolled on the floor with pain. Luckily Te-hsing Hotel was a family-run boardinghouse, and he had been able to book all the adjacent rooms on the third floor, as well as those above and below his own, for only ten yuan. From the room downstairs, Lin heard the man crash to the floor. Ku's subordinates burst in, and he let them drag Morris Jr. downstairs, noting with satisfaction that Morris Jr. still couldn't stand up straight. The fun had only just started. There was no reason why the cell should know that this was a matter of private revenge—the corrupt gangs were their enemies by default. Not only were the gangs the product of a reactionary society, but they had also massacred Communists on behalf of the authorities.

He stood on the third floor of the hotel and looked out toward the barbed fence on Route Ratard, toward the black expanse of the lawn. Backlit, the flower beds glimmered like ghosts. A dim electric light was hung at the entrance to the greenhouse, and someone was smoking beneath it. The huge golden lantern seemed almost to be soundproof. Not a sound could be heard despite the blazing light, which made it even eerier.

He saw Lin and company cross Route Ratard with Morris Jr., whose arms had been tied behind his back. The beefy Morris was nicknamed the "rice dumpling," and now he was tied up like a dumpling wrapped in leaves. None of the passersby paid any attention to the curious group. The casino at 181 Avenue Foch was known for odd goings-on, and no one batted an eyelash. A few of them might have stopped to stare from about a hundred feet away, and then given the group a wide berth. He was worried that Route Ratard might be watched by gang lookouts, but the road was quiet for miles around, and nothing moved.

They were knocking at the door. The shadows near the garden side moved toward the wall. One man tried to open the little window from which the guards collected the mail, but Lin reached out and shoved his head down. His people were crowded to the left of the gate. One of them stood on the right side, with his gun trained on the crack in the gate. Another stood on the street with his back to the gate.

Young people did this the best. They were unafraid and treated the operation like a game. The guards who had come to open the gate were now under their control. The gate itself was half-closed, and the guards in their room on the east side of the building seemed to have overlooked the unusual scene on the lawn.

Morris Jr. was dragged into the dead center of the lawn. Now his legs had been tied up too. He really did look like a pyramid-shaped rice dumpling rolling onto the grass, with his head, ass, and legs at each vertex of the pyramid.

They were waiting.

The man who was about to be executed was waiting.

Ku was also waiting. He glanced at the dark mass that lay under a blue-patterned hotel tablecloth, one end stretched out over the edge of the balcony like the mouth of a giant carnivorous flower. Then he checked his watch and waited for the appointed time.

Eight o'clock. There was a red glow behind the villa, followed instantly by the sound of one explosion after another. The stout lantern seemed to quiver. Two light beams shot out of the guardroom, roving the lawn, and settled on the dumpling.

This was exactly what they had planned. At first they were going to use two hand grenades, but after Ch'i died they had come up with a more elaborate plan, including the fireworks that were going off on the lawn. A handful of their more alert neighbors had opened their windows or even ventured out onto their balconies. As guns rang out, Ku whisked the tablecloth away to reveal a gigantic horn loudspeaker. Holding the microphone firmly, he recited his speech by heart:

"Fellow citizens, fellow residents of Shanghai, on behalf of all my comrades from People's Strength . . . I hereby declare that we are executing this counterrevolutionary." He hadn't realized that the loudspeaker would be so loud. The noise hurt his eardrums, and he could hardly hear his own voice. But sending a message was crucial. He took a deep breath and recited it again. These declarations were a Soviet invention, one of the methods that Mikhail Borodin had brought to Canton when he was advising the Party there.

As he was making his speech for the third time, he saw Lin take aim and fire at the center of the lawn. Guards were pouring out of the building, but they could not get to the black lawn in time. The nighttime dew made the lawn as slippery as the banks of a lake.

Turning around, he bounded down the stairs, and jumped into the driver's seat, with Lin and the others piled into the back. He started the car, and the engine began to warm up. At this very moment, outside the north gate of the building, Park would also be revving his car up and heading east.

Leng could not find a new apartment on short notice, so Ku booked rooms for her in the Singapore Hotel on Rue du Consulat. Of course, she couldn't be spending too much time in crowded public places. This is only temporary, Ku had said. Keep moving. Don't spend more than two or three days in one hotel. But being rootless made her resent her mission. She was no longer passionate about the revolution. How would she survive watching movies and sitting in teahouses with a young dandy?

There's no turning back in what we do, Ku said, but our goal justifies any sacrifice. Any sacrifice is worthwhile. From the moment she accepted Ts'ao's proposal in Lunghwa Garrison Command, there had been no going back. Maybe up until then, things could have been different. But reminding herself that it was all fated forced her to stop daydreaming and focus, like a despairing man who finds something trivial to obsess over, or the musicians on a sinking ship who spend the final hours of their lives picking apart a complex harmonic passage.

She was constantly dissatisfied with her own performance. At night she reeled back to her hotel room exhausted, as if she had just come from a movie set.

Now she was sitting by the dressing table and gazing into the mirror, thinking. She had switched off all the lights in the room and opened the windows to let in the street noises outside. Signs for

Kuan-sheng Yüan, the candy manufacturer across the road, bathed her in neon red light. In the mirror, her face looked mysterious and changeful. When she got home at the end of the day, she often thought back to what she had said and how she must have looked. Did her frankness look too sudden and unthinking? she wondered. Would it have been better to let his questions brew unanswered for half an hour while steam rose from the dishes? She got notepaper and made a list of all the questions she wanted to ask him, so that she would be more sure of herself the following day, neither digressing too far nor panicking about running out of time and asking all her questions at once. He was perfectly aware that she only asked him questions because the cell needed the information, so she wasn't worried that he would suspect her motives. But she did not want their meetings to feel too pragmatic. She cursed her own apathy. She had to be alert, to read the ambiguity in his every look and glance.

When it was over, she was always left feeling tense and worked up. But in just a few moments, her pretend emotions would vanish, as though they had been sucked out of a hole in her foot by an unknown underground force and were seeping into the ground. Then she would feel deflated, as if another self had leaped out of her body and were inspecting her. It would examine all her feeble exaggerations, and pronounce them unconvincing.

If Hsueh were a little more worldly, or if he could watch Leng in slow motion, then yes, her expressions might seem affected. Sometimes she glanced at him coyly while clutching his hand, and then quickly drew her hand back, as if something had just occurred to her. Sometimes she became unaccountably angry and ignored his teasing smile. When she was leaving, she would turn away immediately, but after only a few steps she would glance over her shoulder and grin. She would look up at the sky as though she was thinking about something, or cry in his arms, breathing down his shirt, under his collar. It wasn't the first time she had been with a man, and she knew the effect that had.

Her performance was infectious. It made Hsueh exaggerate his own reactions, as if he was attuning his emotions to hers in order to perfect their double act. He started confiding in her more earnestly than she did in him, as if being earnest were his new game, one that allowed him to flirt even more shamelessly and tease her more mercilessly. He was always having to comfort her and apologize for offending her. It was then that he sounded most genuine.

They sometimes played at speaking lines from movies. That was when she felt truly tender toward him, as if the performance of a performance had to be real.

In the words of the movie *Mata Hari:*

"You want to die so badly?"

"I'm dead now. Just as surely as though there were a bullet in my heart. You killed me."

"No. The brandy." (Here she would playfully raise the coffee mug in her hand.)

"No, no. You."

"Then why don't you give me up?"

They could not count the number of times they had seen that movie. All the movie theaters were showing it. Besides, movie theaters made her feel warm and safe. The strain of being followed everywhere by prying eyes melted away. When she recited these lines, she felt just as beautiful as the secret agent in the movie, just as mysterious and confident.

Now that she knew which police department Hsueh's friend was in, she asked him about the Political Section's view of the incident on Avenue Foch, and especially about what the French thought.

"That was you people too?" Hsueh was cutting up a tenderloin steak with his knife. They were sitting in a restaurant called Fiaker, a small, expensive establishment on Avenue du Roi Albert that only served two tables per meal. It was pouring outside, and the rain licked the entire windowpane with a giant wet tongue that left a viscous trail. The waiter, who was also the chef and owner, served the food and then closed the door to the kitchen behind him, so that his guests could feel as though they were at home in their own dining room. A ceiling-to-ground glass window faced the street. Guests had to enter via the adjacent longtang and walk past the kitchen to reach the long, narrow room.

Instead of answering his question, she frowned and picked at the steak with her fork. It was several inches thick. "I can't eat beef. It makes my heartbeat go faster, I can't breathe, and I get hives here," she said, pointing to her collarbone.

"Oh! I'm so sorry."

"No, no, I should apologize. It must be so expensive, I should have told you earlier."

"Not your fault at all. I didn't say what I was ordering because I wanted to surprise you, to see how you would react to a gigantic steak on your plate."

"Someone wants to meet you," she said affectionately, staring at a stain on the table with an ant-size piece of meat at the center. She was about to pick it up when he caught her hand in his and used his napkin to wipe it up for her. She was touched, but also amused that he was treating her like a child.

She had never met anyone who cared as much about details as he did. He was easy-going and there was nothing he was passionate about, yet he actually thought of himself as a passionate man.

The following day, he told her that the police were consolidating the investigations for the Avenue Foch case and several other cases, and the Political Section would be responsible for the new investigation. A Chinese sergeant called Pock-faced Ch'eng was making inquiries regarding a man in his forties. It appeared a couple of Chinese council members had been making a fuss at the Municipal Office. If the police could not guarantee the safety of Concession residents, then why were business taxes being raised in the name of increased spending on public safety?

He told Leng that the French had set up a working group to investigate Communist violence in the Concession. His friend, the poet from Marseille, the one who always noticed colors and smells, was part of this group. He even brought a photo of the poet, whose expression seemed to indicate that he might be a little weary of his duties. The public water stove in the background was the one on the corner of Rue Conty, and Leng recognized it right away. Hsueh hinted that his literature-loving friend had a leftist bent ill suited to his position, which might prove awkward. The poet had been seen at meetings of expatriates who sympathized with the proletariat. He was known to read reports on the living and working conditions of workers in Shanghai.

Hsueh said they were good friends. He had spent hours listening to the poet's ungrammatical and rambling story of why he had come to China, according to which it was because of a girl in Marseille whose hair smelled of roasted eel and fennel. He had heard the story dozens of times by now, and it always began that way.

That night in the cinema, he found himself scooping her up in his arms. They watched the same movie over and over again, and this time, she went to the bathroom halfway through. When she was coming out of the ladies' room, he was standing at the other end of the red-carpeted corridor. The White Russian girl who worked as an usher leaned against the leather-paneled doors to the cinema and studied him. He stretched his arms out wide, uncertainly, like a sleepwalker. Finally he came up to Leng, put his arms around her, and kissed her. He probably didn't hear her murmur, "What am I doing? What's happening to me?"

CHAPTER 25

JUNE 24, YEAR 20 OF THE REPUBLIC.

9:33 A.M.

It was nearing the end of June, and the rainy season should have started by now. But although the sky sagged with clouds, the rains never came. It was hot and muggy. When Hsueh walked into Lieutenant Sarly's office, he saw that Inspector Maron was also there. There was too much moisture in the air. The walnut wood paneling was mottled with mold, producing a musty smell that mixed with the smoke from Sarly's pipe. He kept stuffing yellow tobacco into his pipe, while shreds of tobacco leaf drifted onto his file. The table was covered with documents: photographs, forms, letters, and several neatly printed reports.

"That Russian princess of yours—Therese, what's she been up to? Mended her ways? Retired early on her money?" The lieutenant was clearly in a bad mood. A change in weather would help, perhaps a dusty Sahara breeze, or a tropical rainstorm from Indo-China.

"Look who's here. You're still knocking about? I thought she'd chopped you into salad and had you for lunch," Maron sniggered.

These days, the thought of Therese made Hsueh's head hurt. Ever since she had extracted a confession from him at gunpoint—though heaven only knew why she had believed him—their relationship had changed unexpectedly. For almost a week after that incident, Hsueh had avoided her. He was afraid that if she kept pressing him for details, he would invent one lie after another until the whole fiction crumbled to pieces.

Maybe the problem would solve itself if he ended their relationship. Now that Lieutenant Sarly had read his file and found that he was the son of an old friend, he was no longer afraid of what the police could do to him, though he was still privately terrified of Maron's motionless fish eyes. He had even less reason to keep following Therese. But just because he didn't want to see her didn't mean that she didn't want to see him. The Concession was tiny, and she had no trouble finding out where he lived. When he saw her men outside his rooms, his heart sank. He must have been found out, he thought, and this time she wouldn't be threatening him with an unloaded gun.

The Cossack bodyguards took him to Mohawk Road. They marched him into the longtang next to the stables, and through a corner gate into what looked like a warehouse. He hadn't expected to be brought here. Did she want him executed by firing squad? Or hanged at the platform in the center of the room?

The building probably used to be a stable. In the center there was a platform with posts at its four corners, linked by ropes. A man stood on it and hollered at the room. The crowd was in a frenzy, and the air was thick with the stench of sweat, tobacco, and of vodka belched up after fermenting in hot stomachs. He stumbled along behind the guards as they wove their way through the outstretched legs, overturned benches, and piles of beer bottles, until he found himself standing in front of Therese.

Unexpectedly, she motioned to a rattan chair next to her. Once he sat down, he realized that this was the underground wrestling ring founded by Cossack gangs and ex-navy officers from Vladivostok. Both groups put up fighters and took bets, and the police saw to it that other gangs did not interfere.

They had the best seats in the house. If you reached out you could touch the corner of the stage, the damp boards beneath the chair in the corner where the wrestlers rested and caught their breath. The timekeeper's bench had been positioned to his right, between the audience and the platform. A bell and a small clock lay on the table.

The wrestler took a heavy punch in the ribs. It sounded like a butcher's hammer hitting a slab of meat. Sweat splashed from his back, and the crowd screamed. People were placing bets, spitting, and cursing at the top of their lungs, as if shouting would make them win.

Therese loved watching men get beaten to a pulp. She also loved betting. She was shivering, and she kept licking her lower lip. Her cheeks were glistening with sweat that could have been hers or the wrestlers'. The way she stared at them, you'd think she could smell their crotches.

Later that night, she screamed as she rammed her thighs at him and sucked the sweat from his shoulders. She got on top of him, and just before the climax, she thumped him on the shoulder.

For the very first time, not only did she permit Hsueh to return to her apartment with her, but they also spent the morning of the following day in bed. She asked Hsueh to lunch at the Odessa with her, and over lunch she declared that she would let Hsueh handle the deal if his boss ever wanted to buy anything else.

He realized he wouldn't be able to just stop seeing her. She believed he loved her because she had been pointing a gun at him when he said so, and the gun was now their witness. Therese was easily swayed by professional pride: if to love a housewife you had to like her cooking, or to love a seamstress you had to appreciate her embroidery, Therese would never be sure you loved her unless you were afraid of her gun.

But his affection for Therese was only one more reason to break things off. He would have to betray her if she had really been selling firearms to Leng's cell. That reminded him of his own conflicting feelings. What was it that made him so desperate to get closer to Leng, to peel away her disciplined exterior, to explore her, analyze her, take her apart and put her together again?

"Your reports connect all these different incidents, from the arms dealer to the suspicious apartment on Rue Amiral Bayle, to the Kin Lee Yuen assassination, the street battle on Rue Paul Beau, and finally the fireworks on Avenue Foch. I'm expecting you to show us what you're made of, to penetrate the cell and find . . ."

"A forty-year-old man, the boss. He usually stays in the shadows, but he's been seen before. Your Therese is the only way we can get to him," Maron added.

"They've never met. They both use agents," Hsueh said. He did not want Lieutenant Sarly to target Therese, at least not through him. In fact, he no longer wanted to see her, although he could now see her whenever he wanted to instead of having to stalk her— not that he himself knew whether he had originally followed her because Maron wanted him to, or for other reasons. She had given him a key to her apartment and let him use the bathroom there. She told him that when he wasn't around, she thought about him every day. In her own words, she was "horny as a peach ripe to bursting."

"I may let this Russian woman off. At the right time, I may decide to overlook her business selling unlicensed firearms to terrorists." Lieutenant Sarly tapped his cigarette ash into a copper ashtray. "The Concession authorities are always sympathetic to commercial interests."

"This lot aren't Communists. That's what the gangs are saying. They work differently. They're acting more like a new gang trying to establish itself," Maron said thoughtfully. Although the weather was humid, he wore his police uniform buttoned up all the way. He ignored the fly buzzing about his ear. Hsueh remembered how solemn Leng looked when she was telling him about her ideals.

"They've got to be Communists," Sarly said. Maron shook his head and yawned.

"Their activity is linked to the Comintern's newest networks in Asia and to the Communist cells threatening colonial authority in Indochina. Consul Baudez told me that once we've cracked this case, we'll have to send copies of all the files to Paris. This information could influence the French government's attitude toward Shanghai."

"They'll be easier to crack if they aren't Communists. The Communists are hard to beat, and we're short-staffed. We should leave the Communists to Nanking."

"We can cooperate with Nanking. But before we do any-thing, we'll need more information. To protect the interests of the Concession, we have to stay one step ahead of our friends in Nanking." Lieutenant Sarly chose his words carefully. He seemed to be keeping something back from them.

"I heard that the Kin Lee Yuen assassination had to do with financial speculation," Hsueh began, seizing his chance to make a good impression. "In the weeks after the assassination, the price of public debt rose steeply. Before then it had been declining steadily for a month. When I looked up the papers around then, I found a rumor that an influential man in Nanking was threatening to split off from the Kuomintang and set up a new government in the south. The warlords there supported him, and when the new government had been set up, he said it would take over the Cantonese customs. But public debt is backed by customs receipts in Canton. The victim, Ts'ao, worked for this man. He'd been sent to Canton to test the waters. But, of course, his assassination scared everyone off, and no one has the nerve to do anything now—they won't even set foot in Shanghai, never mind going to Canton. There were rumors that the assassin was a Nanking special agent, but if that was the case, why would the government's own people spend so much time investigating it?"

Hsueh hardly ever made speeches like this or used this many long words. The jargon made him sound more eloquent. Leng's earnestness had rubbed off on him—she was always bringing up her ideals while they were flirting.

Lieutenant Sarly looked at him approvingly. This young man could be observant when he put his mind to it.

"Excellent work," he said. "But you can't draw any conclusions yet, although the Nanking investigators may think they can. Their so-called experts are all ex-Communists, so you have to take what they say with a grain of salt. There were good financiers among the Communists. Marx himself was one of them."

Inspector Maron was annoyed that Hsueh was getting all the attention. Imagine bringing a stray cat home, feeding it, kicking it, training it to catch mice, and then discovering that the cat has become your boss's pet. Hsueh could tell that Maron was annoyed. To begin with, Maron had never thought of Hsueh as being French anyway, and Hsueh would have to agree with him there. Nor did Maron want the entire detective force supporting Hsueh's operation, although that was clearly what Sarly wanted.

So Hsueh felt a little uncomfortable when Lieutenant Sarly asked Hsueh to stay for a moment at the end of their meeting, as though he had something private to say to him. As Maron was walking away, he happened to glance over his shoulder; Hsueh met his gaze.

Sarly took a photograph from his drawer and showed it to Hsueh. It was an ordinary group photograph of people standing in two rows in front of a building, the architectural style of which was indecipherable because the photograph was overexposed.

"The British Secret Intelligence Service got hold of this photograph, and Martin swapped it for an entire case of my documents."

The dome in the background looked like an Orthodox church, an Easter egg, or perhaps a Russian onion? A few of the subjects wore forced smiles; the rest were unsmiling. Perhaps it was the cold or the food, or perhaps their faces were too numb to smile.

"Look at the third man on the left," Sarly said, directing Hsueh's attention away from the artistic merit of the photograph. "I'm afraid his features aren't very clear. The hat gets in the way."

The man's hat cast a shadow that stretched past his nose, such that only his chin was visible, and the rest of his face lay in shadow. His eye sockets were dark pools.

"Think what question you'd like to ask." Sarly sounded pleased.

"Who is he?" Hsueh knew how to play along.

"Exactly! Who is he? Who on earth could he be?"

Lieutenant Sarly unfolded the note in his hands, and began to read aloud in a resonant voice, as if he had good news he couldn't wait to deliver, and his listener had been anticipating this moment. He might have been eulogizing a philanthropist or announcing the benefactors to a good cause:

"He emerged in 1925 in the Shanghai union movement. Some of the workers thought him intelligent and resolute, while others called him ruthless. It didn't matter either way, because he soon disappeared from their circles. Half a year later, someone saw him driving a car for the Soviet consulate on 10 Whangpoo Road, wearing a driver's uniform, with a military official in his car. He was a good driver, and the consul himself sometimes took his car. That was no surprise—everyone said he could do anything he put his mind to. But no one knew why his career as a driver was so short, or what he got up to after that. In November of 1927, when a White Russian loyalist was caught throwing stones at the Soviet consulate, he was spotted in the crowds. He claimed to be a passerby who had been beaten up by drunken Cossacks, and insisted on filing a police report with the International Settlement authorities. Then he disappeared again. Some said he was in Khabarovsk, while others claimed he had gone to Canton.

"Eventually, his face appeared in this photograph. The people in the photograph weren't classmates. Some of them had been sent to Moscow to study Communist theory, while others were studying electronic communications. Yet others learned how to mix gasoline, rubber, and magnesium powder in a vodka bottle—apparently the trick there is not to put too much gasoline in the bottle, because it can extinguish the detonator. The group disbanded before long, and no one knew where he ended up. Then the British raided a local press in Burma and arrested a few men, one of whom had hidden this photo in the secret compartment of his suitcase, together with his spare fake passports. In fact, if it hadn't been so carefully hidden, no one would have noticed it. As it was, it inspired the police to play a cruel game of identification with their prisoners, rewarding them for correct names and punishing them for wrong ones. Eventually, all the correct answers were printed up and disseminated. Some of these men were arrested, some disappeared, and one was found dead in a prison in Hankow a couple of years ago. Only recently did we become very interested in the man whose face lies in shadow, in part because of the work of several experts in Nanking. I can tell he's a megalomaniac. He kept changing his name: Ku San, Ku Yanlong, Ku Fu-kuang, but he's always refused to change his surname. That's how you can tell he's a megalomaniac."

Sarly exhaled contentedly and leaned back in his chair. His hand wavered over the row of cigars.

"He must be the forty-year-old man, then?" Wait a minute, he thought, this man is Leng's boss? The one who wants to meet me? Hsueh was growing flustered. You're giving yourself away.

"Congratulations, right again!" Sarly still sounded pleased.

He was interrupted by the flurry of policemen assembling on the lawn outside, getting ready to begin their shifts. Drill commands echoed through the dank air, along with the ragged thud of men jogging and a few sharp blasts of the whistle. The man driving the armored police vehicle tested the wail of its siren. Before long, the place was quiet again.

"I don't just want to find him, capture him, and make him give us the names of everyone else in his cell. No, that's not what we want at all. I want you to get to know him, understand what makes him tick, and wait for him to plan something massive."

Sarly stopped speaking abruptly, as though that long speech had exhausted him.

"We need to catch a big fish," he murmured.

Hsueh thought he knew what Lieutenant Sarly meant. He must be thinking it was time he showed he had the patience to crack a big case, and he might as well give Hsueh, the poor son of his old friend, a chance to prove himself as well.

Hsueh never let himself think too hard about ethics, consequences, the meaning of life, things like that. He lived in the moment. The future, to him, was tomorrow, or at most next Wednesday. He often thought of himself as a gambler playing an all-or-nothing game, and in games like that, you can't afford to be distracted by anything besides the game itself. The trickier things got, the more Hsueh tended to resign himself to his fate. That said, he usually erred on the side of going ahead with something and worrying about its consequences later. He didn't know how to stop, to think about whether he had an out. He generally looked ahead and pressed on.

He went along the sidewalk beneath the balconies on Rue du Consulat, and stopped at the door of the National Industrial Bank. At least the job at the police station meant he was suddenly rolling in cash. Sarly had told him to see the poet from Marseille in the Political Section's office before he left. The poet handed Hsueh a check. Hsueh wouldn't be drawing a salary from the police department, so the check was issued in the name of an entertainment company based on Avenue Foch. It was tenable for any amount of money within a specified range, in support of Inspector Maron's special investigations. "Consider it a gift from the Green Gang," the poet had said. Hsueh cashed the check right away. He bought a basket of tangerines at the fruit stall, and went into a stairwell up the creaky stairs past a shoe store and a record company.

The stairs led to the Singapore Hotel, which was advertised by a sign that hung from its second-floor window. The receptionist sat in the stairwell. When he opened the door, Leng was standing right there. He reached out his hand to touch the stretch of bare skin on her arms below her cheongsam, but she ducked. When he drew his hand back and rubbed his nose with it, grinning, she pounced at him and hugged him.

She had been drinking. A wine glass and bottle stood on the table. Her mouth tasted of wine, which she didn't even like all that much—at restaurants she barely touched it. He pretended not to understand what that meant, and passively allowed her to kiss him enthusiastically and too deliberately. He let his hand slide from the nape of her neck down to her waist.

Luckily he was pretending to be unaware of what was happening and didn't take advantage of her right away, or she wouldn't have told him her story. Luckily he hadn't been hugging her tightly—she soon slipped out of his grasp.

Through the window they could hear actors bantering on the radio, with the occasional clang of a zither or thump of castanets, which melted into the endless clatter of dominoes. Hsueh had walked a long way, and after their brief and passionate embrace, his shirt was now soaked. Leng's cheongsam was also stained with sweat.

She told him her story. He used to think that characters and reversals like that could only be found in novels. She had been fated to make such weighty decisions, including a choice about love that had life-or-death consequences. He might have seen parallels to his own life, if it had occurred to him to look. This is your last chance to stop listening and walk away, he thought. One more step and you'll have fallen into the trap.

There was nothing for it—she would have to convince Hsueh to meet with Ku, because it was what the Party wanted. "We must persuade him to become one of us." They would also have to find a safe location for the meeting, because Hsueh's identity had yet to be verified.

She was worried about having lied to Ku about their being old acquaintances, when they had actually met for the first time on the *Paul Lecat*. She had lied to the Party. Of course she couldn't ask Hsueh to cover up her lie, but maybe she could hint at what he could say instead.

She had started by playing the part of a victim, second-guessing her own emotions, and striving to win her audience over. Now she was surprised to find herself getting into character, drawn into an endless debate with herself. While trying to sway him, she herself had been swayed; in attempting to persuade him, she had persuaded herself of her feelings.

She told Hsueh how much she used to admire Wang for being sharp, passionate, making brilliant speeches. He could be arrogant, but he had also been brave in prison. Did she love him? She asked herself the question out loud, while stealing a glance at her audience, and answered, yes. But choosing her words carefully, since this was difficult to admit and she had never even told her cell, she told him that Wang's work was so important to him that everything else was a mere extension of his work. He was uniformly kind to everyone, including all the women, simply because his work trumped all human relationships.

Had she been disappointed? She had asked herself that question, as if Hsueh's silence were a way of probing her for more. And she had to admit that there had been no time for disappointment. She and Wang had been arrested in the same series of mass arrests, when their entire cell had been arrested. She didn't say too much about how she had suffered in jail, which had been such an ugly place that even talking about it felt demeaning.

Now that she was completely in character, she hoped Hsueh would respond by asking questions that gave her another chance to examine herself and defend her actions. She told him about Ts'ao's offer. "He said that given the way things were and the position he was in, he could only get them to release me if we were family, if I married him." She wanted Hsueh to either affirm her decision or argue with her and taunt her for being weak, but he said nothing, playing the part of the admiring audience.

She had been asking and answering all the questions, but this time she wanted Hsueh to ask a question: When Ts'ao first made this offer to you, or rather, when you first rejected it, what did that have to do with Wang's death? That way she could tell him that Ts'ao wouldn't have killed Wang—he wasn't that kind of man. She hadn't dared to say that to the cell. Of course, she had had her doubts, and she had thought hard about Ko Ya-min's question about timing. She had asked about the exact date of Wang's execution, and tried to reconstruct the time of year from the clouds and wind, the uniform the soldiers were wearing. She had counted the days to work out whether Wang was killed in between the time when she rejected and when she accepted Ts'ao's offer. It would be a relief to know for sure. She hazily remembered accepting Ts'ao's offer of marriage after he told her that Wang had already been killed, but she suspected her memories might be warped by guilt. As if in a daze, she imagined sitting in that office in the Military Justice Unit, and relived the flood of immense relief that made her despise herself.

It would be like Hsueh to tell her it wasn't her fault, reassure her that she couldn't have known what was happening, that Wang's death had nothing to do with her. She would probably hate him for sounding so objective, but she wanted him to do that anyway.

Instead, he sighed and exhaled a puff of white smoke that clouded his face. He'll never learn to be serious, she thought. He was silent for a long time, as if searching for the right words, afraid of being a bad listener. Then he said: "It's like a movie with you as the main actress."

She thought she knew what he meant. He was moved that she had been fated to experience such tragic conflict, as though no matter what choices she made, things would come out wrong.

That wasn't what she had expected, and she teared up because he understood her, which made her think she understood him. They both tended to let other people make the decisions and go along with them. She had often tried to explain her own life to herself as she sat at the window of the apartment on Rue Amiral Bayle, but Hsueh had explained it better.

They were sympathetic words—a little ironic, although Hsueh may not have meant them that way. But the more she thought about it, the more they made sense. Something about her life felt unreal to her, like a movie. She couldn't really say what the problem was, whether this was because she had lost the passion for what she did, or because her mission forced her to pretend all the time.

Her cheongsam was stiff with the sweat dripping from her armpits. She felt as though she were drowning in an illusion. Everything sounded indistinct and far away, except the dominoes clicking somewhere in someone's hands.

The sound of the police siren escalated gradually and inexorably, as though it were bubbling up through water. Tires screeched on the road. Then they heard footsteps, and someone rapped at the door.

When they opened it, the steward was standing outside with a few policemen.

"What's happening?" Hsueh drew the wooden blinds and looked down onto the street.

"North Gate police! Don't leave your room. Have your identity papers ready for inspection."

The clatter of dominoes ceased. Someone moved the table, and the teacup fell to the floor, spinning to a halt instead of shattering. Next door, children were crying, and a man was scolding his wife in front of the policeman. The steward tried shrilly to stay in control, like a hapless choir conductor:

"Send word to all the rooms. No one is to leave. Police orders."

Detective 198 came into the room while his French superior stood at the door. He had switched to his summer uniform early, probably because he wasn't used to Shanghai's humid weather. The sweat ran down his calves from his knees. Soaked in sweat, his calves were as white as rotting flesh, and the hairs stuck to his skin. He kept fidgeting to avoid the mosquitoes. He wasn't wearing gaiters—who would, given the weather in this blasted place? Shanghailanders often wrapped medical bandages around their long socks as a precaution against malaria, but surely an officer on duty couldn't be seen in such a ridiculous outfit.

Leng's face was white and she had a blank look in her eyes, as if she had already given herself up for lost. Detective 198 looked like a slapstick actor imitating a street portrait artist. He looked down at the document, up at her, and then down at the photograph. He scrutinized her in profile, as if being closer to the light filtering in through the blinds would give him a better view.

"I've seen this face before," he commented blandly to the French detective. He might as well have been describing a photograph.

They left the building surrounded by detectives, who took them to North Gate Police Station in a police van. After just a few minutes inside the iron compartment, Hsueh was already sweating profusely. He kept wiping the corners of his eyes with a handkerchief. The seats for prisoners were narrow and low, and they were almost squatting on the floor. This was more embarrassing than being seen on the toilet. Leng kept her hands over the slits in her cheongsam so that Hsueh wouldn't see her legs. She had been sweating, and the pores on her legs had dilated and looked ugly. She suddenly didn't know what to do with herself, like an actress who was being dragged out of the limelight and kidnapped.

They were locked up in a wooden cage, and no one asked them any questions. She wouldn't get away with it this time. Everyone would have seen those photographs of her, including the wedding photograph in which she was wearing so much makeup she hardly looked like herself. Ts'ao had insisted on having that photograph taken, as if he couldn't believe she'd said yes, and needed to hang wedding photographs everywhere just to prove they were married. Now the photographs proved that she had been Ts'ao's wife, just as he had wanted.

Although the sweat must have stung Hsueh's eyes, he appeared to be deep in thought. He had noticed neither Leng's imperfect legs nor the look of despair in her eyes.

He began to shout at the top of his voice, making Detective 198 rush over to the wooden cage.

"I am French! My father was a Frenchman! I want to talk to the sergeant! I have something to say!"

Detective 198 opened the cage with a key. He had already stripped his belt off, and put his keys, whistle, baton, and flashlight on the table. He was ready to teach this man a lesson for daring to cause trouble in the lockup.

But then the long-faced sergeant came in and had Detective 198 take Hsueh to his office. The detective was drenched in sweat. He couldn't wait to finish work and find a bar where he could have a long cool draught of beer. He resented the place, his job, and the officers who were making him do all this work despite the weather.

CHAPTER 28

Hsueh was brought to the sergeant's office. His identity papers lay on the table open to the last page, alongside a wooden hat, a catalog of European furniture, and a vial of peppermint oil to keep the mosquitoes away. A green blackboard hung near the door, with a list of to-dos for the day scribbled on it in white chalk. A huge arrow had been added between 3:00 P.M. and 5:00 P.M., hours that should have been spent drinking tea and smoking in the cool of the sergeant's own office. The words SINGAPORE HOTEL had been circled.

The telephone was on the wall next to the blackboard.

"Was there something you wanted to say to me?" the sergeant said.

"I'd like to make a phone call to Lieutenant Sarly of the Political Section. Call and tell him Hsueh wants to speak to him."

"So we think we know a few bigwigs, do we?" The sergeant stretched his legs out to let the breeze filter into his pant legs.

When he got Lieutenant Sarly on the line, he sounded impatient. Hsueh could hear rustling sounds that meant either Sarly was reading something, or there was static on the line.

"And what were you doing in the Singapore Hotel?"

"A friend of mine is staying there."

"A friend." The voice gave no hint of what Sarly was thinking. "A lady friend?"

Hsueh didn't know how much to reveal, and he had to make

up his mind quickly. The line kept crackling. With probably no more than a few seconds left, he remembered that it wasn't Leng the lieutenant was after. She wasn't the protagonist of the story. In that case . . .

"If you trust me, I'll make sure you get everything you want."

"If I trust you? Have you given me any reason so far to trust you?" The static disappeared, making room for a vast silence. Sarly's voice sounded thin, like a piece of thread in the wind, or an echo in a distant corridor.

Hsueh felt his position weaken. He didn't realize that he was shouting. "This is really important! When you come to your senses, you'll see all my reports piled on your desk."

He put the phone down and waited for Sarly's answer. He felt sorry for Leng. He thought about how hard she had tried to pretend to be sophisticated, in the hope that he could be "useful" to her cell. Then he remembered her weeping by the ship railing, and the blank look in her eyes when she had seen him. She never forgot she was a woman. Even when she was terrified, she had held down the slits in her cheongsam, as if the gesture would anchor her in reality. He began to worry about her. For a moment, it seemed to Hsueh that it would be worth risking anything at all, Lieutenant Sarly's trust, even his friendship with Hsueh's father, just to keep her safe.

An hour later, the poet from Marseille appeared.

An hour and a half later, he and Leng were walking out of North Gate Police Station. The poet came to the wooden cages with him, and he noticed that Leng recognized his old friend right away.

The poet told him that the search at the Singapore Hotel had been a coincidence. That morning, a steward at the hotel had found a hand grenade under the dressing table in Room 302, and the manager, Kung Shan-t'ing, had telephoned North Gate Police Station to report the find.

The poet was one of the only policemen Hsueh liked, which was why Sarly had assigned him to be Hsueh's contact point. He was shy. He had hair the color of dried hay, and a weakness for Mallarmé and Verlaine. Before getting in his car, he had privately complimented Leng to Hsueh: she looks so graceful when she is frightened, like a swan.

Leng herself was standing in Hsueh's empty living room, like a swan resting during a long journey, sadness in her eyes. They had politely declined the poet's offer to give them a ride in his car, and when they were sure that no one was following them, Leng had made a phone call from a telephone booth on Boulevard de Montigny. Through the glass window, Hsueh could see her covering the receiver with her hand, trying to explain what had happened. She was beautiful. He wondered whether he felt that way because he had just rescued her from prison. For the first time, he learned what it felt like to have someone look to him for protection.

As she was coming out of the telephone booth, she told him she had nowhere to go, and would have to live with him for now, just to be safe. Her voice was so matter-of-fact that Hsueh was almost a little disappointed.

Hsueh tidied up the table, which was the only thing that needed tidying, since his living room contained nothing but a table and a couple of chairs. He poured out half a cup of cold coffee, and as soon as he came back into the living room, he remembered that he had to boil some water in the kitchen. The old photographs and newspapers could be tossed in a heap in a corner with bottles of developer chemicals. Standing at the doorway, he chucked all his clothes into his bedroom. No sooner had he gotten Leng to sit down than the lid of the kettle clattered in the off-kilter beat of an Irish jig.

Somehow it hadn't occurred to him until now that he owed her an explanation. Wouldn't her cell wonder how they had managed to escape from North Gate Police Station? He told her about the hand grenade, but then he realized that it sounded even more implausible than a lie. He still didn't know what he would say to Sarly. And he had barely given any thought to the fact that he would one day have to betray Leng and her cell to the police. It was true that his mind was always swirling with thoughts, but he would never learn to think ahead.

Right now, he had to make sure he hadn't left anything suspicious lying around. Though he shouldn't have anything to hide—after all, he was a photojournalist, not a detective. All he had were piles of old newspapers and photographs, rolls of film and chemicals. Then he thought of something and shot into the bedroom, leaving Leng alone in the living room.

Ever since Therese's Cossack bodyguards had found Hsueh's rooms, she had been here a couple of times herself. She was the kind of woman who left a telltale trail wherever she went: lipstick smudges on wineglasses and cigarette holders, perfume suffusing the pillowcases and the very cracks in the wall, and of course, stained knickers.

He could not imagine what would happen if Therese were to walk in and find him at home with another woman. That hadn't occurred to him as he was bringing Leng to his rooms. He had better go and meet her so that she wouldn't take it into her head to come here.

Nor could he imagine why Sarly trusted him. In the police van that afternoon, it had crossed his mind that someone might have followed him to the Singapore Hotel, which seemed to be the only explanation for the police search of the rooms. But then he had gotten distracted by the fact that Leng wasn't wearing stockings. It was hot and humid, and her legs had been glistening with sweat.

He was beginning to think that the search might have been a coincidence after all. One thing was certain: Sarly trusted him. Sitting in a trench and sharing a gas mask must forge strong friendships, Hsueh thought.

The sky was growing dark, but it hadn't rained. They were still in Hsueh's rooms on Route J. Frelupt, on the other side of the Concession from the police station, sitting across from each other and near enough to smell each other's sweat.

"So that was the poet from Marseille. Who did you say I was?" He could tell that the performance she had kept up for so long had been shattered like a piece of porcelain and was all jagged edges now. It was her listless face rather than her vacant tone of voice that gave her away.

He looked at her face, her hands, her skin. You could see the pores because she had been sweating.

"My lover," he said.

Her mouth was slightly open, as if she had just swallowed something bitter. He thought he heard her sigh. There was a stain on the side of her nose, from having been rubbed with grimy fingers. Her eyelashes cast long shadows on her pupils.

"Why did you rescue me?"

The pause would make what he was about to say more powerful.

"Because I love you." The words slipped out as if he had been waiting to say them. There is never a good time to tell someone you love them. But then whenever you do, it usually sounds right.

She was weeping noiselessly. A breeze lifted the curtain. She shivered and got up. Then she looked at him and collapsed into his lap, clutching his sleeves and collar, and then punching his head and shoulders.

"But why? Why? Everyone who loves me comes to a bad end!"

It surprised Hsueh that no woman could withstand the power of those three words. They all seemed to be under the same spell, or to have drunk a potion that made them play the same part in the same movie.

Leng felt like a sorry piece of bait, rigged on the end of a line and dropped into the lake. Now that the fisher had abandoned his rod, she was starting to develop feelings for the fish. Her phone call to Ku was brief, and she neglected to mention that they had been arrested or taken to the police station. She was afraid he would expel her from the cell, which was her only connection to the outside world.

Luckily Hsueh had been there—this proved his friends at the police station were as influential as he said they were. Ku was intrigued by this, and repeatedly asked:

"Why would the Political Section be taking part in a North Gate police raid?"

"There wasn't anyone but the North Gate police. The steward found a hand grenade and reported it to the police."

"But you just said they got you out."

"The police were about to burst into the room to check our papers, but Hsueh was standing at the door and started kicking up a fuss. Then he dropped the name of his friend in the Political Section."

"So this poet friend of his must be an important man. Did you say you met him this afternoon?"

"They called the Political Section from the hotel, and confirmed that Hsueh was a journalist at a French newspaper. By the time his friend got here, the police had already left."

This story doesn't hold water, she thought. She felt guilty about lying to Ku for no reason. She felt like an incompetent actress who had forgotten her lines.

"So the police never came into the room? They didn't see you? Didn't his friend in the Political Section see you?"

She said this was all because Hsueh was there. She didn't dare say that she had just been incredibly lucky. She herself could scarcely believe her luck. She might as well put it down to her new hairstyle or careworn face. When she looked in the mirror, she thought being sad made her look different.

Finally, Ku said: "You've got to work harder to win Hsueh over for the Party. We want him to join us. His connections to the police will be useful for the next stage of our work."

"What am I supposed to do?"

"Just live with him. Remember your mission and the Party's goal. You will spend time with him, observe him, and understand his relationships. This is important work."

Leng knew exactly what Ku was hinting at, but she was getting tired of being told to hide her feelings. In movies, the charismatic double agent could develop feelings for the target she was flirting with, or at least trick herself into thinking so. The audience would sympathize as long as the agent believed she was working for good. Leng, on the other hand, always ended up falling into her own trap.

Her pretense had erected a thin film between her and Hsueh, which it was also her job to penetrate, although she didn't know how. She told herself that the Party hadn't ordered her to fall in love. They wanted her to crack the cynical exterior of this Concession dandy, and get at his deepest thoughts and feelings, so that they could gain control of him and make him useful to the cell. There must be something real under his carefully constructed image—if you stripped away the flippant comments, the conceitedness and constant scheming, you would find that he was vulnerable and innocent and naked as a newborn baby at the core. That Hsueh would be idealistic. He would be willing to fight for justice, to dedicate himself to the Party's mission. It didn't occur to her that a lover might thirst to understand Hsueh the way she thirsted to understand him.

She began to seduce him in a spirit of self-sacrifice, which made everything she did absurdly solemn. Making oatmeal for him, she poured the oatmeal into the pan from a rusty tin, and added water and milk powder. They hunted for the sugar jar together, but couldn't find it. Eventually they found several lumps of sugar on top of the coffee jar.

They ate in silence. His mind was elsewhere. She looked exhausted, at the end of her rope. Frowning, she ate her oatmeal in tiny spoonfuls, as though she wanted it to be an anesthetic.

She couldn't remember how she had first been introduced to Party ideals. She tried talking to him, beginning with the events of that afternoon. She pretended to be outraged by the cops' insolence, although no one expected anything different from the Concession Police, because she thought he might be inspired to a simple hatred of imperialism. But then again, an imperialist had rescued them from North Gate Police Station. Making an abstract truth palpable was so difficult. She wanted him to argue with her, to say that there were good people in the police force, or something like that. Eventually she said: "Don't think that your friend the poet is a good man. That may be, but he represents an oppressive system." He looked at her with a crooked smile. I don't think of myself as a good man either, he said.

"Of course you're good! Why else would you want to help me?" She had raised her voice, not realizing that her premise was a little shaky. But then she got caught up in the argument and stopped second-guessing herself or having to force herself to keep going.

As for Hsueh, now that there was someone in his room, in the space where he lived, he felt the need to demonstrate that he had a real profession, and was not a good-for-nothing who spent all his days flirting with women. He began to mess about with his chemicals and rolls of film. Simply drawing the curtains wouldn't make the room dark enough, so he nailed a thick piece of cloth across the window, and lit a red lightbulb. She realized that time was passing, and talking at Hsueh would not help them understand each other any better. She came up to him and hugged him from behind, grasping his wrist, forcing him to put down the canister in his hand. It rolled along the table and came to a stop.

She wanted her voice to be pleading rather than commanding, but it came out sounding more like a whine: "I want some hot water—I need to take a bath."

She was feeling virtuous as she started her bath, which may have been why she only asked for one kettleful of hot water. She could wait solemnly for the kettle to boil once, but having to wait twice would be preposterous. It was cold, but she was feeling too virtuous to notice.

She bathed in a dignified manner. If this were a scene in a movie, the Internationale might make for good background music. Only after she had bathed did a dissonant note of embarrassment creep in. She couldn't find her gown or even a bedsheet anywhere. Her cheongsam was sticky with sweat, and she couldn't face putting it on. But she couldn't just come out of the bathroom naked either. Screw it, she thought, opening the door and striding out.

Hsueh nearly fell off his chair. He had been sitting with his legs up, facing the bathroom door and rocking the chair absentmindedly. Then his eyes opened wide, and he fell backward, clutching at the air for support. Only when the back of the chair hit the table was he able to steady himself. She had pictured going boldly up to him, taking him by the collar, steering him into the bedroom and onto the bed. Somehow she had gotten the idea that she would take his clothes off. But she could only picture undoing his buttons—she imagined the rest would peel off as their bodies pressed together.

What happened next was a sheer accident that interrupted her plan. She covered her face with her hands and dashed into the bedroom by herself, like an actress forgetting her lines and rushing off the stage.

Up until then, she had never thought hard about how to make this happen. You can sometimes be so focused on a goal that you lose sight of the concrete steps toward it. Not that she was completely naïve, like a trapped bird. She had been married twice, and if it were not for a mechanical difficulty of Ts'ao's, she would have a child by now.

Up until then, she had never actually thought hard about how to seduce him. Her mind was empty. She lay on the pillow and tried to take deep breaths. She could detect the sweetness of milk powder on her own breath, and when things came unblurred, she noticed a speck of Quaker Oats on her left nipple. She tried to will herself not to say anything corny, but the trouble was that she believed what she was about to say: "That was good. I didn't know sex could be that good."

When he arrived in Therese's living room, Hsueh saw the man he had been following. Now Hsueh knew his name, Zung Ts-mih, because Lieutenant Sarly had let him read a few of his prized files in the secretariat of the police headquarters. He had rushed to Therese's apartment first thing in the morning because he was worried that Therese would come barging into his own rooms on Route J. Frelupt. Needless to say, Therese could be venomous, and she would have little patience for a man who told her that he loved her while he kept another woman at home.

Things weren't going much better with Leng. These two women had such complicated backgrounds that he felt as though he had been caught between the cogwheels of two sophisticated killing machines, and would answer for his first mistake with his life. Hsueh's life had turned into a terrifying game of mahjong, and he had no idea when he had been dealt this hand or how he had been duped into staking everything he had on it. He had always thought of himself as a gambler, but this time he really was playing for his life.

There was another woman in the apartment, Yindee Zung. The file said that she was related to Mr. Zung. The Zung siblings were staring at him. I should have phoned first, he thought. Therese had Ah Kwai show him into the sunlit sitting room attached to her bedroom. She had sent him to the bedroom, in front of her guests! He might as well be her gigolo.

It was rarely this sunny during the rainy season, and the little room was warm. The steam from the bathroom made him dizzy. He listened uneasily to the voices in the next room. Were they talking about him? It would only take one question from Therese: Have you seen this man at Mr. Ku's? Then Zung would mention him casually some other time to some other people, and the game would be up for him, he would lose everything.

It had never occurred to him that a sunny day could make him this miserable. He let his thoughts wander.

The next thing he knew, Therese's hand was pressing down on his head. Her silk nightgown gleamed silver in the sunlight, like the cape of a heroine in the legends. The sunlight hurt his eyes when he opened them. Therese's guests had left, and it seemed as though only moments ago the nightgown was still lying on the bed. There was a distant rumble.

Almost as if he was thinking out loud, continuing the line of thought with which he had fallen asleep, he heard himself saying, "I saw him."

"Saw whom?"

"Your Mr. Zung. I saw him again a couple of nights ago."

He was making things up, as if his voice was not under his control. What he read in the police files had gotten all mixed up with what he had glimpsed in dark corners, in crowds, on unlit streets, and with his own inventions. He thrust the whole pile in front of Therese, like a gambler plunking a bundle of notes down to bluff his opponent.

Her eyes grew wide. She drew her hand back from his warm hair, and retreated to the recliner between the windows.

"So you say he is still doing business with your boss?"

He had said too much. Anything he said could entrap him, and he barely knew anything. He scoured his mind for any wisp of memory that would help him to answer Therese's next question.

"The night before last, Mr. Ku arranged a meeting."

"The night before last?"

Hsueh lit a cigarette while Ah Kwai sent a pot lid crashing to the floor in the kitchen. Therese frowned. Her hair looked brown in the sunlight.

Hsueh had not meant to disparage his rival. Now he would need to come up with a nebulous story that would buy him time and allow him to cover his tracks. Eventually, Therese asked him a question:

"What was the deal they were talking about?"

He instantly realized his mistake. Mr. Ku, Leng's superior, the star of those police files, did not have a deal on with Therese. Their last deal had closed: it's a pleasure doing business with you, sir, see you next time. Now he had to open the door, bring Zung in again, and have him sit and talk to the famous Mr. Ku about an entirely new deal. His alarming imagination had already created the scene in his mind. He could picture the dim chandeliers, the small table and steaming teacups, and a man sitting in an unlit corner—Hsueh himself, perhaps. Two people sat facing each other at a table beneath the electric light while others lurked in the dark alley downstairs.

But although he had been sitting so near them, just a couple of feet away, he hadn't heard what they were saying. He needed evidence, even if it was tenuous, like a piece of paper he could have seen. In fact, he did recall a piece of paper with a few unfamiliar words on it. He began explaining it to Therese, gesturing with his hands:

"I saw a piece of paper with a cross-section of something that looked like a rifle, but had a mount like a machine gun. It's the newest thing, they were saying, it's extremely powerful." He could barely recall the diagram, and his memory of it was all entwined with images of the Astor, a smell of moldy camphor, seagulls shrieking on the Whampoa. What could Therese be thinking about? What was she searching her memory for?

She appeared to be deep in thought. "Is it real? Does it really exist?" she murmured, as if repeating an ancient nursery rhyme.

"It's apparently quite expensive." Hsueh was regaining his confidence. "Very expensive, actually. Mr. Ku looked a little concerned."

"Why does he have to have it? What would he do with it?"

He didn't have to answer this question. As the architect of this story, his job was to invent the plot, not to explain his characters' motivations to the audience. But the architect also needed answers to questions like this, if only for himself, even if he would never allude to them directly. And Hsueh didn't have a clue what the weapon was for.

He realized that he had just unknowingly launched a side attack on Therese's closest assistant, the *comprador* who liaised with all these dangerous men for her. He had hinted that Zung might be two-timing her by cutting deals behind her back, possibly even with her money. This was not a question of ethics—in the Concession, everyone had to play by the rules.

But the blitz was over, and he decided to clear the battlefield and tend to the wounded before his rival got even with him.

"Why do you keep asking me these questions? You make me feel like a traitor."

He tried his best to sound nonchalant, pouting like the rich young men he saw in movies. Her silk nightgown was bunched up above her knees. She had kicked off her silk slippers, and she was barefoot. Her toenails were painted the same color as her lips. Only now did he notice that the white shape in the center of the colorful canvas, the curves of a huge body that expanded outward, depicted Therese herself in a state of excitement. The lines delineating the distinction between the top and bottom half of her body seemed to curve infinitely inward. But whereas the body in the painting had a black helmet of hair that tapered neatly on either side of her face, the real Therese had a shock of unruly hair. He noticed the calluses around her ankles and thought, there's something the artist left out.

He felt sorry, especially when he remembered that Leng was still waiting for him at home. But then he thought—if it weren't for the two of you, you and everyone else forcing my hand, would I be in this mess? You both wanted me to join your camp, and if I hadn't agreed, chances are you would have had me killed. Come to think of it, that was exactly how he was most likely to have gotten himself killed.

He saw the surprised look on Therese's face as she was distracted from her thoughts. She opened her mouth, and a puff of smoke escaped from the corner of her lips. He could sense Leng watching him from behind, her figure nearly transparent in the sunlight. He felt guilty, but the thought also turned him on.

Her calluses were rubbing up against his ears, and her clothes had been rolled all the way up to her shoulders, like a froth of silver bubbles engulfing her shoulders and arms. Both her hands were twisted awkwardly, cupped around her ass, as if she were a half-painted colored egg that could roll away any moment. And her head was rolling along the pillow like the head of a goddess on a pendulum.

"I feel like a hot water bag that's been burst from the inside."

"A hot water bottle," Hsueh corrected her gently. Therese learned a new word in Chinese.

They both started daydreaming. He was still stroking her wetness. The trams jingling along Avenue Joffre made him shiver. His ears had become very sensitive to noises. Therese's pubic hair was tougher and crisper than the rest of her hair. It rustled like the sugar curls on a pastry.

"Yes. Yes. Just two fingers. Pinch it from both sides. Tell me, if I let you do this deal, if . . . yeah, that's good. I'll put you in charge of this deal. Could you do that for me?"

Therese did believe Hsueh, but not because he mentioned the diagram, though that certainly helped. She believed him because he said he had seen Zung and Ku meet the night before. Zung had previously sent her a telegram from Hong Kong saying he would be back in Shanghai, and he was supposed to have arrived two days ago. But he did not appear until that morning, when he had turned up at her apartment with some absurd story about how his ship had sailed into the first typhoon of the year near Chou-shan and run aground on the muddy banks of Wu-sung-k'ou. Only early this morning at high tide did the pilot manage to steer us back on course, he said.

This, along with the fact that Zung was frequently unable to account for discrepancies in the books (though Yindee could sometimes explain them) made her realize that Zung must be doing deals of his own behind her back. She could not just get rid of him. She had to have a *comprador*. And Chinese *compradors* always did deals behind their bosses' backs. But she would have to warn him. Wresting this piece of business from him might be a good way of doing that without having to confront him directly. All she would have to do was get him to hand over the invoice.

On a deeper level, Therese might have been more willing to believe Hsueh because she was still reeling from a shock she had had two days ago, when Zung claimed to have been violently seasick at Chou-shan or Wu-sung-k'ou. The postman had delivered a note from Baron Pidol with distressing news: Therese's friend Margot, the Baroness Pidol, was in intensive care at Ste-Marie Hospital on Route Père Robert. A gastroenterologist was doing all he could to save her life. Before going into a coma, she had begged to be allowed to see Therese. Therese didn't even wait to call a cab. She dashed out of the lobby, hailed the first rickshaw she saw, and made straight for the hospital.

But by the time she got there, Margot's pupils had dilated, and she had stopped breathing. The cause of death was acute barbiturate poisoning. Margot's face was covered with cold sweat, and Therese couldn't help wondering why she would have been sweating. Her skin had turned a greenish color, her face had shrunk, and the cleft between her nose and mouth looked sunken in.

Baron Pidol drew a bundle of letters tied up with a ribbon from under the sheet covering Margot's body.

"These letters are addressed to you. I didn't read them. She once said she couldn't write her diaries to the empty window she sat at, so she kept it in the form of letters to you. She said if she were alive, she would be too embarrassed to let you read them." The baron's voice was tired, but not terribly sad. Now that the contest had ended with one of them dead and another wounded, the survivor barely had the strength to stumble out of the wrestling ring.

She spent all evening reading those letters, and went on reading the following morning. Margot's letters read like an elementary school student's composition exercises. She used all the forms of the past tense, including the ones peculiar to written French. She must have written them long after the fact, carefully using the verb tenses to distinguish events of the previous day and of an hour ago.

The first few letters were oblique. They were full of phrases like "I am sure Mr. Blair will handle these matters admirably," or "He certainly is a noble and generous (a sympathetic) friend." But then the writer grew more impassioned, more absorbed, more direct.

Have you ever read a detailed account of a secret extramarital affair by a friend after her death?

"Sometimes I think a woman is like a lock, and a man like a key. There's only one that fits every gear and groove of your lock. It's not just a question of common interests or strong emotions. It's like you've always known each other. Even your bodies fit together. His is the right key, and it fits my lock exactly. We're so happy together. You know that afternoon at the Paper Hunt Club? That was our first time, and he was standing, or rather, we were both standing, so he didn't get that far in, but it was the best sex I'd had."

Therese cringed at some of these passages, even though their writer was already dead and her body cold.

"We're trying out something new. I think all women want to be a man's slave, to kneel at his feet, to beg him for happiness. That's what we all secretly want. Semen (forgive me—isn't that what doctors call it?) smells heavenly, like freshly milled wheat or almond flour. Maybe it depends on whose semen it is.

"Nagasaki is a beautiful port city, just as he said it would be. The waitress brought us a poisonous fish called *fugu*, which means the fish of happiness. After eating it I felt faint, as if I myself were a fish floating in water. Wooden clogs click in an unnerving way outside the windows at night, but they are only *geisha*. You wouldn't have thought it, but Nagasaki is paved with long slabs of limestone like a seventeenth-century Dutch city."

Therese could not believe that her friend had gotten so carried away in three short months. Maybe it had started long before that trip to Nagasaki. The letters alluded vaguely to a psychiatrist, but she hardly talked about her husband. Once, she mentioned him when they were together at a holiday resort at Mo-kan-shan, one of the baron's investments. On another occasion, she wrote about sitting in the living room with her husband and several other guests, all longtime Shanghailanders, smoking Luzon cigars and talking about roads to be built beyond the boundaries of the Concession. They were discussing two possible scenarios, the Greater Shanghai Plan and the Free City Scheme, as if they were configurations on a chessboard. Something to do with speculation. Does money equal freedom? she wondered in her letter. Surely only love can set you free.

But Margot's lover was an ambitious young man, and running away to Nagasaki for half a month with her while the baron was away in Europe was the most imprudent thing Mr. Blair had ever done. The local columns of the Concession newspapers followed their trip, and someone even managed to find the hotel where they had stayed. When they got back to Shanghai, Mr. Blair had to start behaving properly again—after all, he was a man with responsibilities. Baron Pidol's new circle disapproved of such goings-on. A young man like Mr. Blair could easily forget his place, they said. All the men who had made their fortunes in Shanghai had a say in the colonial matters of their own countries, especially when it came to Shanghai. That meant the affair couldn't go on, which left Margot stuck like a ship run aground without a skipper.

It looked as though Margot might have died of a nervous breakdown. Therese was astonished by the euphoria of those letters. Her friend seemed to have been living in an endless carnival. Therese could imagine Margot writing those letters in the lulls between those euphoric moments, on rainy mornings, or on evenings when her husband was attending a ball. Claiming a headache, she would stay home and sit at her dressing table calling her happiest memories to mind, with the mysterious Oriental scent of cinnamon trees on the evening breeze.

Therese gave no thought to the parallels between Hsueh and Mr. Blair. It was Margot's euphoria that fascinated her. She wondered how anyone could just decide to die like that, like throwing a tantrum: if you make me mad I'll pretend to ignore you and go to sleep.

She looked at the face in the mirror. Its contours were a little too sharp and her cheekbones jutted out. She would need to find a darker blush. She did not like the color of her nipples, so she brushed some blush onto them too, making them a translucent pink. Next she tried applying some lipstick to her labia, which gave her chills. Women love exploring their own bodies, she thought. We express ourselves in color like tribal warriors.

Therese was the kind of woman who was capable of making decisions and acting on them instantly. The previous afternoon, as soon as Hsueh had left, she had phoned the Zung siblings and summoned them to her apartment to tell them that someone from Ku's gang had contacted her to order the new weapon, and that Zung should return to Hong Kong to prepare the shipment. She didn't look directly at him, and she let the cigarette smoke obscure her eyes. She was proud of having chosen Zung as her *comprador*: his surprise barely registered on his face. She could also tell that Yindee knew nothing of all this. Therese warned Zung not to get in touch with the customer again. She would take charge, so as not to confuse their counterparty.

"Get moving and buy your tickets at Kung-ho-hsiang Pier tonight," she said.

"Are you going to deal directly with them?" Zung asked her.

"Someone here will take care of that. I want to train a couple of new people. We'll need them as we expand," she said gleefully.

"All right then." He sounded a little disappointed, but resigned.

This morning she had gotten up early. It was another humid, sunless day. She had been sitting at home for almost two whole hours. It was a Friday, and by now she would usually have called the Astor to reserve a room. She stared into space for a while, and felt an urge to reopen the bundle of letters, but decided against it. She did not want to have to remove her makeup, and she decided that it was, in a way, appropriate for her friend's funeral. Here I am again, alone and friendless, she thought. In all these years in Shanghai, Margot had been her only friend. Therese was immensely lonely, and she considered asking Hsueh to move in with her. But she eventually decided against the idea.

For one whole day, Hsueh had almost completely forgotten about Leng. He had left her at home as if she were part of a different strand of the plot and could be put aside for now. Or rather, as if she were a character in a completely different novel, and could be left under his pillow for another day. When he got home in the early hours of the morning, and saw her tear-stained face, he felt a little guilty.

When he left Therese's apartment in the afternoon, he had gone straight to the police headquarters on Route Stanislas Chevalier. There was one other thing he had to do that day. He'd been forced to call Lieutenant Sarly from North Gate Police Station, and now he would pay for it.

Lieutenant Sarly had been so readily helpful that day that Hsueh was a little nervous. It felt like a trap. But he intuitively felt he should talk to Sarly, which was why he was going to see him, not because he was feeling brave.

Sure enough, Sarly shouted at him.

"Tell me, what were you doing in Singapore Hotel? There were a thousand better things you could have been doing. What were you thinking, running off with some woman? Who is she anyway? What prompted the sergeant to arrest her? What did she have to do with your work? Why are there so many mysterious women? First the White Russian woman, then the woman in that apartment, and now—aren't there any men in Shanghai?"

Sarly might be pretending to be angrier than he really was, but Hsueh couldn't be sure.

"You're an embarrassment to me!" Sarly raged. "The Political Section, vouch for a couple of philandering lovebirds? The police were extremely suspicious of this woman. Her identity papers were probably forged. Who on earth is she?"

"I'm afraid I can't tell you right now." Hsueh's knees wouldn't stop quivering. He stared at the teak floor, as if that would make it the floor that was quivering, and not his legs. He would tell Sarly everything if it would only make him stop shouting, never mind what would happen to Leng.

"Why can't you tell me? Why not? Have you no shame?" Sarly was scolding like a Chinese market woman.

"Because I am in the process of cultivating this woman as a contact!" Hsueh decided to risk it. He became eloquent like one of those reporters who procrastinated all day and wrote his articles in a single burst of inspiration right before the paper had to go to press:

"This is the biggest breakthrough I've had so far! I've only just gained her trust. Lady Holly wanted me to contact someone from an illegal organization on her behalf. I knew it had to be the Communist assassination squad you're after. The woman at the Singapore Hotel and the one who ran away from Rue Amiral Bayle are the same woman. I saw her on the ship and I'm not mistaken. But you can't arrest her now—this is Shanghai, and you must have patience like the Shanghainese. You must do as we do here. The man hiding behind her is the man you are looking for."

"Then why didn't you just tell me?" Lieutenant Sarly's voice softened, as though his anger had suddenly been deflated. His face grew paler, and his expression was indistinct, like a camera close-up fading out. He gazed at Hsueh, backlit by the sun. He seemed to be talking to himself, or perhaps confiding in Hsueh, explaining something to him, or deliberately making an ominous suggestion.

"Maybe I could have her arrested instead. I'd interrogate her and turn her over to Maron and his detectives. They know how to make people talk."

"But then their operation would screech to a halt! And the ticking bomb would stop ticking." Hsueh thought it was ridiculous to be speaking in elaborate metaphors at this time, but he had to let his inspiration do the talking, let his thoughts swirl between imagination and memory. "It's the boss you want, not one of his underlings. They're planning something big, something that will shock the whole city. I don't know exactly what it is, but it's going to be huge."

He chose carefully from the words he remembered: "In fact, my guess is that they are buying a powerful new weapon."

"A weapon? What weapon?"

"I don't know, but I saw a diagram of it. It looked like a machine gun on a mount."

"A machine gun? What would they do with it?"

"I don't know yet, but when I do know I promise I'll tell you everything. This is going to work, but you'll have to trust me." Hsueh decided that the situation was temporarily under control. He now had time to think about other problems, such as how to protect Leng. But there his innate optimism prevailed, and he brushed these worries off. I'll find a way to fix that, he thought. If it ever came to it, and if Sarly really trusted him, he could ask him to release Leng and Therese. Of course, he couldn't be responsible for all the others.

"How much of the diagram do you remember?"

It turned out that Hsueh remembered most of it. His photographer's brain had unconsciously absorbed the shapes and lines of the object despite not knowing what it was. He made two drawings on the notepad Sarly tossed at him. But it was a precise diagram he was reproducing, and he kept drawing the mount too big, so that it looked more like a camera tripod. When he had finished sketching, he was sure it was a machine gun.

There were also a handful of German words on the page, he said. Sarly agreed that the device could be a machine gun. Hsueh also vaguely remembered something that looked like a cylinder split in two, but he had to put it at the bottom of the page because there was no space on the side. Then he drew the other shape he remembered beneath the mount. That shouldn't matter, he thought, since the two components are completely separate.

Lieutenant Sarly said he would have a weapons specialist look at it. The most important thing was to work out how it would shape Ku's plan.

"What about that woman, where is she hiding now?" he asked.

"She'll get in touch. She won't give me her address or phone number." Having lied to Sarly made him afraid to go straight home after he left the police station, as if the rooms on Route J. Frelupt didn't exist as long as he wasn't home, and no one would realize Leng was hiding there. Of course, he was also reluctant to see Leng. He was the kind of person who liked to bargain with life, and if he could put something off, he always would.

He went to Haialai, the *jai alai* court on Avenue du Roi Albert. They had started holding enough contests that there was betting going on almost every day. But the contests were over for the afternoon. He was sitting in Domino Café, a small Spanish restaurant opposite the courts, watching men with names like Juan and Osa holler at the top of their lungs. The air was heavy with the scent of fried onions and chorizo. The handle of the slot machine creaked every now and again, and a coin would drop with a clang. A pile of *cestas* lay on the table in the corner, like a heap of beaks cut from the corpses of giant slaughtered birds.

As soon as he sat down, he saw Barker, the American, all in white like most of the players. But Barker seemed to be sweating more than they were, and his white shirt had two large yellow underarm stains. He was standing at the players' table, shouting that he would buy everyone a round. If he weren't so loud, Hsueh wouldn't have noticed him right away. A balding man stood to his left; the hairy man to his right looked as though he had shaved this morning but already had a five o'clock shadow.

When Barker saw him, he began to elbow his way out of the crowd. He came right up to Hsueh, and sat down so violently on the chair next to him that he nearly burst the seams of his pants.

"It's been ages, how have you been?" Barker was as loud as ever. A few years in American prisons hadn't taught him the value of peace and quiet. He didn't have the look of a wanted man who had fled to China across the oceans—he could easily have been a businessman chatting in front of any one of the trading houses on the Bund.

Just then, a red armored vehicle sped right past them, outside the glass doors, its machine gun pointed at the sea of people, like Poseidon's trident or Moses's staff parting the Red Sea, the shrill police whistle piercing the glass and hurting everyone's ears. If it weren't for that car, Barker wouldn't have told his story about Dillinger.

The armored vehicle turning onto Avenue du Roi Albert was carrying the newly issued silver yuan from the Shanghai mint to the central bank's treasury. This was neither its usual route nor the usual time of day. Barker spat on the wooden flooring and muttered: If John Dillinger were here . . .

Barker's words made the famous outlaw appear in the room, darting among the coffee cups and ham platters. They had done time in the Indiana State Prison together and were great friends, Barker said. (He was probably lying.) He talked too much, said Barker, you'd never think he was a real robber. (Hsueh wondered whether anyone could talk more than Barker himself.) Dillinger was always daydreaming about bank heists, about barging in somewhere and scaring the daylights out of the guards and customers. The few minutes after someone called the cops and before they got there were the best. Of course you'd tweak the engine on your car to make it go faster than the police cars. You had to be better armed than they were, so that you could be sure of winning a shootout. Barker said he couldn't imagine how Dillinger eventually pulled it off. He also didn't think that Dillinger would actually manage to escape, taking Barker and a few others with him as they dashed out of the prison gates.

Barker talked about Baby Face Nelson and Bonnie and Clyde as though they were all his friends and he was proud of them. He kept talking when they were sitting behind the wire fence in the *jai alai* court. When the server in a blue shirt ran over to give them their bill, he didn't even look at the number on the man's nameplate.

Hsueh won his bet that evening, guessing both the first and second places right. Everything seemed to be going his way. But when he got home in the early hours of the morning, and saw Leng's tear-stained face on the pillow, he began to doubt whether things were going as well as he'd hoped.

The day after what happened at the Singapore Hotel, Leng began to doubt her own influence over Hsueh. In fact, she started doubting Hsueh himself. It all came about because she found herself alone in Hsueh's rooms that morning, after he went out. The sun had come out from behind the clouds, and she was overcome by affection for Hsueh.

When she started cleaning his room, she found a pair of dirty drawers under the bed. They were made of Cantonese crepe silk with lace edges. In the sunlight, they gave off a dusty, moldy scent of old perfume, and a musky smell.

There were other signs. Lipstick stains on a cigarette holder, a scrunched-up powder puff in his woolen Fintex vest, and a photograph slipped under the cover of a notebook in his suit pocket. The woman in the photo was smoking, and a five-digit number was scrawled on the reverse. Leng realized she knew nothing about Hsueh. It wasn't the other woman who upset her, she told herself; she was upset that she had trusted Hsueh.

She told herself not to cry, but she did—though not until late at night, when she collapsed on the bed and found herself sobbing with loneliness into the pillow, too exhausted to be repulsed by thoughts of the scenes that pillow might have witnessed.

But when she woke the next morning to see the sunlight stream through the window onto Hsueh's face, she felt like a new person.

Later she would learn that it was officially the last day of the rainy season. The air was fresher. Actually, this will simplify things, she thought. Her duty loomed before her like a mountain. She was no longer feeling lethargic, and she felt she could outdo the owner of the dirty lingerie. She didn't ask him about it until two days later. She had started thinking of Hsueh as an enemy to be conquered. Keep your distance, she told herself. Provoke him—make him pursue you. It was a pity she couldn't just get up and leave, since she had nowhere else to go. Still, he was confused by her aloofness, which meant her plan was working.

He was out all the time. She didn't ask where he was going. Two days later, he asked abruptly when they were in the kitchen: "Didn't you say your boss wants to see me?"

Then he glanced away without looking her in the eye. He's feeling guilty, she thought. She had been avoiding him for a few days. He kept wanting to say something, and then not saying it. Maybe he had noticed the difference and felt bad about it. Maybe he subconsciously wanted to prove he cared by doing something for her.

"There's no rush. They'll tell us when."

He was grinding coffee beans, and she was cooking oatmeal. The kitchen was full of delicious smells. They could have been an ordinary couple making breakfast together.

"What is he like?"

She looked at Hsueh. His shirt wasn't tucked in at the back.

"Your boss—I mean, Mr. Ku."

"You'll find out when you see him." She could tell he was trying to make small talk. Her plan was working.

"But how will he get in touch with us? Can he call us? He doesn't have a phone number for us here. You didn't give him the landlady's number, did you? It's not like you can have a real conversation in her room, anyway." Hsueh was basically talking to himself. Coffee beans clattered in the grinder.

"I'll call him."

"But you haven't called him yet. Did you call yesterday?"

Leng was suddenly irritated. Hsueh was sounding like one of

those men who get up in the morning and start nagging, finding fault with everything.

"How do you know I didn't call him?" She threw the wooden spoon into the pot and began to scream. "You weren't even home! You've been out all day! Why are you so anxious to see him? Are you—" She cut herself off.

Hsueh was alarmed. She watched his shoulders slump and waited for him to turn around. He looked about wildly, like a thief caught in the act. Ask him now while you have the upper hand, she thought. She grew calmer, and lowered her voice.

"Is there something you should be telling me?" she said slowly. She could tell that he wanted to talk to her, and she was forcing him to talk. But she didn't want him to lie, so she added:

"Why have you been out for the past few days? Why did you leave me at home all day? You have another woman, don't you?"

He sighed, slumping like a tabby cat slinking away from a fight. He can't hide it any longer, she thought—he's going to tell me the truth.

But Hsueh had one last idea. He dashed out of the kitchen to find the evidence. That didn't worry Leng; she knew she would win this round. Striding into the bedroom, she saw him rummaging under the bed, and thought, silly you. Did you toss it under the bed and then just forget it was there?

Reaching into the gap between the closet and the wall, she drew out a package wrapped in an old copy of the *Ta Kung Pao*, the newspaper she was reading. There was a headline about the victory of the Red Army in Kiangsi, where the Communists had executed a local official and put his head on a raft to drift past the town, scaring the remnants of the Kuomintang Army off. She put the package on the table and opened it. The rumpled crepe silk unfurled like a bundle of wilted petals. A moldy powder puff quivered in the sunlight. The victory of the Red Army seemed to echo her own victory over Hsueh.

She sat down, waiting for his confession.

"You probably saw her on the ship," he began. "She's a White

Russian in the jewelry business. But you'd never guess she also sells firearms on the side. I only found that out later. It's true I loved her, but I don't anymore. By the time we were on the ship, I wasn't in love with her." His voice was calm. "You may have seen us bickering onboard." Leng could believe this—she had heard him cursing under his breath by the railing. "Then she slept with someone while we were in Hong Kong, a Chinese man from Vietnam, her business partner. It's true I liked her a lot, but she couldn't stop sleeping around. I came home a day early from Canton, put the key in the lock, and caught them in the act. The couch was shoved up against the window and her legs were propped up on the windowsill. The man looked up at me with a sneer, which was even more humiliating than the thought of her with someone else.

"Do you think that's why I came to talk to you? I can't pretend it had nothing to do with it, but I'd rather you didn't think that. You're such different people. That night, when we escaped from the police station, I thought I was over her. Not just because of you, but because that's all history now. Meeting you felt like a gift, a sign that things would be different. But just to be friendly, I went to see her yesterday. I thought it would be good for me, and it might help you."

He means because she sells firearms, she thought. That was unusually brave for Hsueh. If he had really been thinking that, then perhaps he did like her after all. He wasn't courageous by nature—he was timid and mediocre, but suffering had changed him. Or maybe he gets a kick out of danger, the way some people do from drinking or smoking opium. That doesn't have to be a bad thing, she thought.

Now was the right time to arrange a meeting with Ku. Whatever Hsueh's motives for joining the Party were, once he was one of them the cell would educate him and turn him into a true revolutionary. If that happened, then it would be permissible to accept him, to fall in love with him. Even if he were using her to get over his old love, over time that would change. And his connections at the police station would come in useful.

She came up to him and hugged him. As she reached under his belt to straighten his shirt and tuck it in, she let her hand brush against the back of his waist—no, Leng didn't want to make love right then. There might be time for that later.

For now, she thought, she should listen to him talk about his feelings, without realizing that she wanted to hear about them because she had feelings of her own.

CHAPTER 34

The Nanking commission was convinced that Ku's people were ordinary criminals, not Communists. Their methods weren't like Communist methods. And the investigators should know, not just because they were experts on the Communists, but also because a few of them used to be Communists themselves.

That was precisely how Lieutenant Sarly planned to undermine them. He was attending a meeting at the Municipal Office's Trustees House on Route Pichon in the leafy west of the French Concession. Nominally, the Trustees House was not a government building, and it had been chosen to give the session an informal setting. Consul Baudez had called this meeting in his capacity as a trustee of the Municipal Office, although he was not taking part in it. Ever since M. Brenier de Montmorant, the previous consul, had clashed with the Municipal Office over the police station, the consul had held both posts. At the time, M. Brenier had ordered the trustees dismissed, and surrounded the Municipal Office with police, causing a fracas that escalated all the way to the Ministry of Foreign Affairs in Paris. Three days later, the trustees were set free on payment of 100,000 francs, and the Ministry had to create a special committee to restore the government of the Concession. From then onward, the police headquarters were placed firmly under the authority of the consul, and its main officers were always trusted lieutenants of his.

"Maybe our visitors simply can't bear to think that Communists could stoop to ordinary crime. After all, communism is just a youthful phase, isn't it?" Sarly was taunting the ex-Communists from Nanking. Colonel Bichat of the Shanghai Volunteer Corps also began to laugh—he and Commander Martin, who was also present, supported Sarly's view. Shanghailanders were growing tired of the fight between the Kuomintang and the Communists. The demonstrations and strikes were bad for business, and now shootouts in the streets verged on civil war, threatening to reduce the concessions to rubble. Perhaps there was nothing for it but to turn Shanghai into a—

Horns tooted in the yard. A car was ready for Consul Baudez's wife. Once, when he was in a good mood, Baudez had told Sarly that there were three beautiful women in the villa. His wife and daughter were two of the three, of course. The third must be the half-naked marble statue in the center of the pond, guessed Sarly, but luckily he didn't say that aloud. No, the third was the pond itself, which narrowed on both ends but widened in the middle, curving outward like a woman's hips. Consul Baudez does have conventional taste in women, thought Sarly. Did that make the camphor tree bending toward the surface of the pond a lecher? One of its branches was pointing at the woman's breasts.

"The gangs in Shanghai tipped us off that these people aren't Communists," Mr. Tseng from Nanking insisted.

"The Green Gang is a sworn enemy of the Communists, just like you."

"Speak for yourself!" Tseng retorted.

"Indeed. Maybe the Concession Police should take more responsibility for combating the Red Threat in Shanghai. We can't let Nanking do all the work." Like all Corsicans, Lieutenant Sarly had a way with words. The Nanking investigators were temporarily silenced.

"Nanking overrelies on brute force to suppress dissident parties. That won't work nowadays, but your Kuomintang politicians are stuck in the past. They don't know how to govern a modern city. When the Communists in Kiangsi executed one of your men and set his head afloat on a raft on the Kan River, I heard you shot a bunch of jailed Communists in Nanking and Shanghai to retaliate." Unlike the other Shanghailanders, Sarly read Chinese newspapers and took a real interest in what the Chinese thought. The poetic headline had lodged itself in his mind: *Silently the waves bear him home.*

"Shanghai could be a model city for China, a modern city where law and order prevail," Sarly concluded. Only Mr. Blair, attending the meeting as a diplomatic policy observer for the British government, approved of these abstract musings. Blair listened dutifully, but his eyes looked weary and sad.

"The chaos in Shanghai is all your doing. You only want to appease the Communists so you can make money off the Chinese. Half the problem is that you restrict Nanking's freedom to maneuver in the concessions. The reason why the Communists are based in Shanghai is that you're too shortsighted to crack down on them!" a young man from the investigative commission said indignantly.

"Sun Yat-sen was right about modern China. We're not ready for democracy yet, and there has to be a period of political tutelage during which the Kuomintang governs. But one day we will have this city under control, maybe when the Greater Shanghai Plan has succeeded." The young man sounded a little defeated.

They had strayed from the topic of the meeting. These larger questions would have to be resolved by politicians in London, Paris, or Nanking. Commander Martin said it was time they returned to the matters at hand. If Nanking's people were permitted to move freely in the concessions, they would contribute more to the intelligence exchanged among all parties, Mr. Tseng said as the spokesman for the investigative commission.

On behalf of the two foreign governing authorities in Shanghai, Lieutenant Sarly and Commander Martin negotiated with the Nanking investigators regarding the carrying of firearms, wireless frequencies, and special license plates, and permitted them to set up an operation base in the concessions. But Sarly reminded them that Nanking would have no authority whatsoever to make arrests within the territories of the concessions.

The meeting became more amicable. Whereas all the parties disagreed heartily in principle, negotiating on concrete matters helped them to find common ground. Under the current arrangement, Nanking submitted names to the concession authorities, which would then carry out the arrests. Tseng pointed out that the delay often caused them to miss their best opportunities for interrogations. He suggested that Nanking be allowed to make arrests within the concessions, on condition that they report all names to the concession authorities retrospectively, and share the intelligence so obtained with all parties. But Lieutenant Sarly insisted that the consular jurisdiction of the concessions must be protected. He warned that if Nanking made any unilateral arrests, the French Concession Police would be compelled to view them as kidnappings.

Commander Martin broke the ensuing silence. It is true that the Nanking authorities have a home advantage in dealing with Chinese matters, he said. Perhaps we could agree to call these operations neither arrests nor kidnappings. Let us say the Nanking commission were to invite a couple of individuals to discuss something at their office, eyewitnesses agreed that the parties in question were not coerced into doing so, and the police forces of the concessions were given a reasonable explanation of the circumstances. Let us say that the results of this discussion would be made available in their entirety to the police, and within a certain time, say forty-eight hours, these individuals would be turned over to the police authorities of the respective concessions, and lawfully tried or extradited. I would have no objection to that.

Sarly insisted that all interrogations would have to be carried out in the presence of an observer appointed by the French Concession Police or the Shanghai Municipal Police. Eventually they agreed that written notice of Nanking's actions would have to be given directly to the Political Section within twenty-four hours, upon which the police would send an observer. During those twenty-four hours, the Nanking investigators would be free to discuss matters of interest with their subjects in a friendly manner.

"So who are you planning to ask out on a friendly date?" Sarly brought the discussion to a close with what he intended to be a lighthearted question.

Unlike the other Chinese, who were always too serious around Westerners, Mr. Tseng did have a sense of humor. "As we agreed, whoever they are, we will notify their parents within twenty-four hours of issuing an invitation."

"That's enough time to get someone pregnant," Colonel Bichat added cheerfully.

The Nanking investigators filed out of the temporary meeting room, a side room on the second floor adjoining the large living room. After these five bookish Chinese men had made their way across the balcony and down the exterior stairs onto the lawn, and their black sedan car had driven through the gate, Commander Martin cried: "Did they have to send all that many people to one meeting? Are there really too many people in China?"

Consul Baudez appeared only after the Chinese had left. His position was equivalent to that of a colonial governor, which meant he remained detached from most practical affairs. He handed Mr. Blair a memo his secretary had just written, to be passed on to the British consul. It had been drafted in accordance with Lieutenant Sarly's suggestions.

"We have reliable information that the underground organization we have been discussing is acquiring a more dangerous arsenal of weapons. We do not yet have a full picture of their movements. But this constitutes concrete evidence in favor of our hypothesis that Shanghai is turning into a battleground for the struggle between the Communists and the Kuomintang, which would affect our interests here. The French government has committed to redeploying some French troops from Hanoi to Shanghai, to address recent developments. We urge other European governments with strong interests in the concessions to do the same." Sarly hoped chiefly to influence the romantic Mr. Blair, who acted as an observer for the Foreign Office. He was now infamous for his way with women in the Concession. Surely he could not object to doing something for the men?

"And then there's the Greater Shanghai Plan," murmured Colonel Bichat. Many Shanghailanders felt that the plan would severely damage international interests in the concessions. In fact, Lieutenant Sarly was well aware that Nanking's scheme chiefly hurt foreign land developers. European and now American land speculators had bought up large tracts of land to the south and west of Shanghai. These firms would buy land, wait for the prices to be driven up, sell it, and then buy more land farther south and west.

But according to the blueprint for the Greater Shanghai Plan, the heart of Shanghai was to lie in the northeast. Government buildings, a university, model elementary schools, and even a sports ground were to be built in Chapei and Chiang-wan. Roads and public facilities would bring commercial activity to a part of town that was currently a wasteland, and future residents of Shanghai would buy property there. If that happened, the land in the southwest that foreign developers had acquired for huge sums of money would be worthless, and they would lose their investment. Not only would the speculators and banks suffer losses, but the whole system of profiteering would collapse.

"There's also Tokyo—they keep sending naval and ground troops here, and they've always wanted more clout in Shanghai. The Japanese businessmen in the International Settlement have been getting aggressive, and the Municipal Police has spent the past year breaking up brawls between the Chinese and the Japanese in the streets," Commander Martin said.

"If the Japanese are willing to help, I say the more the merrier," said Colonel Bichat. "What's that piece of cloth they wear at the back of their necks again?"

"Ah, neck flaps—they're just afraid of having their heads chopped off," said Martin, gesturing with a flick of his wrist. "I hear they like beheading people up there."

"The Japanese Army got that idea from our North African troops. The Meiji emperor ordered military hats from all over the world to be brought to him, and he chose that one, despite the fact that it was designed for the desert and Japan is nowhere near one. He thought it looked most like the *kabuto*, a samurai helmet with a neck guard. Except they have two flaps instead of one—for good luck." Sarly got his information from books.

"The Shanghainese are good people," Colonel Bichat said. "I say letting Shanghai become a free city would be a wise decision." But Sarly thought that was a rash thing to say, little better than the rash bets that speculators were making, snapping up farmland around Shanghai. In his view, policy had to progress incrementally, and sending more troops to Shanghai right now would be the right thing to do. The setting sun shone on the pool outside, and the water shimmered like the glistening skin of a belly dancer.

CHAPTER 35

JUNE 29, YEAR 20 OF THE REPUBLIC.

12:30 P.M.

At first, Lin had no reason to be suspicious. But the class struggle had made him more vigilant. He was a quick learner, and he often learned by observing Park. For instance, he had noticed that Park always returned to the scene of even a minor operation, and talked to the shirtless errand boys who stood at the doors of the corner stores all day.

Without telling Ku, he went off to the Singapore Hotel on his own. It was only a short walk from the Rue Palikao candle store. On the way he wondered how he could strike up a conversation. Maybe he could pretend to be a wealthy man looking to set up a private gambling den, but he didn't think he looked the part.

He stood on the opposite side of Rue du Consulat, at the door of Kuan-sheng Yüan, the candy manufacturer. When someone began to climb the narrow stairs toward the hotel, he quickly crossed the road and followed them. He would feel safer if he wasn't the only person at the reception. The receptionist was standing behind the desk at the stairwell, talking to someone. He slipped past him and struck up a conversation with the steward sitting on a bench. He spoke in a low voice, winking to hint that it was sex he was after. But the Concession prohibited under-the-table prostitution, and he'd heard that this place had had a spot of trouble with the cops.

"I live in the longtang across the street," he added unnecessarily. He shouldn't have said that. A real john doesn't tell people where he lives.

"The police were here just last week. You scared now?"

He shook his head and shrugged, rattling the coins in his pocket.

"It was the Communists they were after."

"I heard it was a woman."

The steward was a young man, but he had met all kinds of people. He gave Lin a meaningful look. Then he shook his head.

"She was a single woman. They took her to the police station, with a man." That proved his point: you can always learn something useful by returning to the scene of an incident.

He bungled his exit by simply walking away, as though asking about hookers embarrassed him. That could well have made the steward suspicious enough to mention him to the manager in a spare moment. He rushed out of the building, trying to avoid the beggars who squatted in twos and threes by the colonnade, enjoying a few moments of peace during the police's lunch break.

Leng had lied to the cell! Lin had been there when she called Ku—in fact, he had answered the phone. This has to be reported to Ku, he thought. What did it mean that Leng had been taken to North Gate Police Station? He didn't have the time to think that through. Ku would be leaving the candle store this very moment, to meet Leng and that photojournalist friend of hers, as they had arranged. That man had real connections in the Political Section. He stopped at the corner of Rue Palikao.

Lin didn't know where they were planning to meet, but he realized how serious the problem was. Leng was completely exposed: her photograph was in all the Concession newspapers, and it must have been plastered on the walls of the police station, to fix her face in the minds of all those policemen going off to their daily beat. She must have been arrested because someone recognized her, but despite knowing precisely who she was, they had released her anyway. The police weren't blind, so there must have been some reason why they would turn a blind eye.

He couldn't think straight. Ku wasn't there, Park wouldn't be there, and he always went to one of them when he had questions. His entire unit had been deployed to protect Ku, since this was one of the rare occasions when he would appear in public.

He should go to the new safe house, the apartment rented to replace the one on Rue Amiral Bayle. It was on Boulevard des Deux Républiques between Rue Buissonnet and Rue Voisin. Boulevard des Deux Républiques was the boundary between the French Concession and the Chinese-administered Old Town. The buildings facing the street were under Concession jurisdiction, because the longtang stretching from east to west opened onto Boulevard de Montigny, but the eastern windows opened onto Ming Koo Road, just across the street from the Chinese-administered area. The apartment was rented under his name, but the idea had been Ku's. Ku said that one night, when he was being frisked by Concession detectives at the gate on Ming Koo Road, he had seen the light come on in a second-floor window. It occurred to him that it could be useful to keep a bundle of rope at the window facing east in one of these apartments and let it down in an emergency, said Ku. Then an unusually wistful look had come over him.

Lin never made it to the apartment. He would later think he only got caught because he couldn't stop thinking about Leng's lie.

He had just turned the corner. Afterward he wouldn't for the life of him be able to remember which street he had been on. He did remember seeing basketfuls of peaches between those fingers—pink and flat green peaches. A pair of large callused hands had covered his eyes, digging its fingers into his sockets, making his temples hurt.

The pair of hands had reached over from behind him, and the voice also came from behind, floating toward him like a disembodied voice:

"Guess who I am? Guess who I am?" It was a high-pitched singsong voice, like someone reciting a nursery rhyme. He could hear laughter muffled by the street noises. The hands were also twisting his ears, making all those voices sound as though they were underwater.

He heard a car screech to a halt. Someone was standing in front of him, pushing him, pulling him from the side. There was a brief burst of light, and then he could see nothing. He was surrounded by people breathing heavily.

He didn't notice when they twisted his arms behind his back. He was aware of being dragged to the edge of the pavement, and he noticed the step. Then a stab of pain—a punch, he thought. He was just thinking that when he was punched again in the stomach, his knees buckled, he bent over and collapsed to the ground.

But this wasn't the ground. It was soft and bouncy, with a smell of new leather. Before he knew what was happening, the door had been closed. He knew he was in a car because the door had caught on his pant leg.

As it sped off, the hands pushed his head down into the car seat. It felt as if a thousand people were sitting on his back, and he could hardly breathe. His nose was wedged into the gap at the back of the seat, and his mouth tasted of rust, probably because his lips or gums were bleeding.

Someone put a cloth bag over his head and tied it on tightly. The rope was right at his mouth, and it felt as though the corners of his mouth were going to split open. This must be to stop him from screaming, he thought. It actually hadn't occurred to him to scream. He couldn't make a sound if he tried.

He was dragged out of the car by many pairs of hands. He couldn't see where he was and he had no concept of time; he had never been trained to handle situations like this. But he remembered Park once saying that you could count silently using a regular bodily rhythm like your heartbeat or breathing. Count how many times the car turns a corner—you can always tell, because of inertia. Pay attention to changes in the ground surface, notice whether it's sloping upward or downward, whether it's hard or soft. If you stay calm, you can feel even the gaps between the tiles beneath your feet. Without Park's training, Lin didn't have the presence of mind to start counting. All he could remember was birdsong, the sound of wind in the leaves, and the smell of car exhaust. He didn't remember to count the number of steps they climbed, but he knew that he had been taken to an empty third-floor room, and he noticed the dank smell of slaked lime.

Now there was silence. No more breathing noises, no footsteps. He felt as though he had been abandoned, not just in an empty room, but also in an empty building. Before long, he heard someone talking in low tones through the ceiling. The voice sounded as if it was coming from a room to his left. His hearing was recovering. He could hear someone pouring water from a hot water bottle into a teacup. This couldn't be the police station, he guessed. There were no clanking sounds of metal, no handcuffs, no metal doors. Besides, the police could arrest him openly. No, these men were more likely to be from the Green Gang. At first he thought it must be because of the Singapore Hotel, but he quickly abandoned that idea. Stay calm. He remembered what Park had told him: expand your senses of hearing, touch, smell, and the entire surface of your skin, so that you absorb every bit of sound, warmth, and humidity from your surroundings.

Not long afterward, he remembered about the Singapore Hotel, and realized that he hadn't had a chance to report his discovery to Ku. The entire cell was in danger, and there was nothing he could do about it. Lin began to worry.

The jargon sounded abstract and remote to Hsueh. All those new words came from Europe via the Soviet Union and Japan, and over the past twenty years, they had flooded in so quickly that it had been impossible to keep track of them all. They had caught on faster than imported goods, ships, or cars. Everyone these days was learning the new vocabulary. Even small-time reporters and errand boys could go on about the Left or Imperialism, and you'd have to be a real philistine or country bumpkin not to know those words. To be sure, some of the new words were useful. For instance, having sex with a hostess was now called *sleeping with her,* and being interested in someone could be described as *falling in love.* This made things simpler. If everyone used the same words, the words themselves would have the effect of a spell you could cast on people. Now that "love" had been invented by novels and movies, all the women servants in Shanghai would soon tremble like actresses at the mere mention of falling in love.

Mr. Ku, Leng's boss, was speaking to him. Spells had no effect on him, but Hsueh was intrigued nonetheless by Ku's mystique. They had arranged to meet outside the gate of the Koukaza Gardens, but at the appointed time, Ku was nowhere to be seen. Five minutes later, two young people appeared behind him and Leng. Follow us, they said in a low voice.

They followed them down the road that ran north-south through the park. At the northwest corner of the park, the two students slowed down and told Hsueh to wait there. Without ever looking directly at him, they hurried away.

Two minutes later, someone in a black linen suit came toward them. His face looked familiar, and Hsueh remembered having once seen him in a black leather jacket. He sure likes wearing black, he thought. The man brought him and Leng to a Peugeot, and had them get in the back while he drove. Although they couldn't see out the windows because of the blinds, Hsueh could tell that they were traveling west along Avenue Joffre.

The car stopped in an empty yard surrounded by tall buildings, such that only the northwest corner of the yard was sunlit. There were camphor trees on the lawn and carefully tended flower beds. Cherry blossoms were in full bloom, and the ground was carpeted with petals. They were taken through a glass door into a building. There was no doorman, and the elevator was to the left. It went up to the fifth floor, where Mr. Ku was waiting for them.

He sat in the middle of a horseshoe-shaped table, while Leng and Hsueh sat in soft chairs on either side. The man in black, whose name was Park, sat behind Hsueh. He slouched on his armchair and rocked it, with his legs propped up on a folding chair.

Ku talked about the cell's ideals and mission. The atmosphere was a little awkward. Leng played with a pencil. Park's armchair rocked more violently.

Then they took a break. Have a cigarette, Mr. Ku said. Let's get some fresh air on the balcony. They went through the kitchen and climbed onto the rooftop via a spiral iron ladder that hung outside the building.

They stood by the railing. Hsueh lit a match for Mr. Ku with his back turned to the wind, and then lit himself one. They both smoked silently. The corners of the railing were overgrown with moss, and the uneven floor was partly flooded. Hsueh shivered. He turned his collar up and held his hand up to let the breeze carry the cigarette ash away.

"Tell me why you are helping us. Tell me why," Ku said, almost to himself. He smiled.

Hsueh shook his head. He had nothing to say. No one would believe him—he wasn't very sure if he believed himself. He tried to make himself smile.

"Because of her?" Ku's smile grew wider, as if he wasn't used to telling jokes but was telling one now.

"Because of love. Is that a good reason?" Hsueh said, staring at a puddle by his feet. "I mean, is falling in love an acceptable reason for becoming a Communist?"

"Right. Becoming a Communist." Ku took a long drag of his cigarette, and tossed the stub over the railing. "Are you telling me that what you're doing is joining the Revolution?" Hsueh thought he saw a shadow of loneliness or grief in Ku's eyes.

"Sure. Isn't love supposed to transform you and make you want to alter your life?" This Ku is a canny type, Hsueh thought. He knows how to steer this conversation in the direction he wants.

"We can accept any reason for joining, but you have to be honest with us. Even if you're in it for the money." He waved his hand, as though he himself regretted this policy, as though he had only mentioned the basest possible motive to put Hsueh at ease.

"We always compensate well," he said, stopping Hsueh from speaking with another wave. "No, not you. What I mean is that we can pay our sources if we have to. Your friend at the police station, for instance. Does he need money? Didn't he come to China in order to make money? Of course it would be better if he were truly sympathetic to our cause, but if he would do it for the money, he could still be useful to us." Ku's voice grew fainter, nearly disappearing in the wind, and he spoke quickly, as if to avoid hurting Hsueh's pride.

The break was over, and they went back inside. Leng had disappeared. The next part of the conversation felt like an interrogation. Ku took his place inside the horseshoe, and the curtains were closed. Hsueh's own chair had been moved just opposite the curved table to face Ku directly. Park was still sitting behind him, but he was no longer sprawled on the sofa.

"We have a few questions for you. Standard procedure. Nothing to be nervous about." Ku was laconic but his voice was gentle.

"Tell me your name." Ku did not take notes; it was unnecessary. Hsueh guessed that the interrogation itself was not strictly necessary.

But the questions were full of double meanings, and they had a hypnotic effect on Hsueh, conditioning him to attempt to please his interrogator.

"Tell me where you met her." The first set of questions was about Leng.

"On the ship."

"On the ship?" The voice suddenly grew stern. It occurred to Hsueh that he had completely forgotten what Leng had said to him. The hypnotism was working. Leng hadn't been clear about wanting Hsueh to say they were old acquaintances, so as not to give Ku the impression she had been lying—she'd mentioned it but told him it wasn't all that important. Hsueh had thought it was because she didn't want to look like a flirt. He now realized that Leng might not have been telling her cell the truth.

"How did you meet onboard?" Ku's voice sounded calmer. Maybe he had only imagined it sounding stern.

"We didn't—well, meet isn't the right word. Leng was on deck, walking toward the bow by herself. It was cold and windy. I happened to see her there." She had looked sad but resolute, her face almost transparent in the sunlight.

"She looked familiar, and I kept thinking I'd seen her before. We must know each other from somewhere, I later told her, and she agreed. Maybe sometimes a man and a woman just feel this way about each other. If she told you that we'd known each other for ages, it wouldn't surprise me at all. Do you see?"

"I see. That's a clever way to describe love at first sight, isn't it?" His questioner smiled again. "You didn't even have to flirt with her—it was just meant to be."

"Maybe so," Hsueh said.

"Very clever of you. You're clever, but you're also honest," Ku said generously.

But after a pause, his voice grew stern again: "When was the next time you saw her?"

"In the newspapers, I think. There were pictures of her in all the papers."

"So you fell in love the moment you saw her on the ship. Then her photograph appeared in the papers, and although you hadn't had a chance to see her again, you couldn't forget her face. We know you're a photojournalist. So when you heard the police were planning to arrest her on Rue Amiral Bayle, did you track her down just so you could warn her?"

Hsueh knew he was being mocked. He knew he should get offended, jump up, and shove these questions in his interrogator's face. But he didn't have the energy to do that. He wouldn't know how to justify himself, not even to Leng.

"That's how it was," he said simply.

"Very good. That's how it was. We believe you. We believe you precisely because your story sounds so implausible. And you look like you could be a hopeless romantic. Aren't you half French?"

Well, if Ku was going to fall for that, it only went to prove Hsueh's conjectures about the power of words like *love* and *revolution*. Was a *half-French* man a hopeless romantic, by definition?

"I didn't believe what the papers were saying about her. I'd talked to her. I'd looked into her eyes. I thought I knew her."

But Ku stopped asking about love. Perhaps a few small untruths are permitted when ideals conflict with love.

Instead they started talking about Hsueh's friend. Ku asked for his name and occupation. He was very interested to hear that this man belonged to Maron's new detective squad, although Hsueh had already mentioned this fact in his written report. The previous night, Ku had instructed Leng over the phone to have Hsueh produce a report. Sitting alone at the table in his room, Hsueh had done his best to put something coherent together. Mr. Ku is like Lieutenant Sarly, he thought: they both believe in written documents. Although the report consisted of scraps of intelligence, some of the information was very valuable, and in any case, intelligence is fragmentary by nature. He included the police's conjectures about Ku's background, which he had heard from his friend the poet. They were not entirely consistent—but that only goes to show that they reflect a wide range of opinions, he thought.

Hsueh put all this in his report without fully understanding how valuable the information was. For instance, he did not realize that the police view of the Kin Lee Yuen assassination and reconstruction of events, as well as most of what the poet had told him, came from the Nanking investigators' report. He also did not know that the police interpretation of the incident on Avenue Foch as a revenge killing had been influenced by the Green Gang's view of events. And he had no way of knowing how relieved Ku was that Hsueh had handed him the report directly, instead of giving it to Leng. When he told Ku that Leng hadn't read the report, he was just being honest, not trying to cover for her.

CHAPTER 37

During the half hour in which Park dined with their guest, Ku read Hsueh's report carefully from beginning to end. West Avenue Joffre was lined with expensive houses, and the only shops on the street were custom tailors. Park had had to drive all the way to Avenue du Roi Albert to find a cheap restaurant. He came back with a box of roast duck and rice.

Ku reread the report, smoked a cigarette, and considered its contents. Then he threw the sheaf of papers into the glowing oven. He had to prevent the others from reading it, in part to protect his source, but also in part to preserve the ignorance that kept his troops disciplined. At all costs, he wanted to keep them from knowing that the attack on 181 Avenue Foch had been motivated in part by Ch'i's death.

The report was stylistically and grammatically jumbled. It alternately paraphrased the poet and quoted him directly. A few paragraphs had been cautiously rewritten, but then the writer would lace the facts boldly with his own observations. Ku paid extra attention to inconsistencies. For instance, at one point the poet was quoted as saying that he thought Avenue Foch had been a revenge killing, but the very next paragraph had him saying that "the police are sure these people belong to an underground Communist organization." Could it be that the poet and his superior had different opinions?

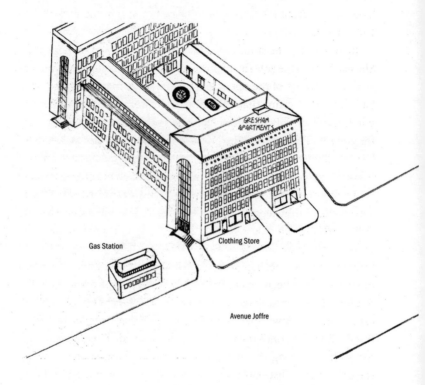

Gas Station

GRESHAM
APARTMENTS

Clothing Store

Avenue Joffre

The safe house where Hsueh was taken to meet with Ku

Ku believed that precisely these inconsistencies made the manuscript reliable. They proved it consisted of casual conversations recounted by one person to another and then crudely summarized by Hsueh—no wonder they had lost some of their original shape. The value of this intelligence lay in the contradictions, Ku thought. They showed that the Concession Police was still in the dark about Ku's true identity.

Before dinner, he summoned Leng and came down on her hard. She had broken the rules by making contact with a complete stranger at a crucial point of the operation, and to make matters worse, she had lied. Why claim that she and Hsueh were old acquaintances when they had only just met? Don't be fooled by a petty bourgeois fling, he told her. And never, never think you can get away with lying to the Party. Only when Leng began to sob did he turn on his reassuring voice and praise her for winning Hsueh over to their side.

The more violent the struggle, the more unexpectedly love can appear, he said. It didn't surprise him at all. He mentioned a few instances in which fellow comrades had gotten married in the face of the firing squad. Who knows, the two of you could have a pair of little revolutionary babies, he teased. When you've completed all the missions you've been given, you can move on to the Soviet Union, to Hong Kong, or to France. Isn't Hsueh half French? He got a little caught up in his own speech until he noticed that Leng looked confused. Of course, once the revolution has succeeded in one country, the proletariat vanguard will have to export it to other countries in the grip of capitalist oppression. Maybe the two of you will have a part to play in the Communist revolution in France.

But after Leng left, he began to think about how difficult it was to maintain the focus of his team. These young people were as naïve as they were plucky, and up until now he had singlehandedly controlled what they thought. But he couldn't guarantee that they would not waver. That was why they had to constantly be moving on to new targets. He felt defeated, somewhat lethargic—maybe the cigarettes were giving him a headache. He had never gotten over Ch'i's death.

He called the safe house on Boulevard des Deux Républiques. Most of Lin's unit was with him at the moment; he had summoned them for this operation. Lin himself had been ordered to wait in the apartment, but no one was answering the phone. Time to plan a new operation, he thought.

The cell was growing. There were three units under his command, all fully equipped. He had an eight-cylinder French-made car. And if he wanted another one, the steady stream of operations was bringing in plenty of cash. He even had a reliable police source. He had established himself in the Concession.

After the operation at 181 Avenue Foch, one of those fixers who seemed to know everyone and have complicated allegiances brought him a message. The Boss was offering him 100,000 silver yuan for a truce. Ku hadn't responded yet. The Green Gang was treating his group as one of those brash new outfits trying to make a name for itself by perpetrating a series of killings, but Ku wanted more. He wanted a revolution that would alter the balance of power in the Concession.

The dark bricks of the building outside reflected the glow of the late afternoon sun. A foreign woman with auburn hair opened the window, through which piano music sounded faintly, in fits and starts, as though the Victrola was spinning erratically. There was a bitter taste in his mouth. Too many cigarettes. He was getting hungry. He came into the living room for dinner.

"All the papers called him a public menace," Hsueh was saying. He was telling a tall tale while Leng picked listlessly at her food. Park was trying to find the holes in Hsueh's story:

"That's impossible. It can't be done. You've never been in a gunfight. Americans love to exaggerate—you can't just drive through a barricade like that, bursting through crossfire."

"Why not? As long as your engine's powerful enough and running fast?"

Hsueh stopped talking as soon as Ku came into the room. Hsueh is telling a story about an American outlaw robbing a bank, when all I want to do is have dinner, said Park.

"Really, the president of the United States nicknamed him the enemy of the people. Think about it. Banks are the heart of the capitalist system." Hsueh sounded ridiculous when he tried to use Communist jargon. He might get the words right, but they all came out sounding wrong.

Ku had considered robbing a bank, but he wasn't sure the cell was ready for an operation on that scale.

He wouldn't want to target a bank branch that was either too small or too big. The biggest branches had scores of guards and direct phone lines to the police station. They were all in the busy heart of the Concession, where police armored vehicles could reach them within minutes. As Park had pointed out, there was no way to burst through a barricade on a big street.

No, he didn't need tall tales. He needed intelligence, real intelligence. He wanted to sit down properly with Hsueh, get a piece of paper, and list everything he needed to know. He would give Hsueh some tips on the right questions to ask the next time he got a drink with his poet friend.

All kinds of questions occurred to him right away. Inspired by Hsueh's story, he wanted to know how many policemen there were and how their armored vehicles were fitted out. Of course, he also wanted to know more about that Inspector Maron who was after him.

Putting himself in Hsueh's shoes, he wondered whether the poet would smell a rat. An ordinary photojournalist at a French paper, asking all these questions about the cops? How could he work them into the conversation without raising suspicions? He would have to coach Hsueh not to ask them all at once. Ask a question in the pause between two toasts. If the poet is quiet, if he looks uncomfortable or tries to change the subject, then act like you were just wondering out loud, as if no one asked and you're not interested in the answer, and never mention it again.

He brought Hsueh to the room where they had originally met. Now they were sitting on the same side of the horseshoe-shaped table. He took out a pen and paper, like a tutor talking to a student. More questions came to mind. Hsueh mentioned the lieutenant in charge, the man from the Political Section. According to Hsueh, the poet had once said that this lieutenant thought Ku's cell was nothing to worry about. It was a "little red flea"—Hsueh hesitated perceptibly before saying the words—that would amount to nothing. Ku didn't lose his temper. He simply asked more questions about the lieutenant.

"The police think there are probably financiers among you," said Hsueh.

"What does that mean?"

"No idea. *Financier*, that's the word he used. I thought he might be talking about banks." Hsueh flashed him a cunning smile.

Ku patted Hsueh reassuringly on the shoulders. He thought he knew what Hsueh was getting at. Only in retrospect, when he was reading the newspapers, had he realized why Ts'ao had to be killed. His contact hadn't told him the truth—that man may not even have known. Ku had no idea why anyone would pay twenty thousand silver yuan to have Ts'ao Chen-wu assassinated. But later he discovered the hidden thread that linked everything together: Ts'ao's mission in Shanghai, the influential Nanking man who was causing trouble in Canton, and the speculators betting heavily on public debt. The discovery didn't upset him. That assassination had only been the first step in his master plan, a chance to give the cell some practice and make their name. Ts'ao was indisputably an enemy of the people. And back then the cell had been brand-new, so he'd needed the cash.

That night the cell members who returned to Boulevard des Deux Républiques sounded distressed when they called. Lin had disappeared. He was supposed to be in the apartment, waiting for news from them, but by 10:00 P.M. he still wasn't back yet. Ku could feel the anger rising inside him. Of all things that could go wrong, the one that worried him most was the discipline of his crew. It was a sign of danger. Young people are capable of doing things you'd never imagined, but give them a moment to themselves and they can ruin it all. The more he thought about it, the angrier he became. That idiot French lieutenant's words came to mind.

CHAPTER 38

JUNE 29, YEAR 20 OF THE REPUBLIC.

7:35 P.M.

Someone undid the piece of rope around his mouth, and tore off the bag around his head. Even so, it took a long time before Lin could make anything out in the dark, narrow room. He had been tied to a chair, and the moldy air made his nose itch. He could tell the room was full of dust and spiderwebs even though he couldn't see them. Light filtered through a small gray rectangle in front of him, probably a louver door with both shutters closed. That was good to know. It meant he was probably in a house, and this dark room must be a storeroom, or perhaps a converted cloakroom.

He knew that some time had passed. But probably less than half a day. He had pissed just before being dragged into the car, and he needed to piss again now, but not urgently. He was in good health, and he had walked quite a way without drinking much water. He guessed that it was probably before sunset, and that he had been abducted about three hours ago.

He remembered what Park had told him about holding piss. In the absence of other information, it's a good way of keeping track of time, Park had said. Lin was testing that out right now. If the darkness and loneliness terrifies you, then say you need to piss—no one will really punish you for that. If they won't let you, they are testing your endurance. The principle is always to do the opposite of what you intuitively want to do. You have two options. If you don't want to give in, and want to keep holding it in, then you should scream at the top of your lungs. But if you can't hold it any longer and want to scream, you should just piss into your pants, because the greatest test of your ability to withstand pain is yet to come. The more you confuse your opponent, the easier things will be for you. I should scream, Lin thought. The ropes trussing him to the chair made it harder to project his voice, but he did his best. No one opened the door. There was no sound of footsteps, and he hadn't disturbed anyone. Maybe I didn't scream for long enough, he thought. Or is that proof that they want to test my endurance? He had too much self-respect to draw the conclusion that he should just piss into his pants. He stopped to breathe deeply and calm himself down.

As he was panting in the dust, the door opened, and he was dragged out along with his chair into an empty room with white walls. It was dark outside the window. They loosened the ropes and slammed him onto the floor. The cement grazed his cheeks. He was lying facedown, and someone had yanked his arms up and was pushing them forward toward his head as if they were switchblades. He felt as though his shoulder ligaments were being torn apart, and he couldn't breathe. The knobby parts of his face—his nose and lips— were scraping against the cement. He felt his rib cage being pulled taut like a bow, as if his insides were about to burst out. They let go, and then it started again. He couldn't even scream. He was sobbing, bawling, and he despised himself.

Finally, they unbound him and tore his clothes off. He was tied naked onto the chair again, but his ankles were pulled back and tied to the back legs of the chair in an odd position, forcing him to spread his legs. The spotlight in front of him shone up into his face and onto his testicles. He felt like a beaker in which humiliation and rage were two chemicals that had been made to react in predetermined proportions. He didn't even know whom to be angry at. He couldn't see anyone around him, and they all looked like shadows in the light.

Before they left, someone poured a bucket of water over him, and someone else lugged an electric fan over and pointed it at him.

He was cold. His teeth were chattering, and there was a rusty taste between them. His skin burned where the ropes were cutting into it. His bladder was distended with pain and about to explode, and the rope stretched across it cut into his skin. Before they closed the door, someone said: Want to piss? Piss on the floor.

Before long he could no longer feel the pain, and the feeling of bloatedness disappeared, replaced by a comfortable numbness. He tried to fall asleep, but as soon as he did, he was awakened by a sharp pain.

Maybe he had fallen asleep after all. As soon as the ropes were untied, he felt as though he was being pricked by a thousand needles, as though the air in the room had been compressed and was coming at him through an exceedingly fine mesh.

Someone held him down by the shoulders. Others were busy bringing tables and chairs and more lights. They didn't want to move him, he thought, they wanted to freeze him in this position. He remembered Park telling him that you have to seize any chance to move or shift positions, that change in your environment makes you more alert and helps you feel less like a slab of meat on the chopping block. But Lin simply couldn't move—in fact, there was no need to hold him down. His whole body ached, and he could barely sit up in his chair.

They began to ask him a load of useless questions. His name. Where he was from. They were asking these questions simply to make the interrogation sound official. He was still in the spotlight. Naked, he felt like a frightened, hunted animal. Eventually the pain subsided and his strength began to return. He planned to resist them as soon as he could pull himself together.

The spotlight shone at him from the left. The shadowy man sitting at a table to the right looked like the leader of the group. He listened, rarely asking questions, and smoked a cigarette that glowed red. Lin wanted to express his anger, but he didn't have the energy to put up a fight.

He refused to answer the question. Where on Ming Koo Road had he been going? Which apartment? Lin remained silent, and the man behind him punched him hard on the back of his head. Unable to contain himself any longer, Lin leaped up and rushed at the shadow, his fists clenched—

But someone reached a leg out and tripped him up, giving him a good kick in the ribs and stamping on his arms. The shadow suddenly spoke. His voice was low and gentle.

"Let go of him. Let him sit down."

"All right. You're not interested in answering this question. Let me tell you a few things we know instead. You were spotted at the scene of both the 181 Avenue Foch bombing and the Kin Lee Yuen Wharf assassination. That makes you a criminal. Someone recognized you."

That was a lie. He hadn't been on Kin Lee Yuen Wharf—he had not yet been tested and found worthy by the cell, so he had only been an observer at the time.

"I'm a student. I just graduated from Nanyang College, and I'm looking for a job."

"Don't think you can weasel your way out of this," the man said, lighting another cigarette. "Your interrogators are all specialists. Who are these people? You must be asking yourself that question. Who are my abductors? The gangs? I can tell you that you have officially been arrested. We're expert interrogators, and we can force the most stubborn suspects to talk. Even Soviet-trained Communists will talk to us, never mind you. You're just a band of ordinary crooks."

Lin was young, and easily incensed. He had been insulted. "We're not crooks! You're crooks."

He saw the face taunting him in the red glow of the cigarette, but it was too late to stop. "One day we'll overthrow your system and get rid of you all!"

"Are you telling me you're Communists?" The man returned to the darkness, but kept taunting him. "All you do is kill people and blow things up. You're a bunch of regular crooks. What you're doing is making money off terrorizing people. And you're wrong about us. We're not criminals. We represent the government. I can tell you our real name: officially, we are the Central Organization Department's Investigative Unit for Party Affairs. We often deal with real Communists, and we can make them talk too."

He was being long-winded on purpose, repeating himself over and over, as if he were casting a dizzying spell.

"You killed Ts'ao to prevent him from going to Canton. Or rather, to prevent his boss from going to Canton. His boss was an important government man who was going to set up a separate government in Canton. His treasonous plans were backed by warlords in the southwest bent on destroying our fragile, hard-won unity, our fledgling state. They even wanted control of the customs at Canton. That drove the speculators here frantic, because they had all bought public debt backed by customs receipts. So they put a price on Ts'ao's head, offering a reward to anyone who would kill him. And they found Ku Fu-kuang, your Ku—isn't that his name? See, we do know a few things."

"You're making this up! It's not true!"

"Don't get too riled up. I applaud you. We applaud passionate young people." He was provoking Lin with his smile and the way he lit a match and let it burn in his hand, gazing at it instead of lighting his cigarette.

"As for 181 Avenue Foch, that was an ordinary crime. A simple revenge killing. For a woman, a prostitute. We know the Green Gang engaged hit men to kill Mr. Ku. They were hit men just like Ku, but on the other side, just as there are always speculators who've bought a stock pitted against others who are shorting it. This time they lost. They weren't professionals, they hadn't planned their attack well, and they only managed to shoot a woman. This prostitute was Ku's woman, we've been told. His lover. His whore."

Lin pounced at the crowd of shadows. He had forgotten his shame, and forgotten that he was naked. He crashed to the ground again.

Tseng knew all about breaking down a man's defenses. That was one of his specialties. He was an ex-Communist who had been trained in Soviet interrogation and counterinterrogation techniques. He had chosen a straightforward method because he judged the subject of interrogation to be a naïve, passionate young man. He had to destroy the foundations of this man's belief, enrage him, confuse him, and make him doubt himself.

He himself was lucky he had seen the light when he did. They had made an exception for him, not because they trusted him, but because they needed him. He and his colleagues had their own snoops inside the French Concession Police, so he was aware that Lieutenant Sarly referred to him and his colleagues as the "Nanking investigators." He considered the description apt. He didn't like using torture. The human ability to withstand physical pain was limited, and torture was the fastest way to break down those defenses and force a subject to surrender and start talking. But people responded differently to pain, and if you crossed a subject's maximum threshold too quickly, then torture would cease to be effective. In fact, he had heard that in some cases it could actually gratify the victim.

Pain stimulated the production of adrenaline, the source of the fight response, which led to aggression, defiance, and hatred. If your subjects managed to stay calm, this hatred could erect mental barriers that would make it impossible to know whether they were telling the truth. They could even be clever enough to feed you false information leading to costly blunders later on.

He allowed his people to rough this young man up a little, just to tire him out. Violence could be used to warm up the subject, to stretch his nerves to their breaking point so that anything would set them off. That was his subject of expertise, and it was exactly why Nanking needed him. He was an intelligent man, and he knew what he was doing. He knew that torture was necessary, but only in moderation—torture was a performance, intended to terrify the subject as much as to cause pain.

With him and people like him around, he thought modestly, the Communists' days in Shanghai were numbered. All those anarchists and revolutionaries with their childish demonstrations and protests, holding meetings and writing articles—all that would have to go. They used to walk openly on the streets and go from their meetings to restaurants where they continued their discussions. But now that the Investigative Unit for Party Affairs had developed a deep intelligence network in Shanghai, the photographs of known Communists had been widely disseminated. Many people had memorized these faces.

Nanking was expanding the Greater Shanghai Plan. He had heard that the authorities were exploring the idea of a large-scale patriotic education movement. The investigation reports had been made available to the functionaries in charge of planning this movement. When their plan was put into action, it would make the Communists' lives even harder. Tseng was certain that Ku and his so-called People's Strength had nothing whatsoever to do with the Communists—they weren't even a fringe organization. On this point, he agreed with Cheng Yün-tuan, the secretary posted to their investigative commission by the Investigative Unit for Party Affairs. This man was supposed to be his deputy, but he was really there to keep an eye on him. Tseng had argued his case to both the French Concession Police and the Shanghai Municipal Police, but no one had believed him.

After tossing out those two grenades, he ended the interrogation abruptly. He wanted to give the young man time to think. He had his subordinates give Lin a meal.

Arresting Lin had been an unexpected piece of luck. The gangs had heard that the cell responsible for the attack on 181 Avenue Foch might have rented an apartment near Boulevard des Deux Républiques. Someone had spotted one of them on the street. He sent an undercover team to investigate the claim and found its source, a gardener at 181 Avenue Foch. On the night of the attack, he had been crouching by the wall, shitting in the shadows behind the trees. He had been so petrified he could barely move, and the faces he had seen in the half-light had made an indelible impression. One of them had come to ask him something about the casino a few days before, and he had recognized the man immediately. Later he had seen that man use a public telephone booth on Boulevard de Montigny before walking in the direction of Boulevard des Deux Républiques, but he hadn't had the guts to follow him. When the news got out, gang leaders sent their foot soldiers to sniff out the area, and they discovered more traces of Ku's cell. The errand boy at a tobacco store on Rue Buissonnet said that an unfamiliar face had started coming in to buy cigarettes, and that he would always buy half a dozen packs of several different brands at once. Someone overheard a suspicious conversation in an adjacent cubicle at Pu-chüan Bathhouse on Rue Voisin. So Tseng had some of his people take the gardener for a drive around Boulevard des Deux Républiques. As luck would have it, they actually ran into the young man, whose identification documents listed him as a student.

He was extremely interested in this case. He thought he liked this man, this Ku Fu-kuang. After comparing a number of different reports, he was convinced that this was the man's real name. People who knew him back when he was a union organizer said that he was a *chi kung* master who could punch through a door or break a brick with his bare hands. He was said to be audacious and extremely intelligent, good at making quick decisions and acting on them even in chaos. Tseng Nan-p'u picked out one incident that seemed to shed light on his character. Apparently Ku had once emptied a sack of night soil over the head of a factory foreman with ties to the Green Gang. The man lost face in front of hundreds of workers, and Ku himself became a union leader overnight. Then he had worked briefly as a guard at the Soviet consulate before gradually disappearing from public view.

There was some evidence that he had gone on to receive training at Khabarovsk. The Political Section of the British Police had acquired a photograph of a graduation ceremony from somewhere in India, and the Investigative Unit for Party Affairs got hold of a copy via an agreement to exchange intelligence. Someone looked at the photo and recognized a prisoner in the Nanking Military Court Model Prison. The man was immediately questioned, and he testified that Ku had been active in Southeast Asia as a businessman until he was caught up in the Soviet purges. As far as he knew, Ku had already been executed.

Tseng Nan-p'u couldn't tell how Ku had made it back to Shanghai, but he was certain that Ku, like him, had completely abandoned his former beliefs (or perhaps he shouldn't say that of himself, since he had never really had strong beliefs).

The door opened slowly, and Cheng came into the room with a half-eaten apple. He had been standing behind the subject during the interrogation, and had slipped out halfway through. Tseng didn't stop him. He guessed that he was phoning in a report to Nanking.

"Did you read the interrogation notes?"

"I just did. We were right—they're all in the dark about Ku."

Cheng Yün-tuan was the man posted to their group by the Investigative Unit for Party Affairs, but the two of them got on very well. That was because he, Tseng, was very open. He used to be a university professor, and he knew how to talk to young people.

"It was a heavy blow for him," Cheng said, commenting as if he were a narrator in a student play. "He's questioning his deepest beliefs. If he is disoriented, we should strike now instead of allowing him to reestablish his defenses."

"Let's wait a while longer. Give him time to weigh the evidence and have him look at a few newspapers."

"We're running out of time. Tomorrow we have to notify the French Concession Police, and the day after tomorrow we'll have to hand him over."

"We'll keep him here for now. I'd like for us to crack this case." Tseng still couldn't work out why the Concession Police kept insisting Ku's group was a Communist cell. He suspected they had their motives for refusing to believe otherwise.

"Why are they so sure that these people are Communists?" he asked softly, not because he thought Cheng would have an answer.

Cheng's apple squeaked as he bit into it. He threw it, half-eaten, into the wastepaper basket. Tseng thought wasting food like that reflected poorly on how a young man had been brought up. But maybe the bad habit made people feel comfortable around him.

"Easy," Cheng said. "It merely confirms what they have thought all along, that the fight between the Kuomintang and the Communists is the source of all trouble in the foreign concessions. Maybe Lieutenant Sarly wants to take credit for a major case, or maybe he wants the case to stay within the remit of Political Section. Maybe arresting a Communist cell will look better on his record of colonial service. Relations between France and the Soviet Union have been deteriorating. There've been trade delegations withdrawn and diplomats expelled. The Soviet Union's biggest enemy is Paris rather than London now, or so they say."

"That sounds reasonable. You could write a report on it. That's all the more reason why we shouldn't hand him over to the Concession Police. It's a conspiracy."

"An imperialist conspiracy." Cheng added an adjective that would make their imagined report sound self-evidently true to the typical Nanking politician.

"Maybe you should talk to him. You're young people, you'll get along. The truth is that he's been taken in. As long as he's willing to talk, we can speak up for him, rig things so that other people get the blame. We can teach him how to talk so that the Concession Police will dismiss him as being harmless. If he is truly willing to work for us, we may not even have to turn him over to the police. We'd send him straight to a training program instead of juvenile detention. These young socialists can be very promising. After all, if a man can't see the injustice in society at twenty, he has no heart."

Tseng wasn't worried that Cheng Yün-tuan would report him to Nanking. The Party Affairs people were all specialists in communism, from the head of the department down to the typists. You could bet their document archives in Nanking were chock full of Communist pamphlets, whereas the Central Bureau had burned most of theirs in case they were surprised by a search.

Hsueh had no idea how to clean up this mess. It was a mess that he had created, chiefly by being unable to say no and not wanting to disappoint anyone. But there were two people involved whom he really didn't want to get hurt. He couldn't even warn them of the danger they were in. He walked along the narrow path by the wall of the police headquarters, toward the stairs.

He had had lunch at Therese's apartment before leaving. He could tell that she was falling in love with him just as quickly as Leng was. Paradoxically, to make a cheeky observation, she was less focused on making love to him, and wanted to talk instead. But Hsueh was aware that he had gotten himself into this mess by talking too much. This morning, for instance, they had barely done anything. She had only allowed him to put his dick in halfway, and while she ran her fingers around the other half, she wanted him to promise to take her to his family home in Canton. He talked about the bamboo mattresses they had there, which printed lines on your face that made you wake up looking like a rice cake cut into squares. She told him about the farm she remembered: the cows, donkeys, barns full of hay, and the swamp of a pond that turned to ice for half the year.

He was lost in thought for a long time. The sun shone into his armpits and on Therese's shoulders. Hsueh didn't have a care in the world until Therese brought up the deal again, over lunch. He was forced to say that Mr. Ku was very keen. It was exactly what he wanted, and money was no object, so he would go through with the deal. All he wanted to know was whether the weapon was as powerful as advertised.

"Is it?"

Ah Kwai was in the kitchen. Therese reached her hand beneath the flowery tablecloth and into his underpants. She gripped him:

"Of course, just like you."

Therese said he wasn't acting quickly enough. Since Ku was sure he wanted the goods, they should settle on a time and place for delivery. There was no need for her to meet him. Hsueh could take care of everything, but he had to give her a clear date and order size, so that she could arrange for someone to deliver the goods.

He already knew it was a weapon called the *Schiessbecher*, manufactured by the German company Rheinmetall. But he couldn't describe it in Chinese or give it a Chinese name. He knew it was extremely dangerous, and powerful enough to penetrate the steel plates on an armored vehicle. He felt that just knowing it existed put him in danger. He intuitively thought he should hide what he knew, so he didn't tell Sarly what he had just learned and only half understood. But now he had a diagram of the weapon and an information sheet about it. He decided to give Sarly the diagram.

As he walked along the corridor toward Sarly's office, he noticed that the door to the detective squad's office was open. Inspector Maron was not in, and the poet from Marseille was sitting at a desk by the door. An idea occurred to Hsueh. He rapped on the door and opened it before the poet even answered. But he could not convince himself to ask his questions, especially now that he knew about this powerful weapon. He sat on a folding chair across from the poet for a few minutes, and decided not to ask. He would just make something up for the report he was going to write this evening under Leng's supervision and hand in to Ku the next day. After all, you could see police vehicles with rifles on their turrets everywhere. He would invent an even number of vehicles, twenty-two armored vehicles belonging to the Concession Police. He liked even numbers as long as they weren't round numbers, which looked fake.

He reached into his jacket pocket for the diagram, and gave it to Lieutenant Sarly. It made his own diagram look like the work of a drunkard, or a child's assignment scribbled at the last minute.

Lieutenant Sarly wanted to know exactly when the delivery would take place. Of course Hsueh didn't have a clue. He was just a go-between, a flighty lover given a task far beyond his abilities. He had only ended up in this mess by sheer coincidence, and Sarly was well aware of that fact.

All the vigilance and tiptoeing around sometimes got the better of him and drove him to start prattling recklessly away. It was happening again.

"Why not just arrest them on charges of conspiring to commit a crime?" Hsueh asked. "They're perfectly capable of shooting people and planting bombs. I've met this Mr. Ku, and he looks dangerous. He should be locked up. He's inciting people to give their lives to his cause, and some of them must be decent people. He should be arrested now before he does anything else. He's planning to rob a bank."

Hsueh suddenly realized he had told a terrible lie, and also revealed something he had meant to keep to himself. It was true he had met Mr. Ku. It was not true that they were planning to rob a bank.

"You've met him?" It was the true statement that first caught Lieutenant Sarly's attention. Without waiting for Hsueh to answer, he asked: "And you say he means to rob a bank?" He paused for a few seconds between the two questions, as though the information was only just sinking in.

"That's right," Hsueh continued, without letting the pause linger too long. "The weapons will be delivered soon, so he had someone contact me to fix a time and place. Of course I couldn't make that decision—I'm just the middleman. Leng sounded frightened. Things aren't going the way she'd imagined them. She said their main goal right now is to rob a bank."

"Why a bank? Since when have Communists gone in for bank robbery?"

"Oh, it's quite possible. You did say once that there were financiers among them." He should sound firm, he thought, and tried again. "It's only natural. Banks are the heart of the capitalist world, circulating the blood of the capitalist system. A bank is like a fortress."

Hsueh wondered whether he was using all that jargon correctly. Jargon is invented to name the inconceivable, to pin down something that's hard to explain. The force of the word itself makes the speaker more convincing, so that he can influence you to do what he wants you to do and think what he wants you to think.

Lieutenant Sarly didn't recognize the weapon in the diagram either. Hsueh guessed that Sarly had never even heard of it. He didn't pay much attention to the diagram: he simply glanced at it while cleaning out his pipe, and tried to smooth out a small crease on the page. Then he stuffed it into his document folder, along with all those photographs, forms, and neatly printed reports.

Hsueh had sprinkled his speech with details that might later come in useful. He did so subconsciously; he simply had a knack for mashing everything together, and he was always trying to be helpful to someone. For instance, he had mentioned that Leng was afraid. This was a reasonable thing to say, he thought, and it would come in useful some day. He thought of Sarly as his talisman, and you can make demands of your talisman. One day, he thought, he would be able to plead with Sarly to let Leng and Therese go. Hsueh was optimistic by nature. He saw them as good people caught up in complicated circumstances, like himself.

He would still be in an optimistic mood when he wrote his report for Mr. Ku that night. Influenced by Sarly's hints, Hsueh imagined that Ku was plotting something that would petrify everyone. He embellished the report, exaggerated somewhat, writing that Ku was the Political Section's most important suspect, and that nearly all their resources were devoted to investigating him. Based on his vague impressions and the dubious snippets of information floating around in his brain, he concocted a story that even he thought sounded crazy. The French Concession Police and the Shanghai Municipal Police were jointly ordering a new fleet of police vehicles from Rolls-Royce, he wrote, not only to patrol the streets, but also equipped with sufficient personnel and firepower to be rented out to private and public entities, such as banks. Then he thought of a way to incorporate his newly acquired knowledge into the report. Current models can withstand ordinary bullets, but not the newest antitank grenades projected from rifle-mounted launchers, he wrote. The new, reinforced fleet of police vehicles will rectify this vulnerability.

For a moment, he was terrified by his own imagination. He felt as though he himself was planning a violent crime, not Ku. Leng stood there holding his hand, puzzled by how much it was sweating.

Leng wished she hadn't told Ku about Hsueh and his gun-peddling woman. It had slipped out when Ku was telling her off for lying to the cell about her and Hsueh being old acquaintances. Maybe she had only told Ku about the Russian jeweler to make herself feel less guilty. But she had to admit that she was jealous. Maybe she had told Ku because it would help her find out who this woman really was. Of course, if she was an arms dealer, that could actually be useful, and Ku might decide to buy something from her.

But right now she regretted it as she clutched Hsueh's clammy hand. She could tell he was nervous, and she shouldn't have gotten him involved to begin with. She stood behind him and gazed at his curly hair, choking up with a sudden feeling of tenderness.

Taking her left foot out of her slipper, she brushed her toe up against her other ankle, leaning closer to Hsueh. The way she was standing wasn't all that sexy, but she still wished he could see her now. She tried picking the slipper up with her toes, but that made her falter.

She had to beat the other woman. That was how this game worked. She had to seduce Hsueh and become his woman, replace all those other women, in order to make him take up his part in the class struggle. That was her mission, and when she didn't know there were other women, she had been certain she would succeed. Now she was less certain.

She had tried all the sexy moves she could imagine, the ones she thought a Russian woman might know. Sometimes she would turn over in bed and crawl onto him. But as soon as she was sitting across his belly, she would realize she didn't know what to do next. That was embarrassing, just sitting there, as if she were perched on an altar surrounded by a waiting crowd. She didn't know whether to prop herself up with her hands—she didn't even know where to look. She avoided meeting his gaze, which seemed to taunt her.

It was her duty to seduce him. Everyone knew that sophisticated men like him only fell for those other women. Her only weapon was psychological, and if she couldn't keep his attention, he would soon find someone else. How else could someone like him be compelled to risk working for the cell?

He went out every day. When he was out, she always phoned Ku, receiving a constant stream of news from the cell and fresh orders. Since Hsueh's meeting with Ku, they had gone from speaking every day to speaking twice a day. That was how she kept reminding herself that this was a mission, not a love affair. Whenever he left the apartment, she would start wondering whether he was off to see that White Russian woman. That always made her upset, until she reminded herself that she had never been all that into him, that she was just using him. That made her feel better.

But when he got home at night, or sometimes in the afternoon, all her resolve would melt away. At some point they had started going for walks through the cobblestone alleys, down to Chao-chia Creek and back via a more roundabout route. On those walks, it often seemed to her that everything she thought of as mere playacting was real, and all the harsh truths that were so clear to her during the day were a sham. She felt as if she lived in two different worlds, night and day, and she was reluctant to admit that she liked the nights more.

Once they got home, they would change out of their day clothes. She didn't want to change in front of him, but he didn't seem to care. She was slowly filling up his space with her clothes, her habits of arranging things, her flowers, food, the books she fished out of his dusty piles of stuff and arranged on the bedside table. Despite not having brought anything with her, she was gradually making the place hers.

At night they talked before falling asleep, and sometimes they made love. Usually she didn't really want to, because it thrust her back into her playacting mode. But when they fell silent and she knew his mind was elsewhere, she would try to get his attention by cuddling or kissing him. That was always how they ended up having sex. Whenever he seemed either too wired or too relaxed, she would get into character and allow herself to seduce him.

Afterward, she often had the strange feeling that Hsueh enjoyed himself most when her exaggerated playacting became ridiculous. Almost as though genuine emotions and playacting were two sides of the same coin, and exaggerating her feelings would make them real.

Hsueh finished writing, folded the piece of paper up, and handed it to her. Tomorrow she would call Ku, who would have her send him the report. It should really be written in code, in chemical ink, and slipped into the pages of a book or inside an inconspicuous parcel. But Hsueh would find that all laughable. He wouldn't understand.

He got up suddenly, and grabbed her by the shoulders. "This is too dangerous! You've got to leave. You can't keep doing this."

She looked silently at him.

"You're not like them! You should leave the cell. They're full of hatred, and that's not for you. Let them do what they do."

Of course his concerns were entirely bourgeois, but she was touched that he cared about her. Maybe he was only trying to obtain information for Ku in order to help her complete her mission and whisk her away. She should really be grateful to him.

"I can't leave. I can't just walk away. This is my job—it's a calling. I'm not like you. I believe in the class struggle."

She was too flustered to know what to say, and her brain was full of abstract phrases that didn't help.

"You know I can't just leave. I'm the prime suspect in an assassination case. I'm wanted by the police."

She was trying to put it in a way he would understand, without realizing that she had already conceded ground.

"I'll come up with something. I can talk to my friends in the Concession Police. I have a good friend in the Political Section, a very senior French officer. We'll find a way to get you out of this crowd."

"It wouldn't work. You couldn't do it. Even your friend couldn't." She could tell she had lost the argument. She should have been talking to him about the evils of imperialism, about class struggle. She was supposed to say that the very idea of running away repulsed her, and she certainly didn't need the help or faux sympathy of a couple of imperialist policemen. But she didn't want to go on about something Hsueh wouldn't understand. Hadn't she spent all this time trying to learn how his mind worked, so she could explain things in a way that would make sense to him?

"Of course it can be done. If that's what you want. We could leave Shanghai together." Hsueh cut himself off abruptly, because he realized he had lied about being able to just pick up and leave. But Leng didn't know that. She had momentarily been tempted by his offer, and she despised herself for it. She thought back to the choice she had made in prison.

She was angry with herself and trying to make up for it by yelling at him.

"Get lost! Don't you try to tempt me! Don't mock me. I'm not in love with you. I'm using you, don't you see?"

She enjoyed seeing the startled look in his eyes. She knew she could conquer him. Oh, she liked knowing that her words hurt him. She went on and on.

She hurled herself at him and started punching him (the hurling was largely imaginary, since they were standing only inches apart). She wanted to slap his face, but they were standing too near each other and he had his arm around her waist, so all she could do was slap him on the back.

He started kissing her, and she realized that her anger was melting away. That's the end of it, she thought, he wants me in bed. She despised herself for not even resisting him.

Ku's greatest worry was that the cell was losing focus. He could tell it was happening. Three days had passed since Lin disappeared. At first Ku thought he might have been arrested, but Leng told him that Lin wasn't being held by the police. He asked about the gangs, and heard nothing. He posted lookouts near the safe house on Boulevard des Deux Républiques, but there were no arrests, nothing out of the ordinary. He began to think that Lin might simply have left of his own accord. He told no one else about this suspicion. To the cell he maintained that Lin had been arrested.

If one member of the cell was arrested, they usually assumed that all the locations that person knew about had been exposed. Lin was the leader of his unit, and he knew about all the safe houses. The unit asked Ku whether they should evacuate the apartment on Boulevard des Deux Républiques, but with another operation imminent, they couldn't afford the time. He told them Lin was being held by the Concession Police, and that he was being very brave and he hadn't said a word, so the apartment was still safe. But he did station a few more guards around the candle store on Rue Palikao.

Lin's dropping out was the worst thing that could have happened, and Ku was always expecting the worst—it helped him to make good decisions quickly in times of danger. Leng's lie had also shaken him. On the deepest level of the cell's workings, in terms of maintaining its focus and planning its next attack, he was alone and no one could help him. When loneliness engulfed him, turning to the concrete details of the next operation usually made him feel better. But he used to deal with despair and lethargy by visiting Ch'i.

He had been left without a woman when she died, and he was not about to get himself another. When he had Ch'i, he had always reminded himself that the woman was his weakness, his vulnerability, but he had found it hard to stop thinking about her. Even now, he found it hard to take his mind off her. How could he? He used to say self-deprecatingly that a woman would be his downfall, but now the words just made him sad.

He could not even remember what Ch'i looked like. He knew she had a round face with long bangs that parted in the center and covered her eyes, a face the shape of a melon seed or an egg. But try as he might, he couldn't picture her eyes or eyebrows or mouth or nose.

Perhaps because of his memory of her death, when he thought of her late at night, it was always her ass that came to mind. If he was happy, he pictured it smiling, and if he was sad, he pictured it crying. The most beautiful part of Ch'i's body was her ass. He imagined it as being larger than life, able to protect him from actual and metaphorical bullets, from his own successes and failures.

Wearing a gray woolen suit, off-white pants with the cuffs turned up, and a dark gray velvet hat, Ku turned the corner from the Bund onto Nanking Road, dressed like a respectable banker who was squinting in the sunlight because he had just come out of an office. He looked as if he was strolling aimlessly about, but he was actually scrutinizing the buildings with a city planner's eye for detail, mentally calculating distances and travel times, and noting where the police were posted: at traffic posts twice a man's height at the crossroads, at guard posts on either side of important buildings, and at the barricades between districts. He also took note of their uniforms and whether they were armed.

He walked past plenty of banks, moneychangers, and bond issuers. He didn't like the look of the foreign banks along the Bund, which were all heavily guarded and housed in buildings too big to properly control. But too small a target wouldn't do either. His wrestling classes in Khabarovsk had taught him that you have to hit your opponent where it hurts. That way you're in control and he's too busy defending himself to go on the offensive.

Perhaps a medium-size bank on the border between the two concessions would be best. He was walking along Yuyaching Road, which was full of people all day long, especially near the Race Course. A few men sat on benches under the trees reading the racing paper. One of them flipped through the whole paper, screwed up his face in thought, and started tapping the edge of the newspaper with a pencil sharpened on both ends to calm himself down. Walking south along the wall of the Race Course, he could hear the crowds clamoring in the grandstands. This is utter madness, he thought. But then he had his own form of insanity, and he was playing for far higher stakes than they were.

Of course, there was nothing special about that. Everyone in Shanghai was always betting on something. One of these days I'll lose everything—but not this time, he thought. Wondering when he would lose gave him a rush of excitement. He realized it was an insane gamble, but then he had been driven insane when the Soviets locked him in the pitch-black room where the Purge Commission imprisoned its victims. Not that he knew that at the time; all he remembered was an oak door as thick as a cliff face. He was lucky they hadn't just taken him out and shot him, probably only because he was a foreigner. And he was twice lucky that they had sent him to a gulag in Azerbaijan, where his insanity turned out to be useful—it allowed him to escape.

To win big, you have to be insane. A madman is terrifying, an insane gambler more so, but if an insane gambler judges risks accurately and thinks clearly, he can terrorize everyone. Power comes from terror, which means, conversely, that terror can alter the present power structure and force existing powers to give up part of their territory. Being weak and complacent, they would rather appease a terrifying new power than risk losing what they already have. Oh yes, they would beg for mercy. They would buy him off.

The Race Club would one day offer to buy him off, as the Green

Gang had. But he wasn't so easily bought. He wanted more than just money. That was what made him different from all those people, and why he thought of himself as a different kind of revolutionary.

He cut across the road and stopped in front of I-pin-hsiang Hotel. Department stores and silk stores lined one side of the street. He went past Sheng-t'ai Dance Hall and the Great World Arcade. He turned from Boulevard de Montigny onto Rue du Consulat, and thought about how much he preferred the Concession to the International Settlement. In the Concession, the streets went every which way, traffic was chaotic, and the crowds sometimes took over half the street. He tried to work out a route that would allow him to speed through the tangle and out of the concessions' jurisdiction. Standing at the entrance to Hsieh-ta-hsiang Silk Store, he found himself looking at the banks on Rue du Weikwé, which were neither too small nor too big. Just what he wanted. It was true that banks are the heart of the capitalist system, but that was why they were always heavily guarded. He imagined himself watching that heart beat inside a rib cage.

He stopped by the butcher's, drawing back its cotton curtains to go inside, and had the shop assistant weigh out a pound of meat for him. Although he had called a meeting of the unit leaders, he didn't want to go back to the candle store just yet. First, he had to find somewhere quiet to think. As he was going into An-le Bathhouse, he decided that Rue du Weikwé wouldn't be a good spot either. It was too near Rue Palikao, and the street was too short. To think that after going all that way, he had realized the bank opposite the candle store was their best bet, he thought ruefully.

As he relaxed into the hot bathwater, sweat and dirty water ran down his head and face. He inhaled the steam, which made him feel faint. Gray bodies floated along like ghosts. Someone stepped on his toe underwater but it didn't hurt. An arm's length in front of him, he could see a dark mass of testicles bobbing near the surface of the water, surrounded by filth the way dirt might collect around a floating corpse on the river. Suddenly, he felt a glimmer of unease, like a flicker in one of the dim lightbulbs on the domed ceiling.

Whenever he felt a chill in his bones like this, he knew it was a sign of danger. It was the same thing he had felt that day on the way to Ch'i's. He could feel it even now, as he lay soaking in hot water, but he didn't know why.

He relaxed and leaned back against the porcelain walls, letting the steaming water come up to his neck. It's just your nerves, he told himself, forcing himself to focus on something positive instead. The best thing he had going for him was that new grenade launcher they were going to buy. In his military technology class in Khabarovsk, he had had to learn about all kinds of weapons, even the ones being developed in Red Army factories, and he had recognized the diagram as soon as he saw it. These grenade launchers would be invaluable to the imminent battle against imperialism. No matter what husk of a vehicle the imperialists were hiding in, the grenade would penetrate it like a poisoned dart and explode in its heart.

He had already instructed Hsueh to have that White Russian woman deliver the goods. Money was no object. He needed to come up with something new, turn a one-man grenade launcher designed for defensive use against armored vehicles into a powerful weapon of urban guerilla warfare. Next he had to figure out how to train his people to use the new launcher. The best thing to do would be to hire boats and sail out to Wu-sung-k'ou. A few of the Pu-tung unit knew how to sail a boat, and others were familiar with the treacherous waterways of the Yangtze. He would also have to hire a car with an eight-cylinder engine that could outrace the police cars.

CHAPTER 43

JULY 12, YEAR 20 OF THE REPUBLIC.

1:35 P.M.

It was already July. The air near the ground appeared to ripple in the heat. There were people playing tennis on the lawn outside on the terrace, straining to swing their rackets in the scorching sun. Lieutenant Sarly had the driver stop directly in front of the door. The pillars in the corridor looked grainier than usual, as though the last drops of sweat had been wrung from them, leaving a knobby bark.

The glass doors were like lines of latitude separating two climate zones. Indoors it was quiet and cool. The Chinese servants wore long-sleeved livery. Sarly went through the golden vestibule, where dozens of naked women cast bashful sidelong glances at him, the mons pubis swelling above their smooth white thighs. He reflected that French people only kept sculptures in order to perpetuate other people's stereotypes of the French.

His hands brushed against the carved brass railings as he went up the stairs. The crimson rose patterns of the porcelain flooring were smooth as glass, and the doors to all the halls were open. A servant sprawled on the floor, rubbing it vigorously, his knees knocking against the pomelo wood flooring mounted on springs. Another servant stood on a ladder, carefully scrubbing the golden mosaic walls as if the tiles were gemstones. If he had the time, he would have breathed on each tile before scrubbing it, so that impurities in the bucket of water he was carrying would not damage it. The day after next was Bastille Day, or the Fête Nationale, and the French Club would be hosting a large ball.

The corridor echoed with the sound of bowling balls rumbling down their lanes. The men had congregated on the balcony of the bar. A bunch of tuberoses nodded sleepily in a vase, and cigar smoke dissolved in the breeze. He sat on a chair beneath the Ionic columns.

"I heard the two companies arriving from Haiphong get in tomorrow?" That was the younger M. Madier of Madier Frères. The elder M. Madier, his brother, had founded a company in Paris to import the raw silk that his brother sourced in inland China and shipped to Lyon. The two brothers had been running their business for nearly fifteen years. They were among Shanghai's most prominent businessmen.

"That's right, they'll be just in time for the review of troops on Bastille Day!" Colonel Bichat roared. The heat appeared to have no effect on him.

It was too early for dinner. The English, Americans, French, and Japanese were all well represented in the select inner circle that had invited Sarly to this weekend banquet, but as a result of the Great War, Germans were never invited. Baron Pidol was new to the group and now very much sought after. He had made a few risky bets that had paid off extremely well, and his eye for deals had quickly earned him the respect of the China veterans.

Lieutenant Sarly knew that all these men cared about was money. When they said they wanted to protect the concessions, what they meant was that they wanted to protect their own privilege. They despised newcomers and thought of themselves as the only true heirs of nineteenth-century imperialist explorers, who would survive in tiny foreign concessions that remained lone bastions of capitalism even if the capitalist world order was swept away. To preserve their territory, they were even willing to countenance a Japanese attack, especially if Nanking insisted on stationing the Nineteenth Route Army in Shanghai. Lieutenant Sarly considered that a suicidal idea.

Although they had little in common, he was now on their side.

These men had their eyes on the next deal, whereas he had the long game in mind.

The scheme they were going to discuss had been dreamed up by a bunch of American real estate speculators. The Americans were just as vulgar and ingenious as everyone made them out to be. When they landed in Shanghai bearing vast sums of money, the best land had already been bought up, and its owners were sitting tight. They had even formed a cartel, making it impossible for a newcomer to find so much as a corner to plant a stake in the ground. When one of them went bankrupt, or died, another would hold priority rights to purchase the land at a price worked out in advance in the cigar room.

So the Americans had no choice but to buy up land on the outskirts of Shanghai. The biggest bets had been made by the Raven Group, a company registered in the International Settlement, which was buying up tracts of barren land along the Yangtze, as though Shanghai would become a second Alaska. But after they had bought and paid for it all, the Americans found that things were more complicated than they had realized. Shanghai was governed by rules of its own. Powerful interests controlled the Board of Works and the Municipal Office, which in turn controlled urban planning in the two concessions. That meant the Americans' land would remain barren for the next hundred years. To add insult to injury, Nanking's Greater Shanghai Plan would encourage development in the northeast of the city.

In desperation, the Americans hatched an interventionist scheme to turn Shanghai into a Free City like Danzig after the Great War, and started hawking their idea to the foreign governments with interests in Shanghai. Danzig had originally been Napoleon's brainchild, a semi-independent state that would be a haven for capitalist gambling, like a medieval city-state. Carving out a free Shanghai independent of the Kuomintang government would allow capital to stream into the city from all over the world and boost the value of even the most barren land. A proposal was drawn up for the League of Nations in Geneva, and the papers began to crackle with the news.

Even veteran Shanghailanders found this a most interesting suggestion. The shrewder among them started inviting the once-despised Americans to discuss the idea over dinner. They soon formed a little lobby consisting of bank executives, politicians, journalists, legal consultants, and professional lobbyists who haunted the capitals of powerful nations. The most preposterous version of the idea was for the boundaries of the Free City to include a fifty-kilometer strip of land on both banks of the Yangtze, stretching from Shanghai to Wuhan, providing a neutral buffer that would protect China from being split by battling warlords, or so they argued. Shanghai would prosper, the Yangtze River Delta would export its wares to the world, and Shanghailanders would get rich all over again.

But Sarly looked at this scheme and saw the germ of an unlikely opportunity for Shanghai to save the world from communism, just as the Comintern was planning to attack it as the weakest link in the capitalist chain. These people had overlooked the strongest reason in favor of their proposal: as a Free City, Shanghai would attract international attention and protection, making it harder for the Communists to gain a foothold, and safeguarding French and European interests in the concessions.

Ku and his band of urban terrorists would be the spark, he thought. Ku's attack would bring Paris and those dim European politicians to their senses, warning them of the dangers of Communist violence. Sarly could easily have had Ku's whole gang arrested, and he was only letting them continue to operate because he wanted them to commit a real crime. He had few qualms about his plan—it was a small price to pay for a Free City. Sometimes it seemed crazy to him, but then the times themselves were crazy. The volcano was about to erupt.

Someone screamed on the lawn. The woman playing tennis had been trying to hit a volley when the ball had knocked the racket right out of her hand. She seemed to have torn her deltoid, and she was sitting on the ground and massaging her shoulder while her racket lay several feet away. Her legs were sweating, and bits of grass were stuck onto her knee. Sarly recognized her. She was the American author who was said to be living with a Chinese poet, a monkey, and a parrot.

Only then did Lieutenant Sarly notice the man on the other side of the court, who was walking toward the net. It was Mr. Blair of the British Foreign Service. "I hear he's going to be posted back to London soon," said an American businessman Sarly didn't know well.

Commander Martin looked embarrassed. He stole a glance at Baron Pidol, who preserved a dignified silence. Mr. Blair had voluntarily withdrawn from this inner circle when he realized that his tryst with Baroness Pidol had aroused public disapproval. Affairs were tolerated, and most of the men in the Concession would turn a blind eye to one. But having an affair that made the papers might be interpreted as a challenge to the authority of old Shanghailanders. Then the woman killed herself, and Blair had lost the sympathy of the foreign women as well.

"No one but this author will talk to him now," the younger M. Madier said. "She's like a Chinese moth. She gets hot every time she sees a fire, and she flutters with excitement in the face of danger."

"All she wants is to put him in one of her stories," the American businessman explained. He clearly knew her work well. "Maybe he'll end up in *The New Yorker*, which could be his new claim to fame."

Baron Pidol tried to steer them all back to the matter at hand. "Just sending more troops to Shanghai from Haiphong won't do the trick. The Ministry of Foreign Affairs in Paris must send an official memorandum to Nanking as soon as it possibly can."

"The best thing would be for Western governments to jointly send a diplomatic note to Nanking." Colonel Bichat sounded impatient, as if he thought his Shanghai Volunteer Corps had a chance of becoming an independent Ministry of Defense.

Lin was wondering why the man who claimed to be from the Investigative Unit for Party Affairs had not been in to interrogate him for three days in a row. He wondered whether this signaled a victory on his part. Had the enemy decided on a change of tactics because he was refusing to cooperate?

They were certainly treating him better. He was allowed to wear clothes and no longer tied up, but they still kept him locked up in that dark storeroom. A man who said his name was Cheng often came to talk to him. He always brought a whole bunch of newspapers like *Shun Pao* or *Ta Kung Pao*, and pointed specific articles out to Lin. Lin didn't believe their irritating claims about the whole chain of events. They thought they could dupe him.

But why was he even listening to the enemy's lies? He knew they always found ways to slander revolutionaries. Nonetheless, he couldn't help leafing through the articles, which was exactly what they were counting on. Even if it was true that Ts'ao's death had swung the price of public debt, then it only proved their cell had chosen their target well, that they had really delivered a shock to the capitalist system. He didn't believe the shooting on Rue Eugène Bard had anything to do with Ku. Ku would never get involved with a prostitute. And he certainly didn't believe that Ku had accepted a reward for Ts'ao's assassination. If speculators had profited from Ts'ao's death, well then that was a coincidence.

They could enjoy their money while they were allowed to keep it, because it wouldn't be long.

It was hot during the day, especially in that stuffy little room. The dust and cobwebs kept making him sneeze. This is the end for me, he thought. Even if he refused to confess, the casino bombing alone would be reason enough for the courts of the French Concession to sentence him to death. Things wouldn't be any different if they handed him over to Nanking as a Communist. But he was not afraid of death. His only fear was that the enemy would paint him as a terrorist. They could blacken his name by forging documents and testimonies that portrayed their cell as a bunch of criminals. He could already see signs of it, which worried him. He had to come up with a way to foil their schemes.

He was eventually summoned from the storeroom on a sunny day. The furniture had been reshuffled since his first interrogation. The spotlights were gone, and the table had been replaced with a square table placed next to the chair he had sat on. The electric fan was still there, in the corner next to the window, and it had been switched on.

The man called Cheng had someone bring Lin a cup of tea. Tea leaves swirled in the glass. The other operatives had left the room. As he sat down, Lin held his cup up so that he was looking at Cheng through the glass filled with amber-colored tea. He might be powerless, but he wouldn't stop trying to irritate his enemy.

The door was locked and bolted. The windows were closed and the curtains drawn.

"Comrade Lin, let's talk some theory," said Cheng with a smile.

"We aren't comrades, not since you betrayed the Revolution in the spring of Year 16 of the Republic. You've been pandering to imperialists and capitalists, and we'll fight you to the death." Lin tried to keep his voice steady.

"Believe me, one of these days we'll be comrades." Cheng's voice sounded fuzzy, like the steam rising from his teacup. "When you finally know the truth."

He coughed lightly, as if his cough was a punctuation mark sig-

naling a new tone of voice. "When I was young, I was leftist like
you. But I knew much more about the Communists than you do."

"Knowing isn't believing. You didn't know anything anyway."

"Believing won't make you a revolutionary. You've got to be
sharp. You've been misled, but you're young, and we want you back
on the right path."

Lin snorted through his teeth. He didn't need to talk theory with
a Nanking operative who had a few half-baked theories about the
Party. And he did not want to be infected by their poisonous ideas.

"Have you been reading the newspapers I gave you?"

Lin decided not to answer. The poison could affect him
subconsciously.

"We know all about your boss, Mr. Ku. We know much more
than you know or can even imagine. We know his entire life
story. He was born at Mud Crossing in Pu-tung. As a young man,
he worked at the China Import and Export Lumber Company and
joined one of the gangs active on the pier. I know you don't believe
he was involved with the prostitute shot in her apartment on Rue
Eugène Bard, but there's proof."

He drew two photographs from his shirt pocket and put them on
the table. He pushed them toward Lin's teacup with his fingertips.
Both photos were blurred, but one seemed to be of a document written with a brush pen on red-lined square paper, while the other was
a printed form filled out with a fountain pen.

He pointed to the one on the left. "This is a guarantor letter
for two second-floor rooms rented on the western wing of a *shih-
k'u-men* house on Rue Eugène Bard. The landlord has asked his
new tenant to sign 'Ch'i' next to her real name, because Ch'i is
what everyone calls her. He doesn't know her occupation, and he
wants a guarantor because he suspects she may be a prostitute. A
candle store's official chop has been stamped beneath the guarantor's signature. We went looking for that elusive candle store, but
it had already moved away, and no one seemed to know where it
was. The guarantor signed his name, which you may or may not
know. But at least you'll know the man's surname: his name is Ku

T'ing-lung. The photographer focused on the name, so you'll see it quite clearly."

He picked up the second photo. "This is the letter of consent for a surgical procedure performed at Nien-tz'u Gynecological Hospital on the corner of Rue Hennequin and Rue Oriou. It's a small private hospital occupying a single *shih-k'u-men* house, not far from Rue Eugène Bard. The only surgeon is Dr. Ch'en Hsiao-ts'un, a doctor trained in Japan, where he may have had his name changed. The patient was in critical condition following a miscarriage. Ku T'ing-lung's name appears again, under 'nearest of kin.'"

Lin could feel the anger rushing to his throat like lava. He wanted to throw up. Instead he picked up his teacup and smashed it on the ground. He could hear footsteps, and a key turning in the lock. The door wouldn't open and was thick enough to be almost soundproof. Someone was battering at the door and shouting unintelligibly.

Lin planted his hands on the table and stared at Cheng, who stared back. Then Cheng turned and shouted in the direction of the door: "There's no need to come in, there's nothing to worry about. Comrade Lin just got a little worked up."

The battering stopped. There was a silence, and then the foot-steps went away.

"Don't get all riled up. If you'd rather talk about something else, we can do that."

He produced something else from his shirt pocket, like a magician.

"What we have here is a copy of the manifesto for your so-called cell, People's Strength," he said, opening the mimeographed pam-phlet and beginning to read. At first he read in a monotone voice, as if he were reading a grocery list or a bad student play. But then his face darkened. Before he had finished reading, he tossed the pam-phlet on the table as if it were toxic to the touch.

"Tell me what you think of this. What did your boss, that Ku Fu-kuang, tell you? That this is the latest Communist communiqué?"

"That we will learn from your massacre of the revolutionaries, and repay an eye for an eye."

He looked at him coldly, and clapped his hands to his pockets, but he didn't have any cigarettes on him. He didn't smoke.

"A real Communist would never write something like this!" Cheng sounded angry, maybe because he thought he had a better chance of convincing Lin that way.

"Ku made this up! It's garbage. In fact, he didn't make it up—he plagiarized it. You joined the Party during the May Thirtieth Movement, right? During the student strikes? Young man, you need to learn some theory. Every Communist should apply himself to socialist theory. This is all plagiarized garbage, the work of a Russian anarchist! Marx rejected anarchism for treating revolution as nothing more than individual political theater, a game of violence. Let me tell you about the author of this manifesto. His name was Sergei Nechayev, and he was a consummate liar who started an organization aimed at terrorizing people. Your Ku is like that—he's a fear-monger!"

The man's voice softened. He curled the corners of his lips into a smile. "Here's a story that might give you a sense of who this Ku Fu-kuang is. Nechayev was a nobody until he came up with the idea of mailing an anonymous letter to a woman he knew. In the letter, a fellow student claimed that he had gone out for a stroll when he saw someone toss a note out of a police carriage. Apparently this was a note from Nechayev, exhorting his classmates to carry on with the revolution, as he was about to be killed. Then he ran off to Switzerland, where he told everyone that he had escaped police custody in St. Petersburg, posing as a hero! That's how men like Ku Fu-kuang scam their comrades and seize power."

The electric fan whirred straight at Lin, drying the sweat on his body. His shirt was unspeakably dirty, and he was shivering inwardly.

CHAPTER 45

They crossed the river on the last ferry of the day, which left T'ung-jen Pier at 5:00 P.M. Hsueh was dressed as a Shanghailander going to Pu-tung to hunt rabbits and weasels for the weekend, wearing a white canvas suit tapered at the waist with a slit at the back. In a trunk under the backseat of the car, they had a single-shot hunting rifle and a picnic basket. Park was dressed similarly, in black. Hsueh didn't recognize the other two men, but Park introduced one of them as Ch'in.

They drove east along the main road that wound along the river, past the piers, and stopped for a break in an empty lot between warehouses belonging to British American Tobacco and the Japanese firm Iwasaki. It was almost sunset. Beyond the warehouse fences and the shipyards, the river shimmered. A Japanese warship was moored at the shipyard awaiting repairs, while its officers were off-duty and had gone ashore. Two men were wrestling on deck while a small crowd hooted and cheered, their cries echoing along the deserted river.

They left the main road at Mitsui Pier, turned onto a dirt road, and took some time crossing a narrow stone bridge. Hsueh got off and beckoned to Park from the other side of the bridge, carefully directing him while the wheels of the car hung partly off the narrow bridge. When they had crossed the bridge, they stopped for some food.

By then it was dark. The rapeseed fields had long since flowered and ripened into pods, but after a long day of sunshine, the soil oozed a residual fragrance of rapeseed flowers. After they had driven past a small copse, the dirt road vanished. The headlights shone into the Pu-tung wasteland ahead of them, and they finally realized that the clumps of soil they could see were actually gravestones. The night was cloudless and patterned with stars; lights flickered eerily in the trees. Hsueh felt as if his heart were being sucked out of his chest with a pump.

An hour later, they drove back onto the main road before turning into a small village just off Min-sheng Road. Ch'in's cousin was a boatman who sailed a fifty-ton cargo boat to villages along Soochow Creek for the Yü clan, a prominent local family, and they had arranged to meet him here. A few years ago, when the Yü clan had had difficulty covering their expenses with land rent, Ch'in's cousin had set up a warehouse to buy hog hair and cattle bones, which he sold on to foreign firms.

It was the Yü clan boat they wanted.

They went into a yard that stank. The boatman stood in dim electric light outside a hut, waiting for them. They all sat around a small table, and Ch'in drank distilled liquor with the boatman. Park picked up the peanut shells littering the table and crushed them one by one between his fingertips. The constant croaking of frogs began to irk them. The mud was plastered with rotting hog hair that bubbled when you stepped on it, which felt like squelching a corpse.

After midnight, when they were finally taken to the boat, Hsueh walked unsteadily onto the pallet, as if he were in a nightmare.

The cargo boat sailed along Yang-ching Creek to the Whampoa. Frogs kept croaking on the banks. All the men were smoking, but the boat stank despite the breeze. Hsueh was sweating, and he couldn't hide how nervous he was. The river made an oily gurgle in the moonlight.

The land along the banks where the Yang-ching flowed into the Whampoa belonged to Alfred Holt and Co., the shipping company that ran the Blue Funnel Line. The goods Hsueh and his companions wanted were on an eight-thousand-ton English cargo ship moored at a floating dock at the confluence of the rivers. The Blue Funnel Line's ships ran almost every day from Hong Kong's Swire Pier, beneath Signal Hill in Tsim Sha Tsui, to Shanghai. The passenger liners Hsueh usually took from Hong Kong to Shanghai set sail from that pier too.

Over years, Therese had built up a transport network involving the seamen on cargo ships. They were always short of money and usually willing to smuggle something onboard for a few extra bucks. Even though the Customs House was just across the river from the Blue Funnel Line's piers, she never had any trouble slipping her contraband through.

As their small cargo boat drew noiselessly nearer to the larger ship, Hsueh broke out in a cold sweat. His hands trembled, and he could feel the sweat in his clammy armpits. "The signal!" Park hissed at him from the helm.

Hsueh started, and his flashlight nearly fell into the water. It wouldn't switch on, so he pushed the button again, signaling toward the port-side stern of the ship, and waiting for the White Russian seaman to return the signal when he saw it. The huge cargo ship blocked out the sky, leaving only a sliver of starlight that outlined its silhouette.

It was quiet. Waves sloshed against the pier, and the odd seagull squawked. Except for a couple of dim lights among the rows of warehouses a hundred yards away, the riverbanks were pitch-black. There were no dockworkers or guards on patrol.

There were no policemen. The previous day, Hsueh had given Sarly the location of the pier and the name of the boat. Then, before setting out that afternoon, he had gone out on the pretext of buying cigarettes to call Sarly from a corner store and tell him the method of delivery. He realized he was putting both Therese and Leng in danger, but he didn't dare to lie. There was no time to think of all that—too much going on. We're taking this one step at a time, he told himself.

A light sparkled on the railing. He sent another inquiry signal, and the light answered. Then it was dark again. Several minutes later, two heavy packages were lowered onto the deck of the boat, shuddering as they descended.

The packages hovered briefly above the helm before thudding onto the deck. Park and the other two went up to untie the ropes and hoist the packages into the hold.

Two more packages followed.

They started the engine. It hummed gently, making eddies that were visible for several yards along the surface of the water. Hsueh glanced toward the shore again. Nothing stirred.

He couldn't imagine why Lieutenant Sarly hadn't acted on his tip. Again he was overcome by gratitude. Sarly must not have wanted to blow Hsueh's cover. When he was flashing the signal just now, Hsueh had flattened himself against the cabin doors and only leaned out slightly, aware that he could be hit by a stray bullet if the police attacked from land. But no bullets came—Sarly must have wanted him to be safe.

He hadn't been able to tell Sarly much. All he knew was that the delivery would take place on the river. He had no access to Ku's plans, and he didn't even know when they would reach Blue Funnel Pier. The Concession Police would barely have had the time to round up enough boats to make an arrest. On the other end of the line, Sarly said nothing for a long while, for so long that Hsueh began to imagine that Park was standing behind him and staring straight at him, that he had been discovered by Ku's people, and would be gunned down as soon as he stepped out of the corner store.

Eventually, Sarly said: be careful. He didn't tell Hsueh what he was planning, and he didn't ask him to drag the meeting out or to disrupt it in any way. So he must have decided right then not to take action.

Hsueh attributed this to Lieutenant Sarly's extraordinary friendship with his father. Sarly genuinely trusted him. He must be waiting for intelligence that would allow him to make the arrests when it was safer. For a moment, Hsueh's gratitude to Sarly exceeded his affection for Therese and even for Leng.

But the hours of mental strain, physical exertion, sweating and stinking had left him exhausted. By the time he got into the Peugeot, all Hsueh's muscles felt pleasantly numb. In the morning, he would go to the police headquarters as soon as he had taken leave of Ku's gang. But first, to repay Sarly's trust, he would find out where the goods were stashed.

Right now, they were under the backseat in the car, still in their packages. As he was carrying them, he had thought he could feel a metallic coolness beneath the tarp and the wax paper. The packages reeked of engine oil, so Park collected bits of cloth from all over the hut, and wrapped the packages in scraps that stank of rotting flesh.

The horizon at Wu-sung-k'ou was growing bright when they left the Yü clan village, and the car sped through the deserted countryside. They rolled down the windows, but the stench of cattle carcasses seemed to have been infused into the leather seats. They were all sweating profusely and extremely tired. Only the Korean, who was driving, still appeared to be brimming with energy.

They couldn't cross the river yet. The first ferry wasn't until seven. They parked by a grove of trees and laid out the food in their picnic basket. Hsueh had no appetite. He grabbed a bottle of soda and tipped it into his mouth.

Park had wrapped his hands around a slender tree and was yanking it upward, to relieve his tense shoulder muscles. He turned to ask Hsueh: "Where are you going after we cross the river? Would you like a lift in the car?"

Hsueh had a check for seven thousand yuan in his pocket. That was Therese's money, and he had to get it to her. That was the sort of man he was. If you didn't trust him, he would string you along for as long as possible, but as soon as you decided to trust him, he would become loyal to you and scrupulously honest. The previous afternoon, Therese had told him that she didn't want her bodyguards involved in this deal; she wanted Hsueh to take charge of the whole process, payment included. Hsueh was moved, just as he had been moved by Lieutenant Sarly's trust. But when he was terrified that night—looking out the window into a cemetery, for instance—he had daydreamed about running away. He couldn't help thinking that seven thousand yuan would allow him to go anywhere he wanted with Leng.

"I have to deliver this money to someone." Hsueh was not afraid of the man in front of him, even though he knew these people to be capable of shooting someone dead on the street. But he felt like an actor playing a possibly fatal role for which he was not yet prepared. Was this a trap? Didn't stories of double-crossing gangsters appear every day in the Concession newspapers? He was exhausted, and probably imagining things.

Therese was standing naked in front of her dressing table mirror, trying on a plaited chain belt. A revolver-shaped pendant dangled from it, brushing against her pubic hair. She plucked out a few hairs with a tweezer, making her hair a neat triangle. She had recently started caring more about how she looked.

She got dressed and came out of her room. Ah Kwai was still at the vegetable market. Just as she was about to leave and meet Hsueh at the Astor, the phone rang.

The caller was silent for a long while. Therese could hear nothing but crackling and the sound of someone breathing.

"How may I help you?" she asked impatiently.

Silence.

"Who is speaking?" she asked in Shanghainese instead.

"I am Hsueh's friend." Therese listened. The woman's voice sputtered, but Therese couldn't tell whether it was because the caller was hesitating or whether there was static on the line. The only word she could make out was the word *danger*.

Then the caller repeated herself, in short bursts punctuated by long silences, still speaking softly: "Don't go to see Hsueh. They want you dead. You're in danger."

"I don't know what you mean."

"I found a phone number on the back of a photograph in his pocket and knew it had to be yours." Therese picked up on one solid fact in this confused speech. She knew exactly which photo the woman was talking about.

"Who are you?" she repeated.

"A friend of Hsueh's," said the woman in a firmer voice.

"And why would they kill me?" It seemed like an odd question to ask, she thought. She might as well be a stranger wondering: Why would anyone want to kill Therese Irxmayer?

"Now that the deal's done, you know too much, don't you see? They don't have the manpower to kidnap you and hold you somewhere." That was a bizarre rationale. It made her sound like a plate of leftovers. Save it for tomorrow? Don't bother, it'll be too much trouble.

"But what about Hsueh? Will he be all right? Why don't you tell him?"

"I don't know where he is, but you know he went to pick up the goods. He'll come to meet you. They'll keep him alive because he can still be useful to them." The voice was cut off abruptly, and there was more static. Before long, the caller hung up gently.

Therese slid down the wall and knelt at the entrance to the living room. The ceramic flooring felt cold on her knees. About fifteen meters of telephone wires curled beside her bare feet. Thinking quickly, she realized she would have to rescue Hsueh. He was probably already on the way to the Astor, and she would barely get there in time. She picked up the phone and rang the jewelry store.

Then she left in a hurry, dashing out of the lobby, crossing Avenue Joffre without even looking both ways.

The Cossacks were ready and waiting in the jewelry store, and the Ford was parked round the back.

They drove north. On Mohawk Road they were held up by a pack of racehorses coming out of the stables, but then the car sped up again. They drove east along the southern bank of Soochow Creek. Therese was riding shotgun. She slipped her hand into her handbag to retrieve a cigarette and quietly chamber a round. The Cossacks already had their guns loaded.

She lit the cigarette and stopped to think. Who was that woman who seemed to know everything? Was she one of Ku's people? She

had never asked Hsueh about his boss or the gang. The French
Concession was swarming with gangs, and she couldn't count the
number of criminal organizations to which she had sold guns.

The car was held up again on Garden Bridge. Three empty
Japanese military trucks rattled along the bridge, forcing the southbound cars and rickshaws into the northbound lane, and blocking off
traffic in both directions. A gang of ragged child beggars swarmed
around the waiting cars.

It was nearly ten in the morning, and in the sunlight a foul smell
began to rise from Soochow Creek. Therese began fidgeting. She
felt something graze the skin on her waist. It was the chain belt, of
course—she had quite forgotten about it.

She lit another cigarette, and rolled the window down to get rid
of the smoke.

When she looked out, she saw Hsueh sitting in a car whose driver
seemed to be deliberately provoking the Japanese soldiers. It was
going north ahead of them but had driven onto the right-hand lane,
edging brashly between the first two trucks and blocking the southbound cars. Provisions had been unloaded from the trucks, and each
had its tarp rolled up behind the hood. A couple of Japanese soldiers
stood by the tailgate of one truck, looking impassively at the little
French car, as though the neck flaps on their helmets could block out
the chaos around them as well as the sun.

She could see movement inside Hsueh's car. He was leaning back
against the headrest, holding a cigarette between two fingers outside the window. She rolled the window down again and pointed
him out to her Cossack bodyguards, both of whom had semiautomatic Mauser rifles on their laps. She had to think fast.

They could drive up to Hsueh's car and gesture wildly at him,
but she wouldn't be able to warn him properly, and knowing Hsueh,
he might kick up a fuss. On the other hand, if she waited for them to
get out of the car, she could suddenly drive up to them, trusting her
Cossacks to keep things under control with their rifles. While the
other men were too frightened to move, she could explain things to
Hsueh and leave calmly with him.

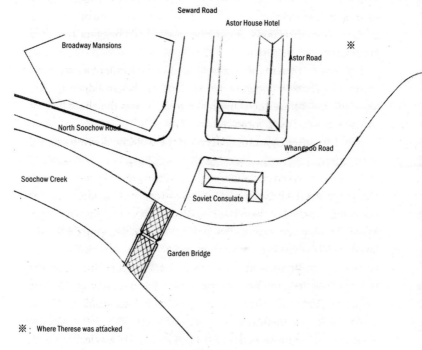

Seward Road

Astor House Hotel

Broadway Mansions

Astor Road

North Soochow Road

Whangpoo Road

Soochow Creek

Soviet Consulate

Garden Bridge

※ : Where Therese was attacked

The Astor House Hotel and environs

They started tailing the other car. It was in the right-hand lane and her Ford was in the left, so she could see straight into it. She rolled the window up, knowing the reflected sunlight would prevent her opponent from seeing into her own car. Gazing at Hsueh's silhouette in the window, she thought what a handsome man he was.

The cars slowly found their way around the roadblock. A few people got out of rickshaws, and the rickshaw men yanked their empty rickshaws onto the sidewalk. One northbound car after another drove slowly up the bridge. The French car merged back onto the left-hand lane, and honked insolently when it passed the last of the Japanese trucks. Therese had her car drive slowly behind them.

The car turned off Paikee Road and past Seward Road toward Whangpoo Road. But Therese directed her driver to turn east on Whangpoo Road instead, and make a U-turn at Astor Road. They could then drive toward the Astor from the other end of Whangpoo Road and cut Hsueh's car off there. At the corner of Astor Road, she asked the driver to slow down. The sun shone on the pale brown facade of the Broadway Mansions. From inside her own suffocatingly hot car, she could see the other car stopping at the side of the road. Behind it, countless windows glittered.

"Now!" she cried.

As the driver slammed down on the accelerator pedal, the car sped toward the Astor at sixty miles an hour, nearly tipping over as it careened to a halt on the pavement. Hsueh leaped aside and hid in the doorway of the Astor. Two other men had just gotten off, and the car sped toward them, forcing them up against the wall. Hsueh's driver was speechless.

The Cossacks leaped fearlessly out of the car, and went straight up to the young men. They ignored Hsueh—he was on their side. Brandishing their rifles, they cried in off-key Shanghainese: "No one move!"

No one moved. The young men had their backs to the wall, their eyes wide open. Their hands wandered to their pistols, but they wouldn't have time to draw.

But the Cossacks had miscalculated badly. Having judged their opponents' position by their own, it simply hadn't occurred to them that the driver of the other car might also be armed. Their most dangerous opponent was just outside their field of view. . . .

Two shots rang out, and both men crumpled onto the porch with the force of the bullets. One was hit in the temple. Another bullet pierced his companion in the left side, just as he was raising the rifle with his left hand, and probably went through his heart. His head thudded onto the white marble porch, exploding like a deranged artist's convulsive oil painting. (Therese had seen a painting like that in the studio of a White Russian artist who kept up with the latest Parisian trends.) Blood seeped from the man's crushed skull onto the gray-flecked marble.

Therese was furious. With one foot out of the car, she had been just about to step out and yell at Hsueh. Instead she leaned back into the car and reached for her handbag, groping for the Browning under the cigarette case. Craning her neck out, she struck her head on the doorframe but barely noticed the pain as she drew the gun in her right hand, pulling the trigger—

The pistol never fired. The trigger had only been partly held down, not far enough to discharge the round. She would have missed anyway, because she hadn't had time to take aim. Her opponent had already leaped onto the pavement and was firing at her from the right flank of the Ford. The bullet lodged in her stomach. She was still sitting there with the door half open when the bullet pierced through layers of silk to bury itself under her skin.

Before she passed out, she saw Hsueh leap at the gun and clutch the driver's arm. The two men who had thrown themselves against the wall only seconds before rushed at Hsueh and bundled him into another car. Just as she was about to faint, a thought suddenly occurred to her: had Hsueh saved her life instead?

If Park hadn't been so incensed by the Japanese soldiers while he was driving, their car would have arrived at the Astor a few minutes earlier. It couldn't be helped, because he was Korean. But that way the shootout at the door wouldn't have happened, and maybe Therese wouldn't have gotten shot.

If they hadn't stopped by Mud Crossing on their way to Putung Pier, and unloaded a few packages into a hut in a field sunken about five meters below the main road, they might have gotten there a couple hours earlier. And if Hsueh hadn't been racking his brains for a way to refuse Park's offer of a lift, so that he could make a phone call to Sarly, maybe they would have gotten there earlier still. Before he passed out, Hsueh realized that he hadn't had a chance to give Sarly an update. Then someone struck him with a heavy piece of metal on the head. A pistol, he realized, and immediately lost consciousness.

When he awoke, he found himself lying in bed. Ku was sitting at the edge of the bed, smiling at him.

"Good, you're awake. That was impulsive of you."

Impulsive? Hsueh was surprised, but he couldn't say a word. There was a hammer thudding against his temple.

"Comrade Leng went missing this morning. She may already have been killed. That White Russian woman showed up at your rooms and found her there. Leng sent a message this morning, but we only just got it. It looks as though Lady Holly came to the Astor because she was after you. They pulled their guns as soon as they got out of the car."

Hsueh needed to think hard about Ku's words, but his brain had turned to jelly, and he could barely make out what the man was saying.

"Don't worry, we know you care about Leng. We're trying to locate her and we will. So have a good rest. Our comrades here will look after you. Ask them for anything you need. You've already met Ch'in."

It didn't add up—there was no reason why Therese would want Leng dead. Although he did see her pull out a gun, he didn't believe she would really have fired at them.

Then Ku left the room hurriedly. From the footsteps clattering on the stairs, Hsueh could tell he had brought quite a group with him. He looked round at the paneled walls. Ch'in poked his head out the window, where someone was shouting up at him from the courtyard. Clearly the window overlooked a courtyard; glancing at the sky, Hsueh judged that their room was in the east wing of a *shih-k'u-men* house. There was someone in the living room.

He tried to get up, but he had no strength in his arms. Ch'in saw him try, and came over to help him up, propping his pillow behind him so that he could sit up in bed. Hsueh's mouth felt dry, and he needed a drink.

After gulping down some water, he realized he was exhausted from having been up all night. He tried hard to picture that hut by the road. He remembered helping to carry those packages down a pebbly slope. In fact, he'd nearly slid into a grassy pit about five meters deep, with a hut at the bottom. The road lay higher than the thatched roof of the hut, and only a few steps away along the road, the hut disappeared from view.

The sun streamed onto the wooden floor in front of him. His coat had been draped over him, but he was getting too warm, and tossed it to one side. He thought of Therese taking the bullet in her stomach, and felt a sympathetic spasm of pain in his own.

He still couldn't figure out why she would want to kill Leng. He thought about Leng. Could it be jealousy? Ku could well be right. Therese did keep a pistol in her handbag.

But you couldn't just pull a gun out in Shanghai and casually shoot someone dead—this was a bustling city with a million inhabitants. Sure, the newspapers were full of stories of murder and arson, and Hsueh himself had seen gunfights on the streets before. In fact, a few years ago, they were actually quite common. But they had never had anything to do with him or with anyone he knew well. This degree of terror and suspense was what he might expect to find at the theater, to be enjoyed and then promptly forgotten.

He felt as though he had been hypnotized by Therese, by Leng, by Lieutenant Sarly and Inspector Maron, and by Ku Fu-kuang. He was in a dream world in which shooting someone dead was a perfectly ordinary thing to do, and he couldn't just decide to wake up. Everyone around him seemed to have gone raving mad. Sarly's words came to mind: Shanghai is like a volcano about to erupt.

Or maybe he wouldn't want to wake up, because this life, so different from his old life, had its own appeal. It felt like a hair-raising and never-ending game of poker in which everyone thought they held the best cards. The same throbbing heartbeat, the same sensation of being numb to everything beyond the game. They were right about what adrenaline did to you, he thought. Poker wasn't a perfect metaphor—perhaps it was more like looking down from the roof of a skyscraper, and enjoying the illusory feeling of tipping forward, the sensation of buoyancy. Or like cutting across the road just as a car was speeding past, letting it brush against his jacket tails.

He wanted to share these musings with someone, but neither Ch'in nor the other man who kept walking past the door to his room were likely to be the right kind of interlocutor.

Ch'in was leaning on the windowsill and staring out into the courtyard. That will make his hair warm from the sun, Hsueh thought as he drifted into sleep.

When he woke it was almost evening. Ch'in was still leaning on the windowsill and looking out when he turned with a startled look, and opened his mouth, as if to shout, but stifled his cry. He heaved his leg off the chair and called toward the living room: "Do you know who—"

But before he could finish his sentence, there was a knock at the door. Opening the door, Ch'in gasped with surprise.

Hsueh recognized one of the shadowy figures at the door. In fact, he recognized him from the night when this man was having dinner with Zung and Park. Hsueh knew that his name was Lin, and that he was one of the comrades Leng trusted most.

Someone said: "I'll go and see if there's anyone outside." Then Hsueh heard footsteps on the stairs.

The newcomer stood motionless in the doorway. In the late afternoon light, you could see that his cheek had been badly scratched, and his neck and chin were bruised. The scar along his nose was so long it looked fake. Nonetheless, Hsueh knew the man at a glance. He did have a photographer's memory for faces.

"Someone wanted to kill him, but we rescued him," Ch'in explained, motioning to Hsueh. "But where have you been all this time? Ku said the police got you. Really, I was afraid you'd been killed." He tugged at Lin's shirtsleeves as if he were his younger brother.

Lin was quiet for a long time.

"Where is Ku Fu-kuang?" he asked abruptly.

"They've taken a boat to Mud Crossing. You don't know what—" Here Ch'in cut himself off, glancing at Hsueh, before realizing that Hsueh already knew all this. "You don't know what we've been up to. Ku is planning a huge operation. We bought some powerful new guns. Ku and the rest of the cell are on boats at Wu-sung-k'ou doing target practice right now. Leng went missing this morning, and Ku says she may have been killed," Ch'in said all in one breath. His listener looked grave. "When is the operation?" Lin asked. But then he, too, glanced at Hsueh, and steered Ch'in into the living room.

They spoke in low voices. Hsueh couldn't make out a word. Lin suddenly cried: "That can't be true! That can't be true!" His voice grew increasingly passionate.

They lowered their voices again. Someone got up and started pacing around. Hsueh suddenly wondered: if he and Therese had arranged to meet at the Astor, why would she go to his rooms first thing in the morning? And why did she bring her bodyguards and guns to the Astor? Why did she say nothing when she got there but point her gun directly at them?

Thinking made his head hurt. Hsueh detected the choking smell of smoke and the clang of a spatula—they must be cooking dinner in an iron wok down in the courtyard. He couldn't hear what was happening in the next room. The Victrola needle was lifted, and a peal of operatic laughter stopped midlaugh, as though the singer had suddenly been stifled. A child was crying. Someone said something mean in a sweet voice.

Hsueh was dead tired, and he wanted nothing more than to sleep. But just then, Ch'in came in to say that dinner was ready. Despite his lack of appetite, he found himself being helped out of bed. There was a dining table in the living room, and at the table sat Lin.

When she put the phone down, Leng didn't know what to do next. She had been waiting all morning for a chance to sneak out, and she did so as soon as Ku left, telling the others that she wanted to go for a walk in the gardens.

She stood by the flower beds, gazing at a white camellia that had bloomed too late and was shriveling up in the July sun. She thought she saw a shadow at an upstairs window, and froze, terrified. She was stalling.

The guard was stationed at the gate on West Avenue Joffre, at the other end of the path, so there was no one by the door. The only words she could make out on the bronze plate next to it were 1230 GRESHAM APARTMENTS. She walked casually along the concrete edge of the flower bed, as if she were following a butterfly. She could feel someone looking at her. Standing at the window, you could see the whole garden without even craning your neck.

But soon she was standing inside Kovsk, a Russian-owned luxury women's fashion store just outside the apartment building. She felt guilty about stalling, but also about what she was going to do, which was a form of betrayal. Then again, not doing anything would also be a betrayal. The previous afternoon, she had been there while Ku was giving Park his orders. Park was to drive to T'ung-jen Pier, where Hsueh would be waiting at the ticket office.

"The day after tomorrow, we strike," Ku said. "No margin for error. Once we get hold of the grenade launchers, Hsueh mustn't be allowed to leave, as a security measure."

He didn't try to hide this from Leng. She should understand that it was a necessary precaution.

"What about this White Russian woman? She knows a lot," Park pointed out.

"We'll have to kidnap her too."

"There just aren't enough of us. It takes two men to watch one prisoner. We'd have to assign three comrades to watch the two of them, and even that would be a stretch."

Ku was thinking. He struck a match, lit his cigarette, and glanced at Leng.

"Hsueh is important to our cell, so we have to protect him. We must treat him as one of our own. But as for that White Russian woman, she knows too much. Even after the operation is over, it'll still be too much."

She couldn't hide the fact that she understood what he was hinting at. Her eyes grew wide.

When a comrade is in danger and the question of whether it is worth attempting a rescue arises, the revolutionary should put aside his own private affection for this comrade, and consider only what would be best for the revolutionary cause. He should carefully weigh the usefulness of this comrade to the revolutionary cause against the revolutionary forces that would be expended in rescuing him. . . . When the question arises as to which individuals are to be executed, and in what order, neither the crimes of those individuals nor even the anger of the revolutionary masses should be taken into account, but only the usefulness of the executions to the revolutionary cause. Those who are most dangerous to the cause are always to be executed first. . . .

The words she had learned by heart came to mind, like intertitles appearing in black in a silent film. There was a ringing in her ears, and she heard their words distantly, as if she were underwater.

"We'll have to execute her then?" That was Park.

Women can be divided into three categories: first, the frivolous, empty-headed, slow-witted kind, who can be used like the third and fourth category of men. Second, those who are passionate, loyal, and capable, but who do not belong to our cause because they have not achieved a truly pragmatic, rigorous level of revolutionary dedication; these can be used like the fifth category of men. Third and final, those who belong wholly to our cause, who can be completely trusted, who fully accept the revolutionary program. These should be treated as priceless treasures, for we cannot operate without their help.

The lines appeared in her mind, one after another. This was the group's manifesto, which Ku himself had written, an oath that all new members of People's Strength had to learn by heart.

"We won't be able to find her," Park said.

"Give this check to Hsueh. It's an enormous sum of money, and he will want her to have it as soon as possible." Leng's ears were ringing again. "Wherever he goes, you must insist on taking him by car. He must be watched from tonight onward, at all times, until the operation is over."

It wasn't like her to speak up at a time like this, but she found herself saying: "If you kill her in front of Hsueh, you'll give him such a fright. She is his friend, his former . . . lover." She paused.

"You'll terrify him," she said softly. "He's always been willing to help us. How will you ever get him to accept her death?"

"But what more could he want? Sure, he'll be frightened, but what is he going to do about it? He's already working for us and he can't stop now. He'll have you, and he'll have all this money. We'll explain things to him—in fact, maybe you could explain things to him. Maybe *you* are a good enough reason for him," Ku said, speaking impassively, as though the thoughts weren't his own.

That night, Ku didn't leave the apartment. He sat there smoking, deep in thought. She went in to bring him some tea, wanting to talk him out of the idea, but when she saw him sitting motionless in the shadows of the desk lamp, she said nothing. Park had already left to execute Ku's orders. The wheels were in motion and no one could stop them now.

Leng couldn't sleep. It wasn't as if she knew the White Russian woman—she couldn't even remember what she looked like. She had only seen her in a photograph in which her face had appeared distorted, and her eyes were staring off to one side. Maybe she was lying down in the picture, which would explain the seventy-degree angle of the smoke rising from her cigarette. Therese was a stranger to her—she only knew that name from Hsueh, and she could barely bring herself to call that woman, of all people, by her first name.

She had first learned of that woman's existence via a pair of stained, musty silk drawers under Hsueh's bed. At the time they had repulsed her. But now she was reminded of them. They proved what the lipstick and photograph could not prove—that their owner was a living, breathing human being.

Her old nightmare was back and crowding in on her. She felt trapped between two choices. She was pacing through an inescapable maze.

I'll go with the first instinct I have when I wake up, she decided. But she barely slept. She couldn't tell when she had woken up because she felt as though she had never fallen asleep. She did try going back to sleep, but her first thought upon opening her eyes again was the complete opposite.

When she finally made a decision, she told herself it was because she wanted Hsueh to feel he was being treated fairly. He mustn't have any doubts about working for the cell.

But when she left the apartment, she was at a loss for where to find Hsueh or the White Russian woman. Finally, she thought of the phone number on the back of that photograph.

She waited outside Yong'an, the greengrocer, for the first cab to come out of the Shell gas station. The driver said he wasn't allowed to pick up a fare on the street, and told her to order a cab at the counters of the cab company. She didn't know what to say, but she gazed sadly at him until he agreed to take her.

Now she was standing in Hsueh's rooms. She knew exactly where the photograph was because she had put it there—in that newspaper package, together with the silk drawers. Together, those two things formed the face of a woman she had never actually met, but whose life she was about to save. She had to warn the White Russian woman not to go to her meeting with Hsueh. I've always wanted them to stop seeing each other, she thought. I've always wanted to wrap her in paper and stuff her in the gap between the closet and the wall. As soon as she picked up the phone, she felt like the jealous wife in the tales, telling the fox demon to stop seducing her husband, telling Therese not to go to meet Hsueh.

When she put down the phone, she didn't know what to do or where to go. By now someone would have told Ku that she had disappeared in the crucial final hours before the operation. They would guess what she had gone off to do, and treat it as a betrayal, but she had nowhere to go. She couldn't find Hsueh, and she was still wanted by the police. It was too dangerous to go out alone. She could be recognized by a policeman, or by an inquisitive but unfriendly journalist.

She eventually decided to return to the apartment on West Avenue Joffre. She had no home or friends. The cell was her home, and her comrades were her friends.

The visitor Lin had brought with him was sitting in a teahouse opposite them on Boulevard des Deux Républiques and looking across to
the east-facing windows of their house. Their rooms were in the eastern wing, and that rascal Hsueh was lying on the bed by the window.

It was the beginning of summer, and at nearly seven in the evening it was still bright outside. Lin sat in the living room. How could
he even begin to explain what was going on? Things were happening so quickly he could barely catch his breath.

Not in his wildest dreams had he imagined that Cheng Yün-tuan
might be a Communist mole who had infiltrated the Kuomintang's
Investigative Unit for Party Affairs. A real Communist! He couldn't
stop thinking about it on the way back, replaying everything that
Cheng had said to him. He realized Cheng had given him plenty of
hints. Believe me, one of these days we'll be comrades, Cheng had
said. Why hadn't he realized what was happening? Why hadn't he
caught the hint of warmth in Cheng's voice?

The previous night after dinner, when the other operatives were
getting sleepy, Cheng had opened the louver door to the storeroom.
He didn't shout at Lin as he had previously done. Instead he gave
him a friendly look, a look that said we are comrades, though at the
time Lin took it for fake chumminess. Cheng even bent over to lean
into the dusty storeroom and extend his hand to Lin.

Lin had no idea what was going on. He figured the operative

had a new trick up his sleeve. Only later, when he had come to trust Cheng and grasp that he was being rescued, did he see how diffi-cult it must have been to plant a mole in the enemy's most secret operations. Cheng had run the considerable risk of exposing his own identity. Liberating even a few misguided young revolutionaries was a tricky business.

He refused Cheng's hand and looked coldly at him, but he did come out of the storeroom.

Comrade Cheng didn't waste a single moment. "First thing tomorrow morning we're sending you to the French Concession Police," he breathed into Lin's ear.

"Why? You don't have my testimony yet," Lin said tartly.

"A comrade at the Concession Police let slip the news that you had been arrested by Nanking. Just this morning, the police called to demand that we turn you over."

"A comrade?"

"There's no time to explain. You'll understand soon enough. But be prepared. The Party is going to rescue you."

Lin felt faint.

"Be careful. Don't be nervous, but don't let yourself relax. There will be another interrogation tonight. Tseng Nan-p'u is in Nanking and won't be able to get back in time, so I'll be interrogating you. Just do what you usually do. The Concession Police will send a car to pick you up tomorrow morning. Our inside man there has bribed someone to make sure the car will spend an extra half hour on the road. Another black car will come and take you away, and it will be a rescue squad sent by the Party. But if the enemy discovers this and there is a fight—whatever happens, you must tell them that the rescuers were sent by Ku Fu-kuang."

That interrogation may have seemed even more brutal than the previous ones had been. Cheng actually came up to him and slapped him on the face. But the questions themselves were run-of-the-mill, and he had been asked them all before. Growing impatient, Lin became brusque with his interrogators, which only made his ques-tioning look more violent.

He barely slept that night. He kept thinking through the conversations of the previous day, trying to absorb them. The storeroom seemed sultrier and the corner he was leaning against narrower than it had been.

Early the next morning, a black Ford did come to pick him up. He didn't see Comrade Cheng again. (Comrade Cheng—that was how he had taken to thinking of Cheng, ten hours later.) Two young operatives handed him over to the armed policemen, one of whom was, surprisingly, a foreigner. Lin had taken two years of English classes in college, but when he asked the foreigner a question in English, the man smiled and didn't answer. Producing a pencil stub, he wrote a few words on the back of a piece of cigarette foil and handed it to Lin:

> For we went,
> Changing our country
> More often than our shoes,
> Through the class war.

Unbeknownst to Lin, this was a poem by Brecht. The policeman told him it was a poem by a German poet who supported the Comintern, and that he had just translated it into English.

The car took him to a *shih-k'u-men* house on Rue Wantz. Lin immediately recognized the man standing beneath the ceiling fan in the living room. "Secretary Ch'en!" Many years ago, Lin had sat in the audience when Ch'en had been speaking on the podium as the leader of the Student Communists.

Several hours later, as he was leaving the house, he had to make himself calm down and not get too worked up. His world had been turned upside down. *This is a conspiracy, a threat to the Party! If Ku pulls this off, it will be a blow to the Revolution. We must expose and defeat him—this is the mission with which the Party is entrusting you.*

Four whole years, he had spent four years under the leadership of a mere charlatan whom he had taken to be a representative of the Party, his only connection to the Party, his mentor. He had lost touch with the Party after the massacres in the spring of 1927. All his comrades were arrested or had dropped out of the Party, and the most important person in his life—not that he had ever had a chance to express his feelings to her—was killed by a blow to the head by a Green Gang thug wielding a baton. When he returned to Shanghai from Wuxi in November of 1927, Year 16 of the Republic, his friends' revolutionary fervor had died down. In March, a classmate from his hometown had come to see him, and spent half an hour talking about the struggle against imperialism and the warlords before saying: my uncle used to be a teacher in Wuxi, but he's unemployed. You couldn't get him a job somewhere, could you? With your position as a Communist on the Kuomintang's Student District Committee? At the time, all schools were governed by a Kuomintang department consisting of representatives from both parties.

But now that classmate ignored Lin and pretended not to know him when they ran into each other on the street. Lin had thought of going to Wuhan to meet up with Party members there, but the persecution of Communists soon spread to Wuhan. He was not angry at the enemy. No, he hated the enemy—he was angry at all his former comrades who had betrayed the cause.

That was when he had met Ku Fu-kuang. He had been coming out of a lonely bookstore which, only months ago, had been full of socialist books and magazines in several languages. The Shanghai Kuomintang hadn't yet been able to shut it down because it was in the International Settlement, and the owner was a German. At the time, he could tell that he was in danger, though in retrospect he could see that the true danger was not what he had feared. Someone was looking at him. He went into the longtang, and as he turned the corner, he glanced over and met the gaze of two men looking at him. Tensing up, he walked faster, and he thought he could hear footsteps behind him. Ku was hiding in the alley. He said in a low voice: "This way!" Lin followed him into a *shih-k'u-men* house, through the courtyard, and out another door.

Now that he thought about it, after hearing Comrade Cheng's anecdote, he realized that the entire incident could have been a crude trap.

He was ashamed of having been so gullible. He had fallen for it because he had been full of hatred, anxious to exact revenge on the counterrevolutionaries. But his enemy was the system, the class, and hatred is a dangerous emotion for a revolutionary. He had to outdo the enemy in staying power. Just thinking about Secretary Ch'en's words filled him with shame.

When Lin requested formal readmission to the Party, Secretary Ch'en told him that the Party had learned its lesson from the violence of the oppression. Its ranks had to be more disciplined, and Party members would have stricter requirements to fulfill. That meant that procedures for rejoining the Party would also be tightened. Most importantly, Lin had a mission to complete and no time to lose. He had to tell the truth to his comrades who had been duped by Ku, and tell them that the Party would welcome their return.

Lin stood at the window and waved at the man in the teahouse on the other side of the road, who was carrying a classified document that would explain the Party's latest strategy to his misled comrades. But first he had to talk to them all and expose Ku's fraudulent schemes.

He looked at Hsueh, who was fast asleep on the bed. There was one more thing he had to know: what happened at North Gate Police Station. When Secretary Ch'en had asked him about Hsueh, Lin had been amazed that the Party seemed to know everything about everything. Their mole in the Political Section said that Hsueh had an unusual position there because of his ties to Inspector Maron's new detective squad. The Party had arranged for a sum of money to be deposited in an account at the National Industrial Bank, and earmarked for dealing with corrupt policemen in the Concession. Party leaders were taking an interest in the new detective squad. Another undercover comrade, a clerk at the National Industrial Bank counter on Rue du Consulat, discovered by chance that this Hsueh had withdrawn some money from the account. The Party investigated Hsueh, and decided that he was not a counterrevolutionary. He had rescued Leng because of their relationship, and Leng's deceitfulness didn't mean that she had betrayed the Party or gone over to the police's side.

Lin had Ch'in wake Hsueh up for dinner. As he was serving Hsueh a piece of smoked fish, Lin asked: "So what happened this morning at the Astor? And tell us about the delivery last night. What is the mysterious weapon?"

"How is she? Therese?"

"We don't know yet. Our man stationed at the scene says she was rushed to Shanghai General Hospital by hotel staff. You have to tell us everything. Ku might well be sending someone to the hospital to kill her."

"I don't know anything. You should talk to Leng."

CHAPTER 50

JULY 13, YEAR 20 OF THE REPUBLIC.

11:55 P.M.

Park sat on the concrete with his back to the gravestone. It was the grave of a Jesuit who had come to Shanghai at the end of the Ching Dynasty, in the Foreigners' Cemetery on Rue Gaston Kahn, and it was oval shaped, a meter deep in the ground, and made of concrete. A south wind from Chao-chia Creek carried the stench of boatloads of night soil toward them. The stench only grew worse when the wind died down. Ting-hsin Dye Factory lay across the road on Rue Gaston Kahn, and a chili factory lay to the north.

They all arrived separately within five minutes of each other, so as not to attract police attention. Park looked at his watch. He turned to Fu and said, "It's time." Then he led them out of the cemetery through a gap in the wall.

The moon hung low in the sky, the summer night was crowded with stars, and the sky was dream bright. An occasional splash of oars came from the direction of the wooden bridge to the south, so faint that it could have been a rat paddling in the water. There were no trees or streetlights on Rue Gaston Kahn. The road was short, and as they walked north, the tarmac road narrowed into a longtang paved with concrete. They turned into T'ing-yüan Lane. The Hua Sisters Motion Picture Studio was at the end of the lane.

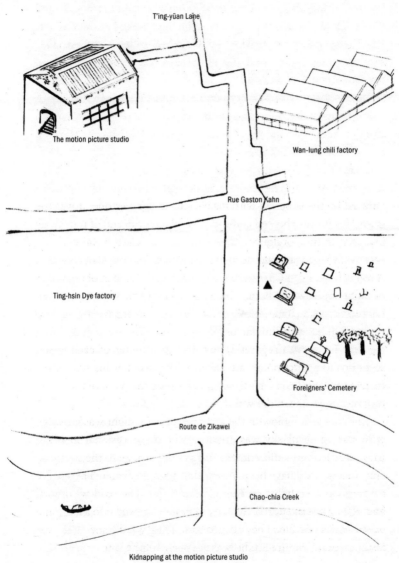

T'ing-yüan Lane

The motion picture studio

Wan-lung chili factory

Rue Gaston Kahn

Ting-hsin Dye factory

Foreigners' Cemetery

Route de Zikawei

Chao-chia Creek

Kidnapping at the motion picture studio

▲ Park's meeting point with the group

Behind the wall, the studio was bustling and brightly lit. Park knew nothing about making movies, and he couldn't understand why Ku had planned this operation. He had looked at the *Guide to Film Photography* Ku had given him, scratched his head, and asked Ku about it. "Never you mind, just make sure you get us the man and his equipment," Ku had said.

Before the guard could cry out, Park punched him in the throat. The black wolf dog pounced at him, but Park ducked, slitting it open along its belly with the dagger hidden in his leather jacket. Man and dog fell noiselessly to the ground.

Inside the studio they were working overtime on a movie slated to open in August. The Concession newspapers were already full of reduced-size posters in which Pearl Yeh was draped in a translucent shawl, reminiscent of the spider demon she had played in a previous movie. A thousand years later, she had accumulated enough Tao to be reborn as a beautiful woman. But just as she was about to lure some man to his destruction, a black-cloaked Taoist priest came to warn her against it. On the poster, he was whispering into her ear, his nose about to touch her shoulder, about a university somewhere in Jambudvîpa called Shanghai. The circle of life had sent Yeh to a big city as a university student. She kept causing trouble for herself and everyone around her, but this time she was a modern woman wearing dresses tailored by a White Russian designer.

They crept onto the set and hid in the shadows. No one noticed them because the three floodlights trained on the stage had large reflectors set up all around them. A technician in a white undershirt stood on the frame of the cardboard set with an eight-meter retractable pole in his hand, shining a spotlight directly onto the bathtub. The scenery depicted a bathroom with thin gauze curtains draped over the windows, outside which painted skyscrapers glittered.

But the bathtub was not painted, and the water in the tub was real. Someone hid behind the bathtub pumping fog into it. Pearl Yeh, who was sitting inside the bathtub, was real too. Her shoulders were white, and her knees floated in the water like jellyfish. They said it was worth buying tickets to ten showings in a row, just to see her.

Park hesitated. He stood there. He had never watched a movie from this point of view. You couldn't see all this on-screen. The camera was propped against the bathtub, and the cameraman was sprawled on the floor. Park was standing behind the reflector, staring at the white shoulders that would appear on-screen in a swirl of steamy mist, but also at the warped refraction of Yeh's body and her bathing suit. He watched her limbs float in the water.

The intruders squatted down, because most of the film crew was squatting on the ground, and politeness seemed to demand that they follow suit. Park was the only one left standing, except for one man on the opposite corner of the set, who was leaning on the wooden frame, and alternately staring down at his feet and looking up at a couple of sheets of scribbled-on paper on a wobbly table. On the left-hand side of the set there was a single wall with a door. An actor sat on the other side of the wall, getting ready for the moment when he would burst into the bathroom.

The director was talking loudly to the cameraman, and to Yeh. "Maybe we'll sit you a bit higher up, with your head leaning back and your neck craning even farther back. Close your eyes and let your head sway a little. You're supposed to be singing. Louder! Don't you ever sing in the bath?"

"Of course not!" a shrill voice rang out from inside the bathtub.

"Well, imagine you're a student and you're relaxing in the shower. Sing out loud! Open your mouth wider!"

Her voice was uglier than Park's own voice when he was drunk. But it was a silent movie, so all she really had to do was move her lips.

"No one move!" Park cried in his textbook perfect northern accent.

No one paid any attention to him. He sprinted into the spotlight and right up to the bathtub. "Who are you? Get out of here!" someone cried.

Park cocked his Mauser rifle and fired a single shot at the roof of the set. Ku had said he could fire a shot or two. It was a movie set, and none of the neighbors would notice a couple of loud noises. To

assert control, you have to come on strong. Watch the director—
he's in charge, and if he defers to you, then you're in charge.

The light wavered. It was the spotlight on the retractable pole.
The technician standing on the frame had nearly fallen off. When
the rest of the crew realized what was happening, they threw themselves on the floor for cover. The stage manager, who had been
standing on one side of the stage, got down and crouched behind the
table. Only Pearl Yeh screamed from where she was inside the bathtub. The bullet had burst a lightbulb, and the glass shattered onto
her shoulder. She struggled to push herself up using the edge of the
bathtub.

Park hoisted her out of the bathtub and flung her on the floor.
Her bathing suit clung wetly to her skin, and the dark outline of her
crotch showed beneath it. She curled up on the floor to hide her private parts.

Brandishing his pistol, Park pointed to the cameraman, whom he
had picked out right away. "You. Come here."

Park had Fu drag the cameraman out of that crowd of squatting
people and point a gun at him while he got all the equipment he
needed to shoot a film. Then he had the cameraman carry his heavy
35 mm camera to the truck. Park pointed to the spools of film on the
ground—they would all have to go in the truck too.

"How many hours will these last?" he asked.

No one answered, and Park didn't really care. They were going
to take it all anyway. They hadn't driven a truck there, because Ku's
sleuthing had revealed that the studio had its own truck, which was
always parked outside at night.

Truss them all up, Ku had said. Don't let anyone leave before
three o'clock tomorrow. It's a small studio, a tiny movie set, and no
one will come looking for them. Filmmakers work at night and in
the morning they're all asleep, so no one will come barging in. Tie
them up and leave a couple of people to stand guard. Easy.

We're short-staffed as it is—do we have to do this? Is it really that
important? he had asked.

"We do have to. It's critical," Ku had said. "You don't understand how powerful movies can be. Have you heard of Eisenstein, the director of the movie *October*? They said more people were killed or injured in the making of Eisenstein's film about the storming of the Winter Palace than during the actual taking of the palace itself. Victory is easily forgotten, and a few deaths are easily forgotten. Only movies will survive."

All this was incomprehensible to Park, but Ku was happy wondering out loud to himself about a theoretical problem.

A camera could turn one dead man into ten dead men by shifting slightly. It could make death look cleaner, elegant, no convulsions or splattered brains, as if death were a mere symbol. This Park could understand. A camera didn't have to show a dead person below the shoulders.

He had them all tied up, including Pearl Yeh and the cameraman on the truck. Park tied the actress up himself. They had brought enough rope with them, and he did a thorough job. He tied her hands behind her back, and bound the ropes over her shoulders and under her arms to cross in front of her and loop twice around her thighs, before tying her ankles together in a secure dead knot. The ropes would grow tighter as they dried.

He deposited Pearl Yeh, now a mass of ropes, under the blinding light where the rest of the film crew was huddled together, thoughtfully draping a curtain over her. He left two people there guarding them. There was no need to stuff and gag their mouths. Even in daylight, they wouldn't dare to make a sound, not with two pistols pointed at them.

There was a tarp draped over the cargo bed. He let the cameraman sit in the passenger's seat. You had to treat people well if you wanted them to do good work for you. They had plenty of time, so he sat in the driver's seat and smoked a cigarette. In the early hours of the morning, he would have to drive the truck to Mohawk Road and drop the cameraman off at the stables. Then he would go to Rue Palikao, where Ku would be waiting for him with another unit.

"How do you hold this thing steady if you're shooting outdoors? Over your shoulder?" he asked the cameraman.

"There's a tripod," the cameraman said.

He had someone get the tripod, which lay in a corner of the studio.

"Will it be stable enough on the truck, even if the truck is moving?" he asked.

"Of course," the cameraman said proudly. "During the Kuomintang's military campaigns in the north, I lugged it right onto the battlefields."

Park clapped him on the shoulder cheerfully, and stuffed a cigarette in the man's mouth.

Leng ached all over. It wasn't just that she was exhausted and hungry. She couldn't turn over, her hands were bound behind her back, and she could only lie on her side. The room was filled with a choking smell of sulfur, which seemed to have coated her nasal membranes with a thin hard shell. But it was her own fault for having turned herself in a second time.

That afternoon, she had run into Li, the most bashful member of Lin's group, a young man who used to be apprenticed to a pharmacist. They saw each other at the end of the path between Avenue Joffre and the gardens.

"Don't come in. Ku says you've betrayed the cell and are to be shot on sight," Li said.

"I haven't betrayed the cell."

"I don't want you to die," Li said, looking at her tenderly. "The White Russian woman came to the Astor this morning with her people, and they nearly killed Park. When we got the news, Ku said you must have warned her. He'd been worried ever since he found out that you'd disappeared, and then we heard about what happened at the Astor."

"I didn't betray the cell."

"Well, there's no point arguing over it. You'd better go." Li was one of the cell members who had come to visit her when she was in Rue

Amiral Bayle. He would haul bags of coal upstairs for her, and bring her water from the public water stove in a neighboring longtang.

"Where's Mr. Hsueh?" she suddenly asked.

"Park brought him back. He is at another safe house. Ku says he is afraid this Hsueh may be a dangerous character too. A man appears out of nowhere, claiming to have contacts at the police station, and the next thing we know, you've betrayed the cell. Ku says he hasn't decided whether Hsueh might turn out to be useful. But you are to be shot on sight. Park shot the White Russian woman, but we heard the bullet didn't kill her, and she was taken to the hospital. Once the operation is over, she will have to be executed too. All three of you are severe threats to the cell, he says."

"Mr. Hsueh is determined to join the revolution. And the White Russian woman helped us too—we can't just kill innocent people."

"Don't you remember the oath we swore? The manifesto of People's Strength? There's no use talking, you'd better go. I won't come after you. Don't go upstairs."

He gave her a gentle nudge, but when she started walking away, he called after her. "Wait!" Rummaging in his pocket, he turned up a handful of coins, a foreign silver coin, and several banknotes. He gave them to her. Then something else occurred to him, and he felt under his shirt for his pistol, and gave that to her too. It was a Browning the size of her palm.

She went back to Hsueh's rooms on Route J. Frelupt, and sat by the table in a daze. Her legs were too sore, and she didn't have the energy to go anywhere. She also didn't know where to go. She buried her face in the pillow to weep. But it smelled of Hsueh's hair, and she suddenly panicked.

He had fallen into Ku's hands. She soon realized she had to rescue him—it was the only thing she could do. She didn't want him to become collateral damage, as she had. She could plead with Ku. She didn't believe that the cell would really harm her, or that Ku would have her killed. This was far from being the hardest decision she had made. But by the time she finally left Hsueh's rooms, found a telephone booth, and made the call, it was almost sunset.

She found the candle store on Rue Palikao using the address she took down during the phone call. Neither Ku nor Park was there, and she hardly knew anyone else in the cell. Strangers took her upstairs and politely bound her to the bed.

There was nothing she could do but lie there and wait.

As it grew lighter, the sky turned a deep blue. She could hear the planks across the door being taken down, and soon the bamboo ladder was creaking with the sound of someone coming upstairs. It was Park.

He sat by the table looking at her.

"Why did you sneak away?"

She looked obstinately at him.

"Why did you warn her? Why betray the cell?"

She didn't think she was in danger. She simply felt humiliated. She had made real sacrifices for this cell. She had been lonely, feigned emotions she didn't feel, and made hard decisions. She looked at Park's haggard face. He hadn't slept or shaved. She thought about how many haggard faces she saw in the cell. They were tense, drained, high on exhaustion, and a little ridiculous. She suddenly saw herself as if she were observing herself from a distance.

Those were faces absorbed in the private world of their top secret missions. They were pale faces glimmering in a dark crowd, full of pride, fear, contempt, and yearning.

Looking at it from an outsider's point of view made her realize that it was all meaningless, but she didn't have the words to explain why. She couldn't help forgiving them—they didn't know what they were doing, she thought. Besides, she also had a pale, haggard face, she hadn't slept a wink all night, and her face betrayed that she was sore all over.

She was thinking about the word Park had used, *betrayal*.

It was words like *betrayal* that tormented them all. They gnawed at your soul, crushing you or filling you with passion, keeping you up all night. Most people never used words like that, but letting them into your life could change it overnight. As soon as she started thinking, a whole slew of words poured out: *operation, manifesto, country, oppression,* and—*love.*

Would she have gotten along better with Hsueh if the word *love* didn't exist? Would she have had to pretend less, if it weren't for the words boxing her into a role she was too tired to keep up?

When it was almost light, she could hear Ku speaking downstairs. She wanted him to come so that she could tell him she hadn't really betrayed them. She had only wanted to make sure Hsueh wouldn't be hurt. She didn't believe that Ku would really have her killed. In fact, she thought Ku might not want to come upstairs because he was sorry, as if it had been his fault that she had sneaked out to warn the other woman. She was no longer ashamed of what she had done; she was beginning to be ashamed for him.

"Ku! Ku!" she cried. Park came up the stairs to tell her that Ku had already left. He untied her and gave her a cup of warm water. She wanted to wash her face and rinse her mouth and change into some new clothes, but most of all she wanted to know how Hsueh was doing.

Park was standing by the table with his back to her. He appeared to be studying the lightbulb.

"Let me take you to see Hsueh," he told her.

She cheered up right away. There would be time to explain everything. Tomorrow, when the operation had been completed, this would all be over. In the meantime, she could go and see Hsueh. As for the White Russian woman, Therese, wasn't she in the hospital? A little pain might even do her some good.

It was early, and Rue Palikao was completely empty. A rat clambered over the heap of coal in the bathroom, on its last scavenging trip before dawn. A pickup truck was parked across the street, with a tarp covering its cargo bed. The tailgate wasn't fully closed. Park opened it to let her get in, and gave her a shove. She fell into the rear bed of the truck.

Park leaped in behind her. She turned in fright to look at him, but the tarp had already been let down, and it was pitch-black. Before her eyes could adjust, there was a stranglehold around her neck. Suddenly it all made sense. She realized that Park was going to strangle her in the truck, so that he wouldn't have to lug her downstairs. But that thought only lasted an instant, because her brain was already short of oxygen, and she couldn't breathe. She started struggling, but he had shoved her into a corner against the tailgate, and he had his knee against her stomach. She tried to kick him, but he was sitting on her legs.

Her hands were empty, but just as she was about to lose consciousness, they brushed against the pistol. In Hsueh's rooms, she had taken off her cheongsam and changed into pants so that she could stick the gun in the back of her pants the way Lin did. Luckily she hadn't left it in her handbag, and no one had searched her.

She pulled the gun out, but she didn't want to kill him, and in any case, the safety was still on. As she flailed, the pistol butt came crashing down on Park's temple, and the hands strangling her loosened their grip. Without stopping to so much as cough, she tumbled out of the cargo bed, and started running toward the front of the truck. She heard the tailgate slam, and something heavy crashed to the ground, but she dared not look back as she dashed across the street.

She saw Lin standing on the corner of Rue du Weikwé. Then Hsueh appeared behind him. She thought she was shouting at them, but she couldn't hear her own voice. She couldn't seem to breathe. She saw them turn to look at her from where they were standing on the curb. She stumbled toward them, waving. She could hear an engine starting behind her. The truck shot out from behind her, its left wheel slamming into the sidewalk. It made a sharp right turn, leaving a twisted skid mark at the street corner, sped onto Rue du Weikwé, and disappeared.

She felt weak all over. She was trembling, crying, coughing. Hsueh clutched her by the arm as she leaned against him. She wanted to stroke his face, but she still had the pistol in her hands. She had nearly died. She didn't have to be embarrassed anymore, or wonder what Lin would think. After all, she had almost been killed, he was handsome, and she'd thought she would never see him again. She hung on Hsueh's neck and wept.

Lin hadn't wasted a single moment, and yet he had almost come too late. A minute later and he would only have been in time to see Leng's corpse. He couldn't let any more of his comrades die. When Hsueh told him what Ku had said as he was leaving, Lin realized that Leng would be in danger. Ku wouldn't want Hsueh to see Leng, so he would kill her and blame the White Russian woman. But later he found out that Li, a member of his own unit, had run into Leng. When Li got back to the safe house on Boulevard des Deux Républiques, he had told Lin that Leng was no longer in danger.

So Lin forgot about Leng. There was too much to do, and he only had one night in which to do it. He sent Ch'in and a few others to gather all the members of his unit for a meeting at the safe house, so that he could tell them the truth. A few were missing because Ku had split up the unit, taking several of its members to Pu-tung with him.

Reaching Lin's own unit was the most important thing, Secretary Ch'en had said. Many of them were students about twenty years old. Ku had deceived them, but they could all play a valuable part in the revolution. He had to find them and tell them the truth. All of Ku's pluckiest fighters belonged to this group. Although he claimed to have several units under his command, these young people did most of the work. Secretary Ch'en told him that the Party had investigated Ku's two other units, and that they consisted mostly of thugs, muscle for the company unions, or ruffians who used to run streetside posts for Hua Hui betting and were wanted by the Green Gang for having absconded with the money. Ku had also attracted an assortment of foreigners: Koreans, Indians, White Russians, and criminals who had fled to Shanghai from all over Asia.

Lin didn't know how to reach all the other comrades he couldn't get in touch with right now. Secretary Ch'en had told him to do anything he could to expose this conspiracy against the Party. After their meeting, he asked everyone to split up and find more members of the unit. He himself stayed to speak to Hsueh. They would have to make the police aware of this intelligence, and he wanted to know what the police would do with it.

"Where's Leng right now?" Hsueh blurted out. The selfish bastard thought of nothing but his own problems. Lin couldn't understand what made Hsueh tick. He might as well belong to a different species. Hsueh had been visibly relieved when he heard that the White Russian woman was taken to the hospital, but now he was asking after Leng. Lin couldn't understand how a man could spend his days chasing two women. He thought it very vulgar.

"She is safe. One of the comrades has told her what is happening, and warned her to stay away from Ku Fu-kuang."

Lin could tell that Hsueh really cared about Leng, but he still couldn't understand how one man could love two women at once.

"Ku isn't a real Communist. He is planning a dangerous robbery, and he wants the Communists to take the blame for it. You should tell the police, via your friend."

Hsueh looked as though he had something to say. Lin stared at him, his own lips salty with sweat. Hsueh was reaching into his pocket, and Lin knew he must be craving a cigarette. Lin himself wouldn't mind one either.

"Why would they believe me?" Hsueh asked. The elegant woman in the Hazeline Snow advertisements on the wall gazed down at them, surrounded by flowers that looked a little lackluster in the dim electric light. Why would the police believe him? The

imperialists in the Concession were terrified of Communists, not
of ordinary criminals—what incentive did the police have to set
the record straight?

Hsueh was deep in thought. Lin gazed at him with a well-
meaning smile. Even though Hsueh was selfish and bourgeois, even
though his conscience had never been captured by Communist
ideals, they were both young men, and Lin hoped to win him over.

"I have an idea," he finally said. Lin waited. "We're in Shanghai.
It's a big city, and cities have their ways of getting the word out. We
could write to the newspapers. We could draft an urgent press statement exposing the conspiracy, or send an open telegram. And then
there are the radio stations," he said, thinking out loud. "All those
places will be busy now, but tomorrow's paper won't have gone to
press yet. We can write something up, make a few dozen copies,
and have it delivered to the newspapers and radio stations. Then the
news will be on the wireless and in tomorrow's papers."

It was a brilliant plan. The more Lin thought about it, the better
he liked it.

They were up all night, writing and rewriting the press statement. Lin had no way of getting a go-ahead from his Party superiors,
so all he could do was write the opening lines himself, with some
trepidation.

*From the Shanghai Committee of the Chinese Communist Party to all
residents of Shanghai:*

Hsueh said the newspapers would never get away with running
that statement on its own. It would be best to attach an article that
framed it as a story. That way, newspapers and radio stations would
take the risk of running it because Shanghai people loved "shocking
crime stories." Lin glared at him.

Lin hesitated to reveal the operation taking place the following
day. He was worried that his message hadn't gotten through to a few
of his comrades. But he eventually decided to put it in. He copied the
statement out twenty times, and Hsueh did some copying too.

Then they got on their bikes and delivered all those copies to various newspapers and radio stations. Hsueh went with Lin, because

he knew where all the offices were. They got back at around four in the afternoon.

A comrade who had just returned from Rue Palikao gave them the startling news that Leng had been seen in the candle store. Park had told him to come back to the safe house and summon the rest of their unit to a meeting at the candle store. But when Lin told him what was going on, he immediately reported that Leng had been tied up and was being held there.

Lin didn't stop to think. He rushed out to Rue Palikao, with Hsueh close behind.

They got there just as Leng was escaping from Park.

Lin now looked at the untidy storefront. It was littered with half-eaten food and cigarette butts, and the neatly stacked cardboard boxes had all been overturned. The guns and explosives hidden beneath the floorboards in the corner had disappeared.

Lin was afraid his cover had been blown. He must have sparked Ku's suspicions by openly calling everyone in his unit to a meeting. Park had sped off as soon as he saw Lin, which meant that Ku knew the truth was out, and he would be desperate.

Lin didn't know what Ku planned to do with the new weapon. He didn't know Ku's target, or when he would attack. The plan existed nowhere but in Ku's brain. One of the comrades Lin had summoned to the meeting said the target was a bank. Another said they were supposed to meet at the stables opposite the Race Course. But there wasn't a single bank anywhere near Mohawk Road. Ku always operated this way—he never revealed his whole plan to his operatives until seconds before it was meant to go into action.

They went into the warehouse behind the store. Ku must have held a meeting here—there was a tin stuffed with cigarette ends, and no one but Ku smoked this many cigarettes. Leng sat on a wooden shelf in the corner, clutching Hsueh's hand.

Lin looked around the dark warehouse. All the windows had been nailed shut. The morning light and smoke were seeping in between the cracks, and the heap of coal smelled smoky in the humid air. He

could hear someone scrubbing a toilet next door in Yu-i Alley. One
of the boxes was only half full of firecrackers. A piece of paper lay on
the side of the table where Ku usually sat.

Lin held it up to the light. He knew what this diagram was for.
Ku always planned each operation very carefully. He would explore
every inch of the location, and make a pencil sketch of the width of
the streets, the doors and windows of each building, where to post
an ambush or provide backup with a car.

But Lin couldn't tell what the rows of little squares on either side
of the street meant. He could see that Ku was planning to post his
men by the squares, two on one side of the road, and one on the
other. The target was on the near side of the road. Ku always drew
a pig face for the target, with two large ears taking up half the pig's
face, and two black dots for nostrils. The triangle on one side of the
diagram probably indicated a guard post. And there was a word
written very small opposite the pig's head. Lin peered at it closely. It
was the word *Kuan*.

The sunlight filtering in between the planks grew brighter. Lin
put the piece of paper back on the table. Leng came over to look at
it, and suddenly cried: "I know where this is—it's Rue du Consulat."

"This is Rue des Pères, and this is Rue de Saigon," she said,
pointing them out. "The word *Kuan* is for Kuan-sheng Yüan. The
squares are columns lining the arcade. The target must be the
National Industrial Bank! And the Singapore Hotel is right there
on the corner."

Lin turned to look at her. He had to ask her this question directly,
so as to get a direct answer.

"When you were arrested at the Singapore Hotel, you were taken
to North Gate Police Station. Why did you lie? Why didn't you tell
Ku the truth?"

"I don't know. I was afraid that if I did, the cell would expel me."

"And could you tell me," said Lin, turning to Hsueh, "what
precisely is your relation to Inspector Maron? Why did you make
contact with Ku via Leng?"

Hsueh couldn't answer his question. "We're friends, just friends," he stammered. "No, actually, we're good friends."

Lin smiled at him. "Don't worry, we know exactly what you've been up to. We would like to stay in contact with you. If you trust us, and trust that we're working for a just cause, you can consider us your friends."

CHAPTER 53

The bigger newspapers, like *Shun Pao* and *Ta Kung Pao*, mentioned the press statement briefly on their local pages. But some of the smaller tabloid-format newspapers that relied on press releases for most of their news printed it in full. The *New Citizen*, for instance, printed the full text on the bottom right-hand corner of the front page. The previous year, it had been temporarily shut down by the Shanghai Committee to Purify the Party for printing a photo of Chiang Kai-shek in full armor in an ad for a libido-boosting drug. Ads poking fun at the commander in chief were everywhere toward the end of the Kuomintang military campaign against regional warlords, but gradually they had been purged. The *New Citizen's* editor on night duty was cautious, but Hsueh pointed out that the Shun News Agency would almost certainly circulate the statement via their wire service, so the editor could attribute it to Shun and let them take responsibility for it. Sure enough, the *New Citizen* printed their convoluted story in a two-page article that consisted more or less of Lin's words, with a few minor changes.

If Hsueh had run into Li Pao-i, he would have given him a copy of the press statement too. Even the *Arsène Lupin* had its regular readers. After seeing Leng safely onto a tram, he bought a copy of the *New Citizen* from the newsstand at the station. Lin was busy making sure that the comrades he had called to that meeting had somewhere safe to go. As for Leng, it would be simplest for her to stay in Hsueh's rooms and rest.

But Hsueh couldn't go home with her—there was something else he had to do. He found a public telephone booth on Boulevard de Montigny, and called Lieutenant Sarly's office at the police headquarters.

Sarly answered the phone on the first ring. He must have been waiting for this phone call since he woke up and read the newspapers. He exploded before Hsueh could say anything.

"What's this in the papers? Is there anything left for you to report to me? It's all over the news! Ku's gang aren't Communists, but there's a conspiracy to blame the Communists? Why didn't you come to me first with this? What is this attack they're planning? Why didn't you report it to the police? What the hell do you think you're doing?"

Afterward he went into the bakery on Rue du Consulat and ordered a coffee. He was pleased to hear the radio broadcast coming from the other side of the house. This was definitely a good idea, he thought.

And when Hsueh told him where Ku was planning to attack, Sarly had to forgive him. If Hsueh hadn't done what these people wanted, he would never have been able to get away, and he wouldn't have been able to give the police the details of Ku's operation. Hsueh sometimes thought that Sarly was playing a game of cat and mouse with him, that he could see exactly what Hsueh was up to from his lofty vantage point, and would tolerate Hsueh's tricks as long as he wanted to keep playing.

At eleven o'clock, he arrived punctually at Mallet Police Station. The poet was waiting for him at the entrance, and Maron's detective squad had assembled in a large conference room.

Sarly was in a smaller, adjacent room. He took the news with extraordinary calm. He had dealt with an indigenous uprising in French-occupied Côte d'Ivoire in 1912, and after the Great War he had searched houses in Hanoi for homemade bomb factories run by the independence activists. When he was in a good mood, he would boast to Hsueh about the highlights of his career serving overseas. Right now he was fascinated by the Communists, and he was disappointed by Hsueh's news. He was especially disappointed that Hsueh had gone to the newspapers and radio stations with it. Hsueh realized that he had let Sarly down. He attributed Sarly's reaction to wounded pride, to having been mistaken about Ku.

Sarly was pleased with the diagram that Hsueh had drawn from memory, and had Inspector Maron take it into the conference room. Successfully thwarting Ku's next operation would help Hsueh to save face with Sarly, but it would also allow Sarly himself to save face. Hsueh sincerely hoped Ku's operation would fail. In fact, he hoped the police would shoot Ku dead on the spot. Lin, his new friend, would want that too—after all, Ku was an imposter misrepresenting the Communist Party. The trouble was that no one knew when the attack would take place.

But Sarly didn't seem troubled. He smoked his pipe and waited.

Inspector Maron burst in. "We'll have to seal the streets off with armored police vehicles," he barked, the boorish ex-wrestler in him coming to the fore. "There are too many pedestrians on the road, and if we don't scare them off, we'll lose control of the situation."

"But they could put the attack off to tomorrow or the day after tomorrow," Sarly said irresolutely.

"Today isn't just any day. All policemen are reporting to duty, and half of them are at the Koukaza Gardens because Consul Baudez and the directors of the Municipal Office are reviewing the troops. The commanding officer of the Indo-Chinese troops will be up on the platform as well."

Only now did Hsueh realize that it was the fourteenth of July; not for nothing had Ku chosen to strike on Bastille Day.

"I'll go myself as soon as we wrap up here. Remember that we want to wait until the robbery is under way before striking. Tell me about your plan of attack." Lieutenant Sarly had put Inspector Maron in charge of coordinating the operation.

"We've stationed snipers at the guard post on Rue des Pères, and the bank is swarming with plainclothes Chinese policemen. It only takes two minutes for a car to get from here to the location of the attack. The police stations on Avenue Joffre and Avenue Foch are both on standby alert, and all police cars are circling the streets near Rue du Consulat. As soon as the alarm is sounded, the entire district will be sealed off."

"Very good. What's there to worry about?"

Sarly drew out the small brown bag that contained his private possessions. He undid the string, took out a copper pick, and started to clean his pipe. But as he was about to pack the pipe, they heard an explosion in the distance, to their west. It was two in the afternoon. Many days later, after things had died down, Sarly said to Hsueh: "It hadn't occurred to me that he would start with an explosion. If he wanted to rob a bank, why start by tossing a grenade? No one does that. I thought he was insane—anyone else would have crept into the bank, quietly taken control, and told everyone to get down on the floor. They would need time to put all that cash in bags or crates. Most of it would be in silver, so the crates would be extremely heavy, and they would have to be lugged into a car. I knew he was armed and could break through a barricade. We were extremely well prepared. We had policemen lying in wait inside and outside the bank with rifles, and as soon as they came out, we were going to open fire from all sides. I told our men that they would have at least ten minutes to take up their positions outside the bank. But they didn't want to give us any time. In fact, they didn't even want to give themselves any time."

The explosions were followed by a barrage of shots as well as single shots that rang out one at a time, as if to avoid being drowned out by the rest of the gunfire. If Hsueh didn't know what they were, he would think these were firecrackers at a wedding banquet. People might assume there was a big banquet at a fancy restaurant like the Hung-yün, or a store opening on Rue du Consulat.

Inspector Maron rushed out with his detectives. They had gotten the tip, and they were ready. The explosions didn't faze them, and police cars awaited them at the gate. Sarly had Hsueh go with himself.

The two of them got into an armored Rolls-Royce. With terrified

pedestrians thronging the roads, it took them seven or eight minutes rather than two minutes to reach the bank, although it was less
than a kilometer away. By the time they got there, the shootout was
almost over.

Hsueh recognized the officer in charge at the scene, Sergeant
Ch'eng of North Gate Police Station. Sergeant Ch'eng glanced
at Hsueh before giving Lieutenant Sarly an account of the
gunfight. Even though his men had been ready, they had been
bewildered when the operation started. It couldn't be said that
they were unprepared. Yes, when they saw that car pull up to
the door of the bank, they had "tensed up," in the words of one
of the snipers. Yes, they had seen three bicycles screech to a
halt by the colonnades, one on the same side of the street as the
bank, and two on the opposite side, exactly where the diagram
had them. But no one would have guessed that the men who
jumped out of the Peugeot would each throw a grenade at the
door of the bank. At the same time, a loud explosion could be
heard coming from each of the bicycles: firecrackers, quantities
of them, rerigged so that a single match would make them all go
off at once.

The robbers were complete amateurs, Sergeant Ch'eng sniffed.
They were terrified out of their wits before they'd even gotten
started. And it hadn't occurred to them that there could be an
ambush. The police had begun to fire seconds later, and it looked
as though they hadn't anticipated that at all. The three men who
had burst into the bank through the smoke of the explosion were
trapped. They were under fire from behind the bank counters as
well as from the steps of the bank.

Then things took a farcical turn. The three men on bikes had
been ready to back up their comrades inside the bank from behind
the cover of the columns, but as soon as they pulled out their guns,
they could tell that things had gone very wrong. They ran out from
the colonnades, jumped into the car, and rushed off before the police
could take aim, abandoning the men inside.

"They went in the direction of Boulevard de Montigny," Sergeant

Ch'eng said. As though to confirm his words, gunfire rang out from the direction of Rue Passejo, to their west.

"They won't get away. They won't be able to get past Boulevard de Montigny," Lieutenant Sarly said, looking at the scene of the explosion. The three corpses lay in a pile of broken glass in the lobby, and who knew how many other casualties there were.

Li Pao-i stopped at Hsieh-t'ai Money Exchange, a small money changer and tobacco shop run on Rue Vouillemont by a man from Ningpo. His takings from the night before were in his pocket, in the form of a ten-yuan note issued by the Chinese Agricultural Bank and printed by Waterloo and Sons. It was covered with foreign writing and had the bank general manager's ornate signature on the back, an anticounterfeiting device. An entire batch of banknotes had once been stolen from a bank before signatures could be printed onto them, and as a result, banknotes with faded counterfeit signatures still turned up every now and again.

He pushed his banknote through the iron railing to the man behind the counter.

"Nine silver coins, and change the last yuan into cents, please." He liked hearing them jingle in his pocket.

Then he bought a bag of fried dumplings at the steamed bun shop next door. He knew it was a fake Ta-hu-ch'un, not a real branch of the well-known dumpling restaurant, but who cared?

He put the small change in his other pocket. He was about to go over to the Morris Teahouse to catch up on the gossip. It was Bastille Day, and the Race Club had organized an extra Champagne Stakes race in honor of the occasion. Last night had been a good night for him at poker, thanks to his new strategy. So he decided not to keep playing that morning. Instead, he would stop by Peach Girl's place to take a nap on her bed around noon, and then continue with his winning streak.

While he was waiting for his dumplings, he could hear the radio playing at the money changer's next door. He heard a name that caught his attention: People's Strength. He'd never forgotten the last time he'd heard those words.

He went along Avenue Édouard VII. It was early, the road was empty, and there were no cars. He was walking right in the middle of the road. Race Course Road arced toward Avenue Édouard VII, which just touched the top of the arc. The two swathes of houses where the roads met spread toward the Race Course like a woman's thighs. A narrow alley between the houses led toward the Race Course, about twenty yards away. To the left of the alley lay a kidney clinic that dispensed traditional Chinese medicine, and a public toilet stood awkwardly in the middle of the road. Li had heard tell that the Race Course's longtime gamblers would all come here to touch the doorframe leading to the female toilets because its *feng shui* gave it especially powerful *yin* luck.

At the tip of that promontory of houses was Morris Teahouse. Li Pao-i went straight up to a window seat on the second floor, and sat on a drum-shaped little stool. He had the waiter make him a pot of jasmine tea, and tore open the oil-drenched wax paper in which his dumplings were wrapped. Then he asked the waiter for a small plate of vinegar.

He was a regular customer here, and even had a tab. But today he wouldn't need his tab. He could even pay it off—in silver yuan coins, no less, playing the high roller. He took out his silver yuan and inspected the bill that the waiter had brought him. He was about to pay with a coin when he realized that he had almost forgotten about his lucky coin, which was jumbled up with all the others. He couldn't just get rid of the coin that had helped him to make good on his losses this morning. He stacked up the coins and sniffed them one by one until he caught a whiff of the familiar smell.

Paying the bill made him feel great. He had the waiter bring him a newspaper. One headline caught his attention, and he read the article carefully, noticing the familiar name it alluded to as its source: an experienced journalist at a French newspaper in the Concession, Mr. Weiss Hsueh. Li spat tea leaves into his cup, irritated that Hsueh hadn't told him about such a big scoop. Ordinary crooks indeed, he spat. He'd known all along that those people weren't Communists. He remembered the questions Hsueh had asked him that night in Moon Palace Dancing Hall.

When he flipped to the racing post, he forgot about the article. Today was the day of the Champagne Stakes, a big race, and all the most famous racehorses would be there. Unusually, bets could be placed up to a week in advance. But Li was in no hurry to place his bet.

For the race with Aussie horses, he had already settled on Bullet, a horse belonging to the British businessman Gordon. It was the kind of horse that always shot to the front of the pack. Horses like that sometimes lost steam and lagged behind, but Bullet wasn't like them. Even in a long one-and-a-quarter-mile race, he knew it would come out ahead. The jockey was well chosen too. Captain Sokoloff was the Concession's only real master of riding with short stirrups, where you had to almost be squatting on the saddle. For Mongolian horses, jockeys usually used longer stirrups, and kicked the horse in the belly to make it go faster. But Aussie horses were taller, and a jockey would need the aid of his reins and whip. Riding with short stirrups would give him more flexibility.

Li decided that he would simply buy a win ticket for the race with Aussie horses. Any fool could guess what would happen in that race, and the betting odds were low. Easy money. But he was going to win big in the race with Mongolian horses by placing a triple bet, going all in. There, an upset would allow him to win dozens of times his wager. In fact, if he was lucky and the horse racing dailies spent a few more inches raving about Mahler's white mare, he stood to win hundreds of times his wager. For a week now, he had inspected the horses at Mohawk Road every day. The gray horse, Illusion, was sure to surprise everyone. It was no longer as timid as it used to be. They said it was startled by hurdles as they sprang up, and that it sweated too much. But he had seen the stable hands wave a net in its face without making it flinch. He'd even seen a groom splash water on its belly before leading it out to the practice track, so that the gamblers clustered by the railing would think it was sweating.

Today would be Illusion's day. Old Mahler had slyly arranged for his own son to ride that mare. Mahler Jr. was fat and too heavy, and with him for a jockey, even the renowned horse could only come second. Illusion would come first, and Mahler's "White Rose" would come second. No one else would have worked this out, and the triple bet only made his bet even riskier and the payoff bigger. He would win hundreds of times his wager because the odds were so long.

He had to go back to Peach Girl's around lunchtime. The previous night he had had the idea of stuffing two silver coins into her drawers. She was fast asleep, and even the two hard coins he wedged right into that sticky cleft didn't wake her. They had absorbed all her female *yin* energy and brought him good luck. He was going to do it again—but with more than ten yuan this time, so that he'd be sure to make a killing.

He gazed confidently around the teahouse, at all the sorry gamblers who were about to lose their shirts, and at the Race Club journalists who thought they knew their stuff. Then he saw a pair of eyes, and panicked.

Yes, he'd seen this man before. His name was—Li racked his brains for the name. He'd only just read it in the papers. The man had sent a bullet in a brown paper envelope to his newspaper office. He'd kidnapped Li, and forced him at gunpoint to print a certain manifesto. His name was Ku Fu-kuang. It was all coming back to him, the name in the news report, the Green Gang gossip, the leak attributed to Hsueh. He thought he could see the man looking at him, and he didn't dare meet his gaze. He lowered his eyes, as though he couldn't be seen by Ku if he couldn't see him.

He didn't dare to kick up a fuss. He knew Ku had a gun. He couldn't see Ku's hands, which were under the table. But he thought he could see his right arm moving, reaching under his linen shirt for something. He felt bloated—the dumplings had been far too oily—and there was something stuck in his throat. He tried to burp but couldn't. He picked up his teacup, and put it down again. He had better pretend he didn't recognize the man, he thought. But he knew he looked flustered, and he was no good at pretending. Ku would have seen him by now.

Li got up and hurried down the stairs. The waiter waved to him, and he waved back irritably—why not wave at someone else, like the man who terrified him, and detain him to give Li time to escape? He didn't look around. He had neither the time nor the nerve. He rushed out of the teahouse and toward a narrow street on his left. The streets were almost empty. The gamblers who'd gotten there early would be on the northern end of Race Course Road, near the stables on Mohawk Road. There were several men clustered outside the public toilets in the middle of the road, so he raced into the toilets. At the door he turned to look back, and saw Ku standing outside the teahouse, looking toward the northern end of the road. He hid inside the toilets, and thought: I'm safe. His stomach ached. He opened the door to a cubicle, undid his pants, and squatted down. His heart was racing. He couldn't shit. He kept farting. His blood ran cold.

He didn't hear the footsteps. But suddenly someone opened the door to the cubicle, and he was blinded by light. He looked up and wanted to smile at him, but he couldn't force a smile. He saw the knife flash, and felt something cold on his neck, as if a gust of wind were blowing straight into his lungs. He couldn't say a thing. He saw his own blood drip onto his clothes, and onto the pants that hung around his knees. His hands relaxed, his legs crumbled, and his pants dropped all the way to his ankles. He could hear the coins jingle in them, and he only had one thought: the coins are there and I haven't used them, so it's still my lucky day.

The moment before he died, he recognized a familiar smell, the smell on those coins, Peach Girl's smell. He saw a streak of gray glide past him, and thought, that's my horse.

Ku's greatest fear had come true. He didn't like what they were saying about him. Whatever he was, he was not an imposter. He was especially irritated by a passage in which he was said to have been caught in bed with a whore and leaped out of bed naked, when he knew he had been wearing briefs. It was Hsueh who infuriated him. He had played fair, hadn't had him killed, and the next thing he knew, that sneak was writing about him in the papers and conniving with Lin to lure all his best people away. Those young people were the boldest operatives he had; they never left a job unfinished. Hsueh must be an undercover detective. As soon as this operation was over, he would have to be executed as an enemy of the revolution.

Ku had deliberately left the diagram on the table at the candle store. As soon as he had gotten back to the store, he had realized something was up. The three people scheduled to meet there hadn't arrived, and they were all members of Lin's unit. He didn't know what the threat to them was, but the candle store was no longer safe. He ordered them all to leave. He made a sign to Park to strangle Leng, so that the neighbors wouldn't hear a struggle. Leng had already betrayed the cell, and her presence would only endanger them. It would be best for Hsueh to think that Therese had killed her. He had originally spared Hsueh because he thought the bastard might come in useful in the future. But Hsueh too could no longer be trusted, and anyone who wasn't going to be useful to the cell and could even harm it would have to be eliminated.

He sat in Morris Teahouse, reading the newspaper article. It made him so mad he almost lost it right there. He pressed his hands into his thighs and thought, take a deep breath. But no sooner had he calmed down than he saw that accursed reporter. He could tell the man had recognized him. What a day, one damn thing after another. He could feel anger welling up in him as he saw the idiot try to slink away.

He couldn't just let him go. An operation was about to take place, and nothing could be allowed to disrupt it.

He finished the man off in the toilet. No one noticed. He shut the low cubicle door gently, and reached over the top of the door to lock it. His clothes were spotless—it had been a clean death. He decided not to go back to the teahouse.

Mohawk Road was crowded. The first pack of racehorses had already been led across the road and into the Race Course via a special entrance. Long lines had formed in front of the ticket offices, and Sikh policemen were patrolling the road nervously. The crowd parted narrowly to let the mounted police through. It was hot, and everywhere there were thinly clad men clutching their wallets to their bellies, to forestall pickpockets.

He went into Te-fu Alley. There was a large field with stables at the end of the alley. He had arranged to rent a stable there months ago, claiming to be a horse dealer from Chang-chia-k'o. The stables were on the first floor of the building, and there were offices upstairs. The whole place was walled off.

Park was sitting at the entrance to the first stall, with a Mauser rifle in his hands.

They were short a few people, but he decided to go ahead anyway. A roar to the east meant the first race had started. A sudden hush followed, as though the earth itself was holding its breath, and the crowd was leaning forward so that their voices became a thin stream of air that melted into the quiet. Then another wave of cheers broke. The winning horse must be making its final dash.

It's now or never, he thought. From now on, he would be notorious and everyone would be afraid of him. Not only did the Race Course swallow huge sums of cash, it was an image of the concessions in its power, wealth, and thirst for money. It was at the heart of the concessions—it *was* the heart of the concessions. Today he was going to explode this heart and send the concessions into shock. The weapons he had bought from the White Russian woman were crucial to this plan. The way they penetrated their targets was a perfect metaphor for how he planned to penetrate his target and blow it to pieces.

He checked the stables to make sure that there wasn't a single copy of that day's paper lying around. Finding a radio in a corner, he opened the back and pulled out the thickest vacuum tube. The photographer was sitting on the sofa, with his camera and tripod lying on the floor. He nodded at the guard.

He breathed deeply and waited.

By three o'clock, it was scorching hot. Ku had asked Park to leave the truck on the corner of Rue Wagner and Rue Vouillemont. At two in the afternoon, he had heard the blast of explosions and gunfire coming from the direction of Boulevard de Montigny, to the east. The planned sham attack was already under way. He had a few people making a stir at the National Industrial Bank on Rue du Consulat. All the policemen in the French Concession would rush there, and Boulevard de Montigny would be completely barricaded. But the gunfire soon stopped. He cursed Hsueh and Lin for taking his best people—the ones he had left were worthless.

At a quarter to three, he saw a motorcade drive past. The two trucks on the end of the motorcade carried French soldiers in wide-brimmed helmets and short-sleeved military uniforms with leggings, bugles of all kinds in their hands. These soldiers were on their way to the Koukaza Gardens for the review of troops. The motorcade would be full of prominent Concession figures. They were heading to the Race Course to see the final and most important race, which would begin at three thirty. The consul, the directors of the Municipal Office, and the commanding officer of the Indo-Chinese troops would all be there for the Champagne Stakes, in the VIP box. At least he hoped they would all be there, so that his message would be unmistakable to them all: he, Ku Fu-kuang, was in Shanghai!

A quarter past three. He rapped on the rear window of the truck cab, signaling to Park to start the engine. The truck edged slowly toward the northern end of Rue Vouillemont. A 35 mm camera peeked out from under the tarp covering the cargo bed, near the front of the truck.

A moment later, their target emerged from Avenue Édouard VII.

The first car was an armored police vehicle equipped with a cannon. The second was a small truck, another armored vehicle that had been newly reinforced with steel plates. It carried the takings from that day's races in cash. According to the papers, the Race Club could make 100,000 silver yuan in a single day. On a day like this, for the Champagne Stakes, there must be at least 500,000 yuan circulating in the Race Course, and Ku was certain that at least 100,000 would be in this armored truck. This was the first cash transport of the day, and it was leaving the Race Course quietly, before the last race ended. It would send most of the Race Club's takings for the day directly to its coffers. This was the truck he would attack.

Marksmen were waiting on the roof of a two-story building on the left-hand side of Rue Vouillemont. They were armed with the grenade launchers that the White Russian woman had sold him. He had recognized them from a glance at the diagram, having seen photos of many different weapons in the Soviet ammunition course he took. They looked like rifles mounted on a two-legged tripod, but they fired grenades, not bullets. He didn't know the precise Chinese name for these weapons, but then they probably weren't available on the Chinese market. The most exciting thing about these launchers, and the reason why he had planned this particular operation, was that they could fire grenades that penetrated armor, straight into the heart of a target, where they would explode.

Unfortunately, he hadn't had much time to train the marksmen. They took their boats beyond Wu-sung-k'ou, where he had them float buoys in the water and sail about fifty meters away. Then his men would lie prostrate on the roof of the boat's cabin, in the exact positions they would be taking up during the operation, and shoot at the buoys. He didn't care about wasting ammunition; he wanted to make sure they would get it right. When the waters were calm, they always hit their targets—he had handpicked the best marksmen. But whenever it was windy, and the buoys began to drift, their hit rates plummeted. They weren't used to these launchers, or to the trajectory of the grenades as they traveled toward their targets.

But he had planned for all that. That was precisely why they were attacking from Rue Vouillemont. He knew the armored vehicle's route inside out. It had to drive along Avenue Édouard VII, the boundary between the French Concession and the International Settlement, and turn onto Rue Vouillemont from there. Those arrogant bastards, he thought. They hadn't even thought to change the route occasionally in case they might be attacked.

The rules of the road differed between the French Concession and the International Settlement. In the latter, cars drove on the left according to the British system, but the Municipal Office stipulated that cars in the Concession had to drive on the right, and it wouldn't budge.

(Ku had no way of knowing that the Board of Works and the Municipal Office were in talks to standardize traffic rules in Shanghai, and that from the end of that year onward, all cars in Shanghai would have to drive on the left. Shortly thereafter, the Kuomintang government would turn that into national law.)

The armored motorcade drove out of the road to the left of the public toilets, and made a U-turn around the opening in the median on Avenue Édouard VII. As it turned into Rue Vouillemont, it would have to stop briefly on the left-hand side of the road.

Shanghailanders had long thought that the traffic rules in the two concessions should really be standardized. At this intersection, for instance, cars making a left turn out of Rue Vouillemont would have to turn onto the far left lane of Avenue Édouard VII.

Drivers often began to turn the steering wheel before they even reached the street corner, to avoid the traffic on Avenue Édouard VII and cut directly into the queue. But this also meant that they were driving straight into southbound traffic on the left-hand side of Rue Vouillemont. Ku discovered that the armored truck always made this turn very carefully. It would stop for about ten seconds, to avoid running into those impatient drivers. After all, it was carrying a truckload of cash.

The sun beat down on the red armored trucks. Snipers hid inside the police vehicle, which had machine guns on the turrets. Ku peered out at the truck from behind the tarp. The camera slid to one side, beneath his chin, to give him room. Once he started shooting, the cameraman appeared to forget how frightened and exhausted he was. There were two parallel rows of rivets along the edge of the armored truck's rectangular body. Ku waited.

The road was white with the sunshine, and he couldn't make out the glow of the launchers. But in the split second before his eardrums vibrated with the explosion, he saw the grenades tear open the armor of the police vehicle and explode its turret, the top of which lifted off altogether and lodged in the branches of a nearby tree.

All the way along Avenue Édouard VII, Race Course Road, and Mohawk Road, firecrackers rang out. He had arranged for them to explode along the route to the Race Course, like a string of those ancient beacon towers used to warn against invasion. Finally, the Race Course itself would be rocked by explosions. The deadliest bombs he had were hidden in the toilets beneath the VIP box.

He saw Park jump out of his own truck and run toward the armored truck. According to the plan, he would kill everyone on that truck, and drive it away to the film studio on Rue Gaston Kahn, where he would hide until it was dark. Then he would drive quietly to the banks of Chao-chia Creek, where a small boat would be waiting for him.

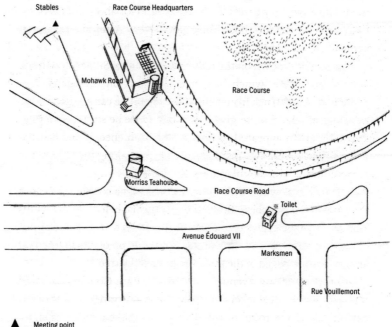

Stables Race Course Headquarters

Mohawk Road

Race Course

Morriss Teahouse

Race Course Road

Toilet

Avenue Édouard VII

Marksmen

Rue Vouillemont

▲ : Meeting point

※ : Li Pao-i assassinated here

☆ : Ambush

The Race Course and environs

With the finish line in sight, he turned to look at the cameraman. He wanted to watch the film of his own masterpiece as soon as he had time. But just then, he saw the steel plate on the right-hand side of the armored truck shift just a crack, and he realized that he had overlooked the rivets. A pale face shimmered behind the dark holes, he saw the glow of a machine gun, and the two men running behind Park fell dead to the ground. Park pulled out his Mauser, and waved his arms, as though he was about to leap into the river. Then his arm was torn off at the shoulder by a barrage of bullets, and it fell to the ground before he did.

He could see them all retreating, rushing out of the longtang, jumping off the truck. Those losers. He could feel his anger welling up through the veins in his neck and going straight to his head. The skin behind his ears pulsed, nearly exploding with rage. He picked up the launcher in the corner of the cargo bed and took a deep breath while his hands calmly loaded another round. Without even bothering to take aim, he fired. The grenade tore off the entire back of the armored truck, which began to smoke. Ku pulled out his gun, jumped out, and made for the other truck. Its driver was unconscious from the impact of the grenade. He opened the door, fired his remaining bullets into the body, and then shoved it aside with his knees. He started the engine. He had no time to wait for anyone else, for his own truck, or even to get the film inside the camera. He sped southward in the armored truck.

For a moment, he mourned for Park. He had lost his most loyal follower, the one who was almost a brother to him. He sometimes wondered whether he had made the anonymous phone call betraying Park's older brother to the police in order to take his place.

He couldn't see behind him, so he didn't know that the chassis of the truck had been completely torn open, spilling a trail of silver onto the road. The inhabitants of the French Concession would celebrate. Three whole days later, the municipal street cleaners would still be digging silver yuan coins from crevices in the drains.

CHAPTER 56

JULY 19, YEAR 20 OF THE REPUBLIC.

3 : 20 P.M.

Days later, Yan Feng couldn't stop thinking about that afternoon. He had slipped away from Rue Vouillemont in the chaos, with his camera and tripod in tow. He had run all the way to the imposing gate of the Foreigners' Cemetery, which towered over it like a city wall. There he flagged down a rickshaw, and had the rickshaw man take him back to the studio on Rue Gaston Kahn.

Dozens of cars were crowded at the entrance to T'ing-yüan Lane. Policemen swarmed in and out, and he didn't dare go in. The actress Pearl Yeh was rushed out in the bathrobe she had been wearing on set. She jumped in her car and hurried away.

What could he possibly say to the police? What would the others say? There was no way they would believe his story that he had been forced at gunpoint into accepting a side gig from a Communist.

A few years ago, he had been a war zone reporter for the National Revolutionary Army, shooting footage that was cut into newsreels and shown alongside Hollywood flicks in the concessions' movie theaters. He even got an award from the Artistic Editing Group of the Central Propaganda Department's Shanghai office. But all those newsreels had been faked. He was never asked to shoot a real battle. As a matter of fact, he wouldn't have been able to follow the soldiers up steep hills or wade through rivers with that 35 mm camera of his. The newsreels all had scripted, pre-determined storylines. Soldiers would lie on the ground dressed as rebels, with uniforms stripped from real corpses on the battlefield, which came ragged with bullet holes.

But in the reel he had shot that afternoon, all the bodies were real. As he hid behind his camera, he thought about how the scene didn't look all that different from a movie set. Bullets crumbled the brick walls as though centuries of weathering had been compressed into seconds. The injured lay convulsing on the ground. Blood didn't spurt from their wounds—it leaked like ketchup from a spilt bottle. The explosions deafened him, and it felt like listening to bombs echo from a distance. The turret on the armored police vehicle looked like an exploding eggshell. In fact, the sheets of metal that tore off and curled up looked softer than eggshells. In the blinding sunlight, he could see bullets spark against the metal sides of the truck from behind his viewfinder.

Only later did he realize that these men were Communists. On Mohawk Road, before setting out, they had sworn an oath and made a statement on camera, declaring war on imperialists and counterrevolutionaries. He even got their hammer-and-sickle flag into the shot.

Not long ago, a few of the ghost movies he had shot for Hua Sisters Motion Picture Studio had been sent to the Shanghai Movie Inspection Committee, which had forced them to cut the movie. It had to be resubmitted a few times, and was only passed after his bosses had put in a few words with the right people, but his best scenes had all been cut. He started feeling that the Communists had a point. The motion picture world had had its own run-in with imperialism just that past year, over *Welcome Danger*, an imported film with a demeaning view of the Chinese. Protesters showed up at the cinema, making speeches during screenings and staging pro-tests outside. Yan went along to chant slogans and wave his flag. He was tagging along at the very end of the procession, but the police arrested him and locked him up for half a day anyway. The film turned Yan into an enemy of imperialism.

He loved cameras, and he loved making movies. He would usually go anywhere with anyone who wanted him to shoot film.

He didn't want anyone touching his camera, and shooting film was his job.

But now that it was over, he was terrified. He was afraid of being questioned by the police. This was a huge deal, and they could charge him with anything they liked. They could even accuse him of collaborating with the Communists and send him to the Kiangsu Provincial Supreme Court. That would mean an automatic minimum sentence of eight or ten years, and whenever they felt like being tough on Communists, they could simply have him shot.

He told the rickshaw man to turn around and head in the opposite direction.

He didn't know whether to develop that reel of film. He wasn't satisfied with his work. He hadn't had an assistant, and those men knew nothing about film—they didn't even bring a light-proof changing bag. From where he had been standing on the truck, his camera was too high up and there wasn't enough depth of field, so the strong sunlight would turn most of the background white. These men would want to be recognizable; they wanted to be heroes. That meant he couldn't make the aperture any narrower, and risked ruining the film by overexposing it. He hadn't had his Watkins Bee Meter with him. It was still in his jacket pocket, draped over the chair in the film studio. An exposure meter like that wasn't easy to come by.

But this film was unlike any he had ever shot in his life. It was real, more real than all the weapons he had ever seen. He shot wide shots, then close-ups, then wide shots, then close-ups, wanting to convey the volatility in every moment.

He didn't dare show up at work. When he finally called in, someone told him that Pearl Yeh had taken fright and announced she would be resting at home. The studio had no choice but to stop production on the movie, and delay its release. But they couldn't complain, because the sensational news would make the movie a box office success. The following night, he could hardly stop himself from destroying the film. It would be so easy. Cellulose nitrate burns instantly, so a single match would do the trick.

Then last night, he had been sitting by the window, reading the papers. It was humid, and the clouds hung oppressively low over the city. Lightning sliced through the night sky. It could rain any moment.

He didn't hear the key turn in the lock. But when he looked up, there was a man standing in the doorway with a canvas raincoat on. His silhouette looked familiar. The man closed the door, locked and bolted it, and turned to face him. He was wearing a sou'wester pulled down over his eyes.

The tea-colored glasses with tortoiseshell rims threw him off, but within seconds, he recognized the leader of the gang. The hero of his latest film, and the protagonist of the day in all the newspapers. His name was said to be Ku Fu-kuang. His newspaper fluttered gently onto the table.

"I've come to get it," he said.

"I haven't got the film. The police came for it." He didn't dare give the film to this man. He didn't know what he wanted with it. Did he want a souvenir to corroborate his shaky memory? What if he decided to show it openly, and Yan's own name appeared in the credits? That would land him a charge of collaboration and ten years in prison. You disagree? Well then the penalty is death, to be carried out immediately.

"Mr. Yan." The man was carrying a messenger bag, like an errand boy at a trading firm. He put the bag on the table and took out a ciga- rette case, matches, and a gun, which he tossed on the table. "I've been watching you for days. You haven't gone to work, you've been hiding at home, and the cops haven't been to see you. You still have it."

I commissioned this film. As the cameraman, you, Yan Feng, have no right to claim possession of it. How dare you fail to hand it over to me? The penalty is death, no appeal, to be carried out immediately with the gun on the table. I'll give you a minute, or perhaps only thirty seconds. . . .

"It isn't here—it's at the studio. Film is delicate, and it fuses into a sticky lump when it gets humid. It's also highly flammable. And it has to be developed, edited, and matched to the sound track, frame by frame."

"Developed?"

"All we have right now are the negatives, which will be exposed and ruined as soon as you take them out. They have to be developed before we can put them on a projector."

"That's fine. I can go to the studio with you right now, and you can develop the film there."

Let's go to your studio to get that reel of film. I need it, and I'll get mad if you don't give it to me. So get dressed and come along to the studio cheerfully, as if we're good friends going someplace together. It's a reasonable enough thing to ask, and you don't have an excuse for turning me down.

"We can't do it today. I'd need the technician's help, and he'll already have gone home."

His visitor considered that for a moment. It started to rain, and the streets began to blur. A white film of rain melted into the vapor rising from the hot tarmac roads. After a single clap of thunder, the sky grew quiet while the rain kept pattering down.

"Very good. In that case, I will come to see you tomorrow."

His eyes flickered behind his tea-colored glasses, but he made no threats. Instead, he slowly replaced the gun in his bag and left, closing the door gently behind him.

The rain kept pelting down. Yan Feng felt as though he were dreaming.

The next morning, he decided to ask the studio technician to help him develop the negatives. They had worked together for many years. It was a Sunday, and the studio was quiet. Watching the film on the little projector next to the film-cutting table, they were both blown away. It wouldn't need to be edited at all. The sound track on the wax record, including the long announcement, could simply provide a background track played on repeat for the twenty-minute film. He had used five spools of film, each four hundred meters long, and every frame was so realistic that he couldn't bear to cut it. This was the best film he had ever shot, and he would probably never get the chance to shoot another one like it. Actually, he would rather not have another chance.

But as he watched it again, he grew dissatisfied. He cut a few sequences out to make the action look smoother. Some actions looked slower once you got them on film, and they didn't convey the brutal shootout he remembered. Then he cut a few more frames to create a montage of fight scenes.

The guard was calling to him from outside the window. He went over and drew the blinds.

It was the police. A Frenchman in a uniform was standing by the car, along with a Chinese man in civilian clothes, who noticed him at the window. The guard was showing him to the stairs. Again, he felt as though he had just woken from a dream.

Finally, they were here, he thought. No matter what happened, this piece would be his crowning piece of work. "Mr. Yan, we know you are in possession of a significant piece of police evidence, a reel of film," they said. "Please come with us."

Hsueh was being held in an isolation cell in the northwest corner of the police headquarters building. He didn't see Sarly until the fourth day he was there. But he had realized long before then that Sarly himself must be under suspicion. Only later did he learn that Chief of Police Mallet had been in charge of the investigation.

It was confirmed that Hsueh was one of the special investigators recruited by Inspector Maron for the Political Section, albeit one who had never passed an examination or been sent to the colonial police school in Hanoi. Hsueh decided that Sarly wasn't just sticking to this story to protect him.

In the many conversations he had had about the incident—no one referred to them as interrogations—Hsueh insisted that he had never heard Ku speak of plans to rob the armored vehicles that transported cash from the Race Course. This was the truth. He never mentioned Sarly's remark that he was waiting for Ku to "plan something massive." That wasn't a lie either—people's memories of past conversations are usually unreliable, and word-for-word recollections often turn out to be false memories. The only thing he did hide from the police was Therese's role in the arms deal involving that new weapon. Strictly speaking he didn't have to lie, since he was never questioned about it. At first he was suspicious that no one ever brought it up, but eventually he decided that Sarly must simply not have mentioned that weapon to anyone. Many years later, when they were longtime colleagues and nearly friends, Hsueh ventured to ask why. Sarly told him that he himself hadn't recognized the weapon, but he had guessed it was a type of machine gun and wanted to get a weapons specialist to look at it. Then everything had happened so quickly and he had been so madly busy that he didn't get around to it right away. By then Hsueh was much less naïve, and he had a hunch that Sarly had had his reasons for choosing to forget about the weapon. But a more worldly-wise Hsueh kept his suspicions to himself.

He decided not to tell Lieutenant Sarly about Lin and the Communists, partly because they had been good to him, and partly because he didn't want any more trouble. As for Leng, she was too deeply implicated in the Kin Lee Yuen assassination to be let off scot-free. The police hadn't yet come after her because they had their hands full with this investigation, but she would have to leave Shanghai before they did. It was time he left Shanghai too, he thought. He even had the money. When they locked him up, he had rolled up the check Ku intended for Therese into a tiny roll the size of a cigarette, flipped up the sole of one shoe, picked open the inner stitching near the heel, burrowed out a hole, and buried the check in it. As soon as they let him out, he told himself, he would go to the bank and cash it before they froze the account—it was a check made out to cash. Then he would go to see Therese at the General Hospital. He both wanted to and dreaded seeing her. But he owed her a visit, if only because of the money he was taking.

He had all kinds of plans for his future life with Leng. They would travel via Haiphong to Europe, or perhaps to America—he wondered whether he would have enough money to start a new life there.

Lieutenant Sarly encouraged him to take a few weeks off before reporting to the Political Section to start work. That would give Hsueh just enough time to wrap up his affairs, buy a suitcase, and book a berth on a ship. He did not tell Sarly of his plans.

When he got to the General Hospital, Therese was lying in a private room, still sedated, with Ah Kwai sitting with her. She had woken up a few minutes ago and murmured something. He held her hand silently, and before long, she fell asleep again.

In the doctor's office, he found the German doctor who had treated her. The surgery was very successful, and Therese would live another fifty years, but the injury had caused irreversible damage. Luckily, Therese had been wearing a chain belt with a huge pendant that dangled beneath her clothes, deflecting the bullet into her womb. It had saved her life, but she would never be able to have children.

He sat by her bedside holding her hand, and feeling her fingers twitch. He didn't leave the hospital until it grew dark.

At home that night, he wasn't able to convince Leng to leave with him. He didn't even get a chance to bring up his plan. Leng was unrecognizable. He didn't know what had happened to her while he was at the police station, but she was energetic and completely refreshed. He soon realized that his plan wasn't going to work.

Hsueh couldn't understand why Leng had changed so dramatically. Ku had deceived her, she said. Now that she was back in the Party, she felt alive again. When he told her he wanted to leave Shanghai, she grew quiet.

"Why not stay here? You could help us," she said.

"Help with what?" he said unenthusiastically.

"You're a good person. You sympathize with our cause," she said, reminding him of his own words.

Again she looked like someone he knew from a movie, as if she were an actress who had just gotten out of a bad rut and was back onstage in top form. For some time now, perhaps because she had been falling to pieces with exhaustion, she had stopped reminding him of an actress. He didn't know which Leng he liked better: the new Leng, glowing with energy, or the old Leng, confused, disoriented, careless of her appearance. Then he decided he liked them both.

"How can I help?" he asked.

"We have a pressing mission for you." Hsueh was amused that Leng had unconsciously used the word *mission*.

"Before that truck robbery happened, Ku kidnapped a cameraman from a film studio and ordered him to film the whole thing. We found out about this through several other comrades misled by Ku. In that film, Ku makes a statement in which he poses as a Communist, and it could really hurt us. We have to find the film and destroy it! The Party has intelligence that if it gets into the hands of imperialists, it could seriously damage our cause."

"How?" He was only half paying attention.

"Our mole reports that a handful of imperialist speculators in the Concession still hope to blame Ku's crimes on the Communists, which will give the foreigners an excuse to send more troops to Shanghai, and turn it into a bona fide colony!"

The plan was for Hsueh to pay a visit to the cameraman in his capacity as a police investigator, and ask him to hand the film over. It had the added advantage that as a photographer, Hsueh would also know what he was doing.

Hsueh got hold of his friend the poet, and asked him to help drive the police van somewhere. Lieutenant Sarly had told the poet that Hsueh was on a special mission he could not reveal; he should simply do as Hsueh said. The cameraman was not at home, so they drove to the studio, where the guard told them that he was in the editing room.

Negatives, a finished print that could be copied, and a wax record for the sound track all lay piled on the living room floor next to the table.

They were waiting for Lin, who would take it all away to be examined by Party operatives, and then destroyed.

It had rained the night before.

During the day it was sunny, but a typhoon was supposed to reach Shanghai that evening. It rained hard, and the windows wouldn't stop rattling. Leng was in the kitchen doing the dishes. Hsueh opened a roll of film and looked at it frame by frame, marveling.

Leng came out of the kitchen with a towel. "It's raining, I wonder—"

She suddenly stopped and stared at the doorknob.

It was turning. He looked at Leng, and turned to look at the door.

It swung open, and a shadow in a canvas raincoat with a hat pulled way over his face stood outside. It was Ku Fu-kuang.

The gun in Ku's hands swung slowly between him and Leng, back and forth. A puddle formed beneath him on the floor. The wind grew louder. Ku's arms were tense, and he appeared to be making up his mind. He looked tired to Hsueh, perhaps even a little wistful.

Hsueh smiled at him and began to say, "Ku—"

But before he could say anything, Ku made his decision, pointing his gun at Hsueh.

"No!" Leng screamed, drowning out the roar of the typhoon and the rattling windows. She leapt at Hsueh, and her cry made Ku hesitate for a few seconds before pulling the trigger.

A shot rang out, cutting off the scream. Hsueh thought he could hear the bullet penetrate Leng's body, but he couldn't describe the sound. It seemed to come from him, as if the bullet had hit him.

He looked up at Ku.

Ku looked disoriented and a little melancholy, as if he had been reminded of something.

Hsueh felt for the gun beneath the reels of film. It was Leng's gun, the pistol she had been given as a present. She had given it to Hsueh that morning, so that he could go out on a mission. The pistol was loaded, and she had disengaged the safety during dinner. At the time, Hsueh had privately made fun of this melodramatic gesture to protect the film reels with her life, as if she were acting. He couldn't understand why she and her friends in the Party cared this much about a documentary film.

He had never fired a gun. He had seen other people open fire countless times, and had taken countless photos of them. But this was the first time he had fired a gun himself. He pulled the trigger several times.

Ku collapsed in the pool of rainwater he had made himself.

The bullet had penetrated Leng's heart. She was convulsing just like all the other gunshot victims Hsueh had seen.

She must be in agony. Hsueh held her, gazing at her furrowed brow. He thought he could feel a spasm of her pain.

Her brain was slowly being deprived of oxygen. The pain was melting away, and her brows unfurrowed. Her lips moved. She was saying something to Hsueh, but he couldn't tell what. She kept speaking. For a moment, Hsueh thought he could understand her, and he thought she sounded more genuine than usual, completely genuine. Right this moment, she wasn't acting at all, he thought. Her expression grew wearier. . . .

Four bombs had struck the *Libia*, an Italian cruiser. That attack and many other bomb attacks in the concessions, as well as plain-clothes Japanese officers attacking shops and harassing civilians, forced the Chinese army to retaliate by dispatching plainclothes officers to arrest Japanese spies and Chinese traitors. Since the bombings of Chinese-administered Shanghai on the night of January 28, many European businessmen had watched the conflict from the safe distance of their expatriate clubs. They now woke up to the fact that war had broken out. No one would be safe from the conflict euphemistically referred to in diplomatic documents as the Shanghai Incident.

Count Ciano, the Italian consul in Shanghai, had the captain of the *Libia* speak to the diplomatic community about their investigation. The bombs had made deep holes in the deck, but fortunately none of them had exploded. Most of the soldiers on deck at the time had been asleep.

They soon discovered markings on the unexploded bombshells that showed they had been made in China, and ballistics experts demonstrated that they had been fired from the direction of the Chinese camp. Baron Harada couldn't help feeling pleased. He had been sent to Shanghai to liaise with foreign powers as the secretary to an important Japanese prince.

The mayor of Shanghai, Wu Tiecheng, expressed sincere regret that the hostilities had affected a neutral country. He promised that the Chinese army would do its best to avoid similar incidents in the future. But Mayor Wu also pointed out that this incident could not be entirely separated from the fact that the Japanese were allowed to move freely within the concessions. Japanese ground forces landed at piers in the concessions, their frontline command headquarters were located in the concessions, retreating Japanese forces could regroup safely inside the concessions, and a Japanese cruiser was moored right next to the *Libia*. We can't very well prevent the Chinese troops from defending themselves, he pointed out.

If this accident had happened at any other time, the Shanghailanders would not have let it slide. But although there were thousands of foreign troops in Shanghai and dozens of cruisers moored in the Whampoa, not to mention the fact that the American naval fleet in Manila could arrive in Shanghai within forty-eight hours, the representatives of the neutral foreign countries said nothing and let the furor die down. Never before had they shown such restraint. But over the past few days, they had all been impressed by the surge of patriotism in Shanghai and the unexpected fearlessness of the Chinese troops.

Lieutenant Sarly was standing at the door to the police headquarters together with the chief of police, getting ready to welcome their guests in the senior officer uniform that he reserved for special occasions. All the foreign police officers were standing to one side of the door in three rows awaiting inspection, carrying rifles and wearing black helmets edged in white. Japanese planes had taken to hovering over Concession airspace, and a number of "accidental" bombing incidents had been reported in commercial areas. Nonetheless, curious spectators had gathered on Route Stanislas Chevalier outside the iron fences enclosing the gardens on the western side of the building. The winter sun gave the porcelain-tiled roof of the octagonal pagoda in the corner of the garden a tranquil, almost lazy glow. Under the sign of Heng Tai and Co., the corner store across the road, several children stopped playing and stood there, as though the mere sight of the policemen had rooted them to the ground.

The police were welcoming the commander in chief of the Japanese Army stationed in the International Settlement, and the first secretary of the Japanese consulate, Sawada-san. They had arranged to discuss public security in the concessions.

Sarly was feeling dejected. Since the events of January 28, when the Japanese Navy and ground forces had begun to attack Chapei, Jiangwan, and other places in Chinese-administered Shanghai, Shanghailanders had grown increasingly pessimistic. But Sarly's pessimism predated the attack. Since the incident the previous July that had rocked the Concession and even piqued the interest of observers in Paris, he had begun to feel that the Shanghailanders' days of colonial leisure were numbered. He used to be very optimistic about the future of the concessions, but he no longer was. Even though no one would blame him for this state of affairs, he blamed himself and people like him, men in positions of responsibility, who had insisted on sticking to old colonial ways. They had thought they could control the concessions and keep millions of Chinese in line with power politics. All these men intent on milking the concessions of their riches had caused its downfall.

The secretary on duty rushed down the steps and into the main door of the police headquarters, to give a memorandum of a phone conversation to the chief of police. The chief glanced at the memo and handed it to Sarly. It was a phone call from the Japanese consulate, informing them that Sawada-san's visit to the Concession Police headquarters that morning would regrettably have to be canceled. Two grenades had landed inside the northeastern walls of the consulate at eight thirty that morning. Although no one had been hurt, the Japanese considered it unsafe for Sawada-san to leave the building. As soon as he received the report, the secretary had made enquiries about the incident, and Commander Martin in the International Settlement had told him that the grenades had been hurled into the consulate from the rooftop of a nearby warehouse on Whangpoo Road.

Baron Pidol was sitting at the bar in the French Club, reading a newspaper. The windows had been shut tight, the lawn was parched, and the parasol tree was bare. Indoors it was warm as spring.

A political cartoon in the newspaper caught his eye. Signed by Mario, the Italian man, it was of a plane hovering over a map of Shanghai, dropping bombs on the city. It had already burned a large hole in the northeast corner of the map, and a gust of wind was blowing the bombs in the center of the map toward the southwest, toward the land that he and his partners had bought for huge sums of money.

Not until the third day after hostilities began did Baron Pidol realize the gravity of the situation. Before then he had secretly been pleased by the turn of events. He and the other speculators privately believed that it wouldn't be a bad thing for the Japanese Army to teach Nanking a lesson. At cocktails at the Japanese consulate, he had even suggested to Sawada-san that many foreign businessmen like himself felt that a civilized Asian country such as Japan could play a greater role in the concessions. In fact, if all the Japanese wanted to do was bomb the newly built northeast of the city, which the government had begun to develop in the name of the Greater Shanghai Plan, everyone would profit.

But three days ago, he had watched Japanese soldiers in civilian clothes toss bombs out of a car into the crowd. He had seen shrapnel slit the throat of a passerby and intestines spill out of a man's belly, a dusty mass of what looked like spaghetti-shaped cream and bread crumbs with jam. He had clutched the hand of a friend of his, a worldly speculator type, who died as blood bubbled out of his throat.

Lin P'ei-wen and Ch'in Ch'i-ch'üan had waited for a break in the bombing before crossing Garden Bay in a sampan boat. The bay was where Soochow Creek flowed into the Whampoa. They moored the boat at a pier in the Chinese-administered Old Town and walked through its streets until they got to Boulevard des Deux Républiques. The French Concession had already been sealed off by military police. Electrified fences had been erected all along the French side of Chao-chia Creek and other canals, and there were armored cars parked behind them.

The gates had also been closed, to stop refugees from flooding into the Concession. But Lin and Ch'in kept slipping in and out of the Concession as they pleased, all because of the unusual location of their safe house, an advantage that no one had anticipated when they first rented it. The *shih-k'u-men* building itself was in the French Concession, but its east wing looked out onto Chinese-administered territory, and the Concession Police hadn't bothered to barricade the full length of Boulevard des Deux Républiques—all they did was block off the major intersections. Lin and Ch'in were able to get into the Concession by climbing up a rope ladder that hung from the window of the apartment. In the early hours of the morning, they wormed their way onto the roof of a warehouse on Whangpoo Road, and lobbed a few grenades into the Japanese consulate as retaliation for the Japanese attacks on civilians.

A few days ago, it had been rumored that the Japanese Army was about to attack the Old Town. Its residents flooded toward the neutral Concession, but the police stopped them with their rifles and armored cars. Lin immediately decided he would help as many ordinary civilians as possible flee the war zone. A few hundred refugees fled into the Concession via his rope ladder.

Hsueh had just come out of Therese's apartment. Via her connections in the White Russian gangs, he had discovered where a certain White Russian businessman was hiding. The man had been renting his trading firm's trucks out to plainclothes Japanese officers who were murdering civilians in the Concession. Someone had made a note of his license plate number, 1359, and reported it to the police. Hsueh passed the intelligence on to the Nanking observers in Shanghai, as well as his old friend Lin. But neither of them was able to find the man, who had long since gone into hiding. Only a tightly knit circle of Russians knew where he was.

Therese had been recuperating for half a year now. She felt stronger on the inside, as if she had died and come back to life. She had been tested before, long ago, both in Talien and in the Japanese marine police prison at Hoshigaura. She had become cold as ice, and hard as iron. Her past hadn't just molded her character, it had also reshaped her memory. From that time onward, all her memories, whether she was recounting them to someone or talking to herself in the dead of night, sounded to her as though they had been made up. They could be beautiful illusions or ghastly nightmares. She didn't hate the Japanese police, even though they had tortured her to make her tell them where Hugo had kept his money. She didn't hate the German either—when she was forced to tell the police something, she described him as a blond Austrian, Hugo Irxmayer, the man who had given her his name. The whole time they were together, he had never told her he was a pirate who commandeered freight ships in the Bohai Sea, and sold their silks and coal on to Japanese businessmen at the piers of the South Manchuria Railway. She had been a happy White Russian woman until the day that the Japanese police barged into her rooms in Talien and found a Lee-Enfield rifle in her trunk—not that she knew the name of the rifle until much later. Only after she was released did someone come to tell her that Hugo, the redhead, had been killed in a gunfight, and left her some money and a pile of jewels.

Hsueh's footsteps faded in the lobby.

For half a year now, she had been wondering about something. A vast sum of money had disappeared, and Hsueh had never told her what happened to it. Ku's assassination squad had bought some expensive German firearms from her, and they had agreed that Hsueh would not hand over the goods until he got the check. He was to make contact via a series of flashlight signals that she had revealed to no one but him. And he was not to send the signals until he had the check in his hands.

But she was very fond of his Chinese ribs, of how they pressed tightly against her body, against the scar throbbing on her abdomen.

Cannons thundered outside the window, to the northeast. She felt the return of an old thrill.

POSTSCRIPT

On a sunny August morning during the gestation of this story, which was then populated only by a few dim shadows, a sentence appeared on the page in front of me. Even I didn't realize its significance at the time. It came like a ray of sunlight piercing the fog on the Whampoa and falling on a desk on the eastern end of the reading room at the Shanghai Municipal Archives:

It was the White Russian woman who first attracted Lieutenant Sarly's attention.

That is how it all started. In 1931, Lieutenant Sarly of the Political Section was attempting to make sense of the chaos in the French Concession in order to crack an unsolved case. He was poring over old files when he found this White Russian woman. Almost eighty years later, I was sitting in the reading room trying to piece together a chain of events that happened at the beginning of the 1930s in the French Concession. As I was reading the same files Sarly would have read, the same woman leaped out at me right away.

The colonial authorities often kept slipshod records, and the Political Section's file on this woman was no exception. After the Japanese invaded Shanghai, the file would have remained within the possession of the Vichy Concession government until Wang Ching-wei's puppet government claimed jurisdiction over the concessions, at which point all the important documents at the Concession Police would have been handed over to "No. 76," Wang's secret police nicknamed after its headquarters at No. 76

Jessfield Road. Either they or the Tokkô, the Japanese secret police, may have removed some of the key documents in that file for an ultimately unsuccessful investigation into the White Russian woman. It is also possible—many things are possible—that Hsueh, who continued to be influential in the Political Section, destroyed part of the file, whether for reasons of national security or for his own private ends. Even if he had attempted to preserve them, they would probably be irrecoverable today.

At the end of the war in 1945, these files were transferred to the recently established police branch in Lokawei, and then, in 1949, to the new Communist government's police branch there. The brand-new country was so pressed for resources that police officers were forced to write on the reverse sides of prewar documents deemed irrelevant by an Intelligence Advisory Committee composed primarily of Kuomintang defectors. Today's historians must understand that dealing with present difficulties was more important to them than preserving the past. Many prewar documents have been destroyed. Some were pasted together out of sequence on the reverse sides of unrelated files, making them difficult to recover. I once found an important document on the reverse side of a report concerning a certain counterrevolutionary industrialist. The pages had been turned inside out and glued together with inferior glue. They came unstuck with time, allowing me to pry apart the page in accordance with the Archives' strict reading rules, without having to damage the binding, so that I could copy out the contents of this page using the brighter light at the seat near the window.

The file itself survived. It was handed over to the Shanghai Municipal Archives and cataloged by staff there. But no more than fragments of the original documents remain, and there is no way to ascertain how they relate to one another. (See appendices for some of these fragments.)

This book must hence be read as a work of fiction. Imagine that a certain kidnapping that took place on a movie set was invented by the author on a windy summer night, with certain familiar rotting smells in the air. Nor can the author hope to reconstruct the plans and hopes brewing in the minds of historical characters. Instead, he employs a shifting narrative perspective, lending his imagined motives a degree of ambiguity, coaxing the reader to believe his fabrications where evidence is scarce. Emotions are the trickiest. How much genuine affection was there between Hsueh and Therese, and how much were they taking advantage of each other? How much of what took place between Hsueh and the innocent Leng can be attributed to passion rather than premeditated calculation?

If an impartial Court of History were to exist, this author would be accused of misleading the jury with a tale spun from incomplete evidence. There are only a handful of documents, and the connections between them are inferred—they would not stand up in court. In fact, the story of what eventually happened to Hsueh and his White Russian lover is instructive. As mentioned, some of the relevant documents had been deliberately mislaid, which led to a postwar investigation into Hsueh's wartime actions by the Kuomintang authorities, focusing on the period between 1937 and 1941 when the isolated concessions had found themselves under increasing pressure from the rest of Japanese-occupied Shanghai. But the investigation itself had to be abandoned because of a lack of evidence, and a dubious statement from Lieutenant Sarly in Hsueh's favor was used as an excuse to wrap it up summarily.

We don't live in the enchanted world of certain movies, in which the sorcerer has a book of infinite pages that writes the never-ending story of everything he does and all his most intimate feelings as they are taking place. If that book were to exist, not only would historians be out of a job, so would novelists.

APPENDICES

Extracts from the archives. (The full documents are not displayed here for reasons of space.)

I. NOS. U731—2727—2922—7620:

Description and extract:

An investigation by the Political Section of the imperialist French Concession Police into an assassination and related firearms deal. Contains a report on the investigation, newspaper cuttings, photographs, and an extract from a wanted list, as well as records of fingerprints, customs searches, and house searches.

Principal suspect: IRXMAYER THERESE. (Italics quoted directly from source material.)

The name "Weiss Hsueh" appears on the back of a photograph. This must be our Hsueh. On closer inspection, the image is revealed to contain a figure in the bottom right corner who is mostly outside the frame. He has his back to the camera and his left hand is reaching for his face. Is he in the habit of rubbing his nose? He is depicted in profile, and he has a nice square jaw. The shot is focused on the White Russian woman, so his figure is blurred, and you can't even see if he is fat or thin. This is the only photograph we have of Hsueh.

II. DOCUMENT FRAGMENT.

Description: These papers may have been removed from the file after 1949 when paper was rationed, or they may never have been added to the file in the first place, which would not be surprising, given the colonial police's halfhearted work ethic. This is a report presented to the Concession Police by the British secret service, concerning European pirates arrested by the Japanese marine police in Talien, in which Therese's name appears. In the margins, someone has drawn a huge question mark in black ballpoint, pointing to Hugo Irxmayer's name, which appears in parentheses.

III.

There are no other documents concerning Hsueh apart from that photograph. Given his position within the Political Section, he would certainly have been able to expunge any record of his own illegal activities. But traces thereof can be found in the collection of personal essays published during the 1980s by retired special agents who escaped to Taiwan with the Kuomintang government. They would have been censored by the Taiwanese authorities, and the deleted portions must exist in an archive somewhere. The clues they contained led me to the records kept by the Tokkô, the Japanese secret police. In them, I found an affidavit written in French and signed with a flourish by our friend Lieutenant Sarly, testifying that he gave Hsueh permission to make contact with the White Russian woman. The rapid progress of Hsueh's career and increases in his salary can be deduced from police salary records. He received many awards, including a medal from a visiting admiral of the French Navy, and his signature appears on many search warrants and police reports.

IV.

During the spring and summer of 1931, Ku's assassination squad appears frequently in Shanghai's Chinese and foreign newspapers. Although certain details of these stories were probably invented by their writers, in aggregate they show that Ku's group made a big splash in Shanghai. Diplomatic correspondence of the time has now been declassified, and several letters to London and Paris from consuls in Shanghai (approved or forwarded by their respective embassies in Beijing) allude to "frequent assassinations in the concessions" and a certain "Free City" plan. They were often mentioned only in the notes appended to an official report, as was standard diplomatic practice for dealing with sensitive subjects at the time.

V.

As regards the Shanghailanders' speculative scheming (the policy of appeasement practiced by European powers in the 1930s being nothing more than the logical culmination of such schemes): in Shanghai, the Kuomintang government's urban development plan, known as the Greater Shanghai Plan, centered on the northeast of the city, putting it at odds with the plans of foreign real estate developers. The latter aimed to increase the value of land to the south and west of Shanghai by building roads beyond the borders of the concessions. After the Japanese attacks during the January 28 incident in 1937, the Greater Shanghai Plan was literally reduced to rubble. Not long after the war, roads were rapidly built to the west of the concession and large amounts of capital for new roads, apartments, commercial buildings, entertainment venues, and high-end spas poured in. It goes without saying that there is no evidence to support any inferences these facts might suggest.

VI.

Ku Fu-kuang, Lin P'ei-wen, and Leng Hsiao-man's activities scarcely appear in these documents. They must be the province of other, highly classified files. But perhaps if the author were to point out that this gives him all the more room for invention, the gentle reader would not blame him?

MORE WORLD FICTION FROM ONEWORLD

French Concession by Xiao Bai (Chinese)
Translated by Chenxin Jiang

The Sky Over Lima by Juan Gómez Bárcena (Spanish)
Translated by Andrea Rosenberg

A Very Special Year by Thomas Montasser (German)
Translated by Jamie Bulloch

Umami by Laia Jufresa (Spanish)
Translated by Sophie Hughes

The Hermit by Thomas Rydahl (Danish)
Translated by K.E. Semmel

The Peculiar Life of a Lonely Postman by Denis Thériault
(French) Translated by Liedewy Hawke

Three Envelopes by Nir Hezroni (Hebrew)
Translated by Steven Cohen

Fever Dream by Samanta Schweblin (Spanish)
Translated by Megan McDowell

The Postman's Fiancée by Denis Thériault (French)
Translated by John Cullen

Frankenstein in Baghdad by Ahmed Saadawi (Arabic)
Translated by Jonathan Wright

The Invisible Life of Euridice Gusmao by Martha Batalha
(Portuguese) Translated by Eric M. B. Becker

The First Day of the Rest of my Life by Lorenzo Marone
(Italian) Translated by Shaun Whiteside

Sweet Bean Paste by Durian Sukegawa (Japanese)
Translated by Alison Watts

They Know Not What They Do by Jussi Valtonen (Finnish)
Translated by Kristian London